"THE O YOU SAFE IS TO MAKE YOU MY WIFE IN TRUTH AS WELL AS IN NAME."

Hugh's blunt declaration made Caroline's breath catch in her throat. "You mean by making love to me," she said.

"Aye." He leaned forward to gently kiss the base of her throat. "But only if it is what you want as well. I'll abide by whatever you say."

Caroline tried desperately to understand the powerful emotions tearing at her. "If the answer is no?" she asked, drawing a shuddering breath.

"Then I will do all that is in my power to keep you safe. You are my wife, and I pledge to do what I must to protect you."

She digested that in silence before finding the courage to speak again. "And if the answer is yes?"

His hard mouth curved in a smile that promised both danger and delight. "Then I will make love to you," he said simply. "Which is it to be, Caroline? Is it yes, or is it no?"

Other **AVON ROMANCES**

A ROSE IN SCOTLAND

JOAN OVERFIELD

AVON BOOKS  NEW YORK

This is a work of fiction. Names, characters, places, and incidents either are the product of the author's imagination or are used fictitiously. Any resemblance to actual events, locales, organizations, or persons, living or dead, is entirely coincidental and beyond the intent of either the author or the publisher.

AVON BOOKS
A division of
The Hearst Corporation
1350 Avenue of the Americas
New York, New York 10019

First Avon Books Printing: January 1998

AVON TRADEMARK REG. U.S. PAT. OFF. AND IN OTHER COUNTRIES, MARCA REGISTRADA, HECHO EN U.S.A.

Printed in the U.S.A.

WCD   10 9 8 7 6 5 4 3 2 1

To Chad Estep, a hero for all seasons who walks the thin blue line for all of us.

This book is also dedicated with gratitude to the men and women of the Spokane Police Department's Chaplaincy Program, and to police chaplains everywhere who offer hope and comfort when the unthinkable becomes a heartbreaking reality. Thank you for your kindness and your compassion.

Prologue

Castle Loch Haven
Scotland, 1771

"*Cladhaire! Fear bradhaidh!*" Douglas Mac-
Colme, laird of Loch Haven, hurled the
invectives at the young man standing before
him. "It's dead I'd rather see ye than wearing the
colors of our enemy! Ye're nae to speak of this
again, do ye hear?"

Hugh MacColme bore his father's rage in stoic
silence, for he'd expected nothing less. At
twenty, he'd grown to manhood listening to his
father rail against the hated English, and had
known how he would respond once he'd learned
of his son's plans. But Hugh had known also that
he could not let it matter. Since the day he'd read
the writ in Edinburgh, he'd accepted what his
duty must be, and accepted as well what that
duty would cost him. Still, his father's words cut
deep, and his silvery-green eyes flashed with
pride as he faced Douglas across the expanse of
the great keep.

"I'm nae a coward, Father," he said quietly,
only the clenching of his jaw betraying his inner

1

turmoil. "Nor am I a traitor—nae to the clan, nor to yourself. It is because of you that I do this thing. Why can you nae be seeing that?"

"Because 'tis a foul lie, that's why!" Douglas surged to his feet, his face twisting with fury. "And if 'twas sense ye had in yer head instead of useless book-learning, ye'd be seeing the truth of that!"

"But a pardon, Douglas," Geordie MacColme, Hugh's uncle, intervened. "Let your mind rest on that for a wee bit, and think on what it could mean to the clan. Ye've seen what's happening about us, how the English seize upon the smallest excuse to take what is ours. If Hugh swears this oath and enlists, it will mean clemency for us all."

Douglas whirled to glare at his brother. "Clemency!" he roared, his voice echoing off the stone walls. "Where's yer pride, mon? Yer honor? Is it a *burraidh* ye are, to be believing in the lies of the English? Did Culloden nae teach you anything?"

A bitter quarrel erupted between the two brothers, with the chieftains soon joining in to offer opinions and criticisms. Hugh watched it all with increasing bitterness. Did his father and the others truly think he wanted to leave? he wondered angrily. Were they so daft as not to know that leaving Scotland and those he loved would tear the heart from him? And did they think there was any other choice? As he listened his iron control slipped, and his temper ran free.

"Honor!" he sneered, breaking into his father's tirade. "Pride! Will honor fill the stomachs of the babes when they wail from the hunger? Will pride keep out the snow and the cold when the winter comes and we dinna have roofs over our people's heads? You know the answer to that as well as I: It will not."

A stunned silence filled the hall as the men assembled there exchanged uneasy looks. " 'Tis nae that we dinna see the truth of yer words," James Callamby, one of his father's oldest friends, said at last, his expression kind as he studied Hugh. "And we mark that ye do this for us. But to accept a MacColme wearing the uniform of the enemy..." He shook his grizzled head. " 'Tis a hard thing ye ask of us, lad."

" 'Tis a disgrace is what it is," his father interjected before Hugh could respond. "A blow to all who have died under the heel of the usurper! Your own mother amongst them," he added, shooting Hugh a glowering look.

The mention of his mother, dead now these last three years, was a stinging lash upon Hugh's soul. He had adored his sweet-tempered mother and grieved for her still, but he knew she would have understood what he was doing. Would have understood and supported him against his father, just as she had when he had begged to be sent to university in Edinburgh. She had stood against his father and the entire clan to see he got the education he craved, and he took comfort in the thought that she would have stood with him now.

"Hugh," Geordie said, regarding him solemnly, "is it set you are to do this thing? Do you truly mean to become one of the English?"

"Nay, Uncle," Hugh said, relieved he could reassure the others on this point. "I'll never be

English. I'll don the uniform; I'll pull my cap and go where I'm told, and do as I am bid; but I'll always be a Highlander. I'll always be a Mac-Colme. Never doubt that."

There was more heated discussion amongst the chieftains and then James Callamby gave him a worried look. "And if 'tis yer own people yer new masters tell ye to kill, what then, Hugh MacColme? Will ye still do as ye are bid?"

This was something Hugh had already considered, accepting that he would die at the end of a rope before ever raising a weapon against his own. He pulled out his dirk and held it high above his head. "If such a time comes," he said, turning slowly around so that all could see his face as he spoke, "if ever I turn against a man of my clan, a man of my blood, I offer my life in forfeit. I charge those here to plunge this dirk in my back if ever I betray Scotland." He turned and hurled the knife into the table where his father sat, the handle quivering as the blade buried itself in the thick wood.

"I love you," he said in the old language, his gaze meeting that of his father. "But I will do what I must to protect the clan. All I ask in return is that you do nothing that will endanger the pardon I have won."

His father's face worked oddly for several seconds, and for a moment Hugh feared to see him weep. "Ye will do this, then?" he asked, his voice hoarse with emotion. "Ye will take the king's shilling and leave all who love ye?"

Hugh blinked back his own tears. "I will."

His father dropped his head. "Then so be it," he said wearily, raising his chin and gazing about the room. "My son is dead," he intoned, ignoring the shocked gasps and cries of dismay. "From this day hence we'll speak his name nae mair."

Hugh stood in painful isolation, accepting his father's judgment before turning away; his head held proudly as he walked away. People looked away as he moved past them, their eyes downcast as if he were a ghost they feared to see. He walked out into the antechamber, and he could tell by the expressions on the faces of the women that they already knew what had happened. More than one pretty lass dried her eyes with the edge of her apron, her private dreams dying as he walked past her. A young lad of some fifteen years stood apart from the others, his hands clenched into fists, and after a moment's hesitation Hugh walked over to lay his hand on the lad's bony shoulder.

"Go to him, Andrew," he said gently, his eyes drinking in every detail of his brother's face. "He'll have need of you now. Mind you have a care for him, and Mairi, too. That one will want a great deal of watching," he added, his heart twisting at the thought of his impish younger sister.

Andrew shrugged his hand off, his young eyes full of hurt and betrayal. "It's true, then?" he asked, his voice caught between youth and manhood, cracking with emotion. "You've enlisted?"

"Andrew," Hugh began painfully, "I beg you to understand. There is no other way . . ."

"Colin MacLorne says you are a coward," Andrew interrupted, wiping his hand across his nose in an impatient gesture. "He says you fear standing against the English, and so you join them instead to murder your own people."

Hugh's desire to soothe vanished at the insulting words. "You are young yet, Andrew," he told his brother sharply, "and Colin MacLorne is a pimple-faced *garrach* who would best be advised to hold his tongue instead of wagging it. I do what I must, and I expect no less from you. I place the family and the safety of the clan in your hands. Guard them until I return."

"You'll never return," Andrew snapped as Hugh turned to leave. "You'll never return because you're a traitor, and a traitor will never be welcomed in Loch Haven!"

Although it cost him everything, Hugh did not respond. He simply kept walking, taking his plaid from the gnarled hands of his old nurse who was standing by the door.

"God have a watch o'er ye," the old woman whispered, tears shimmering in her faded blue eyes as she gazed at him. "I'll nae be seeing ye in this life again."

"Farewell, Annie Kirkcaldy," he said, bending from his great height to press a kiss to her wrinkled cheek. "I'll think of you and your oatcakes when I am far away."

"Hugh! Hugh!" A red-haired whirlwind with a torn dress and a dirty face dashed past the women to launch herself against him. "Dinna go, Hugh! Dinna go!"

"Mairi." Hugh caught his sister in his arms and held her close. *"Mo piuthar*, I love you."

"I hate Colin MacLorne," she charged passionately. "I'm going to bite him the next time I see him!"

Hugh laughed at her fierce tone, his hand shaking as he passed it over the unruly curls that were several shades brighter than the reddish-brown waves streaming past his wide shoulders. "You do that, *kempie*, and mind you bite him hard," he said, giving her smudged cheek a smacking kiss. He treasured the sweet, warm feel of her for a precious second, and then set her on her feet.

"Now off with you, love," he told her, infusing a teasing note in his voice. "I have a hard night's ride ahead of me, and must be away. Mind you do as Father and Andrew bid you."

But instead of going off as she was bade, Mairi resolutely stood her ground, her gaze never leaving his face. "I know you're nae a feardie like the others say," she said, eyes as green as the trees in springtime sparkling with tears. "I know you only joined the English because they made you."

Hugh could not speak for the lump in his throat. Were they alone he would have let his tears flow as they would, and not care a groat for it. But with the others there watching with their sharp eyes and even sharper tongues, he schooled himself to hide his pain.

"No tears now, little one," he scolded gently, raising his hand to brush her damp cheeks. "It's happy I want to remember you."

A tentative smile wobbled on her trembling lips, but her eyes were solemn as they met his. "Will you be back, Hugh?"

Hugh thought of the dangers he would face as a soldier. The chances he would survive the next several years were all but nonexistent, but how could he tell that to a child? Then he saw an adult's understanding shimmering in his sister's eyes, and wondered how he could lie.

"If I live," he said quietly, granting her the honesty she craved. "My word to you, Mairi. I will come back." He reached out to give a tangled curl a playful tug. "I must come back, mustn't I, so that I can dance at your wedding?"

As he knew it would, her small nose wrinkled in disgust. "I'll nae be marrying some pest of a boy!" she declared with conviction. "They're the very devils!"

He gazed down into her face and saw the promise of great beauty in the odd angles of her expressive face. " 'Tis a beauty you will be," he told her, his heart aching that he would not be there to see her grow into womanhood. "Father and I will have to post all the clansmen on the towers to keep watch, so that some love-struck prince from a far-off land doesn't carry you away."

"Let him try," Mairi retorted, tossing back her curls with a sniff. "I'll stick my knife in him as if he was a haggis!"

Some of the women nearby tittered with laughter, while others shook their heads and muttered how wild the cailin had grown. Hugh ignored them all, his concentration fixed on Mairi. She was the image of his mother, and with that thought in mind he reached into the pocket of his jacket, extracting the locket he had carried with him since the day his dying mother had pressed it into his hand. He flicked open the heavily etched silver case, gazing at the miniature it contained.

His mother had been seventeen when it was

painted; it was the year she married his father. She had been young and full of life then, her emerald eyes sparkling with laughter. Eighteen years later she was dead; killed, he knew, by the harsh life and grief over the four small ones who had gone before her. He studied her beloved face for several seconds, and then snapped the locket closed for the final time.

He reached out and took Mairi's small hand in his, placing the locket in her palm and folding her fingers around it. "Keep this safe for me, Mairi," he said, his eyes meeting hers. "The day I come back, you may return it to me. But if I do not, I want you to promise me you will give it to your firstborn son that he might give it to his wife. Will you do this for me?"

Mairi's thin fingers clutched the locket tightly. "I will, Hugh," she vowed, pressing the locket to her heart. "But you will come back; I know you will. And I will be waiting for you."

A single tear Hugh could not stop wended its way down his cheek. "Good-bye, Mairi," he whispered brokenly. "Good-bye, *mo cridhe*." And with that he turned and left, closing the great wooden doors of Castle Loch Haven behind him.

Chapter 1

Castle Loch Haven
Scotland, 1785

All for nothing. Hugh gazed up at the stone turrets of the castle, his eyes narrowing against the lash of ice and rain. The past fourteen years of his life—the pain of it, the hell of it—had all been for naught. His lips twisted in a bitter smile at the realization. 'Twould seem his father had had the final say after all, he decided, his hand clenching about his reins.

"And when was it you say that the soldiers came for my father and brother?" he asked, his voice devoid of emotion.

"Four years last May," James Callamby provided, reaching up to rub his cheek thoughtfully. "I remarked on it because it happened but a week after my Elspeth married Rory Steward. I was to Dunstaffnage for the feasting, and a good thing it was, too," he added, his blue eyes dancing with merriment, "else I wouldna be having this conversation with ye."

Four years ago, Hugh mused, his expression hardening as he did some quick calculations.

That would have been about the time he and his regiment were bogged down in the swamps near Cowpens in the Carolinas. At the same time that he was fighting for his life, killing American rebels for a flag he detested, his father and brother were being dragged off in chains by other soldiers of that same flag. The irony of that was almost laughable, but the feelings tearing at him were too painful for laughter.

"Tell me what happened," he said, banishing the black thoughts from his mind with the experience of many years. "I would know all."

There was a long silence as the older man gathered his thoughts. " 'Twas after the hanging of the rebels in Glasgow, and feeling was running high against the clans," he began, his face taking on a distant expression. "The soldiers came from the border, marching from glen to glen, and those who wouldna sign a pledge of fealty to the king were taken to London for trial—your father, brother, and uncle amongst them. We know some were transported and others hung, but of the men of Loch Haven we have nae heard a thing."

Transported. Hugh's jaw clenched at the fearful word. If his father and Andrew had been shipped to some far-off colony, then they were as good as dead. No one returned from such hellish places, and he knew that in such a circumstance, hanging would have been the truer mercy. It was a horrifying thought, and he felt his stomach tighten in sickness.

"Mairi." He forced the word between gritted teeth. "What of Mairi?" If his sister had been transported as well, he knew he would truly go mad.

"In Edinburgh with your Aunt Egidia," James assured him quickly. "The old lady was fair ill at the time, and Mairi had gone there to care for her. She was well away from the castle when the soldiers came."

Hugh closed his eyes in relief. "Thank God," he murmured feelingly. "I could not have borne it to have lost her as well."

"Ye almost did." James's lips curled in a rueful smile. "For when she heard what happened, what did the lass do but take herself off to London to demand their release. Aye, and her not but seventeen at the time. It was a grand thing, and the clans speak of it still."

Hugh was too stunned to reply. He had been in London but twice, and the filth and the vice of it had horrified him. The thought of his innocent sister alone in such a place filled him with terror, and he made a mental note to give the little *deamhan* a sound shaking when next he saw her. After he kissed her and held her close, he admitted to himself.

"Where does Aunt Egidia stay?" he asked, turning his thoughts to the next thing to be done. "Is she still living on Chambers Street near the kirk?"

James nodded. "Aye. Keir MacKinney is at university there, and writes he saw Mairi not one month past. 'Tis said he is after courting her," he added, twisting in his saddle to cast Hugh a teasing grin. "Though ye'll have to have a word with him on that yerself, MacColme, to be certain the lad's intentions are as they should be."

Hugh was silent on the long ride back to the village. Mairi being courted, he mused, dazed at the very notion. For the past fourteen years he'd carried the image of a dirty-faced urchin close to his heart, clinging to her memory even as he'd gone screaming into battle. Although he'd known she was growing up through the years, until this very moment he hadn't considered the ramifications of what that would mean. A reluctant grin tugged at his mouth as he remembered her passionate declaration never to marry. 'Twould seem a great many things had changed in the years he had been gone.

Despite James's insistence that Hugh stay with him and his family, Hugh returned to the small, rough tavern that passed for an inn in Loch Haven. As it had been when he'd ridden out earlier that morning, the taproom was filled with hard-faced men, and 'twas obvious by their ominous silence that they were no more pleasantly disposed toward him than they'd been when he'd left.

"So, ye've been to the castle and seen fer yerself the truth o' what we told ye," Angus MacColme, his father's distant cousin, snarled, his thin mouth set in a contemptuous sneer. "Yer fine English king nae mair kept his word to ye than did ye to us. Or have ye forgotten the oath ye swore before us all?"

Hugh set his tankard on the bar with studied care. Years of swallowing every manner of insult without complaint had taught him to keep his temper hidden, and none of his rage showed as he raised cool eyes to meet the older man's derisive gaze.

"I forget nothing, cousin," he said, his tone deceptively mild. "Not a vow nor a slight. I remember all."

Angus's cheeks grew red at the implied threat, but before he could speak one of the other men asked challengingly, "And what will ye do to take back what is yers? With yer father gone 'tis the laird of Loch Haven ye be; his obligations and duties are now yer own. What will ye do to fulfill them, Hugh MacColme?"

This was a question Hugh had been asking himself since learning of his father's arrest and the seizure of their lands and title. His years with the army had taught him much about English politics, and he intended on using every bit of that knowledge to gain back what was his. But to do that he would need to journey to London— an action he was certain would make his remaining chieftains even more wary of him.

"I will do what I must," he said simply, raising his tankard and taking a sip.

There was an expectant silence, and when he did not elaborate, the men began shifting their feet and exchanging confused looks. "That is all?" the man who had spoken before demanded in a baffled tone.

Hugh thought of the English major who had been his first commanding officer after he'd been made a sergeant. *"Explain nothing,"* the man had advised, giving Hugh's shoulder a companionable slap. *"Simply issue the orders and act as if they had already been carried out."*

"It is enough," he said, taking another sip of ale. "Now I would speak of the clan. Tell me how fares everyone."

There was an uneasy silence and another exchange of looks, and Hugh braced himself to prepare for anything from an insult to a dirk in the back. Finally a man Hugh recalled from his youth set down his own tankard and began speaking.

"We are better off than many of the others," he said, tugging at his beard in a gesture Hugh well remembered. "The seizure was limited only to yer father's house and lands, and the rest of us were let be. The sheep and cattle are well, and so 'tis enough meat we have to sustain us. Many of the crofts are in sad want of repair, but we have nae the money to see to it."

Hugh thought of the money tucked away in his things. Despite his meager salary he'd managed to put aside a considerable sum, and then there was the money he'd won as part of the booty seized in battle. All in all it was several thousand pounds, enough to repair a hundred crofts and see to the most immediate needs of the clan. Unfortunately, he feared, the money would be needed to buy back his land and title from an English court that would doubtlessly listen better to a man with bags full of gold than to one with pockets to let.

"Talk to the other clans," he said after a moment's consideration. "Offer a trade of meat for the material to help in the repairing of the crofts. That will help them as well as us. What else?"

"We've several widows and women without their men to help them," Lucien Raghnall, a man who had been Hugh's close companion as a lad, volunteered warily. "They stand to lose all if their taxes are nae met by year's end."

Hugh said a mental good-bye to a goodly part of his money. "They will be met," he said. "Are there other matters to discuss? How many men were taken from Loch Haven?"

"Besides yer father, uncle, and brother, there were ten others," Angus MacColme said, the bitterness fairly dripping from his words. "And half a dozen more dragged off by the press-gangs that followed the soldiers, my own Donald included. Dragged from his own home, he was, and taken away as if he was nae mair than a runt to be slaughtered!"

Hugh was silent, his heart aching at the thought of any man under the hell of impressment. Army life was bad enough, often unendurable at times, but it paled in comparison to what befell a man impressed into His Majesty's navy. He'd heard stories horrible enough to give him nightmares, but now he grudgingly accepted there was naught he could do to help the men so cruelly taken away. The best he could hope for was to learn if they even lived, and he doubted that would provide scant comfort to those left behind.

"James told me there was no word on the fate of the men arrested," he said, focusing on the things he felt he could do something about. "Is that so? Were inquiries made?"

"Aye, inquiries aplenty," another man said heatedly. "For all the good it did us! Even yer sister could learn naught when she went there, and 'twas proper determined the lass was, too. Threatened to storm the prison herself and see to their welfare, she did, and was almost clapped into irons for her pains. But she didna back down," he added with an approving nod.

Hugh winced at the admiration in the man's voice. 'Twould seem James had not exaggerated Mairi's heroics, and he shuddered at the image of a flame-haired hellion dressing down some staunch and sour magistrate in a black robe and powdered wig. Well, he was home now, and the first thing he meant to make clear to his sister was that she was never again to do such a foolish thing. He was the laird, and what risks there were would be taken by him.

"What will you do, Hugh?" Lucien was regarding him curiously. "Will you go to London to petition the courts for redress?"

"I had thought to do so," Hugh replied. "I've the king's pardon to show them, and enough groats to grease as many fat English hands as it may take. Although I pray God 'twill not be many." He added this last part with a wry grin, and was rewarded when they broke out into raucous laughter.

"Nae much chance of that, lad," one of the wizened Highlanders chortled, slapping his knee in amusement. " 'Tis greedy as ever the English be, and they'll take yer gold, yer boots, and yer buttons if ye dinna keep yer wits about ye."

"Then I shall have to make certain to do just that," Hugh said, pretending to relax even as he was careful to keep his guard firmly in place. "I haven't survived this long to be buggered by some fat pig of a magistrate."

The crude remark won another burst of laughter from the others, and when he was certain his actions would not be misinterpreted, Hugh bought a round of ale. There was still a distance between himself and the others, but for the first time since arriving in his old village, he cautiously began to hope he would be able to put right what had gone so terribly wrong.

"Will ye be stopping in Edinburgh to see yer sister, lad?" One of the men broke his hostile silence to send Hugh an inquiring look.

Hugh felt his heart race at the thought of seeing his sister again. "Of course," he answered at once. "And had I known Mairi was there, I should have stopped there first. But as it was, I was in a hurry to be home, and in no mind to be read a scold by my aunt, may Saint Giles bless her sweet soul."

More laughter followed, for Egidia Sinclair's sour disposition was known to all. A rich widow, she could have remarried a dozen times over, but her sharp tongue and hectoring ways had driven off any suitor foolish enough to approach her.

The men soon settled back with their ale to reminisce and gossip in the manner of men everywhere, and as he always did, Hugh was content merely to sit and listen in watchful silence.

"When do you leave for London?" Lucien had picked up his tankard and moved to join Hugh at the end of the bar.

Hugh thought of all that would have to be done before taking his leave. "The day after tomorrow," he decided, unwilling to wait any longer before seeing Mairi. "If there is anything left to be done I will leave it to you. Do you mind?"

Lucien gave an expansive shrug. "Not so much," he said, raising his tankard to his lips.

"I've been doing the little I can until now, but it will help if the others know I'm acting on the orders of the laird."

His words had a sobering effect on Hugh. "But am I the laird?" he asked, his glance going to the group of men deep in conversation. "I may have been temporarily forgiven, but that is a long way from being accepted—especially as laird."

Lucien's gray-blue eyes flicked in the men's direction. "Dinna let those old rashers of wind gype you," he said quietly. "I dinna say you will be met with open arms, but there are more here who understand the wisdom of what you did than those who would condemn you for it. Be patient, Hugh. It will come with time, I promise you."

Hugh's plans to leave in two days' time proved optimistic, and it was almost four days after riding into Loch Haven that he was able to ride out again. He attended his duties as laird, riding from house to house to meet with his chieftains and tenants. He was relieved to see Lucien was right, and that most of the men he spoke with, while wary and defensive, seemed inclined to accept him as head of the clan. He listened to their complaints and observations calmly, taking what action he could before moving on to the next house.

He also took the time to lay out his strategy, meticulously plotting each action he would take. In his years in the king's service he had picked up much of English law from watching his commanding officers, and he knew that if he hoped to even win the court's ear, he would first need the aid of a powerful patron. A galling prospect to be sure, but however much it stung his pride, he accepted it nonetheless. Fortunately for him he had just such a patron in his pocket, and upon reflection, he decided it just might be the thing to stop in Bath on his way to London.

It was approaching evening when Hugh rode into Edinburgh, and he was astonished anew how much it had altered in the years of his absence. The area below the castle, which he remembered as being fields filled with flowers and grazing sheep, was now abuzz with construction, and everywhere he looked he saw evidence of new buildings being put up. The style was much like he had seen in London, all cream-colored stone and elegant wrought iron, and he thought it looked as out of place against the fields of Scotland as a wild Highlander would look in the overheated salons of London or Paris.

His aunt's home was the tumbledown wreck he recalled from his days at university, and he felt a wave of nostalgia as he gazed up at the soot-blackened bricks and glass. The creaky butler who answered his knock was another relic from his youth, and he was every bit as dour and disapproving as Hugh remembered.

"So, it's home ye've decided to come, is it?" he demanded, his faded hazel eyes glaring up at Hugh. "About time, I should think. Ye need to be after keeping an eye on that sister of yours, before she disgraces us all with her hoydenish ways. The mistress tries, but she's no' a match for that one."

"Are my aunt and sister at home, Gregors?" he asked, trying not to be too alarmed at the gloomy admonishment. The old butler had strong Presbyterian sensibilities, and had once pronounced Hugh on the road to perdition merely because he'd befriended a young Catholic from Ireland who was a student at the university.

"The mistress is upstairs resting," Gregors informed him, removing Hugh's rain-dampened cape with a flourish. "And that devil's she-cub is the Lord knows where. She doesna tell me where she goes these days, and more's the mercy, I say."

Hugh ignored that, hoping Gregors was but exaggerating. "I would like to see my aunt, if you would be so good as to tell her I am here," he said coolly, adopting the aloof tone he had heard in his officers' voices—the tone of master to servant, even as the shells burst over their heads and the air was screaming with bullets.

Gregors's thin lips twitched in derision. "Suit yerself, lad," he said, clearly unimpressed. "But she'll be in a rare taking, I'm warning ye. Ye know where the drawing room is; take yerself there and I'll inform Mrs. Sinclair ye're here."

The drawing room was small and dark, furnished with faded pieces that had seen better years—better decades, Hugh amended, shifting as a spring in the sagging settee came into painful contact with his buttock. Looking about him, he would almost have thought his aunt a poor widow but one step from the almshouse. Tight as the devil's breeches, was Aunt Egidia.

He cast the darkened fireplace a thoughtful look, and was considering ringing the maid for a bit of coal for the fire when his aunt made her entrance. As he expected, she was already lecturing him.

" 'Tis amazed I find myself you've even remembered this address," she said, studying him regally over her great beak of a nose. "Fourteen years gone, and not a word from you did I have. Well, lad, what have you to say for yourself? And speak up, my hearing is not what it was."

Hugh opened his mouth to apologize but suddenly he was gathering her up in his arms, depositing a kiss on her cheek as he whirled her in a circle. "Ah, Aunt Egidia, I've missed you!" he said, laughing as he set her on her feet once more.

"Dolt!" Aunt Egidia swatted him with the edge of her fan before lifting her hand to tug at her powdered wig, knocked askew by his embrace. "Not yet six of the clock, and you're already drunk as a sailor! A shame on your soul!"

Hugh continued grinning down at her. His entire life had been turned on its head from the moment he'd stepped foot back into Scotland, but here, praise God, was one thing that had remained constant. "If I'm drunk, 'tis happiness and not spirits that 'tis to blame," he told her, reaching out to pull the enormous monstrosity of horsehair and greasy powder into place. "I'm pleased to see you looking so fine, Auntie."

Lined cheeks painted the delicate pink of a young girl's grew even pinker at his compliment. "Wheest!" his aunt exclaimed, her sour expression belied by the sparkle of her dark eyes. "Why are you nae out chasing the hizzies for a wee bit of loving? 'Tis holes in your purse to match the holes in your head you must have, to be wasting your time flattering an old woman!"

The thought of slaking his passions in one of the many prostitutes had occurred to Hugh, but he'd dismissed it with his usual fastidiousness. He'd seen more men laid low by the pox than he'd ever seen felled by an enemy's bullet, and he'd learned to control his baser nature.

"I've no time now to dance the reel o' Bogie," he said, taking an almost boyish delight in using the scandalous phrase in front of his aunt. " 'Tis Mairi I've come to see, and then I'm to Bath and London to learn what's to be done about all of this. Do you know where she's gone?"

"To call upon the son of an old friend of your father's," Aunt Egidia supplied, settling into one of the faded chairs. "I've no doubt you remember him: Iain Dunhelm, laird of Ben Denham."

The image of a fox-faced man with a sharp nose and shrewd gray eyes popped into Hugh's mind. "Aye," he said slowly, "I remember the laird. A clever man, and a mind more devious than that of a wizard. But why would Mairi go to him? Does she think he can be of help?"

His aunt gave an inelegant snort. "Help? Aye, he could well be that, considering the way he's helped himself to the lands about him!" she said, her lips pursing in disgust. "He's more than doubled his holdings since the arrests began, and 'tis nae a secret he's been casting his eyes at Mac-Colme land as well."

"And Mairi went to him?" Hugh demanded, angry and appalled by turns. "For the love of God, why?"

"Because I told her to," came the calm reply.

"And don't be looking at me like that, Hugh MacColme! You're a soldier, and well you know the value of scouting the lay of an enemy's land."

Hugh bit back a furious oath. "And you sent her alone?" he demanded, his hand tightening on the pommel of the sword he wore buckled to his hip.

Aunt Egidia gave him a look of patent long-suffering. "Dinna be a bigger fool than you can help being," she told him with a sniff. "I sent a maid and a footman with her, as is proper. He's his mother living with him, and the poor woman has been sickening this past winter long. Mairi called upon her to inquire after her health and to bring a jar of my tisane. If she can learn what new designs the laird is plotting while she's there, then more to the better, I say."

Hugh digested his aunt's explanation in silence, grudgingly admitting her actions had merit. "And what makes you think Dunhelm has his eye to Loch Haven?" he asked, wondering if he would need to call upon Iain himself, and let it be known that he was returned and would protect what was his.

A crafty look stole into Aunt Egidia's eyes. "He's already acquired half the land between Ben Denham and Castle Loch Haven," she said, watching Hugh for any reaction. " 'Twas also rumored he pressed for the seizing of all Mac-Colme land, not just the properties owned directly by your father, and when the land was put to auction 'tis said he bid upon it. Alas, he did not bid high enough," she added with a smirk, "and it went to some *outeral* from York-shire."

Hugh opened his mouth in reply, but what-ever he might have said was lost when the door to the drawing room was flung open and a woman in an elegant yellow gown, a cape of bright scarlet wool laying crookedly on her shoulders, stood in the doorway. Emerald-green eyes, lavishly trimmed with thick black lashes were wide in a face that was alarmingly pale, and her lips trembled as she took a tentative step forward.

"Hugh?" she whispered, her voice shaking with emotion. "Hugh, is it truly you?"

Hugh gazed at the stunning creature his sister had become, love and anguish making his eyes burn and his throat ache. She was the very image of the mother he mourned still, and seeing her grown was a painful reminder of all the lost years in between. "*Mo piuthar, mo cridhe,*" he said, repeating the endearments he had whis-pered to her in farewell a lifetime ago. "I have missed you, little sister."

"Hugh!" And then she was in his arms as she had been all those years ago, her arms tight about his neck as she held him close. "You're home, you're home," she whispered, and he could feel her tears warm upon his skin. "I knew you would come back! I knew it."

Hugh couldn't speak, his heart too full for words as he pressed a kiss to the top of Mairi's head. This was the moment he had longed for, the moment he had lived for through all the years of danger and death. In his sister's arms he was finally home, and the enormity of his joy overwhelmed him.

Behind him he heard the sound of the door closing, and knew Aunt Egidia had withdrawn to grant them privacy. He savored the feel of his sister a moment longer before gently moving away.

"Let me have a look at you," he said with a half-laugh, drawing back to feast his eyes upon her. "Aye," he said, rubbing his thumb over the curve of her cheek. "I was right, wasn't I, to say you would be a beauty? You're lovely as an angel, Mairi MacColme, although 'tis more the devil I hear you resemble, with your temper and your tongue."

"Oh, fasch with you!" she exclaimed, dashing the tears from her eyes with an impatient hand. "I'm a MacColme, aren't I, and the temper is mine to have. And if the Lord saw fit to grant me a tongue and the wit to use it, I refuse to be ashamed!"

Her vehemence and the sparkle in her eyes had Hugh throwing back his head in laughter. "Ah, Mairi, you've been too long in Aunt Egidia's company," he said, smiling. "But tell me of Keir Mackinney; I hear he is courting you. Do you love him?"

Mairi tossed back her head with pride. "Keir Mackinney is a troublesome brat with dirty hands and nae a thought in his head!" she said decisively. "And the last time he called, I told him did he but attempt to pinch me again, I would stick my dirk in his fat belly."

Hugh's smile faded. "He dared to place his

hands upon you?" he asked, a deadly note creeping into his deep voice.

"Aye, but it's dealt with and done, so there's no cause for you to go off and murder him as you're thinking," she said. "Now, let me have a look at *you*," she added quickly, before he could gainsay her, "so I can see for myself the man you have become."

He stood silent under the intense perusal of those deep-emerald eyes, feeling the gentle touch of her gaze as it moved over the planes and hollows of his face. The last fourteen years had been hard ones. He was a man now, with a man's experiences stamped deep into his tanned flesh, and he only hoped she would not find his appearance too changed.

"And what is this?" Mairi's hand trembled as she traced a finger down the thin white scar slashed across Hugh's left cheek. "A dueling scar, is it? Or was it done from an enemy's sword in the heat of battle?"

In truth, it was the scar left by the riding crop belonging to a pretty-faced lieutenant he had angered by not moving fast enough, but there was no way he'd be telling his sister that. Just as there was no way he would ever tell her of the horrendous scars marring his back.

"Only officers are allowed to duel, little sister," he said, dancing neatly around an explanation. "The rest of us are left to settle our differences with knives and our fists."

"Brawling like a gypsy. I might have known," she scolded, shaking her head at him in disapproval. Then her expression abruptly grew pensive as she took his hand. "Tell me how long you've been in Scotland, and whether you've been to the castle as yet. I've news to tell you, and it's nae pleasant to hear."

"I know about Father and Andrew," Hugh replied, guiding her to the settee. "But I would you will tell me what you know, and what's been done about it."

Mairi wasted little time, giving him the facts he requested in an orderly fashion. She told him of the soldiers riding into the castle, and of his father's reaction to the very suggestion he sign an oath to him he still regarded as a foreign king. Force had been used upon others, Mairi told him, but his father and brother had been treated with what she recognized as a surprising degree of respect.

" 'Tis odd, I know, but the captain did all that he could to make the matter easier for Father to swallow," Mairi confided, head tilted to one side as she recalled the events related to her by a sharp-eyed servant. "Out of his men's hearing he told Father the oath was naught but a piece of paper, and that Father could tear it to pieces the moment they were gone, and he wouldna care a wit. He all but pleaded with Father to sign, they say, but he wouldna do it, and when he drew his sword upon the captain the soldiers had no choice but to take him."

Hugh silently cursed his father's stubborn pride. "And Andrew and our uncle?" he asked, determined to understand all. "Did they draw upon the soldiers as well?"

"Andrew did," Mairi said, shaking her head at her brother's folly. "A hothead he has been since you went away, and he was more fiercely determined than Father that not another Mac-Colme would swear an oath to the English king." She shot him an apologetic look. "I'm sorry, Hugh, but that is what he said."

Hugh waved her apology aside, having long ago accepted his actions had set him apart from his family. "What did he do?" he asked instead, turning his mind away from his painful memories.

"While Father was arguing with the captain he rallied the men of the castle, and they confronted the soldiers in the main keep. Words were exchanged, and from the telling of it 'twas Andrew who fired the first shot. The soldiers were about to return fire, but the captain ordered them to stand and hold their positions. Then he ordered the others to surrender or be shot. They surrendered," she added.

Hugh gave a distracted nod, envisioning the scene Mairi had described only all too clearly. He himself had been in much the same situation, when he and his squad of irregulars had stormed a barn where a group of American rebels had taken refuge. Those men had also opened fire upon them, and been shot dead for their pains. That this unknown captain had spared his brother and uncle was an act of rare kindness, and one he knew he would have to repay if he hoped to count himself an honorable man.

"This captain, do you know his name?"

"Captain Alexander Dupres of the Sixty-ninth," Mairi said, eyeing him with interest. "Do you know of him?"

Hugh thought of the man with coal-black hair and eyes the color of a tropical sea who had been his commanding officer in Canada. "Aye," he said softly, "I know him."

Mairi gave a wise nod. "I thought perhaps you might, although he didna speak of it. When Muireach told us what had happened, Aunt Egidia said it was a blessing you had gone into the fusiliers as you had done, else we would doubtlessly have lost all. They didna even burn the castle, although 'tis my understanding that is the usual way of it."

"It is," Hugh said in an absentminded tone, lost in memories of another time and place. "It's done to punish the enemy, and to make certain the castle will never be used against you again."

"Well, it wasna burned," Mairi said accepting his explanation, "although the *blecks* did sell it away from us, and the land and cattle with it. You'll be after getting it back, won't you?" she added, studying him anxiously. "That is why you've come back?"

He reached out and tugged a strand of bright-red hair that had escaped her elaborate coiffure. "I'm after getting it back," he agreed. "I'm bound for Bath when I leave here, and from there I'm to London."

"Bath?" Mairi gave him an astonished look. "Why would you want to be going there? It's full of naught but rich old English lords who enjoy fancying themselves ill."

Although it was not in his nature to explain, Hugh decided to grant her the courtesy of an answer. She was his sister, after all, and like him, amongst the last of the line MacColme. "I'm going to see General George Burroughs, the duke of Hawkeshill," he said, his voice grimly determined. "I've heard he has retired there, and I mean to request his aid in getting back all that was taken from us."

Mairi digested this information in silence for a long moment. "And why would an English general, and a duke at that, be aiding you?" she asked curiously.

A hard smile touched Hugh's lips. "You might say he owes me something," he told her wryly.

"What?"

"His life."

Chapter 2

London

"Marry Sir Gervase? Are you mad? I would sooner wed with a pig!" Lady Caroline Burroughs declared, her deep-blue eyes spitting with fury as she glared into the dissipated face of her uncle. "I won't do it, do you hear me? And there is no way you can make me!"

Lord Charles Burroughs, earl of Westhall, arched a thin eyebrow at the dramatic pronouncement. "Can I not?" he drawled, his lips lifting in an amused smile. "I should not be so certain of that fact were I you, my dear. And I should have a care what you say about Sir Gervase. Wilmount is one of my dearest friends, and I will not tolerate his being insulted."

Caroline's delicate hands curled into small fists as she choked back a furious retort. Sir Gervase was indeed a "dearest friend" to her uncle: the two of them were as painted and powdered as a pair of aging actresses strutting the boards at Drury Lane, and their manners were almost as coarse. The thought of being shackled for life to such a creature was enough to make her ill, and she knew she would do whatever was required to avoid such a fate.

"Sir Gervase may well be your dear friend," she began, returning to her chair, "but that doesn't mean he would make me an ideal husband. I am but one and twenty, and the baronet is well into his forties. He is too old for me."

Her uncle did not answer at first, seeming far more interested in the taking of his snuff than in his niece's matrimonial concerns, but his indifference in no way fooled Caroline. She had long since learned to distrust such performances, knowing the more indolent he appeared, the more mischief he was planning.

"An older husband has been the making of many a young bride," he observed, after first delicately sneezing into the lace handkerchief he had produced from the sleeve of his satin coat. "And at your advanced age, I should think you would be grateful to receive an offer at all. You've had four seasons to make a match on your own, and you've yet to bring a man to the sticking point." He sent her a poisonous smile. "Your reputation precedes you, my dear, and it would seem that not even the sweetness of your fortune is enough to entice a man to wed and bed so renowned a shrew."

Caroline flushed angrily at the spiteful words. She knew her uncle was well aware she'd received offers aplenty in the four years since making her curtsies, just as he was aware she had rejected each and every one of those offers. She had little use for the brainless puppies clinging to her skirts and professing undying love, and even less use for the calculating fortune hunters who pursued her, their eyes fixed on her heavily laden purse. Neither group could see past her blonde curls and blue eyes to the woman inside, which made rejecting their offers of marriage easy. She had the example of her parents' marriage to draw upon, and like them, she was determined to marry only for love.

"As I was saying, I consider this to be an ideal match, and I have quite set my mind upon it," the earl continued, as usual turning a deaf ear to Caroline's objections. "A summer wedding would be best. Wilmount and I are quite anxious that he not miss any more of the season than is necessary."

The drawling comment had Caroline fighting to keep down the panic rising in her breast. Uncle Charles spoke as if the marriage was already a *fait accompli*, and she knew that boded ill for her. If he had already accepted Sir Gervase's offer, she would have to act before the banns were posted, else she could well find herself shackled to the fat, wretched monster her uncle had selected for her. Schooling her face to reflect none of her fear, she raised her eyes to meet his gaze.

"I will not marry him, Uncle Charles," she said, her tone quietly determined. "You may have control over my fortune, but that does not give you control over my person. The days a woman can be forced into an unwanted marriage are long since past, and I will not be wed to a man I abhor."

Her uncle took another delicate sniff of snuff. "Again I must caution you against insulting the baronet," he warned in a chilling voice. "And as for my not having control over your person, I fear you are sadly mistaken. I do have such control, and if you do not do as I see fit, I will not hesitate to exercise it."

Caroline stiffened warily. "And what is that supposed to mean?" she demanded.

"Merely that your behavior, my dear Caroline, has become most alarming in these past weeks," he drawled, his pale-blue eyes gleaming with malice. "And really, it is quite worrying. You are grown headstrong and willful, and I fear for your sanity."

Despite her air of bravado, Caroline's stomach took a sickening plunge. Last year her dear friend, Olivia Crenshaw, had been locked up as mad by her beast of a husband, and had it not been for the determined efforts of her brother, she might be languishing there still. After winning her release her brother had gone on to kill her husband in a duel, but the damage had already been done. The warm, laughing girl Caroline remembered had been replaced by a hollow-eyed, quiet woman who seldom smiled and never laughed.

"You would not dare," she said, although her voice trembled with a mixture of fear and anger.

The smile he gave her was the stuff of nightmares. "Would I not?" he mocked. "But what else am I to do, dearest niece? You are acting irrationally, and your sudden preoccupation with your fortune, besides being decidedly *declassé*, is an indication of how unstable you have become. Why else should you have accused your loving uncle, who has always shown you every kindness, of stealing from you?"

So that was it! Some of Caroline's terror retreated as understanding dawned. Her uncle had somehow learned of her inquiries into his handling of her inheritance, and meant to threaten her into silence.

"I do not recall accusing you of theft," she informed him, retreating behind a wall of cool indifference. "I but made a few discreet inquiries, and if you are not taking my money illegally, you need have nothing to fear."

The smirk on his lips disappeared. "I fear nothing!" he snapped, his satin pantaloons rustling as he rose to his feet. "Just take care you remember what I have said. You might think yourself a woman grown, but you are still my ward and under the law I have full charge over you. Provoke me again, and you will learn to your cost precisely what that means."

The door had scarcely closed behind him before Caroline rang for her maid. If Uncle was going to post the banns she had to act fast, and clearly the first order of business was to call upon her solicitor. He'd been of great assistance in the past, and she was confident he would be now. Less than an hour later she was sitting in his office on Harley Street, listening in horror as he destroyed her last vestige of hope.

"I am sorry, my lady, but I fear your uncle has the right of it." Mr. Garrett's voice was filled with regret as he regarded Caroline over the rim of his spectacles. "As your guardian he does have legal charge over you, and that does, unfortunately, grant him power to have you committed for your own protection."

"But it's not for my protection, it is so he can

help himself to the rest of my money!" she raged, furious at his apparent acquiescence. "There must be something you can do to stop him!"

"Again, my lady, I fear the law can offer you little protection," Mr. Garrett said, shaking his head firmly. "It is appalling to be sure, but so long as your uncle remains your legal guardian, he exercises full control over you. Naturally if he attempts to have you committed I can petition the courts for cause, but it could take some time to have the case heard."

He droned on, pointing out her uncle's power and what they might do to circumvent him, and with each word Caroline grew increasingly desperate. She kept remembering Olivia's wan appearance after being rescued, how ill she had been, and the way she'd started at the smallest sound. She would not let that happen to her, she vowed, refusing to give in to the panic clawing at her. She would not.

". . . your grandfather," Mr. Garrett concluded, looking thoughtful. "Your uncle would still remain your guardian, of course, but if His Grace lets his displeasure be known, Lord Westhall is certain to abide by his wishes."

Caroline stirred in her chair, annoyed with herself for failing to pay attention. "I am sorry, sir," she apologized, "but would you repeat that?"

"I merely said that as the duke has returned to England, it might well be in your interest to contact him and beg him to intercede with your uncle," Mr. Garrett responded dutifully. "When your father first drew up his will he spoke of having his father named your guardian, but as

His Grace was out of the country more than he was in it, he decided it was best to name his brother instead. A mistake, it would seem," he added wryly.

The solicitor's mastery of the obvious usually amused Caroline, but the situation was far too dire for her to find much humor in it. Even now Uncle Charles could be posting the banns, or having the orders for her commitment drawn up, and speed was of the essence. She vaguely recalled hearing that her grandfather, whom she'd met but a handful of times, had retired from the army to spend his dotage in Bath, but it had never occurred to her to seek his aid. Now she wondered that she could have been so foolish as not to have thought of him herself.

"Do you really think he might be able to help me?" she asked, a tenuous plan already forming in her mind.

"He could scarce hurt you," Mr. Garrett answered with a shrug. "At worst he might side with your uncle, but at best he could petition the courts to transfer guardianship to him. His Grace has many friends in the highest of circles, and it would be an easy matter for him to arrange matters to your mutual satisfaction. Shall I contact him for you?" And he picked up his quill in eager anticipation.

Caroline thought of the look on her uncle's face as he left the house. It was a look she'd seen before, when he was about to beat one of the hounds who had disobeyed him. The pleasure and anticipation was sickening to behold, and more sickening yet to think of it turned in her direction.

"No, there is no need for you to do that," she said quietly, her decision made. "I shall contact him myself."

"Wheest! Will ye stop yer squirming!" Angus Cameron scolded, his thick white brows meeting in a scowl as he struggled to tie Hugh's cravat. "How am I to arrange this thing in a proper fashion with ye hopping about like a flea?"

"And how am I to breathe when you are determined to strangle me?" Hugh shot back, doing his best to remain still. "The men in England cannot be so foolish as to actually wear these cursed things! I can scarce move my head."

"English gentlemen dinna move their heads, they have their servants to do their peeping for them," Angus retorted, still scowling. "Ye saw those painted fops in the taproom and on the street the same as I, and ye'll look no less elegant than they or it's both our heads the mistress will have. There." He gave his creation a final pat and stepped back. "What do ye think?"

Obligingly Hugh turned toward the glass, trying not to wince at what he saw reflected there. At Angus's insistence he'd used some of his precious gold to purchase a new wardrobe, grudgingly conceding he could scarcely call upon a duke looking no better than a ragged beggar, to quote his newfound valet. His new coat and breeches were of black kerseymere, and matched with his new shirt and elegant waistcoat of black and gold brocade, he supposed they helped him pass muster. He was only glad he didn't have to wear a wig as well; he hated the pest-ridden things.

"Will the general see ye today, do ye ken?" Angus asked, regarding Hugh with marked interest. "Or is he one of those who enjoys keeping people dangling forever?"

Hugh thought of the blunt, unassuming man he'd come to know in the months they'd spent in America. "If he is at home, he will see me," he said, reaching out to pick up his sword. He was buckling it about his waist when he caught another of Angus's disapproving frowns. "What?"

"I dinna believe the wearing of swords is permitted in Bath," the older man said, picking up a gold-topped cane and showing it to Hugh. "That's why the men carry these." He pressed a button, revealing the length of narrow steel concealed in the cane's hollow case. Hugh stared at it for a moment and resumed fastening his sword about him.

" 'Tis naught but a bit of foppery," he said, his gaze returning to his reflection. "If trouble comes, I want to kill my enemy, not tickle him."

"Aye, as if the way between here and Edward Street was littered with enemies lying in wait for ye," Angus grumbled, clearly unimpressed with his logic. "Well, if it's determined ye are to wear that pigsticker, then ye'd best be on yer way. I've done what I can wi' ye."

Knowing his fearsome valet only too well, Hugh didn't waste time arguing, but quickly took his leave. He still wasn't precisely certain how Angus had come to accompany him on his journey southward, but ruefully accepted that he was stuck with him until they returned to Edinburgh. The little valet had been waiting in the coach Aunt Egidia had hired for him when he'd left Scotland, and would not be budged by threats or pleas. His aunt had given Angus orders to look after him, and look after him the man would, despite Hugh's feeling on the matter.

Hoping to save money, Hugh had taken lodgings along the river, and now he kept a wary eye open for cutpurses who might mistake him for some useless fop and think to attack him. But after a few blocks it was obvious that the denizens of the area were sharp enough to know their business, and none made to stop him as he strode toward the new bridge crossing the river above the weir.

The wide expanse of Great Pulteney Street, with its rows of elegant homes, put him in mind of the houses being built in the new part of Edinburgh. He wondered cynically if the English meant to make the ancient city as pretty as this one, and if so he wished them luck with it. Edinburgh was like a cantankerous old Scot, and would not take well to taming.

Edward Street was located almost at the very end of Great Pulteney, and a few minutes later he was knocking on the door of number 12. An aloof butler with a haughty expression that put even Gregors's imperious manner in the shade gazed up at him.

"I am Hugh MacColme, laird of Loch Haven, to see the duke," he said, not waiting to be asked his business. "Will you be so good as to tell him I am here?"

A thin eyebrow arched. "His Grace is not at home to those who have not made an appointment," he informed Hugh coolly. "If you would care to leave your card, I shall give it to his valet."

"Bundhi?" The name slipped out as Hugh recalled the Hindu body servant the general had brought with him from India after purchasing him in a slave market.

The butler's supercilious expression faded to uncertainty. "You are familiar with the duke's household?"

"We served together, both in Canada and America," Hugh said, wondering if he should have tried this approach first. "He was commander of the battalion."

The butler's haughty look vanished as if by magic. "You are a fusilier?" he asked, fairly beaming at Hugh.

"Aye, that I am," Hugh answered, judiciously ignoring the fact he had been dismissed from service weeks ago.

"His Grace is always at home to members of his old regiment," the butler said, stepping back from the door to admit Hugh. "What is your rank, sir, if I may ask?"

"Sergeant major," Hugh provided, hoping the general's democratic sensibilities hadn't undergone a change since his retirement. The man he recalled was just as likely to give a junior officer a quick kick to the backside as he was to offer a tankard of ale to an enlisted man whose opinion he valued.

The butler gave a magnificent bow. "Very well, Sergeant Major, if you will come with me, I shall conduct you to the morning parlor. His Grace is dressing, but I shall send him word you are here. I am sure he will wish to speak with you."

The room to which Hugh was directed was a far cry from the drab and dreary quarters he and Angus were sharing, and as he waited for his host to arrive, Hugh made a quick study of the room. The walls were lined with gold brocade, the warm, honeyed color reflected in the richly woven Aubusson carpet covering the highly polished floors. A pianoforte stood in one corner, and the rest of the room was taken up with a variety of chairs and a settee of gilded wood and vibrant scarlet damask.

Normally such things did not concern him, but Mairi had charged him most faithfully to pay close attention to such details, as she was hopeful of convincing Aunt Egidia to have her rooms redone in the new fashion. Hugh wished her luck with it. He doubted his clutch-fisted aunt had replaced so much as a chair cushion since a Stuart had sat upon the throne.

He was admiring a pretty table of inlaid wood with daintily scrolled legs when the door opened and General Burroughs came striding in. Training had him leaping to his feet and snapping to rigid attention, an action that clearly delighted his host.

"At ease, Sergeant MacColme, at ease," he said, blue eyes bright with pleasure as he advanced toward Hugh with his hand extended. "No need to act the wooden soldier with me. I should hope we know each other better than that. How are you?"

"Well, sir," Hugh said, breathing a mental sigh

of relief as he shook the older man's hand. "And you?"

"On my last leg, or so the sawbones of Bath would have it," the general chuckled, waving Hugh toward one of the chairs. "Of course, if they said I was healthy as a strapping young man like you, I should hardly be willing to pay the outrageous sums they charge for their dubious services, would I?"

A servant arrived with a bottle of claret and a tempting array of sweets before Hugh could answer. The next several minutes were taken up with idle chatter, as Hugh fought back his rising impatience. He was trying to think of some polite way to broach the reason for his visit when the general took the matter out of his hands.

"But what brings you to Bath, Sergeant?" he asked, handing a glass of the sweet red wine to Hugh. "I should have thought you would have been back amongst the Highlands and heather of Scotland by now. You are from Loch Haven, if memory serves."

Hugh set down his glass of wine untasted. "That is why I am come, sir," he said. Knowing the general's distaste for dissembling, he began laying out the bare details of all that had transpired four years earlier. By the time he was finished, the general was frowning thoughtfully.

"Like that, is it?" he said, tapping a slender finger to his chin. "Oh, dear, that does not sound at all promising."

"I have the oath I signed when I joined the army," Hugh said, refusing to be discouraged by the general's response. "I am hoping that it, along with a letter from a commanding officer giving details of my service, will help persuade the courts to return the castle and lands to me. And naturally I am willing to pay any fines which may be entailed," he added, doing his best not to choke on the words.

"But not happily so, eh, Sergeant?" the general drawled, then held up a hand when Hugh opened his lips to speak. "No, do not bother denying what I can read in your eyes," he said, his own eyes twinkling. "And rest assured, I do not blame you for being angry. Paying for the return of one's own property is rather like being asked to pay for one's own noose. A double insult, I should think."

"But can it be done, do you think?" Hugh pressed, his hands clasped in front of him as he leaned forward. "I can reclaim that which was taken from me? From my clan?"

General Burroughs's expression grew even more pensive. "It is possible, I suppose," he said slowly. "I should happily give a most glowing report of your service under my command, and if that is not enough, I have friends aplenty in the courts I could approach for help. Naturally, the fact that the castle and the lands have already been purchased provides a bit of a challenge, but it should be easy enough to overcome. We've stormed more than one such obstacle in our day, have we not, Sergeant MacColme?" he added, sending Hugh a grin that was surprisingly boyish.

For the first time in a fortnight Hugh felt a stirring of hope. "Aye, General," he said, his own lips lifting in a rueful smile. "And so we have."

They spent the next twenty minutes laying out their plans, and Hugh was pleased to note the general was as sharp a strategist as ever he was. In Canada they'd called him the White Fox, for his ability to outrun and outthink the bands of rebels and Indians they pursued through woods so dangerous no other commander would have dared enter them. They were poring over a list of other officers they might approach for help when the sound of a disturbance in the hallway brought their heads snapping up.

Hugh rose to his feet, his hand reaching automatically for his sword as the door opened and a stunning blonde came dashing into the room. She paused on the threshold, her sharp blue gaze brushing past Hugh before coming to rest on the general.

"Grandfather, I must speak with you!" she said, hurrying at once to the general's side. "Uncle Charles is trying to force me into marriage with one of his friends, and he is threatening to lock me up as insane if I do not agree! You must help me!"

"What the devil?" The general gazed down at her in amazement, confusion giving way to slack-jawed astonishment. "It cannot be," he said, his voice rough as he raised shaking hands to cradle the blonde's face. "Upon my soul . . . Caroline?" His gaze scurried over her face. "Caroline, is it you?"

She gave a brisk nod, sparing Hugh a frowning glance before continuing. "I am sorry for bursting in like this, but I fear there is little time. Uncle Charles may even now be preparing the writ for my confinement, and I've no doubt he will use it if I do not do as he says and marry Sir Gervase. You must help me, Grandfather; you are my last hope!"

"Of course I shall help you, child!" the general soothed, obviously much-shaken by her pleas. His gaze drifted to Hugh, and at the look of apology he saw reflected there, Hugh's hands clenched in impotent fury. He was being dismissed.

"Shall I call upon you tomorrow, sir?" he asked, accepting the inevitable even as he was fighting the urge to throw the chit bodily from the room. The general might be taken in by her dramatic pronouncements, he thought derisively, but he was not. He'd seen her sort before, among the spoiled and pampered wives of officers who indulged in such theatrics to win their way. Doubtless this Uncle Charles of hers had refused to buy her a new gown, and she'd come running to her grandfather with some wild tale of cruelty on her lips.

"That might be best, Sergeant," General Burroughs said, sounding relieved. "Leave your direction with Campton, and I shall send you word. Good day to you."

"As you wish, General," Hugh said, executing a stiff bow. Frustration and resentment devoured him, and he slid a furious glare at the lady who had usurped his place. She was standing beside the general, her cool blue gaze meeting his with a surprising directness. Her eyes were wary to be sure, but the satisfaction and intelligence he saw reflected in their jewel-colored depths confirmed his suspicions. The little witch was acting.

He continued holding her gaze, making no attempt to disguise his contempt of her. At first he thought she meant to brazen her way out of their silent duel; then he saw her eyes widen first in confusion, and then in horrified understanding. *Good*, he thought, his mouth curving with bitter satisfaction. At least she now knew he had not been fooled by her pretty performance. Taking from that what pleasure he could, he turned and left the room.

"Are you all right, dearest child?" her grandfather demanded the moment the door had closed behind the red-haired stranger. "Shall I send for the smelling salts?"

"No, Grandfather, that shall not be necessary," Caroline assured him, annoyed he should think her so weak-willed a creature as that. "I am fine, I promise you."

"If you say so," he replied, his tone anxious as he continued hovering over her. "But at least let me send for some tea, eh? You are looking dashed pale."

"As you wish, sir," Caroline agreed, more out of the desire to placate him than out of any genuine desire for food. And, she silently admitted with a guilty sigh, because it would give her a few minutes in which to compose herself. A few minutes she realized she desperately needed.

While the duke was off seeing to the food, Caroline hurried over to the mirror hung above the mantelpiece to repair the damages to her appearance. Her first glimpse of her reflection did little to improve her spirits, for she looked a perfect fright. She'd fled from London with little more than the clothes on her back, and the long and dusty ride had had a detrimental effect upon her person. Why was it ladies in novels could indulge in such adventures and emerge looking dewy-eyed and delicate, while she looked as if she'd been pulled through a hedgerow backwards? It simply wasn't fair.

When she'd done what she could to restore her appearance to some semblance of order, she returned to the settee to gather her thoughts. Now that she'd achieved the first part of her objective and had won her grandfather's promise to help, all that remained was convincing him to become her guardian. Certainly he seemed sympathetic to her plight, she thought, recalling the concern on his thin face. If she but continued playing upon that sympathy, she was certain he would agree to whatever she suggested.

Such machinations were foreign to her usual direct nature, and her pride burned at being forced to employ the feminine posturings she'd always disdained. But during the long ride from London she'd had a great deal of time to think, and she decided it might be best to immediately impress the duke with the desperation of her situation, rather than attempting to reason with him. Her grandfather was all but a stranger to her, and she had no way of knowing how he might respond. She knew she had to be very clever in her approach, and had planned each word and gesture with the studiousness of an actress preparing to walk out upon a stage.

At first she feared she'd overplayed her hand with her startling bluntness, but to her relief he had believed her at once. Which was more than could be said of the hard-faced stranger who'd been with him, she brooded, remembering the contempt she'd seen gleaming in his silver-green eyes as he'd held her gaze with a boldness that was just short of insolence.

Grandfather had called him "Sergeant," she recalled, and surmised they must have served together. Certainly he had the look of a battle-hardened soldier, and there was a cold, menacing air of danger about him that made her grateful he was not her grandfather. Had she attempted such a ruse on him, she had no doubt he would have sent her packing back to London without so much as a flicker of remorse. Ah, well. She dismissed the memory of his tall, muscular form with a shrug. She had more important things to think of at the moment than some arrogant stranger.

Her grandfather soon returned, accompanied by a maid pushing a cart laden with food. They chatted while the servant laid out the food, but the moment they were alone, her grandfather turned abruptly serious.

"Now tell me what that rakehell son of mine has been about," he said, his directness taking Caroline by surprise. "Not really attempting to force you to the altar, is he?"

Caroline lowered her gaze to her hands, doing her best not to squirm. What she knew as fact and what she could prove were not the same thing, and she struggled for the right words.

"He informed me yesterday I am to accept the viscount's offer of marriage," she said, deciding it would be best to start with the truth. "I told him I hate—am afraid," she amended, deciding that sounded better, "of Sir Gervase, but it does not seem to matter. Uncle Charles says I will marry his friend, or he will have me locked away."

"I see." The duke steepled his fingers together and looked grave. "Have you any idea why he has set upon such a course of action? You must be all of twenty now, and it seems to me that if he was determined to see you wed, he should have done so by now."

"I am one and twenty, Grandfather," Caroline corrected, feeling a sharp pang that he did not even know her true age. "And as for why he has now decided to marry me off, I think I know the reason for that as well."

"And what reason might that be?"

"My fortune. I've recently discovered that although the majority of the money is entailed directly to me, Uncle Charles has still managed to steal several thousand pounds from my funds. He has also been affixing my name to various documents granting him further powers, and he was attempting to gain possession of some properties belonging to my mother when I was warned of his actions by my man of business. It was shortly after I began my inquiries that Uncle Charles announced I would wed Sir Gervase or pay the consequences." Her lips twisted in a bitter smile. "It would seem if he cannot obtain my fortune one way, he is determined to obtain it in another."

There was a long silence before her grandfather finally spoke. "I greatly esteemed your grandmother," he said, a look of resigned pain crossing his face. "But it is at times like this that I cannot help but wonder if she played me false all those years ago. I find it incomprehensible that such a devil's spawn should have sprung from my loins."

Caroline's fingers twisted together. "Then you believe me?" she asked, cautious hope stirring in her breast.

"Alas, knowing my son as I do, I fear I have no other choice," he replied with a heavy sigh. "It sounds precisely the sort of thing he would do, and in all fairness to the wretch, it *is* clever. By marrying you to his friend, a man I assume he controls completely, he will have all of your fortune rather than the bits of it he has managed to grab. Yes," he went on, nodding his head with reluctant admiration, "it is most clever of him, I vow."

Caroline was not certain how to take that. "But you will help me, won't you, Grandfather?" she pleaded, wondering if she ought to squeeze out another tear or two just to be safe. "You will not allow Uncle Charles to marry me off to Sir Gervase?"

"Eh?" He gave her a blank look, and then his blue eyes, so very like her own, began to sparkle with excitement. "Of course I shan't allow such a thing!" he said, sending her a reassuring smile. "In fact, I have in mind the perfect plan that will put an end to your uncle's evil designs once and for all. Yes, yes, it is the very thing."

"What is it, Grandfather?" she asked, all but weak with relief. "Will you petition the courts to become my guardian?"

"That is one way, to be sure," he agreed, frowning thoughtfully. "But given my advanced age, I fear it would be a temporary solution only.

Were I to die before you were safely wed, your uncle would be upon you like a crow on a rotting piece of carrion before I scarce cocked up my toes."

"Then what shall we do?" Caroline demanded, horrified as she accepted the truth of what he was saying.

In answer, he folded his hands and leaned back in his chair. "Why, the solution is as plain as a pikestaff," he said, looking smugly pleased with himself. "We shall marry you off to someone else as quickly as it can be arranged."

Chapter 3

H ugh was surprised to find a message from
General Burroughs waiting when he came
down to the taproom the following morning.
He'd steeled himself to be kept dangling a good
day or more, and the note ordering him to report
to Edward Street at one in the afternoon was
welcome news indeed.

To his surprise the slovenly innkeeper person-
ally fetched his food, bowing and scraping as he
set the plate of beefsteak before him. The food
was even hot, and Hugh was hard-pressed to
hide his cynical amusement as he tucked into his
breakfast. Corresponding with a duke had its unexpected benefits, it would seem.

As it was scarcely ten of the clock, he decided
to while away the rest of the morning exploring
the city. He'd been too long in the out-of-doors
to relish the thought of returning to his cramped,
airless room, and in any case, he thought it might
be worth his while to visit the Pump Room. Aunt
Egidia had told him it was the best place in Bath
to see who was in town. Before his conversation
with the general had been interrupted by the
pretty blonde, General Burroughs had men-

tioned that Colonel Margate was also in Bath. The affable man had been his last commanding officer, and Hugh was most anxious to see him again. The more power he had behind him, the safer he would feel.

The Pump Room was crowded when he arrived. At Angus's insistence he'd left his sword at home, a fact for which he was most grateful when he saw the notice posted beside the door banning the wearing of all weapons. He thought about the dirk he had tucked in the pocket of his fine coat, and gave brief thought to surrendering it. A man was a fool to go anywhere completely unarmed, though, and unless he was attacked, none would ever have cause to know he was carrying it.

After purchasing his tea and biscuits, he joined the crowds circling the elegantly appointed room. There were easily three times as many people as there were tables and chairs for them, and Hugh shook his head at the folly of it. Trust the English to turn the taking of medicinal waters into an excuse to pack as many people into a place as possible, he mused, wincing as a lady in a hooped skirt squeezed her way past him.

While walking, he took the opportunity to surreptitiously study the well-dressed throng, paying special note to what the other men were wearing. For himself he cared not a whit whether they rigged themselves up like a group of painted macaronis, or went about as naked as a band of savages, but for the sake of Loch Haven he knew he had best care. He wouldn't risk the future of his clan because some self-important prig of a magistrate didn't care for the cut of his coat.

To his relief he noted that his new coat and breeches were more than acceptable, and he felt the touch of more than one admiring glance from the ladies as he moved past them. He was also relieved to see he wasn't the only man in the room who had foresworn the wearing of a wig, nor was he even the only one with unpowdered hair. He heartily disliked the ritual, although as a soldier he'd been required to keep his hair meticulously powdered, a practice he'd considered impractical and even dangerous. White hair made a far easier target for American marksmen than plain hair, and in any case, he'd never seen the sense of a young man trying to look like an old one.

By his third turn about the room he decided he'd had enough, and was about to leave when he saw General Burroughs entering. At his side was his granddaughter, looking even more beautiful than before in a stunning ensemble of French blue silk and blond lace. Hugh admired her beauty, even as he cursed her presence. How was he to conduct his business with the general in private if the chit meant to cling to him like a limpet? he wondered crossly. None of these dark thoughts showed on his face, however, as he crossed the room to make his bows before them.

"Your Grace," he said, inclining his head with grave courtesy. "It is a pleasure to see you again."

"Ah, Sergeant, what a delightful surprise to find you here!" the general responded, looking genuinely pleased. "Did you receive the note I had sent round to your lodgings?"

"Yes, Your Grace, and I am looking forward to our meeting," Hugh answered, noting the blonde had gone rigid as a pole. Evidently her aristocratic sensibilities were offended at being introduced to a common soldier, he decided with dislike.

"As am I, Sergeant, as am I," the general replied, a mischievous light dancing in his blue eyes. "As a matter of fact, I have a rather interesting proposal to put to you that I think you may find worth the hearing."

To Hugh's surprise the blonde gave a jerk, her face first growing pink with color and then paling. She swiftly lowered her gaze, but before she did Hugh thought he detected a flash of resentment burning in her eyes. What the devil? he wondered, giving her a questioning look in return.

As if just recalling her presence, the general turned to his granddaughter and drew her forward. "You must forgive me, my manners have gone to lack," he said, smiling at Hugh. "Allow me to make you known to my granddaughter. Caroline, my dear," he said, giving her arm a paternal pat, "this handsome young gentleman is Hugh MacColme, the laird of Loch Haven, and the man to whom your grandfather owes his life. Sergeant MacColme, this stunning creature is my granddaughter, Lady Caroline Burroughs."

A *lady*, Hugh thought with a derisive sneer; he might have known. He made an elegant bow, and acting on the hope of disconcerting her, reached out to take the hand she had stiffly offered. He captured it in his, his fingers curling about hers with just enough strength to have her eyes flying open. Their gazes met, and when he was certain she wouldn't glance away, he raised her hand to his lips for a mocking kiss.

"My lady," he drawled, his mouth curving in a slow smile at the anger he could see flashing in her eyes. "It is an honor to make your acquaintance."

"Mr. MacColme." Her voice was every bit as rigid as her posture as she jerked her hand free. "My grandfather has spoken of you."

"Has he?" Hugh wondered what the older man might have said to have put that note of loathing in her voice. It had always been his impression the general held him in some esteem. But what did he care what some well-born chit thought of him? He turned his attention back to the duke.

"I was hoping I might see the colonel, sir," he said, ignoring Lady Caroline. "But he hasn't arrived as yet."

"No, no, quite the opposite, in fact," the general said, starting toward a table that had just been vacated. "He and I were here earlier to take the waters as befits a pair of old relics. I daresay he is at home on Gay Street, being cosseted by his wife by now. You recall Mrs. Margate, I trust?"

Hugh remembered the middle-aged, heavyset woman who had bullied her husband and his troops with equal ferocity, and remembered as well the way she had searched the battlefield following an engagement for the wounded men of the company. More than one man, himself included, was alive today because of her. "Aye, that I do, sir," he said, genuine pleasure softening his voice. "I trust the good lady is well?"

"With a city filled with invalids and fops to bully?" The general gave a laugh. "Dear boy, she is in alt. I daresay she will have half of Bath cured and the other half beaten into fighting shape by the time she is done."

They continued chatting as a servant brought them coffee and a plate of Bath buns. After a few minutes of exchanging reminiscences with the general, Hugh's manners got the best of him and he turned to Lady Caroline.

"Are you long in Bath, ma'am?" he asked politely, noting she hadn't eaten a single bite of the sugar-crusted roll.

"I am not certain, sir," she replied, her gaze fixed firmly on her plate. "As you know my arrival yesterday was somewhat unexpected, and there is much that has to be determined."

From that, Hugh surmised the general hadn't yet agreed to become her guardian. "It is my first visit here," he continued, deciding it could do him no harm to be polite. "And a most lovely place I find it. The buildings on the Royal Crescent are especially beautiful, do you not agree?"

That won him the courtesy of a look, as she raised her gaze to his face. "I am afraid I have not had much opportunity to take in the sights," she said, her voice filled with wary civility. "And like you, this is my first visit to Bath. But from what I have seen, I agree it is very lovely; far cleaner than London."

"A stable is far cleaner than London," General Burroughs observed, eating his roll with obvious

relish. "But you must make an effort to see something of Bath while you are here, my dearest,"
he added. "Perhaps after our meeting this afternoon, Sergeant MacColme will agree to show
you about, eh, Sergeant?"

Hugh had served with the general long
enough to recognize a command when he heard
one. "I should consider it an honor, Your Grace,"
he said, dredging up a thin smile. "Providing, of
course, her ladyship has no objections?" His gaze
flashed hopefully to her, although he was certain
she was too polite to refuse his offer outright.

"No, I have no objections, Mr. MacColme."
Her stiff reply confirmed his suspicions. "It
sounds most enjoyable, in fact."

"Excellent." General Burroughs beamed at
them both. "Now that we've settled that, do let
us enjoy our coffee and the excellent music. I
vow, it has been a good many years since I last
enjoyed Haydn in such convivial surroundings."

A silence then descended upon the table, both
Hugh and Lady Caroline having acquiesced to
the general's bidding. And it was no great hard-
ship listening to the music, Hugh thought. The
bright and delicate notes put him in mind of the
wild brooks of the Highlands—although to his
way of thinking, the pretty music in no way compared to the sound of the pipes. Now there was
a sound to stir men's souls, he mused, raising his
cup to his lips. Mayhap when he returned to
Loch Haven with the castle once more in his
hands, the clan would have a feast day to celebrate.

He was envisioning the great hall strung with
victory pennants and ringing with the sound of

laughter and the wail of the pipes, when the general gave a sudden exclamation.

"Upon my soul, is that Lady Hanfield?" he said, setting his cup down with an eager clatter. "I did not know her to be in Bath!"

Hugh glanced to his right, spying an ancient lady in a gown of pink silk, her frail frame all but bent under the weight of her towering wig. She was accompanied by half a dozen footmen, who were doing their best to help lower her onto her chair. A rather difficult task, Hugh noted, since the wig looked near to toppling her over. It was two feet in height, if not more.

"I must go over to her." General Burroughs was rising to his feet. "Her late husband was one of my dearest friends, and I should be remiss did I not bid her hello." He scurried off, leaving Hugh and Lady Caroline alone.

Hugh was expecting a stiff silence, and was surprised when she suddenly leaned forward. "I must speak with you," she said. "At what hour do you call upon my grandfather?"

Hugh arched an eyebrow at the urgent note in her voice. "One of the clock," he replied coolly, wondering what she was about.

"Come at twelve-thirty instead," she instructed, her gaze flicking to the nearby table where the general was bowing over the elderly lady's hand. "Have the butler conduct you to the drawing room; I shall be waiting for you there."

Hugh hid his astonishment at her command. To be sure his knowledge of English noblewomen was scarce, but he was fairly certain they did not normally arrange clandestine meetings with strange men. Certainly he would never permit Mairi to do such a thing, and his cautious nature stirred to life.

"Will you?" he asked, his accent deepening along with his suspicions. "And what might you be waiting for, I wonder?"

Her gaze returned to his, the dark-blue eyes flashing with annoyance. "Not for the reason you appear to be thinking," she informed him with a proud lift of her chin. "I have something I wish to discuss with you, and it is something best done in private. Will you be there, or will you not?"

Tempting as it was to toss her arrogant demand back in her face, Hugh managed to resist. It would do him no harm to hear what she had to say, he reasoned—and a MacColme never fled from a challenge, but faced it head on.

"Oh, I shall be there," he drawled, his mouth curving in a mocking smile. "Indeed, I would not dream of missing it. Only mind you make it worth my while," he added, taking a small satisfaction in seeing her cheeks pinken with anger. "I've no patience to have my time wasted by some schoolroom miss bent on making mischief. Keep that in mind, my lady, and we shall get along fine."

Schoolroom miss, indeed! Caroline fumed less than an hour later, the full skirts of her gown flaring about her as she paced the elegant confines of her bedchamber. And how dare he accuse her of attempting to make mischief? It was beyond all enduring, and for twopence she'd keep the arrogant Scot waiting in the drawing room until he died from hunger! Grandfather might think the sergeant the perfect solution to her difficulties, but for herself, she would as lief bargain with the devil. Heaven knew he couldn't make a more dangerous adversary, she brooded, pausing to glare at her reflection in the mirror.

The past two sleepless nights had left her pale and wan, and far more emotional then she could like. She felt as delicate and brittle as the glass figurines she had collected as a child, and feared that the slightest pressure would shatter her into a thousand pieces. It wasn't right, she told herself crossly. All she wanted was to live her own life as she saw fit. Why should she be forced to wed either a disgusting mound of flesh or a dangerous and mocking devil, to have control over what was rightfully hers? The unfairness of it all made her want to take her fist and smash the mirror.

Then the control that had been her salvation these many years reasserted itself, and she fought her way back from the edge of tears. Now was not the time for foolish weeping, she told her refection. In less than an hour her entire fate would be decided, and if she meant to have the smallest say in that decision, she could not allow herself the luxury of emotion. She would have to be twice as cold and calculating as the man she was meeting if she meant to win—a prospect daunting enough to make the knot of tension in her chest tighten with almost painful intensity.

When Grandfather had first made his suggestion, she'd thought him mad. It had to be madness to believe such a thing could possibly work. And yet the more her grandfather had spoken of it, the greater sense it began to make. *A marriage of convenience,* she'd thought, the idea slowly taking shape in her mind. *Her* convenience, if they could but win the sergeant's cooperation in certain matters. A cooperation her grandfather felt certain they could have, although he would not tell her why.

That was why she wanted to speak with him before he met with her grandfather. The duke might be confident he would agree, but she couldn't afford the luxury of his being wrong. Even now her uncle could be on his way from London with a special license or an order for her commitment in his pocket, and if all was not arranged before his arrival, she'd be in every bit as much trouble as she'd been when she'd fled from London. More in trouble, she amended, thinking of the rage the earl was likely to be in when he arrived. Her uncle hated losing, and those who managed to best him were usually punished in some clever and evil way.

With that thought firmly in mind she'd passed the long night staring at the ceiling and carefully laying out her plans. The first difficulty was to win the sergeant's cooperation, although upon reflection she didn't think it would be so very hard. Her years in her uncle's company had taught her that however much men might like their whores and their horses, there was nothing they cared for more than the gleam of gold. For all he was a Scot and a soldier, she couldn't believe Sergeant MacColme was cut from so different a cloth, and she knew if she but offered him enough money, he would do as she wished.

The next problem she foresaw was the man's pride—a pride she now realized was deep and as fierce as the Highlands from which he came. If she didn't word her offer just so, he was likely to toss it in her face and go storming back to Scotland.

"Excuse me, my lady." The little maid assigned to her bobbed a curtsy from the doorway. "Will you wish to be changing your gown? 'Tis past noon."

It was on the tip of her tongue to say no, but then she thought the better of it. She was woman enough to find confidence in a pretty gown, and upon consideration she also thought it might be best if she were to meet Mr. MacColme looking every inch the lady.

Twenty-five minutes later she was staring at her reflection, her expression critical as she studied the glass for the smallest sign of imperfection. The gown she was wearing was a *robe Anglaise* fashioned of pink and yellow striped silk, draped over an underskirt of pink brocade. Sleeves dripping with lace ended just above her elbows, and her hair, arranged *à la conseiller*, gave her the air of fashionable *élan* she had been striving to achieve. *There*, she thought with womanly satisfaction, brushing one of the long curls back from her shoulder. *Let him call me a schoolmiss now*.

When she walked into the drawing room a few minutes later she saw that a small fire had been laid in the fireplace and she also saw a tray of biscuits and a bottle of madeira were standing in readiness per her instructions. She'd offer him a glass of wine first, and when he was feeling comfortable and pleased with himself she'd present her offer to him. Everyone knew the Scots to be a hardheaded, practical people, and if she could make him see the sense of what she was offering, he would agree. He had to agree, she thought, a small frisson of panic sneaking through her defenses. The alternative was too horrible to contemplate.

The tinkling of the bell interrupted her reverie, and she'd no sooner taken her seat before the fire than the door opened and the butler entered, Mr. MacColme hard on his heels. "Sergeant MacColme to see you, my lady," the butler intoned, his wooden expression mute evidence of his disapproval. "Will you be requiring anything further?"

From that, Caroline gathered he was hinting she should have a maid sit with her for propriety's sake. But what she had to say was too important to risk their conversation being overheard by anyone—especially a servant who was likely to repeat everything she heard.

"No, Campton, thank you," she said, dredging up a smile. "That will be all. You may go now."

"As you wish, my lady." The butler's bow was so stiff it was a wonder he didn't snap in half, Caroline mused, the smile on her lips spreading into a genuine grin. She quickly pursed her mouth, sending her guest a worried glance out of the corner of her eye. To her deep surprise, he was also smiling.

"I had a sergeant in my early days with the regiment," he said, his silver-green eyes twinkling with remembered laughter. "He was a proper terror, with a voice like a bull and a fist the size of a ham. When he pokered up like that, we knew we were in for it."

His easy confidence took Caroline aback, destroying the plans she had laid with such care. She'd been prepared to deal with the cold, hard soldier she'd met that morning, and was uncertain what to do with this smiling, even-tempered man. Heavens, she thought, dazed at the realization, he was almost charming. She was wondering how best to adjust to this new development when the smile vanished, and his eyes grew as cold as a wind off the sea.

"Well, I'm here, my lady," he said, folding his arms and studying her with the cold insolence she remembered from yesterday. "What is it you have to say?"

His mocking tones made Caroline's temper flare, but she controlled her tongue. "I will be blunt, sir," she began, meeting his gaze with cool insouciance. "My grandfather has a proposition he is about to put to you; a proposition which will be to both of our benefits. I wish you to accept that proposition, and am willing to pay you handsomely for doing so."

An eyebrow one shade darker than the reddish-brown hair pulled back in a queue arched, but his hard face revealed not a hint of his thoughts. "Indeed?" he said, his deep voice mild. "And what must I do to be paid so handsomely? Is it someone you want killed, mayhap? This Uncle Charles of yours, who has caused you such distress?"

She struggled to her feet with as much grace as her full skirts and tight corset would allow. "Of course I don't want Uncle Charles killed!" she exclaimed, horrified he could even suggest such a thing, his callousness seemed to imply that he would say yes if that was indeed what she wanted.

"Then what is it?" he pressed. "You must admit 'tis more than passing strange. You ask me to meet with you without benefit of a chaperone, and I no sooner get here than you're offering me a fistful of gold to accept a proposition you refuse to describe in any detail."

Her cheeks grew pink at his blunt summation of the situation. "It isn't like that," she muttered, furious that he could reduce her careful plans to foolishness with a few well-spoken words.

"Then how is it?" he demanded, leaning forward in his chair to hold her gaze. "And before you say another word," he added, even as she was opening her lips to speak, "I warn you I'll do nothing to bring shame to the general. He's a fine man, and I'll not have him upset."

"Upset him?" she exclaimed. "How can this possibly upset him when the entire thing is his idea?"

"What idea?"

Too angry to prevaricate, she said the first thing to pop into her mind. "That you marry me, you dolt!" she snapped, and then watched in satisfaction when he went slack-jawed with disbelief. His mouth opened and closed several times, the gift of speech having clearly deserted him.

"What did you say?" he managed at last, his voice sounding like a rusty hinge badly in need of oiling.

Caroline hesitated uncertainly. Pleased as she was at having knocked the arrogant Scot back a pace, she was already regretting her impetuous tongue. Things were not going at all as she had planned, and she decided 'twas time she tossed in her hand and left the table before she had lost

everything. "I believe I have said more than I
should," she said, walking over to the bellpull
hanging beside the fireplace. "I shall have Campton inform Grandfather you are here, and he can
answer your questions."

But he was not about to be dissuaded. He rose
to his feet and stalked over to where she was
standing. "Why should the general want you to
marry me?" he demanded, reaching out to lay a
staying hand on her arm. "Are you with child
and looking for a man, any man, to give your
bastard a proper name?"

Caroline did not stop to think, but slapped him
full across the face with as much strength as she
could muster. He allowed the blow to land, and
then grabbed her wrist and pulled her against
him.

"That slap I admit I deserved," he conceded,
controlling her furious struggles with contemptuous ease. "But I'll not have you beating me as
if I were no more than a servant."

"How dare you!" she said, furious at his
charge. "I've never struck a servant in my life!"

To her fury, a mocking grin spread across his
handsome features. "That would explain why
you made such a poor job of it," he said, laughing as she tried to free her hand. "I've had puffs
of wind do more damage. Ah, ah—" He tightened his grip, anticipating her next move. "No
more, I warn you. I've never in my life raised a
hand to a woman, but you tempt me sorely."

She ceased her struggles, accepting grudgingly
that she would only be freed when he chose to
release her. She remained rigid in his hold, her
eyes fixed on a point over his shoulder. Several

seconds passed before he finally released her hand and took a cautious step backward.

"Very well," he began, eyeing her warily. "Now I would know what you mean by speaking of marriage. Are you with child?"

Her elaborate coiffure had been disturbed by their grappling, and she brushed back a curl dangling against her cheek. "No," she said through gritted teeth, "I am not."

She felt his gaze go to her tightly cinched waist. "Are you certain?"

"Of course I am certain!" she retorted, feeling more angry and embarrassed than she ever had in her life. "I've never been with a man in my . . . oh!" She broke off, sending him an aggrieved scowl. "Why am I bothering to explain myself to you? It is obvious you are no gentleman!"

"On that, my lady, we are in agreement," he responded, inclining his head mockingly. "And that is something I would caution you to remember. So," he continued before she could speak, "if it is not a babe you are carrying, why the offer of marriage? It is the general's idea, you say?"

Caroline gave a jerky nod, all but seething with resentment at his hard implacability. "He said it was the only way to foil Uncle Charles," she said. "Grandfather said he could hardly force me into marriage with Sir Gervase if I were already wed to you, and as my husband, you would be my legal guardian, not him. He could only commit me with your consent."

A look of obvious skepticism stole across his face. "Then he truly did threaten you with such a thing? You weren't exaggerating the matter to win your grandfather's support?"

Knowing he'd seen through her performance was disconcerting, but matters were too serious for Caroline to care. "Did you know my uncle, sir, you would not ask such a question," she said, her lips thinning in a grim smile. "There is nothing he would not do to get his hands on my fortune."

He still looked far from convinced. "Your fortune?" he repeated, tilting his head to one side as he studied her. "You're so rich, then?"

Caroline wasn't certain how to answer his question. Although the size of her fortune had been a matter of much speculation since the day of her coming out, she couldn't remember anyone ever asking her straight out the depth of her pockets. Perversely, she decided she preferred his blunt demand to the mendacity displayed by most of her suitors. She tilted up her head to meet his gaze. "I am," she said, watching his face to see how her admission struck him. "Does that matter?"

He gave an indifferent shrug. "To me, no, though I cannot help but wonder why you should still be pressing for marriage with a stranger. If you are as wealthy as you claim, I would think there would be more than enough men eager to wed you. So I ask you once more, my lady, why me?"

Knowing it was useless to prevaricate any longer, Caroline surrendered to the inevitable. "Because of the Scottish divorce laws," she said quietly. "Grandfather says if we wed and remain married for one year and then divorce, I can gain legal control over my money and my person. Uncle Charles would never be able to threaten me again."

If hearing she wished to wed him had shocked him, it was obvious her plans to divorce him left him reeling. He stared at her as if she were indeed the madwoman her uncle threatened to name her. "Divorce!" he exclaimed, his hands tightening about her upper arms. "You cannot mean it!"

Caroline pulled herself free. "Of course I mean it!" she returned crossly. "I have no desire to be wed—not to you nor to any other troublesome man—but because of British law I have no other choice in the matter. If I am to be free of Uncle Charles and his vile threats, I must marry. What is so difficult to comprehend about that?"

"Aye, the marriage part I ken well enough," he said, his expression darkening. " 'Tis the divorce part I am finding a wee bit hard to swallow. A divorce would cause a devil of a scandal, and I'll not be dragging my name and my clan through such muck."

"But that is precisely the point!" Caroline exclaimed, recalling her grandfather's careful explanations. "Scottish law provides for the dissolution of a marriage for a variety of reasons, with no scandal attached to either party. And even if there were to be some talk, it seems to me *I* am the one who would likely suffer the brunt of it. If I am willing to take such a risk, can you not at least consider the matter?"

He remained visibly skeptical. "And you are willing to live with society's censure?" he asked, folding his arms across his broad chest. "Even knowing it could well make you an outcast, and ruin forever your chances for a proper marriage?"

Caroline had already considered and accepted the dangers of her grandfather's shocking proposal. "As I never desired to marry in the first place, I do not see that I have any chances left to ruin," she said, her chin lifting with quiet resolve. "I want only my freedom, and there is nothing I won't do to achieve it. All I ask is that you listen to Grandfather's proposal before deciding whether or not to agree. Will you do that?"

At first she didn't think he would reply, and then he dipped his head. "Aye, my lady," he said, his expression betraying nothing of his feelings, "I will listen."

Chapter 4

❦❦❦

"**Y**ou're mad," Hugh said with quiet conviction, his gaze never leaving his former commander's face. "Mad as a loon to even suggest such a thing, and I'm madder still to be sitting here listening to you. It will never work."

"Nonsense, dear boy; you must know I never act without knowing precisely what I am about," General Burroughs responded, his brows lifting with icy displeasure at what he obviously considered a rebuke. "The plan is flawless. You marry my granddaughter, remain wedded to her for one year, and at the end of that year you divorce her. What could be simpler? It is swift, decisive, and completely unexpected. The battle would be won before the enemy was even aware it had been joined."

"Aye," Hugh agreed, still stunned to realize the general was in complete earnest. "But 'tis rather like using a brace of cannon to bring down a quail. Surely we need not employ such drastic measures to achieve our objectives. The earl is your son; he cannot be the villain Lady Caroline would have him."

A look of infinite pain flashed across the older

man's face before he spoke. "He is my son," he said quietly, "though it would give me much pleasure were I able to deny the wretch. And he is every inch the villain Caroline has named him. There is no doubt in my mind he wouldn't hesitate to carry through with the threats he has made against her. Indeed, I fear he will do so whether she does as he commands or not."

Hugh stiffened at the general's grim observation. "What do you mean?" he demanded, growing worried despite his determination to remain disinterested.

General Burroughs remained silent for several seconds before responding. "A husband has complete control over the fortune and person of his wife," he began in the careful tones Hugh remembered from their days on the battlefield. "And if Caroline were to bow to Charles's demands and marry this Sir Gervase creature, there is nothing on this earth to prevent him from having her locked away. And did he choose to do so, there is precious little I could do to stop him."

Hugh hid his astonishment. "But you are a duke," he protested, sickened at the thought of the proud and beautiful Lady Caroline locked away in the filth of an asylum. "Surely were you to set up a howl, they would have to release her."

"And so they would, to be sure," the general agreed, "but by then who knows what damage might have already been done? The child could already have been driven to madness by her confinement, or worse still, have perished altogether. Oh, I daresay afterward I could kick up a devil of a scandal, make all sorts of accusations, but short of a trial, that would be the end of it."

Hugh's hands closed into fists as he silently accepted what he was hearing. The general was a man who weighed every possibility with calculating care, and if he said a situation was hopeless, it was hopeless indeed. Still . . .

"Could you not make yourself her ladyship's guardian?" he asked after a moment, wishing he knew more of such matters. "That should keep her safe from your son."

"Yes, but it would be a temporary safety only," the older man replied, suddenly looking alarmingly frail. "I'm not in the best of health, you know. That is why I am come to Bath."

Hugh sat forward, genuinely alarmed. "Are you ill, sir?"

There was another silence before the general spoke. "I am as well as any man who has reached his seventh decade and who has led the sort of life I have," he said, his blue eyes meeting Hugh's with unwavering courage. "I may live another decade, I may die tomorrow. No one can be certain."

Hugh glanced away, unable to answer for the painful lump lodged in his throat. He'd seen death in all its harrowing forms too many times to count, and he'd thought himself inured to grief. But the thought of the wily old general closing his eyes in death left him reeling.

A tired smile touched the general's lips. "Not that I am complaining, mind," he said with a laugh. "Had you not been there to put a bullet through that rebel, I should have died five years ago. Rather ironic when you think about it, don't you agree?"

Hugh shook his head, failing to see any humor in the situation. He was closer to the general than he ever thought he could be to an Englishman, and it grieved him sorely that this time there was nothing he could do to save the older man from death. And it shamed him more to realize his next concern was for himself. If the general should die, who would help him recover his lands?

"Now you can see why I am so desirous that you wed my granddaughter," General Burroughs continued, ignoring Hugh's silence. "Caroline's only protection is a husband, even a temporary one. Someone smart enough and ruthless enough to protect her from Charles when I am gone."

Because his granddaughter's plight seemed uppermost on the general's mind, Hugh reluctantly made himself think of it as well. "Aye," he said, accepting at last that the outlandish scheme was indeed the chit's only hopes of salvation. "But what I cannot understand is why you should want that someone to be me. I understand about the divorce laws, but a man need not be a Scot to make use of them. Why should you be so determined I marry your granddaughter? It makes no sense."

As usual, the general tumbled to his meaning at once. "Because I am English, and a duke, do you mean?" he asked, then chuckled when Hugh gave a terse nod. "Sergeant MacColme, do you know how I came by my title?"

Hugh's shoulders lifted in a shrug. "Inherited it from your father, I would suppose."

"From my uncle," the general corrected. "A thoroughly reprehensible man whose vices and villainy make Charles look like a dashed choir-boy. He died of the pox, but before the disease took him it left him withered and unable to produce heirs. He died without issue, and the title passed to Richard, my elder brother. Richard was a good enough fellow in his way, but he was wild and reckless in the extreme. He died drunk, attempting to walk blindfolded across a section of the roof, and the title fell to me. So you see," he added, a smile of amusement curving his mouth, "that is how I came to bear the noble title of duke. A case of the pox and a drunken wager."

Hugh felt an answering grin tugging at his lips. "I wondered why a duke would be a soldier," he admitted wryly.

"Especially considering I never desired to be a soldier in the first place," the general said, shocking Hugh with his casual confession. "I was enamored of the stage in my salad days, and quite longed to try my hand at acting. But Hawkeshill tradition had the second son taking up the sword, and so I was content to do my duty to the family name.

"Too content, mayhap," he frowned. "Even after I became the duke I kept to my soldiering, avoiding my duties to the title whenever possible. I had a wife and two sons, but I seldom saw them. I had an obligation to the land and the people, but I was happy enough to pass it on to others. Edward, my eldest son and Caroline's father, loved the land, and had he lived, he would have made an excellent duke. Alas, he and his wife died a number of years ago, and still I stayed away, leaving my responsibilities to others. Dereliction of duty, Sergeant Major, wouldn't you say?"

Hugh realized he did think almost that very thing and was appalled. "You're being too hard upon yourself, sir," he said, hastily pushing his traitorous thoughts aside. "You did as you thought best, and none would fault you for it."

"Perhaps." The older man inclined his head with touching humility. "But even as I fault myself, it is of no consequence. That is why I am so determined to help Caroline now, you see. I failed her all her life; I do not intend failing her now."

"General—"

"There is something else to consider," the general said, his tone urgent as he leaned forward. "So far we've only discussed how marriage will help Caroline, but we've not yet addressed how it might benefit you as well."

"Me?" Hugh asked, recalling Lady Caroline's condescending offer of money. He wasn't certain how he would respond if the general should make a similar offer.

"I've been considering your request for assistance in regaining your lands," General Burroughs began in his usual forthright manner. "And it occurs to me that while I may be of some help to you in this regard, there are limits to what I can do. As your friend," he added, the emphasis he placed on the word bringing Hugh to immediate attention.

"Go on," he said, wondering what the wily general was about.

"As your friend, I would be more than happy to write letters on your behalf, and perhaps petition friends of mine who are in positions of some authority. I would even be willing to pay whatever fines and damages may have been levied against your estate, although I'm certain that Scots pride of yours would never allow such a thing. But that is all I can do.

"However," he continued, "were you to marry Caroline you would become my grandson, and as my grandson you would command the attention of some of the most influential men in the land. Men who would give far more credence to the grandson of the duke of Hawkeshill than they ever would to a displaced Scottish laird. The return of your lands would be all but guaranteed."

Hugh sat frozen, unable to respond. Loch Haven his again, he thought, his heart racing with almost unbearable hope. The lands his ancestors had bled and died for, the castle whose stones were laid more than three centuries past—once more in the possession of a MacColme. It was everything he wanted and had prayed for since returning to Scotland, and the price was but a year or so of his life. As he had over fourteen years ago, Hugh made the only choice there was to be made. He rose to his feet, his hands clenched at his sides as he faced the general.

"Very well, Your Grace," he said, his gaze meeting the older man's with cold determination. "With your permission, I wish to request the hand of your granddaughter in marriage."

The general regarded him for several moments before responding. "Permission granted," he said, a pleased smile playing about his lips. "With provisos, of course."

Two hours, Caroline thought, pausing in her pacing long enough to cast the elegant clock on the mantel an impatient glare. Her grandfather and Mr. MacColme had been locked away in her grandfather's study for the past two hours, and not a peep had there been from the pair of them. It was doubtlessly Mr. MacColme who was at fault, she decided, scowling as she resumed her pacing. From what she'd observed of him, the stubborn soldier would argue with the devil himself.

By the time another twenty minutes had passed, Caroline had reached the end of her tether. She was giving serious thought to sneaking downstairs and listening at the keyhole when her maid tapped on the door and came bustling into the room.

"I beg your pardon, my lady," she said with a hasty curtsy, "but His Grace requests you join him in the drawing room."

Finally! Caroline thought, hiding her eagerness as she turned toward the door and hurried downstairs to join the others. At the door to the drawing room she paused briefly, pressing a shaking hand to her stomach to calm its sudden churning, then she stepped inside without knocking. Both men were standing before the fireplace, glasses of brandy in their hands, and looking very much like two gentleman at their leisure. She gave Mr. MacColme a curious glance, wondering what thoughts were going on behind that coldly handsome face, before turning to her grandfather.

"You wished to see me, sir?" she asked, doing her best to appear cool.

"Indeed, my dear, indeed," her grandfather said, setting his brandy aside and walking forward to take her hand. "The sergeant and I have been talking, and you will be happy to know I have given him permission to pay his addresses to you."

Although this was the answer she had been expecting, indeed hoping for, Caroline's stomach gave another uncomfortable lurch. "I see. When is the marriage to take place?" she asked, wondering how she could sound so calm when her entire world had just been set spinning.

"Tomorrow morning," her grandfather informed her, giving her hand a soothing pat. "I have contacted the bishop, and a special license is being prepared. It should be here by nightfall."

Tomorrow morning! So soon as that? Caroline fought back panic. When her grandfather moved, it would seem he moved quickly, she thought, swallowing in sudden fear. She was trying to think of what else to say when Mr. MacColme walked over to join them. Without speaking he took her hand from her grandfather, a gesture which struck her as oddly symbolic.

"If you will forgive me, General, I believe it might be best if my fiancée and I were to discuss the rest of this privately," he said, his warm fingers wrapping around her chilled flesh. "With your permission, I should like to take her for a drive."

"Eh?" Her grandfather blinked, and then to her astonishment he acquiesced at once. "Oh, of course, MacColme, of course. You always were one to take command of a situation. Very well, you may consider yourself dismissed. Only mind you are back within the hour," he ordered with an admonishing wag of his finger. "You are not yet husband and wife."

"Very well, sir." Mr. MacColme sketched a stiff bow before turning to Caroline. "I will wait for you in the hall, my lady, while you are fetching your shawl and bonnet. I ask you do not tarry long, as we've much we must accomplish."

The desire to toss his peremptory command back in his face was strong, but Caroline managed to control the impulse. Now was not the time to indulge her temper, she told herself as she hurried up to her room to retrieve the requested items. But it was plain she and the sergeant would have to come to some sort of agreement if they had the smallest chance of making this "marriage" of theirs succeed. She hadn't escaped one tyrant only to place herself under the control of another.

A quarter of an hour later, she and Mr. MacColme were in her grandfather's elegant coach making their way down Great Pulteney Street. Instead of sitting across from her as she expected, her fiancé settled onto the seat beside her. The feel of him sitting so close to her that their knees and shoulders brushed was disconcerting, and she wondered if he'd done so with precisely that intention. If so, he was in for a disappointment, she decided, her chin lifting with pride. She turned her head, her manner cool as she met the diamond-hard gaze of the stranger who in less than twenty-four hours would be her husband.

"Before we begin, Mr. MacColme, I wish to thank you for your kind assistance. I shudder to think what might have befallen me had you not agreed to this."

He remained silent for several seconds before slowly inclining his head. "You are welcome, my lady," he drawled, an unexpected dimple flashing in his tanned cheek. "But are you certain this is what you want? You hardly seem the eager bride, if you do not mind my saying so."

His mocking words took Caroline aback, and her control wavered dangerously before she managed to rein it in. "As ours is a marriage of convenience and a temporary one at that, I see no reason for subterfuge."

"To be sure," he agreed, capturing her hand and carrying it to his lips. "But sometimes subterfuge is the best defense one can hope for—and in our case, you could say it is the only defense."

The feel of his lips over the back of her hand was unnerving, but Caroline refused to lower herself to anything so undignified as a struggle. "And what does that mean?" she asked, praying she sounded more confident than she felt.

"Merely that while you may be content regarding our arrangement as a simple act of commerce, your grandfather and I cannot be so sanguine. For you to be truly safe, ours must be seen as a marriage in every sense of the word. The world must be made to believe we have married for the usual reasons."

Caroline's brows puckered as she mulled over

his words. Understanding dawned, and her eyes flew wide with horror. "Are you saying you are going to pass this off as a love match?" she gasped, shocked to her toes. "You cannot be serious!"

"Can I not?" His silvery-green eyes danced with amusement. "But if it will help ease your mind, my lady, I believe I said the *usual* reasons. It is my understanding your world would never dream of marrying for so base a thing as love. We will put it about that ours is an arranged marriage and leave it at that."

"Arranged by whom?" Caroline demanded, feeling as if she was on a horse that had bolted and was dashing unchecked toward the edge of a very high cliff.

"Your grandfather, of course," he replied in the cool, imperturbable tones that were beginning to grate on her nerves. "He will let it be known that I am the husband he has selected for you, which is no more than the truth, when you think about it. As he is the duke of Hawkeshill none will dare question the matter—to our faces, at least," he added with a cynical laugh. "Behind our backs, I've no doubt tongues will tie themselves in knots from the wagging."

"The prospect doesn't seem to fill you with undue alarm," Caroline grumbled, blushing to think herself the object of malicious gossip.

His broad shoulders lifted and fell in an indifferent shrug. "I have no care for what a handful of English gossips might say of me. And in any case we shall not be in Bath long enough for it to matter."

Caroline did her best not to panic. "And where

will we be?" she asked, visions of being dragged off to the wet, windswept Highlands swirling in her mind.

His casual answer verified her fears. "Scotland, of course. Although I'm afraid we must first be paying a visit to London."

Caroline thought of Uncle Charles, and her concerns over Scotland vanished. "London!" Fear made her pale.

The hand holding hers tightened in comfort. "I've business which must be seen to before we can return to Scotland," he said, coolly. "His Grace will be accompanying us, and we will be staying in his town house. If it's your uncle you're worrying over, you've nothing to fear from him. If he dares to try and harm you once you are my wife, I will deal with him—on that I give you my pledge."

The firm words gave her an odd sense of comfort. For the first time since the awful death of her parents, she suddenly felt less alone, a sensation that left her feeling more than a little bewildered. The man holding her hand and promising to protect her was still a stranger, and a dangerous stranger at that, she reminded herself. She would forget that at her own peril.

"When do we leave?" she asked, discreetly withdrawing her hand and shifting away. She needed to think, and that was something she couldn't seem to do with the feel of him overwhelming her.

He stared down at her, those eyes of his narrowing with some dark emotion. "Directly after the wedding," he said, closing the distance she had just set between them. "Now that we've put that behind us, there's something else we need to put behind us as well." And without warning he pulled her against him, his arms as tight as iron bands as they closed about her. Furious, she opened her mouth, but before she could utter a word of protest his lips were taking hers in a kiss of blazing passion.

The taste and feel of him were dazzling, and despite her anger, Caroline could feel herself responding. Although she had been kissed before, nothing she'd experienced in the past could compare with what she was feeling now. It was deep and raw, and more than a little frightening. It had to be fear to make her tremble so.

Delicate as her shudder was, he must have felt it, for in a heartbeat she was free. Lashes she couldn't remember closing fluttered open, and she found herself staring up at his hard, implacable features. Not for the first time she noticed the thin white scar slashing across his tanned cheekbone, and as if they possessed a will of her own, her fingers reached up to stroke the puckered flesh. Her fingertips had barely brushed over his face before he jerked his head back, his eyes flashing with an emotion she could not identify.

"We should be turning back soon," he said, pushing her gently from him and moving to the other side of the carriage. "Your grandfather will be waiting for us."

His icy withdrawal was almost as confusing to Caroline as his passionate assault. What on earth ailed the creature? she seethed silently. He was the one who had kissed her without so much as a by-your-leave, so why was he now acting with such rigid propriety? Anger warred with pride, and after a brief struggle, pride won. Not for the world would she let him know his kiss had the slightest effect upon her. In her mind she'd already made a thorough fool of herself, and she was cursed if she would compound that sin. With that thought firmly in mind she drew the tatters of her dignity about her, and forced herself to ape his coolness.

"If you do not mind, Mr. MacColme, there is a question I should like to ask of you first," she said, taking pride in her calm tones.

He regarded her warily. "What is it?"

She clenched her hands to hide their trembling. "I can see how our marriage will benefit me," she said, meeting his gaze with a nonchalance she was far from feeling. "But I do not see how it will benefit you. Did Grandfather offer to pay you?"

A look of black fury flashed across his face, and in that brief moment she feared she had gone too far. Then as quickly as it came the look was gone, and he was once again as cold and unmovable as a block of Highland stone. "I am nae a cicisbeo to be purchased for a lady's pleasure," he informed her, his accent more pronounced than ever. "The general is helping with a matter pertaining to my estate, Loch Haven, and that, my lady, is all you need to know."

Caroline took great issue with his answer, but she decided she'd already pushed harder than was perhaps wise. Not that she intended letting the matter drop, she told herself, turning her head to gaze out the window. Mr. MacColme might think his reasons for marrying her were none of her concern, but she did not. Until she knew what he was doing and why, she would never feel safe from her uncle's machinations.

Idiot! *Gaupie!* Hugh berated himself as the duke's carriage returned him to his rooms. How could he have been so foolish as to kiss the chit? The greenest lad faced with taking his first woman would have shown more finesse, and it infuriated him he should have so little control over his actions. It was plain the lady had the most disastrous effect upon his senses, and had he any say in the matter, nothing would have given him greater pleasure than to give her the widest berth possible. Unfortunately, he didn't have such a say, and he cursed again at his impotence.

At least she hadn't gone running to her grandfather to complain of his behavior, he brooded, grudgingly giving the lady her due. Granted, an engaged man was allowed some liberties with his intended bride, but he was grateful he'd been spared the indignity of explaining himself to the general. Instinct told him the old soldier would not view the matter with any great forbearance, and he valued the general's good opinion too much to risk losing it over something so foolish as a kiss.

Unbidden, the memory of her mouth, soft and supple beneath his own, flashed in Hugh's mind, and he gritted his teeth as his body hardened in response. He'd always been a man of deep hungers, hungers that evidently had gone unfulfilled for too long. Why else would he find himself burning for a wench who was buying him as if he were no more than a bauble in a shop window?

The thought was infuriating enough to cool the passion firing his blood, and Hugh latched on to it as a drowning man would to a lifeline. Buying him. That was precisely what the Lady Caroline was doing. Oh, to be sure, the general had wrapped it all up in pretty linen, doing his best to convince him it was naught but a simple business arrangement, for his benefit as well as Lady Caroline's. But Hugh had learned long ago to accept the unvarnished truth for what it was. He'd sold himself to buy back Loch Haven, and that was that. He would forget that at his own peril, and he was a man who protected himself at all costs.

Angus was waiting when he entered the room, and Hugh had scarcely set down his hat and gloves before the elderly valet pounced upon him. "What did the general say?" he demanded, hurrying forward to help Hugh out of his tight-fitting jacket. "Will he help or nay?"

Hugh's fingers tore at the cravat that suddenly seemed to be choking him. "He will help," he said shortly, having already worked out how to explain the unexplainable. "For a price."

"Aye," Angus grumbled, "with the English there's always a price to be paid for what an honorable man would offer for free. How much did the *gileynour* ask for, then?"

Hugh paused to cast his valet a warning glare. "The general is not a swindler," he said, his voice edged with menace. "He is an honest and fair man, and he asked not a pence for his help. I'll thank you to remember that."

"Then it's land he's after." Angus ignored the admonishment, concentrating on helping Hugh out of the brocade waistcoat. "The English are forever lusting after good Scottish soil."

The man's unreasonable hatred put Hugh in mind of his father, and he wondered what Douglas would say were he here now. If the thought of his son's taking up his sword for England had driven him to disown him, Hugh mused, how would he respond to the knowledge that same son was about to take an English bride?

"General Burroughs is a duke with a fine estate and more than enough land for any man," he said, an unbearable weariness making him sigh. "He's no use for ours."

"Since when has more than enough satisfied the English?" Angus asked rhetorically. "Well, if it's not land and money the duke's after, what is it? What are ye giving him for his help?"

"My name."

The blunt reply had Angus's brows meeting in a scowl. "Eh?"

"My name," Hugh repeated, deciding the simpler the explanation, the better. "He wants me to wed his granddaughter, and in exchange he has promised to throw his support behind me. I have agreed."

The look of shock on the valet's face would have been amusing had Hugh been of a mind to laugh. "Marriage!" Angus gasped, his eyes all but bulging from his face. "Ye canna be meaning it! A MacColme would never wed an English bi—"

Hugh whirled on him. "Guard your tongue, old man," he warned, the glitter in his eyes sending the other man stumbling back. "You are speaking of the lady who is to be my wife. Insult her and you will regret it, I promise you."

"But you are the laird of Loch Haven," Angus protested, gazing at him in horror. "The people have suffered too greatly under the heels of the English to accept one as your wife. You owe it to the clan to—"

"Never speak to me of what I owe the clan!" Hugh exclaimed, a great fist of pain striking at his heart. "All I do, all I have ever done, is for the clan! I have fought for it, bled for it, nearly died for it, and now I am marrying for it! So dinna tell me what is owed and what is not. I'll nae be hearing it."

"But MacColme, you—"

"*Enough!*" Hugh roared the word. It felt as if he was being ripped to pieces by wild beasts, and he knew that if he didn't get out of the stuffy room he wouldn't be responsible for his actions. Cursing beneath his breath, he stalked over to the corner of the room where his clothes hung neatly on pegs. The jacket he'd worn from Edinburgh hung there, and without pausing to don a waistcoat he yanked it on. Where he meant to go, he doubted anyone would remark on his casual dress.

"What are you doing?" His actions brought Angus scurrying to his side. "You cannot go out without a waistcoat and cravat!"

Hugh shot him a look that made it plain he would tolerate no interference. "I can, and I will," he said, buttoning the front of his jacket. "And if you're a wise man, you'll hold that poisonous tongue of yours. I'm in no mood to haggle."

Angus sniffed loudly, raising his great beak of a nose in disdain. "If ye wish to go about looking no better than a penniless beggar, it's naught to me," he said, sounding as disconcerting as Aunt Egidia. "But mind ye leave yer watch and fob wi' me, else the cutpurses will slit yer throat for certain."

The request struck Hugh as sensible, and he surrendered the items without comment. He also took the precaution of slipping a dagger up his sleeve and another in the top of his boot; a pistol went into the pocket of his coat, and at last he felt ready to partake of Bath's less elegant entertainments.

"Do not wait up for me," he advised Angus, pausing to snatch up his hat and cane. "I'll be out the rest of the evening."

"Out whooring is what ye mean, and ye a man handfasted to another," Angus muttered, disapproval evident in his stiff posture. " 'Tis shamed of yerself ye ought to be."

Hugh's jaw set. His original plan had been to go out and drink himself into oblivion, but he liked the sound of Angus's plan better. Mayhap a willing female was just what he needed to quiet the beast inside him. It had been longer than was comfortable since he'd last lain with a woman, and the notion was sweetly tempting. He closed the door behind him.

Less than twenty minutes later he was seated comfortably in a tavern, a tankard of ale at his elbow and an agreeable wench on his knee. Both had materialized magically when he had tossed a gold coin on the table, and in his black mood, he was of a mind to slake himself with both.

"Such pretty hair you have," the woman cooed, running her hands through the waves streaming to his shoulders. She had untied his queue and unbuttoned his jacket within moments of latching on to him, and was doing her best to arouse him. That she wasn't succeeding worried him, and he decided it was time he took a more active role in the situation.

"Not nearly so pretty as yours, my sweet," he lied, giving her too-bright blonde curls a playful tug, and doing his best to drum up some enthusiasm for her expert caresses.

The compliment obviously pleased her, and the blonde preened and wriggled closer. "I don't usually get so many as handsome as you," she confided, placing one hand over the front of his trousers and running an audacious finger down his cheek. "Even with this scar, you're better-looking than most. Gives you dash, it does."

The image of Lady Caroline flashed in Hugh's mind, and the memory of her touch and the passionate kiss he had stolen from her brought forth the result the prostitute had been seeking. She murmured with delight and gave him a gentle squeeze.

"My room is on the next street," she said, kissing the side of his neck. "A few shillings, love, and we'll have a lovely time."

For a moment, Hugh almost said yes. His body was throbbing with a desire more potent than anything he'd ever experienced, and he literally ached for relief. The woman's breasts, lush and ripe, tempted his mouth and hands, but even as he was reaching for them his conscience stayed his hands.

Tomorrow was his wedding day. Never mind the marriage was a temporary one and not of his making; tomorrow he would stand before God and pledge his troth to a woman he scarcely knew. He would vow to honor her, and how could he do that, he wondered, if he took a whore to his bed this night?

"Sorry, sweeting," he said, easing her off his lap. "I'm expected elsewhere." He dug out another coin and pressed it into her hand. "Some other time perhaps."

The money did much to soothe the woman's ire, but Hugh thought he detected a flash of genuine regret in her sulky pout. "Like that, is it?" she said, rising to her feet and shaking out her skirts, her eyes already scanning the smoke-filled room for her next customer. "You can tell her for me she's a lucky woman. There's not many men as would turn down Polly."

Hugh's mouth twisted in an ironic smile. "I'll be certain to mention it to her," he drawled, and then turned and left the tavern, his tankard of ale forgotten.

Chapter 5

❧

It was her wedding day. Caroline stood before the glass, her expression composed as she studied her reflection. Her gown of rose and blue striped satin over a brocade underskirt was suitable, and she supposed the lace cap and wreath of roses wound through her blonde curls made her look the perfect bride. But the feelings in her heart were far from bride-like. This was to be the happiest day of her life, but instead of trembling with joy she was shaking with fury.

"Jug-bitten, he is," one maid had confided to another.

"Drunk as a lord and sick as a cat," came the reply, and both had shaken their heads with sad sighs.

Neither knew she was listening to their every word, her anger mounting as she heard their assessment of her bridegroom's deplorable condition. Granted theirs was but a marriage of convenience, but that didn't mean she was without her pride. What bride could possibly relish the notion of a groom who had arrived for the nuptials thoroughly in his cups? It was not to be borne.

"Oh, how lovely you look, my lady," the first maid exclaimed, her plain face wreathed in smiles as she beamed at Caroline. "You look just like one of the princesses, you do."

Caroline, who had met the king's plump and homely daughters many times, was far from flattered by the comparison, but her smile was no less kind for that. "Thank you, Grace, it is sweet of you to say so," she murmured. "Is it time to go downstairs now?"

"Yes, my lady." The other maid came closer to admire her gown and hair. "The bishop's assistant is officiating, and he arrived while you were dressing. Everyone is waiting for you, your groom included." She gave a high-pitched giggle that grated on Caroline's exacerbated nerves. "He's most handsome, they say. Lucy all but swooned when she saw him."

Then she must have been standing downwind of the sergeant, Caroline thought sourly, since Lucy had said Mr. MacColme smelled as if he'd been swimming in a keg of brandy. An exaggeration perhaps, but it was her experience servants' tattle wasn't without a grain of truth. She only hoped her groom could repeat his lines before passing out. A fat lot of good he would do them snoring through the ceremony!

With her maids' eager assistance she was soon downstairs, fighting for composure as she waited to walk into the formal drawing room where the wedding was being held. She was about to give the footman the signal to open the door when she noticed her grandfather's elderly butler studying her, the oddest expression on his face. She waited for him to speak, but when he remained silent she motioned him forward with a wave of her hand.

"Yes, Campton, is there something you wish to say?" she asked, assuming he was waiting to offer her the best wishes of the staff.

"I . . . er . . . indeed, yes, my lady," he stammered, turning an alarming shade of red. "I . . . that is to say, Mrs. Brown, His Grace's housekeeper, suggested I speak with you. She wishes to know if you wish to speak with her about anything."

Seconds before she was to be married struck Caroline as an odd time to be discussing household matters. "No," she said slowly, "I cannot say that I do. Was there anything in particular Mrs. Brown thought I might wish to discuss?"

Mr. Campton's thin face turned even redder. "She thought that as you have no mother, there might be matters of a . . . er . . . delicate nature you may wish to discuss with another lady," he said, looking as if he might swoon at any moment. "Questions or worries which may be plaguing your mind. She has offered to counsel you, should you have need of it."

Understanding dawned in a blaze of light, and it was all Caroline could do to keep from bursting into laughter. Only the knowledge that poor Mr. Campton would doubtlessly expire from embarrassment kept her from doing just that, and she managed to dredge up a polite smile on his behalf.

"You may thank Mrs. Brown for her kind offer, Mr. Campton," she said in a strained voice. "It is very good of her to consider my . . . er . . . sensibilities, but my governess believed in a thorough education. I have neither questions nor worries about anything, I assure you."

Mr. Campton's thin shoulders sagged with relief. "Very good, my lady," he said, offering her a formal bow. "And pray accept the best wishes from the staff and myself. Sergeant MacColme strikes me as a most worthy gentleman, and I know this marriage will make His Grace very happy."

"Thank you, Mr. Campton," she murmured, glad this farce of a marriage was pleasing someone. The Lord knew she was less than pleased with the prospect, and if there was the slightest bit of truth to the tales of his inebriated state, neither was Mr. MacColme. Still, she didn't see that they had any choice. They might neither be the other's dream intended, but they were stuck with each other. For just a year, though, she reminded herself, turning back toward the door. At the end of it, she would be free. *Free.* She savored the word, drawing strength from the promise of it, and then stepped forward, motioning the footman to open the door.

To her surprise there were at least half a dozen people waiting for her in the sunlit drawing room. She saw her grandfather first, impressive in his regimentals, and then her gaze settled on the tall, russet-haired man waiting beside him. He was also in his uniform, and the sight of him made the breath catch in her throat. Gazing at his broad shoulders and muscular chest, shown to their best advantage by the cut of his scarlet coat, she could see why the unknown Lucy should have grown weak at the sight of him. He was without doubt one of the most handsome men she had ever seen.

"My dear." Her grandfather stepped forward to meet her, his blue eyes shining with happiness as he carried her hand to his lips. "How beautiful you look. Your father and mother would be so proud if they could see you."

"Thank you, Grandfather," she said, a painful lump lodging in her throat. Her parents had married for love, and she knew it had been their hope she would follow in their footsteps. That she was not made her feel as if she was betraying them on some fundamental level, and for a harrowing moment tears threatened. She blinked them back, and gave her grandfather a bright smile.

"How dashing you look," she said with a light laugh. "I hope you don't go about in your regimentals very often, else there won't be a feminine heart safe in the whole of Bath."

He preened at her words. "Oh, I much doubt the ladies would pay an old warhorse like me any mind," he chuckled, guiding her to where Mr. MacColme was standing. "Not with so many handsome soldiers littering the Pump Room and assemblies. And speaking of handsome soldiers . . ." He took her hand and placed it in Mr. MacColme's. "Your groom, my lady."

"Lady Caroline." His gaze held hers, his gloved fingers warm as they closed around her own. "Are you ready?"

She gave a jerky nod, a sudden burst of sheer terror rendering her speechless. Now that the actual moment had arrived, her courage wavered, and she wanted nothing more than to pick up her skirts and run screaming from the room. Her muscles tensed in readiness, but before she could give in to the panic clawing at her, Hugh did the most extraordinary thing. He smiled at her.

"There's no need to break rank and flee," he murmured, his deep voice reassuring. "It will be all right. Everything will work out in the end; you'll see."

Would it? Caroline didn't see how such a thing could be possible, but she let herself be persuaded. If he could be so calm, she told herself, then so could she.

The ceremony was brief, and she kept her attention firmly fixed on the minister; her voice was cool and steady when she repeated her lines. Finally the blessing was given, and she turned to the man who was now legally her husband.

His expression was surprisingly solemn, his green eyes full of shadows as he gazed down into her face. Standing so close, she could feel the warmth emanating from his strong body, and catch the faintest whiff of the spicy cologne he favored. It made her remember the servants' gossip, and she breathed a sigh of relief it had been so wrong. His face might be strained and his eyes the slightest bit bloodshot, but Mr. Mac-Colme—Hugh, she corrected herself—was far from bosky.

He moved closer, his gaze steady as he cupped her face in his hands. "You are a MacColme now, Caroline," he said, using her given name for the first time. "Mind you remember that."

She was puzzling over his meaning when he bent his head and gave her a kiss that was all that was proper, and all that was not. His lips were firm and warm, and she felt the teasing flicker of his tongue before he drew back to smile down at her.

"Come, *annsachd*," he said, tucking her arm beneath his and turning her toward the others. "Our friends await."

The next several minutes passed in a blur as Caroline found herself meeting the strangers who had been invited to witness the wedding. The men were all in uniforms similar to those worn by Hugh and her grandfather, and she assumed them to be members of the same regiment. Her theory was proven correct a few minutes later when a heavyset woman with a huge bonnet stuck on her head came striding forward to meet her.

"I am Mrs. Margate," she said, grabbing Caroline's hand and pumping it up and down much as a man would do. "The sergeant here was a member of my husband's regiment, and if there is anything you wish to know you have but to ask me. I know all your secrets, eh, Sergeant?" And she jabbed her elbow in Hugh's stomach in a blow that would have felled a lesser man.

"More than I dare consider, Mrs. Margate," he said, giving the woman a wink. "But as I know a few of yours as well, I am confident I can trust your discretion."

She threw back her head and let out a loud bark of laughter. "If you're counting on discretion from a soldier's wife, my lad, you're the biggest dolt to ever draw breath. But you were ever a gentleman, I must say."

The others soon ventured forward to offer their felicitations, and as she accepted them, Caroline couldn't help but note the regard with which her husband was treated by the other men. They all held the highest of ranks, yet their attitude toward Hugh was as equal toward equal. Given what she'd heard of the strict distance normally kept between officers and enlisted men she was more than a bit surprised, and it made her wonder about the nature of the man she had just married.

"I hope you don't mind my inviting Colonel Margate and the others," her grandfather said, pausing beside her to give her a smile. "But they're as devoted to Sergeant MacColme as I am, and they'd have been most hurt not to be invited to his wedding."

"It's fine, Grandfather," she assured him, watching as a man wearing the braid of a major laughed and clapped Hugh on the back. "And their presence will give credence to the tale that ours is a marriage arranged by you."

"Eh?" He looked momentarily baffled and then gave a quick nod. "Oh, yes, there is that, although I hadn't considered it in quite that light. But it's a brilliant piece of strategy, now that I think of it. Once it is known this match has my approval, Charles will be hard-pressed to make mischief."

The mention of her uncle killed the fragile peace Caroline had found. Amazing as it was, she hadn't given Uncle Charles or his foul threats a single thought all morning. She'd been too busy brooding over her wedding and her enigmatic groom to consider anything else, but now she could not help but worry. She knew her uncle well enough to know he'd be furious at having been thwarted, and there was no saying how he might respond. She was considering several unpleasant possibilities when she became aware her grandfather was talking.

"... in two days' time," he concluded, studying her carefully. "It will be better that way, as I am sure you will agree."

Too embarrassed to admit she hadn't been attending, Caroline merely nodded. "Yes, Grandfather, whatever you say," she said, wondering what she'd just agreed to. Campton had come in, signaling her with a raised eyebrow that it was time to go into the dining room for the wedding breakfast her grandfather had arranged. She turned to see if she could find Hugh, when she felt his hand slide around her upper arm.

"Come, my dear," he drawled, his voice smoothly polite. "It is time to lead our guests into breakfast."

Her heart gave a jolt as much at his proprietary manner as at the ease with which he used the casual endearment. Listening to him speak, one would think they had been married several years instead of a matter of minutes, she thought, and was instantly furious, both with him and with herself. She knew her response to be childish, and the realization only added to her irritation. Well, she decided, her spine stiffening with pride, if he could conduct himself with such cool aplomb, then she was hanged if she would behave any other way. Aware of the interested glances being cast their way, she gave him her most dazzling smile.

"Very well, darling," she purred, gloating at

the way his eyes widened in surprise. "If that is what you wish."

He said nothing, but she thought she detected an answering smile playing about his mouth as he turned her toward the door.

The first hint something was amiss came after the lengthy breakfast. Caroline had gone upstairs to change into her traveling clothes, and as she walked outside she came upon her grandfather bidding Hugh what looked like a fond adieu.

"The staff should be expecting you," he said, handing Hugh a letter with the Hawkeshill crest stamped on it. "But if there should be any problem, you are to give this to the butler—Begley, I believe he is called. It will explain everything."

"Very well, General," Hugh answered, tucking the letter inside his surtout. "Will there be anything else?"

Before he could answer, Caroline came hurrying down the last few steps. "What is going on here?" she demanded, her gaze going first from Hugh's face to her grandfather's. "Will you not be journeying with us to London?"

"I knew you weren't listening," he chuckled, giving her chin a gentle pinch. "The nervous bride, eh?"

Because it was so close to the truth, she scowled. "I am not nervous," she denied indignantly. "I'd forgotten, that's all."

"Mmm," her grandfather responded, his eyes twinkling with laughter. "Well, as I explained, it will look better if the two of you make your bridal journey without me tagging along. I will travel up after you."

"Oh." Caroline considered the matter and decided he was right. Still, that didn't make the thought of spending the next several days alone in Hugh's company any more palatable, and she swallowed uncomfortably.

Taking her silence for assent, her grandfather turned back to Hugh. "Will you be calling on Lord Farringdale tomorrow?"

"And Sir Anthony Covington," Hugh replied, nodding. "Colonel Margate gave me a letter for him, and said he was certain we could count upon his cooperation."

"As he is Mrs. Margate's cousin, I daresay we can," her grandfather agreed wryly. "He is also a solicitor, and clever as a monkey, I am told. He will know what to do."

Caroline was about to demand an explanation when her grandfather handed Hugh another letter, this one sealed. "For my banker," he said, his gaze stern as it met Hugh's. "Mind you give it to him."

Caroline could sense Hugh's reluctance as his fingers closed around the paper. "General, I do not think—"

"I believe we have already had this discussion," her grandfather interrupted, his voice cool. "And I believe it was agreed then how such matters would be handled. Consider it an order, Sergeant," he added, a smile softening his stern features. Hugh hesitated a moment longer, and then took the letter and put it in his pocket. "Very well, sir," he said brusquely. "I will report once we have settled."

"Mind that you do," her grandfather said, and turned to give Caroline a gentle smile. "Godspeed on your journey, my dear," he said, placing a kiss on her cheek. "And do not look so downcast. Your grandpapa shall see to all, I promise you."

Caroline was embarrassed to find herself fighting tears. She had only just found her grandfather, and it felt as if she was already losing him. She rose on tiptoe to throw her arms about his neck. "Good-bye, Grandfather," she said, giving him an impulsive hug. "I love you."

He gingerly returned the embrace before setting her aside. "Here now, what's this?" he demanded, frowning down at her in mock sternness. "I shall be seeing you in but a few days, you know. No need to get all teary-eyed."

"I'm not," she denied, half-laughing as she swiped at her damp cheeks. "It's just the wind making my eyes water."

Although there wasn't so much as a breeze stirring the feathers on her bonnet, neither man mentioned the fact, and she was grateful for their forbearance. The time to leave was upon them, and for a brief moment the feminine panic she'd been holding at bay threatened to slip the reins. A tremble she couldn't contain shook her, and her grandfather gave her an alarmed look.

"Poor dear, you are cold!" he exclaimed, laying a worried hand on her arm. "Sergeant MacColme, get my granddaughter out of this wind before she catches her death!"

A hard arm stole about her waist, and she was drawn back against the solid wall of his chest. "I'll do that, General," he said, his arm tightening possessively about her. "We'll see you in

London." And with that he bundled her into the waiting carriage, ignoring her feeble protests.

Thank God that was done. Hugh collapsed against the leather squabs, his eyes closing wearily. Except for the terrifying moments just before a battle, he'd never known time to drag by so slowly. This had been one of the longest mornings of his life, and the knowledge that it was far from over was all that kept him from giving in to the exhaustion tugging at him. There was still one final duty to be performed, and with that thought firmly in mind, he opened his eyes to study the woman sitting opposite him.

My wife. The possessive phrase exploded in his mind, and he took a few moments to savor its unexpected sweetness. Concern for Loch Haven and the simple struggle to stay alive had occupied all of his thoughts for more years than he cared to remember, and marriage was something he'd never allowed himself to consider. But the few times such thoughts had crept into his mind, he'd imagined marrying some fire-haired Highland lass, a woman of a neighboring clan who'd fill his days with contentment and his nights with searing passion. The last thing he expected was that he'd one day agree to a temporary marriage of convenience with a golden-haired English aristocrat. It was too ludicrous by half.

"Mr. MacColme?" A soft, hesitant voice jolted him out of his musings, and he glanced up to find Caroline regarding him with a worried look on her face.

"Is everything all right, sir?" she asked, her blue eyes filled with concern as she studied him.

He unfolded his arms, forcing himself to relax as he met her gaze. "We are husband and wife, Caroline. I do not think we shall risk censure were you to call me by my given name," he said, his lips curving in a teasing smile. "It is Hugh."

Her cheeks grew delightfully flushed, but her expression remained somber. "Hugh," she agreed, still studying him. "Is something amiss? You look as if something is troubling you."

Her acuity surprised him, and he cast about in his mind for some explanation. "I am only thinking of all that is to be done." It was as close to the truth as he dared go. "We've some hectic days ahead of us, so perhaps it is best we were making our plans."

She looked surprised and then intrigued. "What sort of plans?" she asked, leaning forward in her seat.

"Your uncle and how best to deal with him is our first concern," he said. "The general sent him a note yesterday announcing our marriage, so I think we can expect him to be waiting on our doorstep when we arrive. Don't worry," he added when he saw her eyes widen, "I'll keep you safe. If the *rabiator* thinks to cause mischief, he'll learn soon enough the error of his ways."

His vow of protection seemed to reassure her. Her look of uneasiness vanished, only to be replaced by a puzzled frown. "What is a rabiator?" she asked, stumbling over the unfamiliar word. "Is it Scottish?"

"Aye," he said, managing not to laugh at her pronunciation. "It means a ruthless scoundrel, and from what I've heard of the earl, it is a term that suits him well."

She nodded, not bothering to deny his charge. "That other word," she began, peeking up at him through her lashes, "the one you called me after the blessing. Is it Scottish as well?"

He knew which word she was referring to, and reached out to capture her hand in his. "*Annsachd*," he said, his gaze holding hers as he slowly removed her glove. "And 'tis Gaelic." He lifted her hand to his mouth and pressed a soft kiss on the warm flesh. "It means *beloved*."

Her cheeks heated once again, but she didn't attempt to free her hand. "*Annsachd*," she repeated, her voice sounding slightly breathless. "It's a beautiful word."

Hugh's fingers tightened about hers. How easy it would be to use his hold to pull her into his arms and taste her sweet lips, he mused, gazing at her lush mouth with mounting hunger. She was his wife; his to kiss and make love to as he pleased. It was a heady realization, made all the more intoxicating by the knowledge she didn't seem repelled by his touch. For a moment he was wildly tempted to follow the urging of his body, but instead he released her hand and leaned back against the squabs.

"As I am not of your social class, I leave it to you to decide what is to be done," he said, frustration and anger making his voice harsh. "But I warn you, if you think to parade me about in silks and velvet, my face painted up like a macaroni's, you had best think again. And I'll not wear a wig for anyone."

Eyes which only moments before had been as luminous as a moonlit sea grew distant. "Wigs are usually worn by gentlemen of the court," she informed him, her manner as rigidly polite as his own. "But as they are no longer required, I am sure there will be no problem. What of your hair?" she added, her gaze briefly resting on his queue. "I note you do not powder it."

"Nor do I intend doing so," he said, scarcely believing he was spending his bridal journey discussing his coiffure. "I had enough of that nonsense in the army. You don't powder yours either," he added, gazing at the thick blonde hair arranged in an elaborate pile of frizzes and curls.

"It is falling out of fashion," she replied, reaching up to touch her hair. "This new style is called *à le hérisson*; it is French, and all the rage. Do you like it?"

Hugh didn't answer at first. As it happened, he spoke French, having learned it at university, and it took him but a few moments to translate the word. "Hedgehog?" he repeated, a wide grin splitting his face. "You are wearing a hedgehog on your head?" And he burst into laughter.

"It's not a hedgehog, you wretch!" she exclaimed, tossing one of the long curls over her shoulder. "It is obvious you know nothing of fashion!"

"So I do not," he agreed, his dark mood vanishing. "And I pray I may never learn if it means putting rodents upon my head. You English— you never cease to amaze me."

They had gone several miles before his wife deigned speak to him again, and when she did it was with a brisk formality that made Hugh chuckle. It was obvious he had wounded her vanity with his laughter, and he knew he would have to work fast to put himself back in her good books. Fortunately she wasn't so miffed as to refuse to cooperate, and he listened to her plans for the next few days with growing respect. In addition to her deep-blue eyes, it was obvious she had also inherited her grandfather's skill for organization as well.

"It seems a great deal of work for naught," he commented, when she finished outlining her plans to introduce him to Society. "What does it matter what your London friends may think of our marriage? Once my business is done we shall be leaving for Edinburgh, and from there, God willing, to Loch Haven."

There was a brief pause before she replied. "Grandfather and I are agreed that the more who know and accept our marriage, the better," she said, her gaze fixed on the scenery outside the carriage window. "Uncle Charles will be hard-pressed to cause difficulties once everyone knows we are wed."

Since it made sense, Hugh swallowed the rest of his objections. However much he might dislike the notion of scraping and bowing to a bunch of rich and arrogant lords, Caroline's safety must come first. And, his common sense added, the more people he had on his side, the stronger his case. For the clan's sake, he supposed he could drink a glass or two of punch.

"When do you think we should make our first appearance as man and wife?" he asked, putting aside his own feelings to concentrate on what must be done.

"Grandfather's announcement should be in the papers in a matter of days," Caroline replied. "But I think it best if we are established by then.

We could go to the theater; that is always a good place to be seen. Or we might attend a ball," she added, looking thoughtful. "I am promised at a ball at Lady Gresham's this evening. I'd thought to send a note of apology, but perhaps it might be better if we put in a brief appearance instead." She glanced at him for a hint of his inclinations on the matter.

"The ball sounds fine," he said, after a moment's consideration. "What rank does her ladyship hold? A countess?" The name was familiar to him, but he could not seem to place it.

"Duchess. Her husband is John, duke of Gresham."

He was also one of the powerful men the general suggested he contact, Hugh remembered, and felt smugly pleased with the easy way everything was falling into place. He settled back against the cushioned seat when a sudden thought had him shooting straight up. "Will I have to dance?" he demanded, sending her a horrified look.

The smile she gave him was closer to a smirk. "It *is* a ball," she reminded him, her tone dangerously sweet. "Some dancing is to be expected."

"Hell." He uttered the curse with heartfelt conviction. It had been over a decade since he last stepped foot upon a dance floor, and he could only imagine the fool he would make of himself. Mayhap 'twould be better to attend the theater instead, he brooded, turning his head toward the window. At least then it wouldn't be him who was providing the entertainment.

They stopped for tea at a small inn outside of

Reading, and while they dined Hugh took the opportunity to observe his wife. Her manners were impeccable, he noted, watching as she treated the inn's staff with unfailing courtesy. Having been on the receiving end of snapped orders, oft accompanied by a swift kick to the backside, he could appreciate the degree of consideration she displayed to the servants.

As if sensing the weight of his gaze, she glanced up to give him a quizzing look. "Is your tea not to your liking, sir?" she inquired worriedly. "I can ring for another cup if you wish."

"No. 'Tis fine," he assured her, and to prove his point he lifted the cup to his lips for a healthy sip. "I was but trying to recall the last time I had so lovely a lady prepare my tea."

A pleased flush touched her cheeks, and her lashes swept down over her eyes. "I wish my uncle might be present to hear you say so," she said wryly. "I fear he thinks little of my feminine skills. Indeed, the last time we spoke he called me a shrew."

The artless confession made Hugh pause. "And are you?" he asked, his curiosity piqued.

She gave a light laugh. "And how am I to answer that, since I do not know what you might mean by the term?" she asked. "Have you much experiences with the species, sir?"

Hugh thought of Aunt Egidia and grinned. "Aye, that I have. But that doesn't answer my question, Caroline. Are you a shrew?"

Her flush grew more pronounced, and he was amused to note she appeared to consider the matter before replying. "If speaking one's mind and refusing to suffer fools gladly makes one a shrew, I suppose there are many who would name me such," she said, her gaze level as it met his. "And I am the first to admit I am possessed of a rather independent nature. That is why I had yet to wed. I treasure the little freedom I do enjoy, and I see no reason to place myself under some man's thumb."

Hugh stared at her with something akin to horror. He'd been comfortable regarding her as no more than a spoiled chit, too rich and too willful for her own good. Learning she was capable of feelings so similar to his own was decidedly disconcerting, and he felt an uncomfortable stab of guilt.

"Caroline," he began, setting his cup aside and leaning forward to take her hand, "we've not yet talked about how we mean to conduct this marriage of ours, and I think this might be a good time to do so. To begin, I want you to know I have no intention of keeping you 'under my thumb,' as you put it. Within reason you may enjoy whatever freedom you please, and I'll not try to stop you. I hope you would not think me such a tyrant as that." He offered her a teasing smile. It was not returned.

" 'Within reason,' " she quoted, eyeing him coolly. "Might I ask what you mean by that?"

Hugh frowned. He'd thought his offer more than magnanimous, and could not like having it tossed back in his face. "I mean, ma'am, that short of picking up your skirts and dancing a jig in the middle of Piccadilly, you may do as you please.

"But," he added, annoyed by her obstinacy, "I would caution you to remember you are now my wife, the lady of Loch Haven, and I expect you to conduct yourself accordingly. I'll countenance no behavior that reflects poorly on either my name or my honor."

She was silent for several more seconds. "I see," she said at last, pouring fresh tea in her cup and raising it to her lips.

He waited impatiently, but when she made no further comment he shot her an impatient scowl. "And what, madam, is it that you see?"

"That I was right to avoid the married state," she informed him in a voice edged with ice. "It would seem to contain little to recommend it to a lady of even moderate intelligence. I thank God I need only endure it for a year before being truly free. I shall live for that day, Mr. MacColme. It cannot come soon enough to suit me."

Chapter 6

It was early evening when the carriage halted before her grandfather's residence on Hanover Street. Caroline cast the imposing edifice a worried glance as Hugh lifted her down from the carriage. She'd walked past the house any number of times, but she'd never been inside. Now she would be entering it as the temporary mistress, and as a married woman. The prospect was most daunting.

"Caroline?" Hugh's hands lingered on her waist, and she glanced up to find him studying her. "Is something wrong?"

She shook off her trepidations to give him a quick smile. "Everything is fine," she replied. "I was but wondering if Uncle might be waiting inside."

Hugh's expression darkened ominously. "If he is, you are to leave him to me. I've dealt with bullies before, and I know how best to deal with his sort."

Caroline's gaze dropped to the sword he'd buckled about his lean hips. "You aren't going to kill him, are you?"

"Only if he deserves killing," came the oblique

117

reply as he turned her toward the door. "If he keeps a civil tongue in his head and makes no move to cause you harm, he may live to be one hundred for all of me, If not . . ." He shrugged, leaving the threat to dangle tantalizingly.

The alacrity with which the front door was opened made it plain their arrival had not gone unnoticed. A short, plump man in butler's togs stepped forward to greet them.

"I am Begley, His Grace's butler," he said, bowing first to Caroline and then to Hugh. "Pray allow me bid you welcome to Hawkeshill House."

"Thank you, Begley," Caroline said, standing quietly as Hugh removed her cloak and handed it to the waiting footman. "Have we had any callers?"

The butler proved his worthiness by not pretending to misunderstand. "The earl of Westhall was here not a quarter of an hour past," he said, his gaze flicking to Hugh. "He wished to wait, but I had orders from His Grace he was not to be admitted under any circumstance. His lordship was . . ." He paused delicately. ". . . most distressed."

Beside her Caroline felt Hugh tense. "Was he now?" he said, a hint of steel in his voice. "Then he shall have to learn to live with his distress. The general's orders stand. If the earl should find fault with those instructions, notify me. I would be pleased to explain the situation to him. Is that clear?"

The butler bowed again a look of newfound respect softening his austere features. "Quite clear, Mr. MacColme," he intoned. "Will there be anything else?"

In response Hugh turned to Caroline. "I'm sure you must be feeling weary," he said, his green eyes meeting hers. "Why don't you go to our rooms and lie down? You'll want to be well-rested for the ball tonight."

His suggestion was all that was polite, but by his tone it was clearly a command. Caroline's independent nature rebelled at such high-handedness. Trust a man not to realize there were a hundred things to be done, to settle in.

"Very well, sir," she said, not wishing to wrangle in front of the servents. "I shall see you later this evening." She turned to go, when he caught her arm in his hand.

"A moment, my lady," he drawled, drawing her back against him. She frowned in confusion, guessing his intentions only as he bent his head and claimed her with a kiss. As if he were oblivious to the presence of the butler his warm lips clung to hers, and he flicked his tongue against her closed mouth with a daring sensuality that had her gasping. He took advantage of her shock to deepen the kiss, and she briefly tasted the potent sweetness of his mouth before he released her.

"To remember me by," he murmured, the smug satisfaction stamped on his handsome features adding to her indignation. "Rest now, *annsachd*. I look forward to escorting you to our first ball as man and wife."

Once she'd completed her tour of the house, Caroline spent the next few hours elbow-deep in work. In between sending out letters to friends

advising them on her new address, she arranged
for her clothing and other personal effects to be
brought from her uncle's house. She also met
with the housekeeper, going over even more lists
and making tenuous plans for the remainder of
their stay. She didn't know how long they would
be in London, but if they were going to be here
more than a few weeks, she knew they would be
expected to host some small entertainment.

It didn't help that Hugh had abandoned her
within an hour of their arrival, leaving no word
as to where he had gone or what time she might
expect him to return. The only message he had
left was that if he wasn't home by nine of the
clock she was to begin preparing for the soiree
without him. His casual treatment hurt her, a reaction she was careful to keep from the prying
eyes of the servants. She had her pride, if nothing
else, and she was hanged if she would allow
them to pity her.

When the clock struck half by nine and there
was still no sign of Hugh, her hurt gave way to
embarrassed anger. This was their wedding
night, she brooded, and although theirs was but
a marriage of convenience, it was still a marriage.
The least Hugh could do was to be there to escort
her to the Greshams' ball. So much for his fine
vow to protect her from Uncle Charles, she
thought, slamming her brush on to the dressing
table.

"Is something amiss, my lady?" The middle-
aged maid who had been her abigail since her
coming out inquired, eyeing her anxiously. "Is
your gown not to your liking?"

"What?" Caroline blinked, flustered at having

been caught woolgathering. "Oh, no, Helene, everything is fine," she assured the maid, casting her reflection a quick glance. The gown she was wearing was cut in the French style, and the rich gold brocade robe with its low, square neckline and three-quarter-length sleeves lavishly trimmed with silver lace made her look quite the woman of the world. A woman, she told herself, reaching up to touch her pearl and diamond necklace, who would not sit about waiting for an errant husband's return.

"Have my carriage summoned," she said, her heart pounding as she rose to her feet. "I will be going out for the evening."

"Out?" Helene's dark eyes bulged in horror. "But—but my lady, 'tis your bridal night! You cannot go out alone! What will your husband say?"

He can say what he pleases, and may he choke on the words, Caroline thought, although she was too wise to voice such things aloud. For all she knew, the servants, Helene included, could be in her uncle's pay, and she was not about to provide him with the fodder to have the marriage overturned. Thinking quickly, she gave the maid a haughty glare.

"As it was Mr. MacColme's suggestion we spend part of the evening at Lady Gresham's soiree, I assume he will say precious little," she said, her voice edged with ice. "Now kindly have my carriage summoned. I do not have all evening."

While the chastised maid rushed to do her bidding, Caroline fought not to feel guilty. She seldom spoke to servants so harshly, but in this case

she didn't feel she had any other choice. Not for
the world would she let anyone know she was
going out because she refused to spend her wedding night meekly awaiting her husband's return. And in the event Hugh did return and
inquired after her, he would know she had gone
ahead of him. Provided he even cared enough to
ask, she thought resentfully, settling the folds of
her scarlet domino about her shoulders.

Thirty minutes later, she was being helped
from her carriage in front of Lady Gresham's
town house. The duchess was a vicious gossip
whose company she usually eschewed, but unfortunately her soiree was the only function to
come to mind. Hiding her trepidations she went
inside, and had scarcely surrendered her cloak
when her hostess was upon her.

"Lady Caroline, how utterly delightful to see
you!" the older woman gushed, her welcoming
tones at odds with the malice evident in her
sharp eyes. "But I must say I am surprised you
came. One would think a bride had better things
to do on her wedding night than sip punch and
gossip."

Caroline stiffened at the taunting words. She
was fairly certain the announcement had yet to
be published, which left but one source for Her
Grace's information: her uncle.

"Indeed?" she asked, raising an eyebrow with
cool hauteur.

An angry flush bloomed beneath the powder
and paint on the duchess's fleshy cheeks, but her
insincere smile remained firmly in place. "But
where is your husband?" she demanded, making
a great show of peering over Caroline's shoulder.

"I hear he is a soldier, and a Scotsman as well. Will he be wearing a kilt? He must look quite handsome in it, I am sure."

Although she had yet to see Hugh in a kilt, it took little effort to envision what he would look like in one, his broad shoulders swathed in plaid and his muscular legs bared beneath the folds of the kilt. "Quite handsome indeed," Caroline replied, willing herself not to blush. "But the last I saw of him, my husband was properly attired in a cravat and breeches."

She knew the words to be a mistake the moment she saw Lady Gresham's eyes fire with malevolent glee. "The last you saw of him?" she repeated in a voice meant to be overheard. "Poor child, do not say the beast has abandoned you already? You cannot have been married above twelve hours!"

Caroline could sense as well as feel the sudden silence that descended upon the room, and she mentally cursed herself for foolishly giving in to her impulses. "He had important business that would not wait, and he wished to dispose of it before joining me here," she said, taking care to keep her own voice level. "But I shall be certain to mention your concern to him," she added, smiling sweetly. "Not many hostesses would be so solicitous of a guest's welfare."

The uncomfortable titter behind her made it plain her point had not gone untaken. No hostess with any claim to gentility would dare attack a guest in her own home, and by doing so the duchess had displayed a shocking want of breeding. The tale would soon be on everyone's lips, and Lady Gresham would be the one to suffer most. Caroline took from that what comfort she could, her chin held high as she moved past the furious duchess.

The next hour passed in a blur as she was besieged by other guests pressing for more information on her sudden marriage. At first she remained rigidly aloof, saying as little as she could about the matter. But as the questions grew more pointed and her annoyance grew stronger, she became less reticent, a feeling of deep resentment destroying her usual caution. If society should think it so remarkable she would marry a man she'd known less than twenty-four hours, she thought, clutching her glass of champagne more tightly, how much more would they be amazed were they to think it a love match?

"Of course," she said, interrupting one of the gentlemen, "I should never have been so amenable to Grandfather's request had I not been so taken with Mr. MacColme. He is a most worthy gentleman."

"Never say you are enamored of the fellow!" A dandy in pink silk Caroline recognized as an intimate of her uncle's gasped, his quizzing glass held high as he gave a delicate shudder. "From all accounts he is naught but a rough and crude Scotsman! A common soldier who never rose above the rank of sergeant!"

That he knew so much about Hugh verified her suspicions that her uncle was already spreading his venomous lies, and she decided it might be wise to begin dispelling such untruths now.

"Sergeant Major," she corrected, recalling her grandfather's many references to Hugh's rank.

"And he is not a rough and crude Scotsman. He is the laird of Loch Haven."

"How passionately you defend your husband, dear Lady Caroline," one of the women said, giving a low purr of laughter. "I find that simply enchanting. Perhaps there is something to be said for these arranged matches after all."

"Your husband's name is MacColme, did you say?" an older man in a powdered wig inquired, his brows wrinkling in thought. "I remember seeing his name in the dispatches while I was in the Foreign Office. He was decorated for bravery under fire for saving your grandfather's life, as I recall. 'Tis said Lord Cornwallis himself offered him a commission, but he turned it down because he didn't wish to leave his men."

"Ah, but it would seem the good sergeant received his promotion after all." The dandy who had first spoken simpered daintily, his thick lips twisting in malevolent pleasure. "Tell me, precisely what does one call a man who has married so high above his station?"

"A most fortunate man, I am thinking," a cold voice said as a strong arm slipped possessively about Caroline's waist. "What would *you* call him?"

A stunned silence descended upon the crowd and for a brief moment Caroline gave careful thought to swooning. She'd been hoping Hugh would come, but she hadn't imagined his arrival would be quite so dramatic. Several of the ladies were gazing at him as if he were a devil sprung from the bowels of Hades to carry them off, and the dandy who'd made the snide observation looked close to engaging in a real swoon. Thinking quickly, she moved out of his embrace and turned to face him.

"It is about time you made your appearance, Mr. MacColme," she scolded, pouting as she offered him her hand. "I was beginning to think you'd forgotten we were to meet here."

He took her hand, his green eyes glittering with icy fury as he raised it to his lips. "Absentminded I might be," he said, his accent more pronounced than she'd ever heard it. "But I'm nae so forgetful as to misplace my bride on our wedding night. Are you ready to leave now?"

There were several nervous giggles behind her but she ignored them, determined to escape without creating an even bigger scandal. The terrified dandy was even now beating an undignified retreat, and several other men were moving away as well, not in the least fooled by his easy words. He had a hard-edged look of violence about him, and it was plain they wanted none of him.

"I am ready," she said, her tone as nonchalant as she could manage given the circumstances. "Shall we go?"

He said nothing, his jaw set as he led her out of the crowded drawing room. There was a short, uncomfortable wait while their wraps were fetched, and then he was hurrying her out of the house and into the waiting carriage. The moment they were off, he turned to face her.

"It's an explanation I am wanting from you," he said, his voice as sharp-edged as a sword. "What do you mean by leaving the house without me? Do you nae have a care for your own safety?"

The arrogant demand had her bristling in instant defense. "I was hardly bereft of protection," she retorted, furious he should dare lecture her after leaving her to her own devices for the better part of the evening. "I had a footman with me, and the coachman is carrying a pistol. I was perfectly safe."

"Aye, a pimple-faced boy and a doddering old man who is as like to put a bullet through himself as through a footpad," he shot back, plainly unimpressed with her escorts. "London is the most dangerous city in the world, and I will not have you going out alone again, do you hear?"

Caroline's jaw dropped in astonishment. "You won't have?" she repeated furiously. "May I remind you, sir, that I have lived the whole of my life in London? I am more than capable of getting to and from a soiree without being attacked."

"And if you were attacked?" he demanded, leaning forward to grab her arm. "What then, my fine lady? What would you do to save yourself?"

The grip of his fingers hurt, but it was the waves of icy anger emanating from him that frightened her most. "Will you kindly let go of my arm?" she asked, seeking refuge behind a facade of cold pride. "You are hurting me."

He released her at once, but didn't shift away. "What you may have done before is of no matter to me," he said, his voice all the more intense for its softness. "It's what you do now that counts. You are my wife, Caroline MacColme; I took a sacred vow to protect you, and protect you I will, despite how you may feel about it. Is that plain enough for you?"

Caroline opened her lips indignantly, but then shut them without speaking. She'd been up since just after dawn, and the toll of the endless hours and the stress of the day's events was suddenly overwhelming. Pride and protest would have to wait, she decided with a weary sigh. She was too exhausted to care.

"Aye," she said stiffly, moving away from him to lean back against the seat. "It's plain enough."

Now he'd done it, Hugh thought, studying the rigid figure of his wife. He'd set her back up good and proper, and he couldn't say as he blamed her. Ordering her about and snapping at her had been a foolish thing to do, and he was deeply ashamed of himself for it. He would have to handle himself and her with a great deal more finesse if he hoped to make this marriage of theirs work. Which was not to say he meant to let her go racketing about free as she pleased, he amended, folding his arms across his chest and gazing out the window at the darkened streets. Now that he knew what that uncle of hers was up to, he was damned if he would let her out of his sight until they were safe inside his castle's thick stone walls.

He'd spent the better part of the evening closeted with her solicitor, and what he'd learned appalled him. Her uncle had already begun investigating the process to have their marriage decreed invalid, and had gone so far as to hint that the very haste of the marriage showed how unstable his niece had become. The solicitor, a Mr. Garrett, was certain the earl's efforts would be for naught, but Hugh was less convinced.

When he returned home to find Caroline had left for the soiree without him he'd all but choked on his panic, and he'd been in a fine temper when he'd gone storming into the drawing room. He'd been fully prepared to drag her out of there by her hair if that's what it took, and he might have done just that had he not heard her defending him to that circle of simpering jackals.

For as long as he lived he would never forget the picture she made, looking like a queen in her dress of gold and silver, her chin held high as she declared him "a most worthy gentleman." Had she meant it? he wondered. And if so, what did he intend doing about it? He spent the rest of the ride back to Hanover Street considering various intriguing possibilities.

The windows were ablaze with lights when the carriage rattled to a halt before the town house. Caroline gathered up her skirts in preparation of climbing out, and he reached out to lay a staying hand on her arm.

"The staff will have prepared a light supper for us," he said, taking care to make his words a request instead of a command. "It would please me greatly if you would consent to dine with me. There are things we must discuss."

She hesitated, and for a moment he feared she would refuse, but then she gave a dainty shrug. "If you wish," she said, holding out her hand to the footman who had already opened the carriage door and was waiting to help them alight.

Her reply was hardly fulsome, but Hugh took comfort in the fact she hadn't hurled the offer back in his face. They surrendered their cloaks to the waiting Begley and then went into the dining room, which had been set up in anticipation of their arrival. Per the instructions he'd issued before retrieving his bride, the table was laid out so that they could serve themselves without servants hovering over them.

"I didn't know if you had eaten," he said, holding out a chair for her. "But for myself, I've not eaten since we stopped on the road, and I am near to fainting from hunger."

"I had some tea earlier, but I suppose I might have a bite of something," she replied, and he thought he detected a slight thawing in her reserve as she took her seat. "I would not wish you to eat alone."

The stiff words were as close to a peace offering as he was likely to get, and Hugh accepted them as such. After making certain she was comfortably settled, he moved to the sideboard where several covered dishes were sitting and began filling their plates. At her direction he placed a slice of salmon pie and cheese on her plate, and to make himself feel better he added some fresh fruit and beef to it as well. He dished up a similar meal for himself and then took his chair beside her. He'd just started eating when he saw the bottle of wine standing in the silver cooler, and his eyes lit with pleasure.

"Champagne," he said, his mouth curving in a wry smile as he lifted up the bottle to examine it. "I've not had a drop since my men and I liberated a case from some French we captured."

Her lips lifted in an answering smile. "Liberated?"

"A more respectable word than *thieving*," he admitted, expertly removing the cork. "Although as spoils of war, the wine was ours to take. What a head we had the next morning," he added, chuckling at a memory made poignant by the fact that many of the men who drank with him that night died in battle the very next afternoon. He poured some of the frothy wine for each of them before setting the bottle down.

"I know there were toasts aplenty this morning," he said, handing her a glass. "But that was for the show of it. Now I would that we toast each other and mean it. To us, Caroline. To our marriage."

He saw the confusion and distrust in her dark-blue eyes, and wondered if she would refuse. He held his breath, waiting, and then she lightly tapped her glass to his. "To us," she said, raising the glass to her lips and drinking deeply.

He followed suit, savoring the burst of the wine upon his tongue and watching her. Her beauty stunned him as it always did, and he felt a flash of hot desire that was almost as potent as the exquisite champagne in his glass. This was his wedding night, and he gritted his teeth against the tantalizing images his fevered brain insisted upon conjuring.

"You said there were things we needed to discuss. May I ask what they might be?"

It took a moment for Caroline's words to penetrate the sensual fog filling Hugh's head, and another moment for them to make sense. He gave himself a mental shake, trying to think of something beside the ache in his body.

"I've spoken with your Mr. Garrett," he said, doing his best to think of practical matters. "Your uncle is already making mischief and speaking of having our marriage annulled. Mr. Garrett is certain he won't succeed," he added when he saw her pale. "But he wanted us to know that we might better protect ourselves."

"What does he suggest we do?" she asked, only the slight tremble in her voice giving any hint as to her emotions.

"Nothing, unfortunately," he admitted, hating that he should feel so impotent. "Expressing concern for your safety is no crime, and until he makes an overt move there's little we can do to fight him."

Caroline gave a bitter laugh. "Overt moves aren't Uncle Charles's way," she said, passing the half-finished glass of wine from one hand to the other. "It's more like him to have me kidnapped than to openly face a fight he may lose."

"Which is why I was so furious to arrive home and find you gone," Hugh said, sliding quickly through the door she had opened. He was pleased she had the wit to fear her uncle; now all that remained was seeing that she made use of that wit to keep herself well out of the bastard's way.

To his surprise she had the grace to flush. "I am sorry," she murmured, sounding genuinely penitent. "I have been left to my own devices for so long it didn't occur to me you would worry. Since we had already decided to attend the soiree, I saw no reason why I should not proceed on my own."

Hugh thought of all that might have happened, and sent her a cold look. "But now you can see there *is* a reason," he said, determined she would not repeat her foolish mistake. "Until

I decide otherwise you are not to leave the house without me, or without men of my choosing. Do you agree to this?"

Her lips thinned in obvious anger, but she met his gaze with a cool control he could not help but admire. "I agree," she said calmly. "Although I do think you might have explained yourself, instead of snapping orders at me as if I was a green recruit," she added, her chin coming up.

Even as Hugh acknowledged the truth of what she was saying, he was reaching out to cup her jaw in his hand.

"But it's orders I'm used to giving, and receiving as well," he said, brushing his thumb across her lips. "In battle it was my duty to keep my men alive, and they either obeyed me or they died. There was no time to explain myself, or for worrying about hard feelings. So don't look to me for explanations or soft words, Caroline; I've none to give you. Only accept that what I tell you, I tell for your own good."

His touch brought the sweet bloom of color to her cheeks, but her gaze was remarkably steady as it held his.

"Very well," she said somberly. "I accept that, so long as you accept I may not always do as you say. I will try to be prudent, that much I can promise you, but I will not be blindly obedient. I cannot. It would be like living under my uncle's thumb again, and that I will not do.

"I know ours is a marriage but for a short span of time," she added, lifting her hand to touch his face as he was touching hers. "But so long as we are man and wife, I mean to treat you with as much honesty as I can. I have never been the meek and compliant sort, and I do not intend to be so now. If it's a submissive wife you're after, Hugh, I fear you have struck a very poor bargain."

Honesty. The word was like a sword thrust to his soul. It was the one thing she seemed to value above all else, and it was the one thing he feared he could not give. How could he, he wondered, when he had yet to tell her the truth regarding Loch Haven? To distract himself, he reached out to give one of her long curls a playful tug.

"So you do know my given name," he teased, his tone deliberately provocative. "I was beginning to think you would never call me anything but *Mr. MacColme* or *sir*."

He caught a gleam of laughter in her blue eyes before she lowered them. "I would not have you think me forward," she said, her tone as demure as the smile curving her lips.

The smile drew his attention to the fullness of her mouth, and the passion he'd been unable to fully conquer rose like a tide in his blood. He could feel the beating of his heart in his chest, and the wild pounding of it made the breath thicken in his throat. *Just a kiss*, he thought, and gently touched her chin. Just a taste of the sweetness of her, and then he'd let her go.

"Caroline," he murmured, leaning closer until he could smell the intoxicating scent of her perfume. "Have you a kiss for your husband on our wedding day?"

He saw her eyes widen in surprise and not a little fear, and the sight had him silently cursing. He might desire her until he was half-blind with it, but he would sooner die than force himself upon her. His pride would not tolerate a bride who endured his caresses instead of welcoming them. Digging deep, he found the control to limit himself to the single chaste kiss he brushed over her lips.

"There," he murmured, drawing back to give her a reassuring smile. "That wasn't too painful, was it?"

She looked dazed, then thoughtful. No," she agreed, her voice sounding slightly breathless. "It wasn't."

Not certain if he was amused or insulted by such faint praise, Hugh moved away from her with a wry chuckle. "Good," he said, settling back in his chair. "Now let us eat, and then we can discuss what is to be done about your uncle. I would be interested in hearing your thoughts on the matter."

Chapter 7

The rest of the bridal dinner passed quite pleasantly, and Caroline was stunned to discover a new side to her husband she would never dream existed. She was so accustomed to his hard, rough edges, it hadn't occurred to her he could he charming as well. But he was, surprisingly so. He was also well-educated, articulate, and possessed of a sly humor that had her chuckling more than once. It was odd to learn that the man she viewed as pure warrior should be so much more. Odd, and more than a little disconcerting.

After the luscious meal was over they rose to their feet, and Caroline experienced a sudden unease when he reached out to take her by the hand.

"You are looking tired, *mo céile*," he said, giving her hand a gentle squeeze. "Why not retire to your rooms? It has been a long day for us both."

A warm tide of color washed over Caroline's cheeks at his words. She was neither wholly innocent nor a fool, and she knew well what intimacies a marriage, even one of convenience, could entail. Theirs might be a temporary arrangement, but it was plain Hugh desired her in the way a man desired a woman.

"Yes, it has," she replied, hiding her trepidation behind a cool smile. "Good night to you, sir."

His green eyes danced with sudden amusement, and he carried her hand to his lips for a quick kiss. "Good night, madam," he intoned, mocking her formal words. "Mind you rest well."

Blushing, and furious with both him and herself, Caroline snatched her hand free and hurried from the room. There was no respite once she reached the sanctuary of her bedchamber, for waiting for her there was a trio of giggling maids eager to help her don her wedding-night finery. She endured their cossetting and shyly teasing remarks in silence, too embarrassed to act the haughty lady. Finally they took their leave, smirking and winking as they shut the door behind them.

The moment she knew herself to be alone, she leaped to her feet to begin nervously pacing. From the other side of the door connecting her room to Hugh's she could hear the deep rumble of his voice, and realized he'd followed her to bed. Would he come to claim his rights and privileges as a husband? she wondered, casting the door an uneasy look. And if he did, how would she respond?

Hugh was a most handsome man, and if she were to be honest with herself, there was something in his blunt, abrasive nature she could not help but admire. Perhaps it was because he was so very much his own master, she decided, moving to stand before the mirror. Other men, even those with wealth and title, might play at being the lord of their domain, but with Hugh there was no pretense. He might have married her because of some pressure brought to bear by her grandfather, but he had also done so for reasons of his own.

More time passed, and as it did her agitation increased. Perhaps he wasn't coming after all, she mused, chewing on her lip. The faint light flickering beneath his door winked out, and she could only assume he had retired for the night. A feeling of profound relief warred with a touch of feminine pique as she accepted he would be claiming no rights this night.

She knew she should be grateful for his consideration of her maidenly sensibilities, and so she was—or at least part of her was grateful. The other part wasn't certain how she felt, and the admission had her turning toward the door with an impatient mutter. Her fingers were fumbling with the ribbons fastening her white silk gown when the door behind her opened, and Hugh stepped into the room.

"Caroline? Is something amiss?" he asked, closing the door and moving toward her. "I thought you would be abed by now."

"I . . ." Her voice trailed off, the words turning to ashes in her mouth as her mind went abruptly blank. She cleared her throat and tried again. "I was just getting ready to do that."

"I feared you might be worrying about your uncle," he said, continuing toward her with that same inexorable stride. "Are you?"

"Uncle?" Caroline blinked in confusion before remembering. "No," she said, giving a forced laugh. "Although I suppose I should. Heaven only knows what new mischief he may be plotting."

"I have been worrying," Hugh replied, his eyes blazing in the soft lights of the candle as he came to a halt before her. "Your grandfather warned me the earl is as clever as he is dangerous, and I've no intention of being taken unawares. I shall sleep with you this night."

The frank declaration of his intentions had the blood draining from Caroline's cheeks. "I beg your pardon?"

"If your uncle is half so quick as we fear, we can only assume he has already bribed a servant to spy upon us," he continued, peeling off his dark-colored robe with apparent unconcern. "And it is imperative he be led to believe I have made you my wife. It is the only way to ensure you are truly safe."

Caroline stared at the broad shoulders straining against the white cambric of his nightshirt, her heart pounding so hard she wondered it didn't burst from her chest. "I see," she said, trying to force her frozen mind to think. She thought he would prevaricate, or wrap his purpose in soft words and pretty phrases, but it seemed she had misjudged him.

"Angus and Begley have pledged to keep their eyes and ears open," Hugh said, his voice so cool one would think they were still in the dining room instead of in the intimacy of her boudoir. "But 'twould be best if you behave as if you are always under observation, because like as not, you are. Remember that."

Since it seemed a logical precaution, she managed a jerky nod. "I will," she said, her voice sounding as rusty as an ancient hinge. "But I still don't see why—"

"I've contacted some former comrades and hired them as footmen." Hugh moved to draw down the sheets on the bed. "You are to take them with you when you leave the house if I am not with you. They will be armed, and will guard you with their lives. If your uncle thinks to seize you, he won't find it easy."

When she saw him climb into the bed, Caroline's heart shot up into her mouth and then plummeted down to her toes. "N-no, I don't suppose he will," she stammered, watching wide-eyed as he settled back against the plump pillows.

"And I shall carry a pistol when we are out of an evening," he said, stretching his arms above his head and yawning. "You are my wife, and I will do what I must to protect you."

"That is very good of you," Caroline said, too stunned at the sight of him in her bed to do more than gape. He looked so devastatingly attractive, his russet hair tumbling unbound to his shoulders and that knowing gleam lighting his pale-green eyes. It drove all thought from her mind. She had never felt desire before, but that didn't mean she didn't recognize it when it stirred warm and sweet in her blood.

"Tomorrow I thought we might go to the theater," Hugh told her with that same maddening calm. "As you say, 'tis a good place to see and be seen. I fear we left the duke's soiree rather precipitously."

Remembering the way he'd all but dragged her from the Greshams' ballroom, Caroline felt a flush stain her cheeks. "Yes," she agreed. "We did."

"Not that it matters; I hadn't planned to stay overly long in any case," he continued, cocking his head one side and regarding her with bright-eyed interest. "Caroline, might I ask you something?"

She jolted and did her best to hide her nervousness. "Of course," she said, relieved when she managed not to stutter. "What is your question?"

"Do you mean to stand there all night, or are you coming to bed?"

The frank inquiry, accompanied by a dimpled grin, shredded Caroline's pretense of control. Her whole face turned bright-red, and the desire she'd been cautiously experiencing turned to a confusing blend of irritation and mind-numbing dread. The moment she'd been both fearing and anticipating was here, and she was at a loss to know what she should do next.

"Caroline?" he prompted gently. "Will you nae come to bed?"

For the briefest of moments Caroline hesitated, pride, fear, and desire all warring inside her. In the end pride proved the strongest of the emotions, and she squared her shoulders in determination. She was bedamned if she would quail before him like some timid virgin, she decided grimly. A virgin she might be, but she was also the daughter of an earl, and wasn't about to let some arrogant Scottish brigand get the best of her.

With her chin held high she advanced toward the bed, and if her legs weren't quite steady, she could only pray it didn't show. She slid into the bed before her courage deserted her. The iciness of the sheets was offset by the heat emanating from Hugh's body. Caroline felt the warmth, and it made her all the more aware of the man lying beside her.

She pulled the sheets up to her chin, her fingers clutching the crisp bedclothes in a death grip. Minutes dragged past, and her heart pounded in painful anticipation as she braced herself for an assault that never came. Finally, unable to bear the agony another moment, she turned her head to give him a wary look. Her mouth dropped open at what she saw. He was asleep!

The thought had no sooner formed than his thick lashes lifted, and he met her astonished gaze with equanimity. "It's all right, *annsachd*," he told her softly. "Go to sleep."

"But you said you were going to ... to sleep with me," she stammered, then winced in embarrassment. If she didn't take care, he would think she *wanted* him to make love to her.

"Aye, and so I shall," he replied, his lips curving in a smug smile. "By tomorrow morning there'll not be a servant in this house who won't know I passed the night in your bed, and make of that what they will. Your uncle will hear of it soon after, and know you are beyond his reach."

Caroline stared at him, comprehension dawning. Put that way, his presence in her bed made perfect sense, and she silently applauded his efficiency. Her grandfather had chosen her champion well, she decided with reluctant admiration.

"Now if you've no more questions, I should like to be getting to sleep," he told her, patting back a yawn. "I've a full day ahead of me tomorrow, and have no desire to spend the night chatting. Unless there is something else you'd rather be doing?" He arched a dark-red eyebrow inquiringly.

To her fury, Caroline felt her cheeks flame again. "No," she said stiffly, thinking it would be easy to learn to hate the heartless rogue. "There is nothing."

"Good." He raised up and dropped a chaste kiss on her forehead. "Good night, Caroline. Pleasant dreams to you." And with that he turned his back to her, settling down to sleep with a contented sigh.

Beside Caroline, Hugh lay in tense silence, his body clenched in an agony of pain and unquenched passion. He could hear the evenness of her breathing as she slumbered in sweet innocence, and it was all he could do not to scream in frustration. He was so hard he was desperate with it, and the hell of it was there was not a thing he could do about it. His bargain with Caroline didn't precisely deny him the rights of a husband, but neither did it grant them to him. Theirs was but a marriage of convenience, and he would not allow himself to forget that.

A sudden image of his bride arching beneath him as he thrust into her burst into Hugh's fevered mind, bringing a sheen of perspiration to his brow. He was experienced enough to know he could overcome her maidenly objections with his touch, but he knew also he would never so besmirch his honor. He'd never forced his attentions upon a reluctant woman, and he wasn't about to do so with his own wife.

Eventually his exhausted body demanded respite, and he dropped into a deep, dreamless sleep. He awoke several hours later to find that in his sleep he had turned to Caroline, and she now slept in his arms. He stared down at her tousled curls, not certain if he should give in to the demands of his body and make love to her, or toss his head back and howl like a moonling. In the end he gently shifted away from her, knowing if he didn't leave the bed he would lose all right to regard himself as a gentleman.

He returned to his rooms in a sour mood, cursing roundly as he poured out tepid water from the pitcher on his wash stand to begin his morning ablutions. He was in the process of impatiently tying his cravat when Angus made his appearance.

"Ye ought to have rung for me," the elderly valet grumbled, knocking Hugh's hands aside to finish tying the cravat. "Look at the sad mess ye've made of this."

"I've dressed myself for the past fourteen years and managed well enough," Hugh shot back, although he remained still. "I've no reason to have someone dancing attendance upon me now."

"Which just shows what ye know," Angus retorted, going to the clothespress to remove a jacket. " 'Tis the grandson of a duke ye now be, as well as the laird of Loch Haven. Ye canna go about dressed like a beggar."

Because he knew the valet was speaking the truth Hugh swallowed his black temper, sullenly enduring the older man's scolds and admonishments until he finished dressing. The one thing he would not endure, however, was Angus's sly innuendos about his wedding night. When the remarks grew too personal Hugh whirled on him, his fists clenched in anger.

"And what makes you think I bedded her?" he demanded, pinning the valet with a burning glare. "I am a gentleman, you know."

Angus gave a derisive snort. "And how else would ye be keeping that limmer who is her uncle from having your marriage overturned? Once ye've taken her maidenhead, not the king himself can have the marriage set aside. Married ye are, and married ye will be until the year is ended and ye petition the courts in Edinburgh to end it."

Hugh didn't bother with a response, although the matter preyed heavily upon his mind as he left the house. He was fairly certain he could trust Angus to keep his silence, but now he couldn't help but wonder what would happen should anyone else learn the truth of his wedding night. Unconsummated marriages were easily reversed by English law, and he realized that in his misplaced gallantry he had just placed a deadly weapon in her uncle's hands.

He was still mulling over the matter when he raised his hand to hail a hack. The duke had given him a letter of introduction to his solicitor, and Hugh was anxious to see to the matter as soon as may be. He had appointments of his own regarding Loch Haven, and little time for patience. When a carriage stopped before him he entered it without thinking, not realizing it was occupied until it was too late.

"Come aboard Sergeant, come aboard," a well-dressed man in an elegant powdered wig drawled, smiling even as he leveled a pistol at Hugh's chest. "This is an unexpected pleasure, I must say. I was hoping for the chance to make your acquaintance."

Cursing himself for his carelessness, Hugh took his seat with studied caution. His gaze swept over the other man, taking his measure in a single glance. Here was one he'd not care to turn his back upon, he thought, deciding he was doubtlessly in the presence of the infamous earl of Westhall.

"I cannot say the sentiment is returned," he said, slipping his hand into the sleeve of his greatcoat to clasp his dirk. "I've no liking to have a pistol pointed at me before I've even taken my breakfast."

The other man's lips curved in a thin smile, and his blue eyes sparkled with malice. "I am sure you do not," he said, affecting an exaggerated concern. "Have I the honor of addressing Mr. Hugh MacColme?"

"Aye, that you have," Hugh responded cautiously, deciding he had nothing to lose by feigning ignorance. He also made his accent more obvious, hoping it would lull the other man into a false sense of ease. "And who might you be, sir?"

"Do you mean you do not know who I am?" The earl's pale-blue eyes widened with feigned shock. "Oh, dear, how very remiss of my niece not to have at least shown you my portrait, although I must confess I have never liked the wretched thing by half. It makes me look tiresomely plain. I am Charles, earl of Westhall. You know my father, I believe?"

Hugh gave a nod. "Aye, I served with the general a great many years. I know him well," he said, stalling for time. He wanted to get word to Caroline, and let her know her uncle had made his first move. He hated to think of her being faced with him unprepared.

Westhall's smile slipped a notch. "Yes, and so you must," he simpered, venom all but dripping from each word. "Considering he handed you dearest Caroline in marriage. That is why I am here. I am come to offer you my felicitations on your marriage."

"That is good of you, sir," Hugh said, wondering what deep game the earl was playing.

"I should have liked to have been at your nuptials," the earl continued, his drawling tones beginning to grate on Hugh's nerves. "It was held so quickly, was it not? The very day after you met her, if I am not mistaken."

" 'Twas the day after that, to be accurate, my lord," Hugh corrected coolly. "And as for the haste of it, 'twas your father's doing. He wanted Caroline protected, you see. He had some fear for her safety." He smiled, letting his mask drop to show the earl he knew precisely what the other man was about.

The earl's fatuous expression tightened, and his painted lips tightened in chilling fury. In that moment he looked every bit the monster Caroline had named him, and Hugh sent his wife a silent apology. Now he believed that she had indeed fled her home to escape this creature, and he shuddered to imagine what it must have been like for her under his power.

"Yes, my father was always one to fly into a panic," the earl said stiffly. "And Caroline, of course, is possessed of a most excitable disposition. High-strung, just like her dearest mama."

"Indeed? I have found Caroline to be a most sober young lady," Hugh said, his voice soft as he gently called the earl a liar. "And as for the general, he has never panicked a day in his life. Did you have the opportunity to serve with him in battle, when the air is thick with lead and men are dying all about you, you would know he is a man who stands ever firm. Such men do not waver. They see what is to be done, and they do it."

There was a brittle silence as Westhall studied him with narrowed eyes. "I see," he said, taking snuff from a porcelain box and sniffing delicately. "And you are also such a man?"

"I pride myself that I am," Hugh said, his eyes full of unspoken promise as he met the earl's malevolent gaze.

The earl regarded him a long moment before nodding. "Yes," he said, "I can see that you are. How interesting. How very interesting. I see I shall have to rethink the situation. Evidently things aren't as simple as I thought they would be."

Hugh wondered what the devil he meant by that, but the earl was already rapping on the roof with his gold-topped cane. The carriage pulled over to the side of the street, and the earl leaned over Hugh to push open the door.

"I thank you for taking the time to chat with me, Mr. MacColme," he said, his voice edged with mockery. "I can assure you I found it a most edifying experience. Do give my dear niece my best, won't you? Tell her I am looking forward to seeing her soon." And with that he slammed the door and drove away, leaving Hugh to glare after him in frustrated silence.

The sunlight was streaming through the opened drapes when Caroline opened her eyes the following morning. The first thought to register in her sleep-dulled mind was that it was far later than her usual rising time, and the next thought was that she wasn't alone. She opened her eyes to see Helene setting a tray on her bedside table. Seeing she was awake, the maid stepped back from the bed, hastily averting her eyes as she dropped a stiff curtsy.

"Good morning, my lady," she said, her gaze not meeting Caroline's. "I trust you slept well?"

To her chagrin, Caroline felt her cheeks flame with hectic color. "Quite well, Helene," she managed in a strained voice, grateful Hugh had possessed the sensitivity to return to his own rooms afterwards. "Is my husband awake as yet, do you know?" she asked, striving for a casual tone as she reached for the pot of chocolate sitting on the tray. She had a vague memory of his mentioning he had several appointments for the morning, and wondered if he'd already set out.

"Oh, awakened and gone, my lady," Helene told her. "He left word with Mr. Beg-ley that he would be gone for the rest of the morning, but that he hoped to be home for luncheon."

"I see." Caroline ignored a sudden stab of disappointment. "Did he leave a note for me?"

"No, I cannot say as he did," Helene replied, her brow wrinkling in thought. "If he did, Mr. Begley has yet to tell me. Shall I go and ask him, just to be certain?"

"No, that is all right," Caroline said swiftly, not wanting anyone else to know of her humiliation. "I will just enjoy my chocolate, and then I believe I shall dress for the day."

Anxious to inspect her new home, Caroline bathed and dressed quickly. She'd seen but the first two floors yesterday, and the housekeeper had promised to show her the rest. The inspection took the better part of the morning, and the sheer size of the place astounded her. She'd thought her uncle's house large by London standards, but her grandfather's residence was easily twice that size. Knowing of her uncle's greed, she wondered why he hadn't attempted to claim it as well as his own residence, and when she asked the housekeeper the elderly woman gave a disdainful sniff.

"As to that, my lady, his lordship was forever trying to lay legal claim to the place," she said, her pleasure he had failed at his attempts obvious. "But His Grace's man of business was too sharp for him. Your grandfather's terms made it plain the earl could only claim those properties entailed directly to him as earl, and that everything else was out of his reach."

"Did he ever attempt to force his way inside?"

Caroline asked, recalling the butler's conversation with Hugh.

"A time or two, yes, but like yesterday we were not allowed to grant him entry," the housekeeper admitted, then cast her an uncertain look. "Do you wish us to continue denying him entrance should he return?"

Caroline thought of Hugh's warning and nodded. "I think that might be best," she said reluctantly, envisioning her uncle's wrath at such humiliating treatment. "At least, so long as my husband is from the house. He has asked that I not receive my uncle alone."

To her relief the housekeeper accepted her orders without quibbling. "Very good, my lady," she said, giving a brisk nod. "And pray allow me to offer the staff's best wishes on your marriage. Mr. MacColme seems a very worthy gentleman."

As she'd spoken those very words herself not twelve hours earlier, this was a sentiment with which Caroline could heartily concur. "Aye," she said softly, unaware of the glow lighting her eyes. "He is a most worthy gentleman indeed."

Following her tour of the house Caroline retired to the library, where she discovered a stack of letters placed there by the ever-efficient Begley. She was sifting through them, deciding which to open first, when there was a knock at her door.

"I beg pardon, Lady Caroline," Begley intoned with a stiff bow. "But Sir Gervase has arrived and is insisting he be allowed to speak with you. Shall I admit him?"

A frisson of fear shot through Caroline, but she

was quick to suppress it. Sir Gervase was an overfed buffoon, she reminded herself sternly, and the day she couldn't deal with him she had yet to see. Then she thought of Hugh's probable reaction, and shook her head. "I do not believe that would be wise, Begley," she said, meeting the butler's astute gaze with aplomb. "You will please inform the baronet that I am not at home to him."

Begley allowed himself the tiniest of smiles before inclining his head. "It will be my pleasure, my lady," he intoned, stepping backward and closing the door behind him.

Caroline thought that the end of the matter, and returned her attention to the mail piled before her. She reached for her letter opener and was about to open what looked to be an invitation when the door was unceremoniously thrown open. Sir Gervase stood in the doorway, his face flushed with drink and temper as he glared at her.

"Bitch!" he said, hurling the insult at her with undisguised contempt. "Presumptuous whore! Who are you to refuse to see me? You are in sad want of manners, my girl, and I am of a mind to teach 'em to you!"

Caroline pushed her chair back, clutching the letter opener as she rose to her feet. "You are a fine one to speak of manners, sir, when you insult me in my own home," she said coldly, refusing to give him the satisfaction of seeing her fear. "You will leave at once. You are not welcome here."

"Ain't I?" Her brave words seemed to further incite the drunken man, and he staggered forward, a meaty hand raised in a threatening fist.

"We'll see how welcome you'll make me after I've beaten some sense into you."

"You will not threaten my mistress, you drunken lout!" An indignant Begley had returned, several large footmen at his heels. "You shall leave, or else we shall throw you bodily from this house!"

Sir Gervase whirled around to face this new threat. "Do you think I'm afraid of a servant?" he sneered. "Touch me, old man, and I'll break you in half! Then I'll have you whipped for daring to lay hands on your betters!"

Angry that he should use his position to threaten her servants, Caroline charged from behind the safety of her desk. "You braying bully!" she exclaimed, the letter opener raised high. "If you think I won't use this on you, you're mistaken! Get out of here before I bury this in your back!"

Sir Gervase swung around, looking much like a bull preparing to charge. He took a threatening step forward, but before he could utter another word Hugh stepped into the room, a deadly-looking pistol in his hand.

"Take one more step and you die," he said, his voice cold as he trained the pistol on Sir Gervase's head.

Sir Gervase stopped, the sight of the pistol clearly having a sobering affect upon him. "Eh? What's this?" he blustered, doing his best to salvage what he could of his dignity. "Who the devil are you?"

"I am Hugh MacColme, of the clan MacColme." Hugh moved inexorably forward. "And the lady you have just insulted is my wife." He placed the tip of the barrel in the center of Sir Gervase's forehead and gave a terrifyingly calm smile. "You will pay for that mistake with your miserable life."

Temper and bravado drained from Sir Gervase along with his color. "You can't shoot me!" he protested, his voice rising in panic. "I am a baronet!"

"And I am a man defending his wife," Hugh returned, drawing back the hammer until it locked into place with a loud click. "English law gives me the right to kill you where you stand, and none will say a word against it. All here heard you threaten Caroline, and they will support me whatever I do."

A loud chorus of agreement rose from the servants crowding into the hallway, and Sir Gervase grew even more alarmed. "Now see here," he began, licking his thick lips, his eyes rolling with fear. "This is all a mistake . . ."

"Aye, a mistake it was, and you are the one as made it," Hugh said, his accent more pronounced than Caroline had ever heard it. "I've killed a dozen men better than you before taking my breakfast, and not a thought did I give it. If you don't want my face to be the last thing you see in this life, you will apologize to my wife, and you will do it now."

Sir Gervase gulped visibly, sweat pouring from his brow as he cast Caroline a look of sheer terror. "My lady, I—"

"On your knees," Hugh interrupted, his voice as implacable as death. "You will apologize to Caroline on your knees."

Caroline opened her lips in automatic protest,

but the baronet was already doing his best to comply. Trembling so hard it was a wonder he could stand, he dropped awkwardly first to one knee and then the other, his hands clutched before him.

"Please, my lady," he pleaded, his voice scarcely audible. "I implore you will forgive me for my words. I meant no insult, truly I did not."

"Caroline?" Hugh glanced at her, his eyes almost silver with deadly anger. "Do you accept this pig's apology, or would you prefer I put a bullet through his head and be done with it?"

"No!" An almost inhuman wail rose from Sir Gervase. "No, please, do not kill me! I'm sorry! I'm sorry!"

Despite the fact she bore the baronet the deepest enmity, Caroline could not bear to see anyone groveling like a beaten dog. "I accept!" she exclaimed, terrified Hugh would ignore her and kill Gervase anyway. "I accept, Hugh!"

There was an agonizing wait, and then Hugh gave an indifferent shrug. "As you wish," he said, stepping back and handing his pistol to Begley. He then reached down and pulled the baronet to his feet, despite the other man outweighing him by several stone.

"Listen well, you disgusting piece of *cack*," he said, shaking Gervase as if he was but a rat. "The next time you come near Caroline, I will kill you. Not cleanly, not painlessly, but in ways that will send you screaming into hell. Do you hear me?"

Gervase nodded, speech having deserted him.

"Then mind you believe me." Hugh turned and hurled him into the arms of the waiting footmen, who staggered under the weight of their unexpected burden. "Take this bastard from my sight," he ordered coldly, "and from now on have better care who you let though the door, else I'll dismiss the lot of you." He turned back to Caroline, the anger already fading from his face as he gave her a brazen smile.

"Good day to you, my wife," he said, bowing deeply. "And how was the rest of your morning?"

Chapter 8

The next several days passed quickly as Caroline adjusted to her new life as a wife. Of Uncle Charles there had been not a sign, but Caroline knew him too well to think he would surrender so easily. He was doubtlessly holed up somewhere nursing his anger and plotting. He would reappear when and where he would have the best advantage, and she grew increasingly tense as she waited for him to make his move.

Of Hugh she had also seen little, a circumstance which added to her mounting anxiety. Admittedly she knew little of what passed between other husbands and their wives, but it seemed to her that if Hugh had any regard for her at all, he might at least attempt to spend some time in her company. Other than accompanying her to the theater and a handful of balls, he seemed more interested in his own concerns, and his apparent indifference hurt.

Another thing which troubled her was the memory of the casual violence he had shown the day he had confronted Sir Gervase. She had never before witnessed such brutality, and she was not ashamed to admit it had frightened her.

Not for the first time she found herself questioning the true nature of the man she had wed, and she wondered if she had made an error that would cost her more than she could ever have anticipated.

A week after she and Hugh had arrived in London, they were to attend a ball being given by one of her grandfather's oldest friends. She had been surprised when Hugh insisted they go. Until now he had shown a marked disdain for such frivolities, and she could only assume it had something to do with that mysterious business of his that seemed to occupy so much of his time. She was adding the finishing touches to her toilette when the door between their two rooms opened and Hugh walked in, as casual as if this wasn't the first time he had been in her room since their wedding night.

"Ah, Caroline, how lovely you are," he said, straightening his cuffs and studying her with an approving smile. "Your hair looks grand. Is that another hedgehog you're wearing?"

She shot him a dignified glare, determined not to be charmed. "This style is called *à la conseiller*," she corrected him, turning back to her glass. "And I will thank you not to insult it. It is all the rage amongst the ladies."

He chuckled, shocking her by bending to drop a husbandly kiss on her neck. "I am sure it is," he drawled, his eyes twinkling as they met hers in the mirror. "Although why a beautiful young woman should want to look like some fat old dullard of a lawyer, I am sure I do not know. Still, on you 'tis lovely."

Caroline set her brush down with care, afraid

she would betray herself by dropping it. "Thank you," she said, picking up her fan and gloves and rising to her feet. "Now I am afraid we must leave. We shall be late if we do not hurry."

"This is London; everyone is late," he replied, his gaze drifting over her in silent appraisal of her toilette. His gaze came to rest on the triple strand of pearls looped about her neck, and he reached out to touch it.

"I've not seen you wear these before," he commented, stroking a finger across one of the creamy pearls. "Are they new?"

She did her best to ignore the sudden acceleration of her heart. "No, quite the opposite, in fact," she said, her voice sounding breathless to her own ears. "They were my mother's."

"Were they?" An odd look stole across his face and he took a step back, his hand dropping to his side. "In any case, your beauty does them justice. Come now—as you say, it will not do for us to be late."

The earl of Farringdale's home was easily within walking distance, so she was surprised when he insisted they take the carriage. She also noted the full retinue of servants who were to accompany them, and turned to Hugh with a raised eyebrow.

"I know his lordship has the reputation for being something of a high stickler," she remarked, taking the footman's hand as she climbed into the torch-lit carriage. "But I do not believe even he would expect us to travel two blocks in such grand style. Surely four footmen is a trifle overdone."

Hugh climbed in after her, securing the door

before turning to her. "As I've said before, London is a dangerous place, and footpads are everywhere, even on this fine street," he said, his guarded tone increasing her suspicions. "In these uncertain days 'tis better to be over-prepared than underprepared."

Caroline digested that in silence before deciding it was all a hum. "Perhaps, but arriving with a carriage full of servants armed to the teeth is certain to cause comment," she said, determined to have the truth. "Now, tell me what is going on. Has Uncle Charles said or done something I should know of? Tell me, Hugh," she added when she saw him hesitate. "I have the right to know."

He remained silent for several moments before sighing. "Aye, that you do," he said, closing his eyes and pinching the bridge of his nose in a gesture that betrayed his weariness. "And if it will ease your mind, your uncle has done nothing untoward. That is precisely why I am taking such care. An enemy you don't see is a greater danger than the one who is marching straight at you. I learned that fighting the rebels in America, and 'tis a lesson I've not forgotten. Your uncle is up to something, of that I'm certain, and I prefer not to be taken unawares."

Caroline would have liked to discuss the matter further, but he turned toward the window, the hard cast of his jaw making it plain he would welcome no further conversation. His obvious rebuff stung her pride, and she also turned toward the window, determined not to speak unless he spoke first. Their carriage had encountered the line of coaches clogging the street before the earl's elegant town house, and from experience she knew it would be several minutes before they could leave the coach. With nothing to do but wait she soon grew restive, and despite her resolve to remain indifferent, her gaze kept returning to Hugh.

His hair was unpowdered as always, although she noted it was arranged with more style than he usually affected. He was wearing a frock coat of dark-green velvet with a high collar and cuffs that were fashionably rounded, and she thought the rather austere style suited his harsh countenance. Still, she thought, a bit of decoration wouldn't have gone amiss.

Some buckles for his shoes, perhaps, she mused, or even a ring. She'd already noted that save for a small signet ring his tanned hands were unadorned, and she wondered if she ought to buy him one as a wedding gift. Due to his pride, she knew it would be no easy thing getting him to accept, and she was trying to decide how best to broach the matter when she realized he had finally spoken.

"I am sorry, sir," she apologized, raising her gaze to meet his. "I fear I was not attending. Did you say something?"

"Only that we might as well get out," he said, watching her thoughtfully. "Unless we mean to sit here half the night, 'tis unlikely we'll get any closer."

When they alighted, Caroline noted three of the footmen closed ranks behind them while a fourth walked ahead of them, a torch in one hand and a pistol in the other. Hugh walked between her and the street, and she could feel his wariness in the iron-hard arm beneath her fingertips. Something more than ordinary vigilance was going on here, she decided, noting how he avoided the shadows spilling from the narrow alleyway. It was plain as a pikestaff he was expecting some sort of attack, and that made her even more alarmed.

Once inside, Hugh kept her close to his side, refusing to let her dance with any of the men foolish enough to approach her. His wary, distrustful attitude was drawing more than a few amused glances, and she could hear the whispers and laughter swirling about them. When his cutting glare sent a dainty fop scrambling away in panic, she decided enough was enough and turned to pin him with a stern frown.

"I appreciate your concern for my safety, sir," she said, taking care to keep her voice pitched low. "But if you don't wish me to dance, may I ask why you brought me to a ball?"

To her amusement she saw an embarrassed flush steal across his tanned cheeks. "'Tis not that I object to your dancing," he muttered, keeping his eyes carefully averted. "Rather 'tis the sort of men who would claim you as their partner I cannot like. Useless, painted fops, the lot of them. I'd not trust them to guard my hound, let alone my wife."

His description of the men who had approached her was, alas, all too accurate, but Caroline decided that was beside the point. "Because a man wears a bit of powder, it doesn't make him any less of a man," she said, her tone severe. "Mr. Crandall, the man you just sent packing, is accounted a deadly shot, and one hears he is quite handy with his fists as well. Besides," she added, frowning as a new realization occurred, "why do I need guarding? I thought you said Uncle Charles hadn't done anything."

Hugh muttered what sounded like a curse before casting her a glare. "He hasn't, and I intend to see things remain that way," he said, looking decidedly harassed. "And as for my not wanting you to dance with those *brolachans*, did it not occur to you that I might want to dance with you myself?"

Caroline's mouth opened and closed several times before she managed to find her voice. "Then why don't you?" she asked, thinking she would never understand the masculine mind.

"Because I don't know the bloody steps!" he snapped, sounding more like an irritated parent than an ardent suitor. "Now will you say no more of the matter? You're giving me a headache."

Caroline was considering dumping her glass of punch over his arrogant head, when their host suddenly appeared before them. With him was a man with black hair and turquoise-colored eyes who was almost startlingly handsome. Caroline was wondering who he might be when Lord Farringdale reached out to take her hand.

"Ah, Lady Caroline, Mr. MacColme, so delighted you could come," the earl said, beaming at them with every evidence of pleasure. "You are enjoying yourself, I trust?"

"Indeed we are, my lord," Caroline said. Unable to resist getting some of her own back from Hugh, she added, "And I must say the music is lovely. I do so love Bach."

The earl look baffled. "Is that what they're playing?" he asked, and then shrugged his bony shoulders. "All sounds the same to me, if you want the truth of it. But now I should like to make you known to my wife's nephew, Captain Alexander Dupres. I believe the two of you are already acquainted, Mr. MacColme?"

"We served together while in Canada, my lord," Hugh replied stiffly, inclining his head to the other man. "Captain, I was hoping I might see you again."

"Sergeant." Captain Dupres's greeting was equally restrained. "General Burroughs wrote me you were safely back in England, and asked that I say hello to you. Your regiment saw a great deal of action in the Carolinas, I heard. I trust you were not badly injured?"

To Caroline's relief some of Hugh's wariness vanished, and he gave the other man a wry smile. "Not that warrants mentioning, Captain," he drawled. "We fusiliers are of slightly hardier stock than your regulars. It takes more than a bruise to send us crying for the camp's doctor."

An answering smile softened the harsh planes of the captain's face. "I shall be certain to mention that to Lieutenant Trevellyn, MacColme," he replied, his icy demeanor dissolving. "He still talks of the day he had to knock you unconscious so that Dr. Warren could remove the bullet from your shoulder. You were holding him off with a Hessian saber, if memory serves."

Caroline's stomach churned at the image of a wounded Hugh lying on a blood-soaked cot, defiant as ever even as he lay bleeding from a bullet wound. She thought of the scar on his cheek, and wondered what other marks his tough, muscular body contained.

"Soldier's talk, so tiresome, do you not agree, my lady?" Lord Farringdale's jovial voice recalled Caroline to the present, and she glanced up to find the earl regarding her quizzically.

"Not at all, my lord," she replied, giving herself a mental shake. "Hugh seldom speaks of his days in the army, and I would know more of his grand adventures."

"So speaks the besotted bride," Farringdale chuckled, patting her hand. "You had best take care, m' dear, else the world will take this marriage of yours for a love match."

Caroline was trying to think of the best way of responding to the outrageous sally when Hugh grasped her elbow in his hand.

"I was wondering, my lord, if you would be so good as to stand up with my wife," he said, his fingers squeezing a silent warning. "These new dances are not known to me, and I've no wish to disgrace her ladyship with my poor attempts."

The earl beamed with delight and bustled forward to grab Caroline's other arm. "Be happy to, lad," he said. "May not be as light on my feet as some of these younger fellows, but I daresay I can still turn a pretty leg. Come, my lady," and he led her off, giving Caroline no chance to protest.

As she and the earl took their positions for the contradance that was forming, Caroline kept a cool smile pinned to her lips. Hugh was up to something, all right, she decided, curtsying to the lady on either side of her. And if it was the last thing she did, she would discover what that something was—and more importantly, what she was to do about it.

"So that is your bride," Alex drawled, his gaze following Caroline as she moved gracefully through the quadrille. "You are to be congratulated, Sergeant. She is every bit as lovely as the general claimed. I can see why the pair of you are so determined to keep her safe. Her grandfather has told me everything, and I am come to offer my services should you have need of them."

"That is good of you," Hugh said, having already deduced as much. "But do not be blinded by her beauty; the little vixen is also clever as a cat. She's already remarked on the precautions I've taken, and she's started asking some pointed questions as well. Deceiving her won't be as easy as I thought."

"Deceiving women is always a dubious proposition," Alex agreed. "That is why it is best to tell them the truth. They will have it sooner or later, in any case."

"Aye, but this is a truth that would give her nightmares," Hugh muttered, recalling the information the general had sent by special courier. Between the two of them, he and Caroline's grandfather had successfully contacted every magistrate in London, showing them the marriage lines and convincing them Hugh was indeed her husband. The tentative attempts Westhall had already made were easily routed, and they'd thought the matter resolved. The last thing they expected was for the earl to go to a magistrate in another town and cleverly plead his case.

"Oxford." Alex shook his head. "One would think a rogue of Westhall's stamp wouldn't even know where the place is, let alone to actually have connections there. How do you think he managed to convince the magistrate to sign the commitment order?"

"Bribery, I would suppose," Hugh said, recalling his cold fury at having learned of the order. "English judges seem unusually susceptible to the practice. Doubtless the earl greased the old bastard's palms with enough silver to make him willing to commit his own mother."

"Doubtlessly," Alex echoed, giving Hugh a disapproving frown. "And English judges, I'll have you know, are no more susceptible to bribes than their Scottish brethren. You are allowing your prejudice to cloud your judgment, MacColme."

Hugh didn't bother denying the charge. His dealings on his own behalf had deepened the contempt he'd already held for English justice, and there were times he was tempted to say to the devil with it and walk away. The general had been right in one thing: as his grandson, Hugh was catered to by a court that seemed eager to do whatever he asked.

The rights of the man who'd bought Loch Haven were dismissed as being of no importance, and he was assured he would have his lands and title returned as soon as the law allowed. The man, he learned, was naught but a rich shopkeeper from York. Naturally his claims weren't given the same credence as those of the grandson of the duke of Hawkeshill.

"Never mind that now," he said, turning his thoughts back to his wife. "The solicitor tells us the order is good only in Oxfordshire, which is why we are so certain an attempt will be made to kidnap her. His lordship must take her there. It is the only way for him to get his hands on her money."

"But what of you?" Alex asked, frowning as he tried to make sense of the earl's stratagems. "You are her legal guardian; it is your money now. Locking her away won't change that."

In answer Hugh gave him a pitying look. "You know me, Captain," he said, folding his arms across his chest and meeting the other man's gaze. "Do you truly think I would allow my wife to be taken while there was breath in my body?"

"Ah." Alex nodded in understanding. "Like that, is it? They mean to kill you as well."

Hugh also nodded. "Aye, and it pains me to admit that 'tis a possibility that never occurred to either the general or myself. We were so set on keeping Caroline safe, we never once considered I would be at risk along with her. The earl is as thorough as he is treacherous, 'twould seem."

"So he is," Alex conceded, studying Hugh thoughtfully. "I don't suppose you could lower that Scots pride of yours enough to put a bullet through him and have done with it? You must own it would solve everything if the bastard were out of the way."

Hugh shifted uncomfortably. He'd already considered the expediency of taking just such an action, but it wasn't something he was willing to do as yet. Only when he was convinced there was no other way would he kill the earl. In the meanwhile, there was another matter he needed to discuss with Dupres.

"I am glad to hear you speak of my Scots pride," he began, straightening his shoulders with grim determination, "for there is something I wish to say to you. I know of your efforts on my family's behalf on the day my father and brother were arrested, and I would thank you for it. I am in your debt."

The captain raised a black eyebrow. "Are you now?" he asked, his voice clipped with ice. "That was a fine, stiff-necked speech to be sure. I don't suppose it occurred to you that I don't want your thanks, or that I've no wish for you to be in my debt?" He gave a cold smile at Hugh's stunned expression. " No? I thought not."

"I do not understand," Hugh said, genuinely hurt and perplexed by Dupres's reaction. "My family could have been killed, my home burned had it not been for you."

"And I might have died screaming my guts out while those Indian braves took their time torturing me, had you not raided their camp to rescue me!" Alex shot back, his eyes burning with the intensity of his memories. "Do you think I've forgotten that? Or how you carried me on your back all those miles to the post, and nursed my wounds afterward? Do you think when I returned to England that I thought no more of the Scottish sergeant who had risked everything to save me?" He shook his head.

"When I was transferred to the border and

given the mission to clear out the clans, I nearly resigned my commission. I saw your face in the face of every man I forced to sign that damned oath, and I hated myself for it. Then one day I rode into Loch Haven, and I realized I had been given the chance at last to repay you for what you'd done."

"Alex," Hugh said, feeling a painful lump forming in his throat. "I do not know what to say . . ."

"I begged your father." Alex continued as if Hugh hadn't spoken. "I pleaded with him, I damned near committed treason to get him to sign that oath, but he would have none of it. And then when that idiot brother of yours opened fire upon us . . ."

"My sister told me what happened," Hugh interrupted, unable to listen another moment. "She told me what Andrew had done, and how you ordered your men not to return fire. Thank you, Alex. I know you may not want the words, but thank you."

"He looked like you," Alex said, his lips twisting in a smile. "And sounded like you as well, when he raged at us in words too filthy to repeat. I almost thought for a minute it was you, but when his shot went wide, I knew it was not."

"Aye." Hugh was amazed he could laugh at the foolish thing his brother had done. "Had it been me, you would have died where you stood. I was always a better shot than Andrew."

"I am sorry I could not prevent them from being transported." Alex laid a hand on Hugh's shoulder. "It was all I could do to keep them from hanging. And I'm sorry about your cousin as well. The press-gangs took him?"

"And several other men from the village with him," Hugh said, accepting at last that nothing could have been done to prevent what had happened. Even had he been there, the result would likely have been the same, so great was his father's hatred for the English. It was a stunning realization, and he felt a considerable lessening of the terrible guilt he had been carrying since learning of the fate of his family.

"The general writes he is hopeful of having their sentences commuted," Alex remarked, studying Hugh. "I hope he succeeds."

"As do I," Hugh said, his eyes smarting at the thought of his family. "I've not seen them in over fourteen years, and my heart aches from missing them. I thank God for Mairi."

"Mairi?" Alex looked puzzled. "I thought your wife's name was Lady Caroline?"

"And so it is. Mairi is my sister."

"Ah, the Scottish goddess." Alex gave a rueful laugh. "I was away from London when she stormed the post, but I heard the tale upon my return. Half the garrison was for marrying her on the spot, and the other half was ready to hang her. Quite the little termagant, from what I heard."

"That's Mairi." Hugh smiled to hear his sister described as a goddess. "I almost swooned upon learning of it when I returned, but I cannot say I am surprised. Even as a child her temper was as fierce as her will."

"I wish I might have had the pleasure of meeting her," Alex said, chuckling softly. "Although

I doubt the sentiment would have been returned. From the tales I heard, she holds the English in as low esteem as do your father and brother."

"You're not her favorite people, that is certain," Hugh agreed.

"Then one can only imagine her reaction when she heard you had taken an English bride," Alex said, and then frowned at Hugh's expression. "You *have* told your family you've married, haven't you?" he demanded incredulously.

"Not precisely," Hugh grumbled, feeling like a lowly private being dressed down at muster. "There was the business with Loch Haven to be seen to first, and this mess with Caroline's uncle as well. I mean to write her and my aunt before leaving London, but there's not been time for it as yet."

"Then I suggest you make time for it, Sergeant Major, and at once." Alex was staring over Hugh's shoulder, his face setting in harsh lines. "You may be leaving London sooner than you think."

"Why would I be doing that?" Hugh asked, turning to see whatever had caught the captain's attention. Several men had entered the ballroom, and there was something about the tall, cadaverously thin man in the middle that looked unsettlingly familiar.

"Because the earl of Westhall just walked in, and he is heading directly toward us. Guard up, Sergeant MacColme. The enemy has been sighted."

Chapter 9

Hugh had barely absorbed the shock of Alex's pronouncement when the earl was upon them. "Good evening, gentlemen," he said with an exaggerated bow. "Mr. MacColme, how delightful to see you again. I trust you are well?"

"Quite well, my lord," Hugh replied, skills honed on the battlefield on full alert. He didn't think the earl would attack him with half of society looking on, and more was the pity, as far as he was concerned. He would have derived a great deal of satisfaction in taking the limmer apart piece by bloody piece.

"But where is my dear niece?" the earl asked, glancing about him with every show of eagerness. "I am come to offer her, and you, of course, my felicitations on your marriage."

Hugh was willing to wager his last groat the earl knew precisely where Caroline was, but before he could say as much Alex stepped in front of him.

"Lady Caroline is with the earl of Farringdale, my lord," he said, inclining his head to Westhall respectfully. "I am sure she will be overjoyed to learn of your arrival." He glanced next at Hugh, his eyes sending out an urgent warning for caution. "With your permission, sir, I should be happy to fetch her."

"That is good of you, Captain Dupres. Thank you," Hugh said, grateful for Alex's quickness. At least Caroline would now have some preparation, and he knew Alex would defend her with his life.

The moment Alex had gone the earl turned back to Hugh, his eyes alight with some secret delight. "It will be good to see Caroline again," he told Hugh in languid accents. "She is such an innocent, I have been most concerned for her."

What was this, now? Hugh wondered, hiding his trepidation behind a mask of cool control. Was the earl even now laying the groundwork to have Caroline declared mad? If so, then the situation was even more dangerous than he had feared—he would have to contact the general at once.

"Caroline is fine, my lord," he informed the other man coldly. "You needn't concern yourself with her."

"But I do concern myself, you see." The earl simpered. "What sort of uncle would I be if I did not? And this marriage of yours was held so precipitously; you cannot fault for me for wishing to assure myself all is well. If it is, then I shall say no more, and if 'tis not . . ." He lifted his padded shoulders in an elegant shrug. "Then I shall have to do what must be done."

Hugh straightened, his eyes narrowing with fury. "There is naught that is to be done," he said, his hands clenching into fists. "We are legally wed, and that is the end of it."

The earl cast him a look dripping with malice. "Is it?" he all but purred. "Marriages may be set aside for a variety of reasons, you know. 'Tis difficult, I grant you, but not impossible. Nothing is impossible if one is determined enough."

Before Hugh could respond to this blatant threat, Alex returned with Caroline on his arm.

"Uncle Charles! What a pleasant surprise," Caroline said, a smile of polite welcome pinned on her lips. "I didn't know you were back in town."

At first glance Hugh thought her remarkably self-possessed; then he saw the strain darkening her blue eyes, and moved forward to take her hand. Even through her gloves he could feel how cold her fingers were, and he gave them a reassuring squeeze before turning back to face the earl.

"Caroline, your uncle has come to give us his blessing," he said, addressing his wife although his gaze never left Westhall. "It is very good of him, do you not agree?"

"Very good," Caroline echoed dutifully, dropping a demure curtsy. "Thank you, Uncle. I am pleased to think my marriage meets with your approval."

Little minx, Hugh thought, delighted at the adroit way she had helped maneuver Westhall. Now there was no way the earl could repudiate their marriage without risking public scandal.

"I might have approved of it even more had I been aware it was to take place." The earl's stilted response made it plain he was also aware of having been manipulated. "I was remarking to Mr. MacColme that the ceremony was held

with what some unkind souls might consider undue dispatch. The old adage about marrying in
haste and repenting at leisure springs to mind.
And I should so hate to see you repenting, my
dear," he added, directing a knife-edged smile at
Caroline.

To Hugh's amazement Caroline slipped her
hand into the crook of his arm and gave him a
melting smile. "You need not worry on that
score, my lord," she said, her blue eyes lambent
as she gazed adoringly up at Hugh. "How could
I ever regret marrying so noble a man?"

Hugh was aware of the amused murmurs
from the crowd that had gathered around them,
and decided it was time to beat a strategic withdrawal. He was abruptly tired of the ridiculous
charade, and he wanted to get Caroline out of
there as quickly as possible. He turned to her,
lifting her hand to his lips for a gentle kiss.

"Are you ready to leave now, *leannan?*" he
asked softly. "I hate to rush you, but we are
promised elsewhere."

This was a bald-faced lie, of course. They had
no other plans for the night, but it was the only
way he could let Caroline know of his desire to
be gone. As he'd hoped, she was quick to seize
upon the hint.

"Very well, Hugh," she said, tilting back her
head and sending him a smile of such sweetness
that he was momentarily dazzled. He took her
arm to leave, only to find the way blocked by the
earl.

"A moment of your time, MacColme, if you
please," Lord Westhall said, his smile not reaching his icy eyes. "I was wondering if you'd be

so good as to have a word with that relic my grandfather employs as butler. The old fool has taken it into his head that I am denied admittance to your house. Naturally you will wish to disabuse him of this absurd notion."

Now it was Hugh who realized he had been manipulated by a master, and the realization was not to his liking. But with half of society looking on and licking their lips in anticipation of a scandal, there was naught he could do but smile stiffly.

"I shall see to it, sir," he said, and then, unable to resist a final dig at the earl, he added, "But in Begley's defense, I must say I cannot fault him for his caution. There have been reports in the neighborhood of several undesirable men lurking about, and as butler, it is his duty to keep such men from gaining admittance to our house. Good night, my lord." And he led Caroline from the ballroom, feeling much like a Daniel fleeing the lion's den.

Several hours later Caroline lay in her bed staring at the ceiling, her mind too troubled for sleep. Seeing her uncle again had shaken her more than she cared to admit, but it was Hugh's reaction which troubled her most. She'd expected the encounter to draw them closer together, but instead he had withdrawn into himself, his manner cold and distant on the short ride home.

No, she amended, shifting onto her side with a sigh. That wasn't quite the truth. At first he had been kindness itself to her, gentle and reassuring as he sought to assuage her fears. But beneath

the soothing words and comforting touches she
had sensed his remoteness, and it made her feel
even that much more alone. When he'd taken his
leave less than an hour after their return home,
she wasn't surprised. She'd expected as much,
just as she expected his request that she not leave
the house again that night. His protectiveness
was something she was beginning to accept,
even if there were times she couldn't help but
resent it.

What the devil was going on? she brooded, her
mind returning again to the confrontation with
Uncle Charles. Beneath his brittle civility her uncle's fury had been all too apparent, just as
Hugh's cold determination had been obvious.
They might have spoken in the most cordial of
terms, but she sensed there was more to their
seemingly idle conversation than might first be
supposed. It was as if they were speaking in a
code only they could understand, and it vexed
her to be excluded.

She was mulling the matter over when she
heard the door between her room and Hugh's
creak open. She lifted her head to see him sil-
houetted in the doorway, but even as she was
absorbing the sight of him he turned as if to
leave.

"Hugh?" she blurted out, and then blushed at
her boldness. "I—I'm not asleep."

He hesitated, and then started toward her. "I
am sorry for disturbing you," he apologized,
walking over to stand beside the bed. "But there
is something I must discuss with you and it will
not wait. May I light the candle?"

"Please," she said, gathering the bedclothes

around her as she sat up. In the warmth of the
night she had foresworn the use of a nightcap,
and her hair was streaming about her shoulders
in untidy disarray. She'd just brushed an errant
lock back from her face when the candle flared
to life, the dancing flame illuminating the harsh
planes of Hugh's face. He looked so grim, so for-
bidding, that she reacted without thought.

"What is it, Hugh?" she said, reaching out to
gently touch his cheek. "What is wrong?" A terrible fear made her stomach clench. "Has something happened to Grandfather?"

He reached up and closed his fingers around
hers. "No, he is fine," he assured her softly. "It
is your uncle. Tonight, before you joined us, he
spoke of having our marriage overturned."

A tremor of fear shook Caroline. "Can he do
that?" she asked, her voice not quite steady.

Hugh nodded, his expression growing even
more grim. "He claims he can," he said. "And
he does not strike me as the kind to make idle
boasts. He has one magistrate in his pocket already; who is to say he does not have another?"

This was news to Caroline, but upon reflection
she was not in the least surprised. She already
knew her uncle to be dangerously well-
connected, which was why she had taken his
threat to have her locked up so seriously.

"What do you think we should do?" she
asked, raising her gaze to meet Hugh's intense
scrutiny.

"I have been thinking," he said slowly, brushing a calloused finger down her neck. "And the
more I think on it, the more I realize there is but
one way to put an end to your uncle's plotting.

One way to make forever certain he can never have our marriage declared invalid by the courts."

Caroline's heart began pounding in an uneven rhythm. "And what way might that be?" she asked, although she already knew what his answer would be.

"I thought by sleeping in your bed I could convince others ours was a marriage in fact," he said, the music of the Highlands rich in his voice. "But now I know it will not serve. The only way to keep you safe, Caroline MacColme, is to make you my wife in truth as well in name."

His blunt declaration had the breath catching in her throat. "You mean by making love to me," she said, the rush of her own blood roaring in her ears like the sound of a mighty sea.

"Aye." He leaned forward to gently kiss the base of her throat. "Make love to you. But only if you decide it is what you want as well," he added, his silvery-green gaze burning into hers. "I'll not force you, not now nor ever. 'Tis a choice only you can make. I'll abide by whatever you say."

Caroline tried to think, tried desperately to understand the powerful emotions tearing at her. "And if the answer is no?" she asked, drawing a shuddering breath.

"Then I will do all that is in my power to keep you safe," he answered with such honesty she believed him at once. "You are my wife, and I pledge to do what I must to protect you."

She digested that in silence before finding the courage to speak again. "And if the answer is yes?"

His hard mouth curved in a smile that promised both danger and delight. "Then I will make love to you," he said simply. "Which is it to be, Caroline? Is it yes, or is it no?"

Caroline continued gazing at him, her emotions tangling themselves into a Gordian knot before smoothing out in a single strand. She drew another breath, held it, then let it slowly out again. She lifted her other hand to frame his face in her palms. "The answer is yes, Hugh Mac-Colme. Make love to me."

There was a tense silence, and at first Caroline didn't think Hugh had heard her. He stood so still, his countenance betraying nothing of what he was feeling. She bit her lip, desperately wishing her impetuous words unsaid, when he reached out and cupped her face in hands that weren't quite steady.

"Are you certain, Caroline?" he asked, his voice harsh.

She nodded, swallowing the last of her lingering doubts. "I'm certain."

He stared at her for a long moment, his gaze searing her as it moved slowly over her face. When it came to rest on her lips she felt its touch as vividly as if it was a kiss. Then his mouth was closing over hers, his kiss deep and strong as he swept her up into his arms and pressed her down on the bed.

She clung to him, her head spinning with an intoxicating mixture of anticipation and dread. She should be afraid, she thought, while thinking was still possible. She should be shrinking in horror at the intimacies they were about to share, and crying for him to stop. But it was hard to think of such things when her heart was racing and her breath was thick as honey in her throat.

"*Mo leannan, mo maise,*" he groaned, whispering the exotic words against her throat. "You are so beautiful, so sweet. I burn from wanting you."

"Hugh..." His name eased through her parted lips like a sigh. She could feel his touch as he slid the robe from her shoulders, leaving her bare save for the transparent silk of her gown. She should have been embarrassed, would have been, she was certain, had it not been for the look of wonder in his eyes.

"How pale your skin is," he said, his fingers brushing over the soft swell of her breasts. "Like the purest of cream." His touch slid lower, circling her aching nipples. "And these, they are as pink and dainty as the first roses of spring."

The ardent praise had her feeling pleased and more than a little flustered. She was a stranger to lovemaking, and did not know how to respond. Was she expected to return his lavish compliments? she wondered, her hands clutching at his broad shoulders. If so, she could think of much she could praise.

"Easy, little one." As if sensing her confusion he dropped a reassuring kiss on her throat. "I will nae rush you. Relax now, and let me show you how it can be between a man and a woman."

Emboldened by his words of comfort, she gazed solemnly up into his face. "I'm not afraid," she said, brushing back a strand of russet hair that had tumbled across his forehead. "It is just I do not know what to do. That is to say," she added, blushing at his startled expression, "I know what will happen, but not what my duties are to be. I don't wish to do anything wrong," she concluded, shooting him an anxious look.

His expression lightened, and he gave a low chuckle as he brushed another kiss over her mouth. "Your duties, my sweet, are to enjoy yourself. Nothing more, and certainly nothing less."

He was making a very good start of it, Caroline mused, her lashes fluttering closed as his fingers resumed their soothing strokes. His touch was like fire on her skin, and she shuddered with pleasure.

He continued murmuring to her, daring compliments that made her blush, and exotic words she could not understand. She noted that the bolder his caresses, the more pronounced his accent became, and the insight brought a womanly smile to her lips. It was pleasing to know he was as affected by their lovemaking as was she. Intrigued by the notion, she slid her hands up his neck and buried them in his thick hair.

"That's it, sweeting," he groaned, clearly delighted by her caress. "Touch me. I want you to touch me as I am touching you."

She tipped her head back, opening her lips to his as he kissed her deeply. When his tongue flicked against hers she responded, shyly at first, and then with increasing boldness as he trembled in her arms. Their caresses grew increasingly heated, and each brush of his fingertips across her sensitized skin was more arousing than the last. Her gown melted away, and she noticed only when he bent his head and drew the tip of her breast into his avid mouth.

"Hugh!" She squeezed her eyes shut, her body arching as pleasure shot through her arrow-sharp.

"Easy, dear one," he said, nipping playfully at her breast and slipping his skillful fingers lower to tease and torment her womanly flesh. "Dinna fight it. Let go. Let go."

She heard his husky chanting as if from a great distance, but she was too dizzy to care. He suckled at her breast like a babe, alternately nibbling and licking until she was certain she would go mad. Her body was tightening with an unbearable pleasure that grew so strong, so full, she wondered she did not burst from it. Then abruptly she *was* bursting, a keening cry tearing from her lips as she convulsed with ecstasy.

Even as the overwhelming sensations pulsed through her, she could feel him shifting away from her, but before she could protest he returned, gently parting her thighs as he settled between them.

"I will try to be gentle," he promised, his voice strained with passion. "You must let me know if I hurt you. Tell me, and I give you my word I will stop."

She tensed, but he was already easing into her, his entry gentle but inexorable. The sensations were overwhelming, and she felt dazed anew as he continued pressing forward. There was a quick flash of pain as her maidenhood gave way, but before she could gasp it was already fading, and in its place was a return of the ecstasy she had experienced moments before.

"Caroline," Hugh moaned against her neck, his body shivering in her arms "Are you all right, *leannan?*" He lifted his head to study her anxiously. "Did I hurt you?"

Caroline took a moment to consider his words. Was she hurt? she wondered, a delicious languor making her bones feel as if they were made from water. "No," she said at last, her voice soft with satisfaction. "You did not hurt me. I am fine."

A relieved look stole across his face and he lowered his head once more, lightly biting her nipple just as he surged forward to seat himself more deeply in her welcoming warmth. She cried out, her arms tight about his massive shoulders as she gave herself over to the dazzling magic he wielded with such stunning skill.

She thought what had come before was the most wondrous thing she could ever have imagined, but he showed her how wrong she was as he brought her again and again to passionate surrender. Time slid away as he loved her through the long night. Sometimes he was gentle, tenderly solicitous of her as he stroked and kissed her to ecstasy. Other times he was more impatient, hungry and ardent as he rocked her to fulfillment, his head thrown back as he groaned out his release.

It was the most incredible experience of her life, and as she settled down to sleep she thought that perhaps this temporary marriage of hers mightn't be as bad as she feared. In fact, she decided snuggling against his sweat-dampened chest, it would seem it had much to recommend it. The thought had her lips curving smugly, and she tumbled headlong into a deep and dreamless sleep.

* * *

Hugh woke to the sound of his wife's gentle breathing, and to the weight of her head resting on his chest. Feeling dazed, he sifted a handful of her golden curls through his fingers; impossibly erotic memories brought a smile to his lips and an unmistakable hardness to his lower body. He gazed down at Caroline, lazily pondering the possibilities before shaking his head with regret. Too soon, he decided, brushing a kiss across her creamy shoulder. He'd give her time to recover before showing her any more of the delights to be found in the marriage bed.

Marriage. The smile faded from his lips as realization dawned. He had made his marriage to Caroline a true one. Never mind that there had been no other choice for either of them, that they had only done what was necessary to stymie her uncle's devious plans. The fact remained he had made love to her, and by doing so he had put an end to any chance of a simple dissolution of their marriage once the year was ended. Even if he never touched Caroline again, it could already be too late. She could already be carrying his child.

The image of a babe with his red hair and Caroline's vivid blue eyes filled his mind. If it was a boy, the lad would be his heir; a son he might never be able to claim. Children had never been part of the bargain he and Caroline had struck, and he wondered how they could have been so shortsighted.

Some of his tension must have communicated itself to Caroline because she stirred restlessly, her eyes blinking open as she gazed at him in sleepy confusion.

"Hugh? What is it?" she asked, her voice slurred with exhaustion. "Is something wrong?"

"No, *annsachd*, nothing is wrong," he soothed her, even as he wrestled with this new dilemma. "Go back to sleep."

"I'm not sleepy now," she protested, albeit with a yawn. "What time is it?"

Hugh judged the weak light filtering in through the closed drapes. "Early," he told her, unable to resist brushing a kiss across her sleep-flushed cheek.

"Mmm," she said, and then stunned him by snuggling closer. "What are your plans for today?" she asked, sounding surprisingly prosaic considering she was laying naked in his arms. "Do you wish to spend the afternoon together?"

Hugh thought it was as well the room was in shadow, else he knew he would have been hard-pressed to hide his astonishment. He would have thought Caroline would be uncomfortable around him now that they had made love, and that she was not filled him with cautious hope.

"I have several appointments that will take up most of the day," he began, reviewing the tasks he had set for himself. "But if all goes well I should be home by four o'clock. Would you care to go for a drive in the park?"

She gave another yawn. "That sounds lovely," she said, and by the way she was slurring her words Hugh could tell she was already half asleep. He held her closer, gently stroking her arm until her breath softened and then deepened. He was beginning to think she had drifted off to sleep when she spoke.

"Will you tell Grandfather of Uncle Charles's

threats?" she asked, sounding surprisingly coherent. "He may wish to come to London after all."

"That might be best," Hugh agreed reluctantly, accepting that in the inexplicable way of women, Caroline was now eager for a chat. "I will send him word first thing tomorrow morning. I had planned to do so, in any case."

"It will be good to see him again." Caroline sounded contented as she brushed her fingers through the hair dusting his chest. "What is he like? It is odd; he is my grandfather, but you know him so much better than I do."

Reluctantly at first, uncertain what details to share, Hugh began speaking of the man he had come to admire more than any other man he'd ever met. He spoke of the general's intelligence, his bravery, and the compassion he showed to the men who served under him. In the process he revealed a great deal more of himself than he ever had, a fact he wasn't even aware of until Caroline was pressing a gentle kiss to his shoulder.

"Poor Hugh," she murmured, her eyes full of sympathy as she gazed at him. "It can't have been easy for you, serving a king who had done you such a disservice. I only wonder that you stayed with the army as long as you did."

Hugh gaped at her in horror, realizing belatedly what he had let slip. He had been speaking of the campaign in the southern colonies one moment, and in the next his feelings of ambivalence and resentment were spilling out of him. He'd spoken of things he'd never told another living soul, and his sense of embarrassment was compounded by the odd sense of relief he was experiencing. It was as if a wound long infected had been lanced, and the poison could at last seep out. It was a startling revelation, and one he impatiently brushed to one side.

"It was all I knew," he answered her observation curtly. "All I had. There was nothing for me in Scotland, and so I stayed. Too long, it seems," he added, remembering what had greeted him upon his return.

"Why do you say that?" She studied him curiously. "Had your father died while you were away?"

Hugh's lips twisted bitterly. "No, he was not dead. He was worse than dead. He and my brother Andrew had been charged with treason and transported to a penal colony. It is doubtful I shall ever see them again."

Her eyes filled with tears. "Oh, Hugh, I am so sorry . . ."

"As if that were not enough, the king I had bled and killed for had taken my land," Hugh continued, not caring now that she should know the truth he had been so careful to keep from her. "Loch Haven was seized and sold at auction to some rich merchant from York. That is why I sought out your grandfather. I was hoping with his connections he might be able to help me recover what was taken from me."

She bent her head, her attention focused on the broad plains of his chest. "I see," she said softly, not looking at him. "That explains why you married me. I'll own I was curious."

He was at a loss to know what to make of that. He slipped a hand under her chin and lifted her face to his. "Does it matter?" he asked, studying her somberly.

She hesitated, then shook her head. "No," she said, her gaze meeting his. "It is not as if there was any pretense of love between us, after all. I married you to secure my freedom, and you married me to secure your land. It seems a perfectly straightforward arrangement to me."

He frowned at her cool tones. "Aye," he agreed. "So it is." He remembered his earlier troubling thoughts, but decided now was not the time to bring the matter to her attention. Later, when they were both feeling less raw, he would broach the subject again and decide what was to be done. In the meanwhile, he was determined not to make love to her again. He might desire her, but that did not mean he wished to trap either of them in a cage that had no way out by getting a child on her.

"It is early, dearest," he said, gently easing her down beside him. "Close your eyes and go back to sleep. We've a busy day yet ahead of us."

He could feel the stiffness in her, and thought she would argue. Instead she finally relaxed, the tension easing from her as she lay her head on his shoulder.

"As you wish," she said, her tone giving away nothing of what she was thinking. "Good night, Hugh."

"Good night, *annsachd*," he replied, holding her against him as he drifted into an uneasy sleep.

Chapter 10

⌒◯◯⌒

Two nights later, Caroline sat before her dressing table adding the finishing touches to her toilette. She and Hugh were expected at the home of Sir Henry Gillmore, an old friend of her grandfather's. He was also a member of the Privy Council, and she wondered if Hugh meant to enlist the baronet's help in regaining his seized estates.

Not that the wretch would tell her if he was, she brooded, dabbing rose-scented oil behind her ears. Since the night he'd made such passionate love to her, he had retreated behind a facade of civility, never speaking to her unless it was to issue clipped commands or utter the most commonplace of pleasantries. Attempts on her part to bring the conversation to a more personal level usually met with stony silence, and in the end she abandoned the attempt. He might have his pride, but she had hers as well, and she refused to lower it by attempting to fix the attentions of a man so clearly indifferent to her.

At first she feared she'd disappointed him in the marriage bed, and that their heated lovemaking hadn't been as pleasurable for him as it had been for her. But then she would catch him watching her with such naked longing and desire that she did not know what to think. One thing she did know, was that she refused to endure his black moods much longer. He might bite off her head for her pains, but she was determined to know what the devil was bothering him.

"Oh, my lady, what a sight you look!" Helene exclaimed, clasping her hands together and beaming at Caroline like a delighted parent. "You are beautiful!"

"The gown is beautiful, Helene," Caroline corrected, pleased nonetheless by the maid's effusive praise. "Madame Clare is to be commended for her skill with a needle and thread."

"Oh, no, my lady," Helene insisted loyally, stepping forward to hand Caroline her fan. " 'Tis you who do the gown proud!"

Caroline smiled in gratitude before giving her reflection one final glance. What would Hugh think when he saw her? she wondered, patting an errant curl into place. Would seeing her dressed so elegantly remind him he had wed a flesh-and-blood woman, and not some untouchable stone statue? She was debating the possibilities when the door opened and Hugh stepped inside, halting abruptly when he saw her.

"Good evening, sir," she said, a hopeful smile touching her lips as she turned to greet him. "Have you come to fetch me? I do hope I haven't been keeping you waiting."

He gazed at her in heavy silence before speaking. "No. I have come to tell you the general has arrived. He is in the drawing room and asking for you."

Caroline shot to her feet. "Grandfather is here?" she exclaimed. "Why did someone not tell me?" She rushed past Hugh, her trepidation forgotten as she dashed down the stairs. She ran into the drawing room and threw herself into the duke's arms with a glad cry.

"Grandfather! Oh, Grandfather! It is so good to see you!" she said, giving him an exuberant hug. "I have missed you!"

"So I gather." The duke chuckled, gingerly unwinding her arms from about his neck. "Have a care of my cravat, dearest. My valet will give notice if you crush his masterpiece."

Caroline gave a soft laugh, savoring his closeness for another moment before stepping back. "But what has kept you?" she asked, catching hold of his hand and guiding him to the settee. "We were expecting you in London days ago!"

"Business, my dear, business," he replied, smiling secretively. "And I had no desire to intrude upon the newly married couple. Be somewhat *de trop*, eh?"

To her chagrin a rosy blush darkened Caroline's cheeks. "What are your plans for the evening?" she asked. "Hugh and I are promised at the Gillmores', but I'm sure they would understand if we sent our regrets."

"No such thing, child," her grandfather insisted, his white brows meeting in a frown. "An obligation is an obligation, and ought not to be set aside for convenience's sake. Besides, old Dillydally has invited me as well, and I must say I am looking forward to seeing the fellow again."

Caroline thought of the stern and pompous baronet, who was widely known for the air of grave majesty he affected. "Dillydally?" she repeated, her lips twitching in amusement.

"A name from our youth," the duke explained with a wave of his hand. "He could never make up his mind about anything, not even what coat to wear. Ought to have known he would end a politician." He turned on the settee and surveyed Caroline with every indication of approval.

"You are looking dashed well," he said, giving her hand a paternal pat. "You look just like a queen. Doesn't she, Sergeant?" He addressed his remark to Hugh, who had just walked into the room.

His silvery-green eyes rested briefly on Caroline before moving on to the duke. "Aye, general, that she does," he said, his voice lacking any inflection. "Are you ready to leave now? I have a carriage waiting outside."

Her grandfather accepted the unspoken command with a grumble. "Always were one to keep tightly to a schedule," he muttered, accepting Caroline's aid as he rose to his feet. "Tell me, my dear, is he always such a tyrant? If he is, you must tell me; I shall give him a sharp talking-to, and make no doubt."

Caroline's gaze met Hugh's and then she glanced away. "It is all right, Grandfather," she said, her voice mimicking Hugh's cool tones. "You must remember I have lived the last several years with Uncle Charles. I know well how to deal with tyrants."

Her answer seemed to amuse her grandfather. "You do, eh?" he asked. "And how is that?"

She gave her husband a pointed look. "Why, Grandfather, 'tis simple—you ignore them." And with that she sailed past Hugh, her nose held high in the air.

She is a goddess, Hugh thought, pride and desire warring within him as he followed his wife's progress about the crowded ballroom. When he'd walked into her boudoir to find her looking like something out of a dream, it had taken all of his will not to throw her on the bed and make love to her. It was a sensation he had become depressingly familiar with over the past two days—a sensation that was growing almost impossible to resist.

"Looks like her grandmother," the general observed, his gaze following Hugh's. "Those are her rubies she's wearing. Tildie willed 'em to her before she died. Good thing she did so, else that scoundrel Charles would have sold them off by now."

Hugh merely grunted, not bothering with a reply. He had already noticed the fortune in blood-red stones draped about his wife's neck and dangling from her ears. He would have to have been blind not to, and the sight of them only seemed to emphasize the vast difference in their stations in life. Given the current state of his finances it was unlikely he would have been able to buy her so much as a single stone, and there she was dripping in them. It was something he had best remember, for his own sake.

"Glad to see her looking so well," the general continued, sounding thoughtful. "I'll own I was a trifle worried. Not that I thought you would do anything ungentlemanly, mind," he added before Hugh could speak. "You're the finest man I know, else I would never have entrusted her to your care. I know you would sooner face a firing squad than lay a harsh hand upon her."

Hugh thought of the night he had made wild love to Caroline. Would the general consider that a harsh hand? he wondered, trying not to squirm like a schoolboy facing his headmaster.

"It is good of you to say so, sir," he said, his voice sounding wooden even to his own ears. "I appreciate it."

"Not at all, Sergeant, not at all. Only the truth, after all. You're a good man, and I know you will do what is right. That is what I wish to discuss with you."

"What is right, sir?" Hugh asked, his eyes narrowing as a man in a purple and gold jacket made an elaborate bow in front of Caroline. Hugh recognized him as being one of Westhall's crowd, and he disliked the attention he was showing his wife.

"I have been thinking." If the general noted Hugh's distraction, he did not say. "At my age there's not much one can do but look back, or look forward. I've always thought dwelling on the past to be a dashed waste of time. What's done cannot be undone, eh? Just as the poets say. But the future, the future, Sergeant MacColme, is another matter entirely. And it is the future that most concerns me."

"What about the future, General?" Hugh relaxed when the overdressed fop moved away from Caroline.

"The future of my family, and yours," the general replied, and something in his tone brought Hugh snapping to attention. It was the tone the general used when he was planning something audacious.

"My family?" he repeated warily.

"Your brother and father—I have been thinking about them," General Burroughs said, tapping his chin thoughtfully. "I have a friend in the Admiralty, capital fellow. I mentioned the sad fate that had befallen them, and he said he did not see why something could not be arranged to bring them home. A parole, perhaps, or even a full pardon, if all was well."

Hugh's heart began pounding. "A pardon?" he asked, wanting with all his heart to believe 'twas possible, but afraid of the crushing disappointment were it not so.

"A parole, more like," the general warned, stabbing his finger at Hugh. "But it could be done, it shall be done—if you would do but one thing for me."

Hugh thought of his father and brother, home again at Loch Haven where they belonged. "Anything," he said fervently, his eyes burning with tears. "I would do anything, General."

"Excellent. Then you can give Caroline a child."

Hugh stared at him in blank shock, certain his ears had failed him. "I beg your pardon?"

"A child," the general repeated, as if Hugh was the greatest simpleton to draw breath. "Someone to carry my blood into the next generation. Oh, I know what you're thinking," he said, holding up a hand to halt Hugh's sputtering protest. "Yours is but a marriage of conven-

ience, and will end in a year's time; I am aware
of that. But I know Scottish divorce laws, you
see. I know that when properly handled, anything, even the matter of offspring, can be easily
dealt with.''

Hugh could only gape at him, realizing in horror that the general was in dead earnest. He had
always admired the wily old warrior for his
courage and daring, for the impossible plans that
always seemed to work, no matter the odds. But
this . . . Hugh shook his head. This was madness.

"You canna be serious!" he said, slipping into
his Scots accent in his shock. "It would never
work!"

General Burroughs gave him a knowing look.
"Are you telling me you are not attracted to my
granddaughter, nor she to you?" he asked dryly.
"I may be an old man, MacColme, but I still have
eyes in my head, and the wit to make sense of
what they tell me."

Hugh's cheeks turned a dull red. "Of course I
am attracted to Caroline," he said, his gaze going
automatically to the corner where Caroline was
standing. "She is a beautiful woman, but—"

"Then it should be no great matter for you to
seduce her into your bed," the older man continued in his relentless manner. "Only mind that
she is seduced," he warned, bending a stern
frown on Hugh. "I'll not have the child forced."

"But . . ." Hugh's voice trailed off. A dozen objections leaped to his mind, but he seemed unable to articulate any of them. What the general
was asking of him was an affront to any man of
honor, he told himself. It was an outrage. It was
indecent. It would bring his father and brother

home. He drew a deep breath, praying for guidance.

"General, I—"

"Think about it, that is all I ask," the general interrupted, snapping to attention and glaring at a group of men who had just entered. "In the meanwhile we've more important concerns. Charles has arrived, and he is making straight for Caroline!"

"Caroline, dearest, dearest girl, how perfectly wonderful to see you again!" Her uncle simpered, bowing over Caroline's hand. "You are looking as lovely as ever."

"Thank you, Uncle Charles," Caroline replied, doing her best not to jerk her hand away. Where were Hugh and her grandfather? she wondered, and then drew a deep sigh of relief when she felt a familiar arm slide about her waist.

"Your lordship," Hugh intoned, inclining his head to the earl in a cold show of civility. "It is good to see you again."

The earl turned his gaze on him, his blue eyes filled with malevolence. "Then there is delight all around," he said with an exaggerated drawl. "For I was only telling Caroline of my joy in seeing her again. And Father." His reptilian gaze flicked next to the duke. "I am glad to see you safely home."

"Are you?" The general gave him a disdainful look and glanced at the two men standing behind Charles. "And who are these fellows, eh?" he demanded imperiously. "Are they with you?"

Her uncle feigned instant chagrin. "Where are my manners?" he cried, motioning the two men forward with a wave of his hand. "This is Dr. Harrison, from Abingdon," he said, indicating a plump man in a badly cut jacket of black serge. "And this is his associate, Milkins." He gestured at a hulking brute of a man with thick shoulders and a sullen expression. "Gentlemen, my niece, Lady Caroline Burroughs—I beg pardon, MacColme." He smirked at Caroline. "I am having trouble remembering your wedded name, my dear. I pray that you forgive me."

Caroline gave him a cold look. She had no idea why her uncle had introduced her to two such rough-looking fellows, but she didn't doubt he had a reason for it, and like as not a bad one. She opened her mouth to issue a stinging set-down when she felt Hugh give her waist a warning squeeze.

"It would be best for you, my lord, and for others if you did remember that," he said coldly. "Caroline is my wife, and I will defend her to the death, if need be. Now if you will pardon us, we must be going. Come, Caroline." And he swept her from the ballroom without another word.

Later Caroline lay in her bed, puzzling over the bizarre incident. What was her uncle up to? she wondered. Why would he introduce her to two men who were so obviously not of his circle? Charles was an insufferable snob, and that he should appear publicly with such men was indeed troubling. She was no closer to solving the mystery when there was a tap on the door connecting her room to Hugh's. She sat up at once, her heart beginning to race with anticipation.

"Come in," she said, and was surprised when

Hugh walked in still dressed in evening clothes. "My apologies for coming to you without changing," he said, setting his candle on her table. "But I've only just left your grandfather, and haven't had time to change."

"That's all right," she said, nervously twisting the bedclothes between her fingers. "Is something amiss?"

He stared down at her for several seconds before replying. "We must leave London at once," he said without preamble, sitting on the bed beside her. "Your uncle has secured an order for your confinement, and I have proof he means to seize you before the week is out."

Even though this was something she had been half-expecting, half-fearing since seeing her uncle, the news still hit her with the viciousness of a blow. "But he can't!" she cried, her fingers clutching the hand he'd offered her. "He is no longer my guardian—you are!"

"A fact he took care to hide from the drunken sot of a magistrate who gave him the writ," he answered, his strong fingers gently chafing her chilled flesh. "Your solicitor has assured me that legally speaking it is quite invalid, especially here in London, but that may not be enough to prevent him from making use of it."

This was her most dreaded nightmare come to life, and for a moment Caroline feared she would be ill. "What makes you think he will have me seized?" she asked, trying to think her way past the overwhelming terror consuming her.

"The writ was issued in Oxford, and you would need to be taken there for it to be valid. I put some men to watch your uncle, and they informed me he has already hired a coach and four." There was a brief pause, and then he added grimly, "There's more."

Caroline didn't think she could endure hearing anything else, but she knew she must. "Go on," she said, steeling herself to hear the worst.

"That man he introduced you to tonight, Dr. Harrison—he runs an asylum near Abingdon," Hugh told her bluntly. "And I would say his associate Mr. Milkin is here to make certain you give them no trouble."

Caroline gave an involuntary shudder, and Hugh gathered her to his chest. "Do not worry, dearest," he said, his arms tightening about her. "You must know I would die before letting that *deamhan* place his filthy hands upon you! You do know that, don't you?" he added, drawing back to send her a fierce scowl.

Caroline managed a weak nod, realizing that it was nothing less than the truth. Although she didn't truly know Hugh, wasn't all that certain she trusted him, she accepted without question that he would guard her with his life.

"Where will we go?" she asked, closing her eyes and laying her head on his shoulder.

"Edinburgh," he said, brushing his hand through her tangled curls. "My Aunt Egidia lives there with my sister, Mairi, and we will stay with them. I'd hoped to take you home, to Loch Haven, but that will have to wait."

The gentle movement of his hand eased the last bit of fear from her, and Caroline snuggled closer. "What is she like?" she murmured, trying without success to envision a feminine version of her fiercely masculine husband.

"Who? Aunt Egidia?" Although she couldn't see his face Caroline could tell from his warm tone that he was smiling. "A proper scold she is, with a tongue that will flay you alive, and a disposition that would make vinegar seem sweet as honey."

Caroline's lips curved at the telling description. "She sounds delightful," she drawled, a warm sense of contentment filling her. "But as it happens, I was speaking of your sister. Is she younger than you? Older?"

"Younger," he said, and now there was no doubting the deep affection in his voice. "She was a child when I went away, and now she's a woman grown. She's your age, I think, and the image of our mother. She'll be surprised to learn I've wed, and will no doubt make my life a misery for not telling her of it sooner."

The rueful remark shattered Caroline's fragile peace. Until this moment, she'd never given Hugh's family and their possible reaction to their marriage a single thought. Indeed, it hadn't even occurred to her he was possessed of a family. He seemed so solitary, so completely self-sufficient, that she assumed him to be as alone in the world as was she. The revelation was vaguely disturbing, as was the sudden concern for what her new sister-in-law might think of her.

"Will it bother her that I am not Scottish?" she asked, raising her head to gaze into his eyes.

A shuttered look stole into his eyes, and he glanced away, visibly uneasy. "I don't know," he confessed, his gaze fixed on the front of her nightgown. "It will shock her, to be sure, and hurt her as well. But she has a warm heart and a sweet nature, and she will welcome you as my wife, if I tell her to do so."

Caroline was about to remark that ordering his sister to make her welcome would hardly endear her to the other woman, when another consideration struck her. "What of our marriage?" she asked curiously. "Will you tell her the truth of it?"

"That is another reason I needed to speak with you," he said, stroking a finger across her shoulder. "Aunt Egidia's home is a small one, with scarce ten rooms to it, and if we stay with her we will need to share a bedchamber, and a bed," he added, raising his head to meet her stunned gaze.

Caroline's mind went abruptly blank. "I see," she said, trying her best not to blush as images of their first night together filled her head.

"Will it distress you?" he demanded bluntly, his brows meeting in a worried scowl. "If it does, I would that you will tell me that I might begin making other arrangements—"

"No!" she interrupted, and then flushed at how abrupt she sounded. "That is," she added, making a desperate grab for her dignity, "it won't be necessary to make other arrangements. I—I have no objections to sharing a b-bed with you." Despite her best efforts she stumbled over the words.

"Are you certain?" he asked, sounding far from convinced. "I'll not force myself on you, if that's what you're fearing."

"Of course I never thought you would force me!" she denied indignantly. "You certainly didn't force me the first time!"

Her vehemence seemed to give him pause, and it was several seconds before he spoke. "Then you enjoyed what we shared that night?" he queried, his hands sliding down her back to lightly cup her hips. "It pleased you?"

Caroline tilted her head back, her breath catching as he feathered a kiss down her neck. "Very much," she admitted, her limbs turning deliciously to water. "It was wonderful."

His tongue flicked out to tease her sensitized flesh. "And you've no objections if we do it again?"

Her hands lifted to settle on his broad shoulders, her mind already hazing with pleasure. Did she have any objections? It took her less than a second to reach her decision. She opened her eyes and met his heated gaze. "No, Hugh," she said softly, "I have no objections whatsoever." Then, taking her courage in both hands, she reached up to untie his cravat.

At her touch he stilled, only the narrowing of his eyes and the quickening of his breath betraying his passion. The cravat was soon dangling from her fingers, and she waited for him to gather her in his arms and press her down against the pillows. When he remained where he was she cast him an uncertain glance, fearing she may have misunderstood his intentions.

He was watching her, his face dark with desire. "Remove my jacket," he ordered, his deep voice making her shiver.

The command both shocked and intrigued her, and her fingers trembled as she reached for the gilded buttons holding the jacket closed. It took a few fumbling tries, but at last she managed to unfasten the double row of buttons, and the jacket hung open. Having never acted as a valet, the most expedient way of removing his coat stymied her at first, but she solved the puzzle by leaning forward and pushing it from his shoulders. The movement brought her close against him, and for a moment their bodies were perfectly aligned. She could feel his arousal in the pounding of his heart and the hardening of his masculine flesh, and she choked back a soft moan.

"My waistcoat," he said, his breath hissing between clenched teeth. His whole body was quivering, and his fingers were as hard as steel as they dug into her hips.

She complied, her fingers more sure as she dealt with the remaining buttons. The waistcoat was soon discarded, leaving him in his shirtsleeves. Her hands rested on his chest, and through the soft cambric she could feel the heat of his skin searing her palms. She could also feel the rapid thudding of his heart, and its strong rhythm echoed the frantic beating of her own. She held his gaze and with his assistance, lifted the shirt over his head.

The sight of his muscular, hair-dusted chest had the breath catching in her throat. The first time they'd made love it had been too dark for her to truly see him, and now she was dazzled by the strength and beauty of him. It was odd to think of a man as beautiful, she mused, shyly stroking her hand across the strong swell of his breast, yet she could think of no other word to describe the perfection of him. His shoulders were broad and roped with heavy muscles, and not an ounce of softness to be found on him. Her gaze came to rest on the small, star-shaped scar just below his left shoulder, and she raised her head to find him watching her.

"Is this where you were shot?" she asked, gently running her finger across the puckered flesh.

"Aye," he said, his eyes glinting silver in the light of the candle. "A small price to pay for not having the sense to better keep my wits about me."

"It must have pained you," she murmured, recalling the lighthearted way he and Captain Dupres had spoken of it. She stroked the scar again, realizing that a few inches either way and the bullet he could make such sport of might have cost him his arm ... or his life. The horrifying thought brought the sting of tears to her eyes, and she quickly blinked them away. Without pausing to consider her actions, she placed her lips on the wound and gently kissed the damaged flesh.

"Caroline!" Hugh gave a tortured cry and pressed her closer. "Christ, woman, you're killing me!"

Caroline responded by sliding her mouth down his broad chest to the masculine nipple peeking through the cloud of dark-brown hair. Remembering the pleasure he had given her, she lowered her head and gently flicked it with her tongue. Hugh's reaction was immediate; in a flash she was on her back, blinking up in surprise as he loomed over her.

"My turn, I think," he drawled, a wolfish smile curving his mouth as he slid the gown from her shoulders. "If you wish to play love games, *cairdeas*, I shall be happy to oblige you."

He treated each breast in turn to the sweet suckling, the play of his lips and tongue making her writhe with mindless pleasure. His clever hands soon had the gown off her, and the brush of his legs, still clad in satin breeches, against her softest flesh was almost unbearably erotic. When his fingers began teasing her as well, she gave a keening cry.

"Hugh! Oh, Hugh, please!" she pleaded, her head moving restlessly on the pillows. She could feel the wondrous tension building in her once more, but this time she knew where it led, and she was eager for the wild release to take her.

"Please what, my angel?" he demanded, biting her neck and brushing his thumb over her moist folds. "Tell me, Caroline, tell me how to please you. I want to please you, to pleasure you until you are wild with it."

She opened her lips to tell him he was already doing just that when the tension inside of her was unleashed in a flash of white-hot desire. The strength of the explosion left her drained of reason, even as it filled her with a sense of glorious power. As he plunged deep inside her, she was hurled once more into the heart of the storm. There seemed to be no beginning or end to the glorious sensations tearing through her. There was only pleasure greater than anything she had ever known; pleasure, and the feel of Hugh's arms holding her close as he took them once more into madness.

The candle was still burning bright when Hugh managed to open his eyes. He was laying half on and half off the bed, with a drowsing Caroline draped once more across his chest. This time there was none of the deep remorse and troubling doubts he had experienced the last time, and Hugh let himself bask in the warm aftermath of loving.

Aye, but the wench was a passionate one, he thought smugly, letting his fingers tangle in the blonde curls rioting down her back. He'd suspected as much, but having it proven had been glorious indeed.

He was wondering if he might interest her in another demonstration of her sensual nature when she asked, "How did you come to be shot?"

The question caught him unawares, and he stared at the top of her head in confusion. "What?"

"You said you were shot because you weren't paying attention," she said, stroking her finger across the old wound. "Were you with my grandfather when it happened?"

Since she genuinely seemed to want to know, he could see no harm in relating the story. "No, I was in Dupres's command," he said, settling back against his pillows. "We were a day's march from the fort when a band of Indians attacked us. I lost two men before we even knew they were there, and I was shot before I could even aim my rifle. Once Dupres knew I'd recover, he put me in the stockade for three days."

"He arrested you?" Her head shot up, her eyes flashing with outrage. "But that is infamous! I thought he was your friend!"

"And so he was," he told her, amused at the

way she leaped to his defense. "But he was an officer first, and I had bungled things badly. I knew bands of rebels had slipped into the country and were agitating the local tribes, but I didn't post guards. I had let myself relax, and because of that two men died. I was lucky not to have been court-martialed. Or hung," he added, knowing the likely outcome of such a court-martial.

"How did you get this?" Her fingers brushed over a ridge of angry pink flesh that snaked around his waist.

"A close-quarter engagement just outside of Charleston," he said, recalling the pain of the saber slash, and his terror as he'd fought grimly for his life. "I was carrying orders to your grandfather and a rebel group ambushed us."

"And this?" A small horseshoe-shaped scar on his thigh was next treated to her tender examination.

Her touch distracted him, and it was a moment before he could remember. "A piece of grapeshot from Cowpens," he said at last. "The fire was murderous that day."

"What about this?" A scar on the other side of his waist drew her attention.

"More grapeshot, from King's Mountain, if I'm not mistaken," he said, becoming more than a little aroused by her solicitous inspection. He hadn't spent his fourteen years in the fusiliers prancing about a parade ground, and his body was well-marked from the active service he had given the English king. If she kissed and cooed over every scar he possessed, he'd be a raving maniac before the night was half over.

She was leaning over him, tracing a thin scar along his ribs. "What about . . . oh, my God!" Her words ended in a cry of horror.

"What?" he asked, and then too late understood what had so appalled her.

"Your back!" she cried, her eyes filling with tears as she gazed at the network of white scars laced across his tanned flesh. "Oh, Hugh, your back!"

Embarrassed and uneasy, he tried to shift away from her touch. " 'Tis nothing," he said, wishing he'd stopped her while it had still been a game. "Don't concern yourself."

"Nothing! There must be a dozen or more such scars here!" she exclaimed, her hands gently stroking and soothing the torn flesh. "They're everywhere! What happened to you?"

"I've already told you 'tis nothing," he said, sexual contentment giving way to a rising tide of memories too bitter to contain. "Leave it be, Caroline, I'm warning you."

"Were you in a fire?" she continued as if he hadn't spoken. "Oh, Hugh, how awful to have been burned. It must have been so painful for you! Do they hurt still? I have some salve—"

Abruptly he'd had enough, and caught her hands in his, his face twisting with bitter anger as he glared at her. "I wasna burned!" he exclaimed, fury buried deep for ten years spilling out of him. "I wasna burned, do you hear? I was flogged."

The color fled from her face. "Flogged?" she whispered.

"Aye, flogged," he said, his accent growing thicker with his temper. "Tied to a post in front

of the entire company and beaten like a disobedient dog. And do you know why?'' he added,
giving her an angry shake. ''Do you know what
terrible crime I committed to be given twenty
lashes?''

''Twenty lashes?'' She trembled in his grip,
tears streaming down her cheeks. ''Hugh, I
don't—''

''I was slow in saluting some wet-nosed officer, that was my crime,'' he said, even now infuriated by the injustice of it all. ''And when they
discovered I was Scots they called it dissention,
and added another ten lashes to the total. They
wanted to make an example of me, you see, to
show the rest of my traitorous race what happens to impudent young Scotsmen who think
themselves the equal to one of the lofty English.

''Well, I took their flogging,'' he said, tossing
back his head, his eyes shining with bitter pride.
''I took every one of those thirty lashes, and not
once did I cry out. Not once,'' he added, thrusting her away. ''There is the truth you were so
eager to have; I hope you are satisfied with it.''

He expected her to burst into tears, or perhaps
slap his face and rage at him for daring to handle
her so roughly. He expected anything except for
her to throw herself back in his arms, her arms
closing tightly about his neck.

''I'm sorry, Hugh,'' she whispered in a broken
voice, pressing her tear-dampened face against
his throat. ''I am so sorry.''

Her response stunned him, destroying the last
vestiges of the old anger and hatred he had carried with him for the last decade. The loss of his
overwhelming emotions left him feeling oddly

hollow, and for a moment he simply lay there, unable to think. His arms shook as he folded them gently around her.

"It's all right," he soothed, pressing a kiss on the top of her head. "I am the one who should be sorry. Sorry for raging at you, and for making you pay for something that was none of your doing. Sorry for taking out an anger on you that should have ceased to matter a long time ago."

She drew back to gaze up at him, her blue eyes luminous with tears. "No wonder you seem to hate us English," she said, a profound sadness stealing into her soft voice. "How you must have suffered because of us."

He felt his own eyes beginning to smart with tears. "Caroline, I do not know what to say," he whispered rawly, cupping her face with hands that weren't quite steady. He felt as if something inside him was raging to be set free, and he feared that if whatever it was succeeded in escaping, he would never be completely whole again.

"You seem so angry," she said, touching his cheek and studying his face as if searching for some deep truth. "There are times when I would almost swear you hate me as well."

"Not you, *mo cridhe*," he told her, using his thumbs to brush the tears from her cheeks. "I could never hate you."

He saw hope flare in her sapphire-colored eyes. "Are you certain of that, Hugh?" she asked wistfully. "Are you certain you do not hate me because of this marriage we have made? A marriage that is more farce than fact?"

Hugh didn't answer. He could think of no words to explain his tangled emotions regarding their marriage. He only knew that he didn't hate her, that he cared for her in ways he had never cared for another woman. He wanted to tell her as much, but he could not. Instead he showed her, lowering her to the bed once more and demonstrating his feelings for her in the only way he could.

Chapter 11

The journey north to Edinburgh was an arduous one, made all the more difficult by the haste with which it was conducted. Because he feared her uncle might be in pursuit, Hugh insisted upon keeping a brutal pace, driving himself and her as hard as he drove the teams of horses. Harder, in fact, Caroline corrected wearily, for at the least the horses were changed several times daily, while she was afforded no such opportunity for respite.

If there was any consolation to be found in the situation, it was that the forced confinement afforded her and Hugh the chance to become better acquainted. However intimate they might have become, they were still strangers in many ways, and as the miles flew past Caroline did her best to understand the complex and often difficult man who was her husband.

She learned that while he would speak openly of many matters, there were other topics that were strictly forbidden. He would never refuse to answer, precisely, but his eyes would grow more silver than green, and his voice would take on a clipped, cold edge that had her eager to turn the conversation to other subjects. Among the forbidden topics, she was quick to discover, were his father and brother, and Loch Haven.

But however cold he might be during the day, there was no faulting the warmth he showed her each night. They didn't always make love, but he would hold her in his arms, tenderly stroking her hair and murmuring words of comfort until she drifted into an easy sleep. It had been years since anyone had shown her such tender care, and she reveled in the time they spent together.

Four days after leaving London, they pulled to a halt before a row of cramped town houses looming over the narrow Edinburgh street like brooding giants. But such was Caroline's relief at not having to climb back into the racketing coach that she wouldn't have cared had she been expected to enter a stable.

"I must warn you again about Aunt Egidia's temper," Hugh cautioned, gently helping her down from the carriage. "I took the precaution of sending a messenger ahead with news of our arrival, but there's no saying we haven't beaten him here."

"I'm sure all will be fine," she soothed, amused that a querulous old woman could set her formidable husband to quaking in his boots. "She can be no worse than Uncle Charles. At least she is not trying to put me in a madhouse."

"Aye, that is so," Hugh chuckled as he tucked her hand in his arm and guided her up the uneven granite steps. "Although 'tis to a madhouse she's likely to drive you, with her lectures and her scolds. Do not say you were not warned."

Before he could raise his hand to knock, the

door was thrown open, and a young woman with bright-red hair rushed out to throw herself against his chest.

"Hugh! You're home!" she cried, hugging him enthusiastically. "We've been looking for you since last evening! What kept you?"

"The roads." Hugh laughed, dropping Caroline's hand to give the young woman who was obviously his sister a hug. " 'Tis a long way from London, little one, and we came as quickly as we could."

The young woman drew back from him, her emerald eyes growing cool as she turned next to Caroline. "You must be the Lady Caroline," she said, dropping a graceful curtsy. "Welcome to my aunt's house and to the clan MacColme. I am Mairi MacColme. *Beannachd Dhé leat*—may God's blessing be upon you."

The polite greeting paled in comparison to the warm reception afforded Hugh, but it was no more than Caroline expected. "Thank you, Mairi," she said, offering the other woman a warm smile. "I should like to say as much in your own tongue, but fear I don't know the proper words."

Mairi's lively features betrayed her surprise, and there was a thaw in her reserve. "*Thoir buidheachas*," she supplied, her lilting accent making the words sound like the sweetest music. "But don't think we shall expect you to speak Gaelic. At least," she went on, her eyes sparkling mischievously, "not until after we've given you a cup of tea with a wee drop of whiskey in it to help loosen your English tongue."

"Wheest! What are ye aboot, standing on the

steps and kimmerin' like a pack of old women?"
a wizened old man with hazel eyes demanded
sourly. "Into the house wi' ye, before ye've the
whole of the town knowin' our business!"

"Och, Gregors, you are shaming us for certain," Mairi responded, surprising Caroline by
taking her hand and pulling her forward. "Is that
a proper way for a butler to be greeting his new
mistress? And she the daughter of an earl, and
accustomed to the fine-mannered servants of
London. For shame!"

The butler's disapproving gaze settled on Caroline. "When the daughter of an earl conducts
herself like the daughter of an earl, she'll be
greeted as such," he said dourly. "In the meanwhile, the mistress is in the parlor waiting for ye.
Just the lassie, mind," he added, his thin lips
twisting in a crafty smile. "She's wantin' a word
wi' the new bride."

"And if that's not enough to send you running
for the border, then my brother's nae done his
duty by you," Mairi murmured, her arm still
linked with Caroline's as she guided her forward. "Or has he warned you already of our
aunt's temper?"

"He has mentioned her character is . . .
strong," Caroline said, choosing the most diplo-
matic word she could think of.

"Strong?" Mairi threw back her head and gave
a rich laugh. "Aye, strong as an ox, is Egidia Sinclair, but there's no harm in her harping and cutting at you. Cut back, if you want my advice.
She'll think the better of you for it."

"That's enough, Mairi," Hugh scolded, slipping his arm about Caroline's waist. "I'll not

have you scaring my wife with your wild tales. And I've no intention of leaving her to Aunt Egidia, either. We shall go in together."

Mairi gave another laugh. "You've been too long gone from home, *brathair*, to think Auntie will talk with you if she wishes it otherwise. Poke your nose in there when it's nae wanted, and she's likely to bite it off."

"It's all right, Hugh," Caroline said quickly, not wishing to cause any discord. "I've survived London's most fearsome grand dames; I am sure I can survive your aunt as well. Besides," she added, giving his nose a playful tweak, "I've grown rather fond of this nose of yours, and I should hate to see it damaged."

He smiled at her words, a look of undisguised relief stealing across his face. "Very well, my lady," he said, capturing her hand and carrying it to his lips. "But if she should turn too fearsome, call out, and I promise to come dashing to your rescue."

Even though she knew he was but teasing her, Caroline's pride rebelled at the idea she would be so poor-spirited. "I won't call out," she said, straightening her shoulders with resolve. "I am a Burroughs, and we do not quit the field so easily. Take me to your aunt. I am anxious to make her acquaintance."

Her bravado lasted until Hugh escorted to a room located at the back of the house and rapped on the closed door. When an impatient voice from inside called out and querulously bade her enter, her courage failed her, and she shot him a panicked look. To her surprise he answered with an encouraging smile.

"You'll do fine, *leannan*," he said, brushing a soft kiss over her mouth. "Only mind she doesn't devour you whole; I've plans for you later this night." He gave her a lascivious wink and then walked away, leaving her alone to face the dragon.

The sight that greeted her when she stepped into the room and closed the door behind her was hardly terror-inducing. A tiny bird of a woman wearing a hideous wig and a gown many years out of fashion was perched on the edge of a faded chair, regarding her over the bridge of a hooked nose with obvious distrust. She looked like nothing more than an ill-tempered fairy, and the sight was so incongruous Caroline could not help but smile.

"Well, dinna stand there grinning at me like a daft!" the older woman snapped, her thick brows meeting in a disagreeable scowl. "Come closer so I can have a proper look at ye. Unless ye're so plain of face as to prefer the shadows."

Inexplicably, the astringent comment appealed to Caroline's sense of the ridiculous. "Actually I am accounted a passingly pretty female," she said, wisely hiding her amusement as she moved gracefully toward the woman. The light of the tallow candle fell across her features, and she smiled again as she met Mrs. Sinclair's dark gaze. "I trust my appearance meets with your approval, ma'am," she added, dropping a low curtsy.

Color flooded the heavily painted and powdered cheeks, but Caroline thought she detected a flash of approval in the bright eyes before the older woman lifted her great beak of a nose and gave a disdainful sniff. "Hmph! Full of pride, aren't ye?" she grumbled, sounding vaguely pleased with the fact. "And not without some cause, I'll grant ye that. Although ye're too small-boned for my liking. MacColmes need strong women to bear them strapping sons, and ye dinna look equal to the task. Are ye breeding now?" Her gaze fastened on Caroline's narrow waist.

Caroline's amusement grew thin at the audacious demand. "As we have been married for scarcely a fortnight, Mrs. Sinclair, I should think that most unlikely," she said coolly.

"Fah!" Mrs. Sinclair dismissed her objection with a wave of her gnarled hand. "A man like my nephew could give you a babe the first night of yer marriage, did he desire it. Ye are laying with him, are ye nae?"

So much for the legendary Scot prudishness! Caroline wished Hugh had warned her of his aunt's utter lack of discretion as well. "That, Mrs. Sinclair, is a private matter between Hugh and myself," she said, feeling decidedly pressed. "I prefer not to speak of it, if you do not mind."

"Ye're laying with him," Mrs. Sinclair said, nodding wisely. "Ye're too bonny of a lass for him to keep away from yer bed, and ye've the look of a woman who's well-loved by her man. Why did ye marry him?"

Caroline seated herself on one of the chairs facing the older woman. "What?" she asked, fighting the urge to scream and laugh all in the same breath.

"If 'tis gold ye're after, then ye've been played for a fool," Mrs. Sinclair warned, her jaw jutting

out as she leaned forward. "For all he is a laird,
Hugh has nae a groat to his name, save for what
he earned as a soldier. And dinna be thinking to
inherit from me when I pass," she added, indicating the shabby parlor with another wave.
" 'Tis promised to Mairi."

After so many years of being ruthlessly
courted for her money, Caroline found being
called a fortune hunter a diverting novelty. "I
didn't marry Hugh for his money," she said,
raising her chin with cold pride. "And that is all
I am prepared to say. If you wish to know anything else, you may ask him."

"Hmph! As if that *cowlie* would tell me aught,"
Mrs. Sinclair muttered, folding her arms across
her chest and pouting like a thwarted child.
"Closemouthed as a clam, he is, and stubborn as
a block of stone. Although I suppose that is
something ye've already learned for yerself, eh,
lassie?" she added, ducking her head and shooting Caroline a sly look.

It was the sly look that won Caroline over.
"There are times when I could cheerfully throttle
him," she agreed, dropping her wariness and
settling back in her chair. "He is also very fond
of issuing orders and expecting them to be carried out with the greatest dispatch, I've noted."

"Aye, and for keeping things secret from ye
because he's trying to protect ye," Mrs. Sinclair
sighed. "But dinna be thinking 'tis some failing
of Hugh's that makes him act so. All men are
equally doltish. They think we women weak, ye
ken, and because it pleases them to believe so,
we let them.

"Now," she continued before Caroline could

respond, "if 'tis married to Hugh ye mean to be, then 'tis best ye were learning how to handle the devil. Tell me what else ye've learned of his shortcomings, and I'll tell ye how to correct them. Consider it my wedding present to ye," she added at Caroline's shocked stare. "Ye'll have need of it, I promise ye."

"Hugh? Are you busy?" Mairi poked her head into the cramped room where Hugh was sitting. "I have something for you."

Hugh glanced up from the letter he had been perusing and sent his sister a warm smile. "I'm never too busy for you, dearest," he said, folding the letter and putting it aside. "What is it you've brought me? Some tea? I could do with a cup."

"No." She came in, a look of apology on her face. "I tried getting some from that beast Gregors, but he said we must wait for Aunt Egidia, and she's still shut away with your wife, the poor lamb. Don't you think you ought to be rescuing her? You did promise to save her should she have need of it."

Hugh smiled, although he was also beginning to grow alarmed. Caroline had been alone with his aunt for the better part of an hour, with not a sound from her. He didn't want to dwell on what that might portend.

"I've heard no shrieks nor the breaking of crockery," he said, seeking to reassure himself as well as Mairi. "If they are much longer, we can always send Gregors in to check. Unless you want to go?" he asked, shooting her a hopeful look.

Mairi made a rude noise as she joined him on

the settee. "Me? Do I look that big of a fool? I've lived too many years with Auntie to interfere when she's interrogating a prisoner. If they're not out in a quarter hour's time, we'll set fire to the drapes. The smoke will drive them out."

Hugh scratched his ear as if considering her plan. "Done," he said, and then gave one of her bright-red curls a playful tug. "Now what is it you wish to show me?"

In answer she took his hand and placed a familiar-looking object in the palm. "For you," she said, her eyes shimmering with tears as she folded his fingers over the locket. "I'm returning it to you, just as you bade me to. Welcome home, Hugh."

Hugh slowly opened his hand, his throat growing tight as he traced a shaking finger over the etched silver case. "Mother's portrait," he said, his voice raw with emotion. "I never thought to see it again."

"I kept it hidden away," Mairi said, resting her head on his shoulder and lightly touching the locket. "When I heard the others say you were likely dead and lying in some forsaken grave, I would run up to my room and take it out, and I would hold it tight in my hand and say your name over and over again. I told myself you could hear me, and if you heard me, I knew it meant you were alive. Alive," she repeated, and threw herself into his arms with a sob.

"I heard you, *luaidh*," Hugh whispered brokenly, pressing his lips to his sister's head. "Sometimes I would be so cold, so weary from the fighting I did not think I could go on, and 'twas then I would hear your voice, calling my name. It kept me alive, Mairi. It brought me safely home again."

"Oh, Hugh." Mairi tightened her arms about his neck. "Why did you never write? I understand about Father, but why could you nae have written me? For years I waited for some word, some message from you, but there was nothing. At first I feared you dead, or captured, and then I thought mayhap you'd forgotten about us, or that you hated us. That you weren't coming home because you didn't want to."

Her anguished words were more painful than the lash of the whip all those years ago. "No, dearest, not that, never that!" he said, holding her tightly. "How can you think such a thing?"

"Because you didn't write!" Mairi cried, raising tear-filled eyes to study his face. "What else was I to think when you didn't write?"

Hugh gathered her against him again, unable to speak for the pain of his memories. He didn't know how to tell her he didn't write for the simple reason he couldn't bring himself to do so. Thoughts of Scotland and her were so hurtful that he learned to push them from his mind. He'd survived his exile by pretending he had no home, no family; he'd lived from one day to the next with no thought save survival. It had kept him alive, and at the time he'd thought 'twas enough; now he wasn't so certain.

"If I could go back and undo what I've done, *kempie*, I would," he said, his voice shaking with regret. "I would write you so many letters you'd groan at the sight of another one."

She gave a weak laugh and wiped at the tears staining her cheeks with an impatient hand. "As if I would ever do that," she said, levering herself away from him. "Now, tell me when you will give this to Caroline. Tonight?"

Hugh didn't answer at first, his emotions in too much of a whirl to think coherently. "No, not tonight," he said, opening the locket and gazing down at his mother's face.

"I like her," Mairi said, surprising him with her candid confession. "I was determined not to, you know, but she seems a nice enough sort, for an Englishwoman." She tipped her head to one side and studied him with bright eyes. "And I don't suppose you'll tell me why the devil you married her within a day of your arrival in Bath, either. Or more to the point, why she married you."

Hugh closed the locket and slipped it into his pocket. " 'Tis a long story, Mairi, and one I promise to tell you later," he said, helping her to her feet. "But in the meanwhile I think I will rescue my bride. You can help."

"Me?" She was laughing as he led her from the room. "What is it you want me to do?"

"Create a diversion," he said, feigning a lightheartedness he was far from feeling. "An old military tactic I learned in America. Marching in to get what you're after just gets you shot, so you send in a unit to distract the enemy and while they're shooting at them, you nip in and get what you want."

"Which sounds a fine thing, unless you're the one drawing the fire," Mairi retorted, pouting as they stopped before the closed door. "You know Aunt Egidia will skin me alive for this."

"I know." He kissed the tip of her nose. "But

remember: you're a MacColme, and we die proud." Without waiting for an answer he pushed open the door and stepped inside.

His gaze flashed to Caroline, and he noted with relief that she seemed relatively unscathed. "Ah, Aunt Egidia, there you are," he said, dragging his reluctant sister forward. "Mairi has something she wishes to discuss with you, and I need to have a word with my wife." And while Mairi was busy stammering an apology to their irate aunt, he grabbed Caroline's hand and made good their escape.

"That was really too bad of you, Hugh," Caroline chided several hours later as she cuddled against his chest. "Your aunt and I had almost finished our discussion; there was no need for you to sacrifice poor Mairi."

"Complained to you, did she?" Hugh asked, wincing as he shifted his cramped legs. "I thought better of her than that."

"She did not complain," Caroline corrected, giving his bare shoulder an admonishing slap. "She didn't have to. I saw the black looks she cast you, and I cannot say that I blame her."

"Needs must where the devil drives," he muttered, repeating a quote he had often heard as a lad. "The devil or Aunt Egidia, which is much the same thing if you want—damn!" He swore furiously, tossing back the covers and climbing out of the bed.

Caroline also sat up, gathering the covers about her to cover her nakedness. "What is it?" she asked, gazing up at him in alarm.

"What do you think it is?" he demanded ill-

temperedly, snatching up his robe from the floor
and shrugging into it with a scowl. " 'Tis that
instrument of torture Aunt laughingly calls a
bed! I've slept on ground strewn with rocks as
big as my fist and been more comfortable!"

"It is rather lumpy," she conceded, shifting in
discomfort. "And I will own it is a trifle small."

"Small?" He gave a disbelieving snort. "A
bairn couldn't fit on that thing did he bend himself in half! She's done this deliberately, I am telling you," he added, his dark glare daring her to
disagree. "She's getting back at me for this afternoon, the vindictive old hag!"

Caroline's lips twitched with humor. "I'm sure
that's not true," she murmured, and the quivering note in her demure voice had him stalking
over to bend over her.

" 'Tis so true," he said, cupping her chin and
tilting her face so he could study her. "And I can
see by that smile you're doing your best to hide
that you approve of her devious methods. Con-
verted you to her evil ways, has Aunt Egidia?"

Although her eyes remained downcast, he
could tell she was doing her best not to laugh.
"Your aunt is a most intelligent lady with many
sterling qualities to recommend her," she said,
her cool, precise accent enchanting him.

"Indeed?" he asked, his annoyance with the
bed forgotten as he began brushing kisses across
her mouth. "And what might those sterling qualities be? I cannot say as I've noticed them."

"She is very direct," Caroline said, tilting her
head to grant his lips freer access.

"Rude," he translated, nibbling the scented
flesh.

"She has excellent advice which she freely offers." Her hands drifted to his narrow waist.

"Meddlesome," he corrected, and cupped her breasts, his thumbs lightly caressing the sensitive tips.

"She told me to let you make love to me whenever you wished."

Hugh's head snapped up at the soft words, disbelief giving way to delight as he gazed down into her flushed face. "Did she now?" he drawled, a slow smile spreading across his face. "Well, then, 'tis as I have always said; Aunt Egidia is a woman of rare good sense, and you are to do just as she bids you."

In answer Caroline flicked open his robe, smiling up at him as she boldly stroked him. "Very well, sir," she said, her voice a wanton's sultry purr. "If that is what you wish."

The next morning Caroline was awakened by a loud thump, followed by a stream of the foulest language she'd ever heard. She opened her eyes and found Hugh sprawled on the floor.

"The plague take that tightfisted, black-hearted daughter of the devil!" he raged, rolling onto his back and rubbing his head. "She is trying to kill me!"

The picture of her handsome husband sitting on the floor naked and cranky as a babe had Caroline biting her lip. "Are you all right?" she asked, doing her best to sound solicitous.

The black look he shot her made it plain her efforts had been for naught. "No, I am not all right," he retorted furiously. "My legs are numb, my back is in agony, and now my bloody head

feels as if 'twas kicked by a horse! I'm nae spending another night in that hellish thing," he
added, pointing an accusatory finger at the bed.
"I'll be crippled for life if I try!"

Despite her best efforts a strangled giggle escaped her lips, and she was instantly pinned by
a narrow-eyed glare. "Are you by chance laughing at me, wife?" he queried silkily, reaching up
to capture her ankle in his strong hand.

"I shouldn't dream of it, husband," she said
demurely, and then spoiled the effect by breaking out in a wide smile. "Do you need assistance
getting up, or is it your intention to remain
where you are? If so, I shall have to warn the
maids. I would not wish them to be shocked by
your dishabille."

His fingers tightened warningly. "One good
tug, *leannan*, and you're down here with me.
Then we'll treat the maids to a sight that will
have their eyes popping from their heads."

"You would never be so ungentlemanly," she
said, then gave a squeal of laughter when he
proved her wrong.

"You were saying, my lady?" he asked, pinning her to the faded carpet with a supple shift
of his body.

"I was saying I shall have the bed replaced by
nightfall," she said, thrilling to the unexpected
love play. "Now, will you please let me up? Your
sister has promised to take me about the shops,
and I don't wish to keep her waiting."

"And what of our aunt's sage advice?" he queried, ignoring her efforts to free herself with
lordly indifference. "Or have you've already forgotten her words to you?"

She slipped her hands into the thick russet hair cascading about his face. "I've forgotten nothing," she assured him, wrapping her fingers about a strand and pulling firmly. "She also advised me to box your ears at least once a day, lest you become too full of yourself is how she phrased it, I believe."

Hugh scowled. "Witch," he muttered, rolling to his feet before pulling Caroline to hers.

"That is no way to talk about your aunt," she said, shaking back her hair and sending him an admonishing frown.

"Who said 'twas Aunt Egidia I was speaking of?" he asked, spinning her around. "Now go ring for my breakfast, wife," he ordered, adding to her outrage by giving her bare behind a playful slap. "I've a powerful hunger this morning."

Although she'd been joking when she'd promised Hugh to buy a new bed for them, Caroline made the cabinetmaker's shop her first stop. To her relief she found exactly what she needed within minutes of her arrival, and by employing a judicious mixture of flattery and bribery she was able to secure the shopkeeper's ardent promise to have it delivered by nightfall. Pleased with the bargain she'd struck, she ordered several other pieces to be delivered as well, only stopping to think how her purchases might be received after she and Mairi had left the shop.

"You don't think your aunt will be angry, do you?" she asked, sending Mairi a worried look. "I wouldn't wish to give offense."

"Och, no!" Mairi assured her with a lilting laugh. "Knowing Aunt Egidia, she'll like as not lift her skirts and dance a jig when she sees all this fine new furniture. She's a Scot, after all, and there's nothing more pleasing to a Scot than to be getting something for nothing. Dinna fash yourself over it."

"Then perhaps she wouldn't object if I purchased some new drapes for our bedroom?" Caroline asked, thinking of the dusty, rotting shreds of velvet dangling crookedly from the broken rods. "And a new carpet would not go amiss as well. The floor is dreadfully hard." She clapped her hand over her mouth, her cheeks suffusing with color as she realized what she'd said.

Mairi gave another lusty roar of laughter. "Purchase what you like, Caroline, and never mind what Auntie may say," she said, giving Caroline's arm a sisterly squeeze. "But don't you think you should wait until after you and Hugh buy a home? Not that you aren't perfectly welcome to remain with us," she added quickly at Caroline's stunned expression. "And of course, once Hugh gets Loch Haven back, you'll live most of the year there. But you'll be wanting your own house, won't you? For when the bairns start coming."

Caroline could think of nothing to say, the art of dissembling beyond her. From Mairi's remarks, she gathered Hugh had decided to keep the truth from her, just as she'd neglected to tell his aunt more than was necessary. She'd become so adept at avoiding the stark reality of their marriage that there were times when she managed to fool herself as well. An obvious error on her part, she decided, struggling to draw a shaky breath.

"Caroline? Is something wrong?" Mairi was regarding her with genuine alarm. "Oh, I've hurt you, haven't I, with my heedless tongue and prattling ways!" she cried, her green eyes full of distress. "I'm sorry, I didn't mean it, truly I did not!"

Her sister-in-law's anguish brought Caroline back to herself, and she gave a quick shake of her head. "No, no, Mairi, that's not it at all, truly," she said, giving the unhappy girl an impulsive hug. "It is just I've never had a home of my own, and I—I am a little overwhelmed at the thought, that is all."

"Are you certain?" Mairi eyed her worriedly. "Hugh will pin my ears back if he should learn I've upset you."

"Of course I'm certain," Caroline said decisively, reaching a swift conclusion. "And you've not upset me in the slightest. In fact, you've just given me the most wonderful idea I have ever had. Come with me!" And she turned back toward the street they had just left.

"Wait!" Mairi hurried to keep abreast with her. "What is it? Where are we going?"

"To find a solicitor," Caroline said, recalling the office she'd seen on the last corner. "I am going to buy a house."

Chapter 12

$\sim\!\!\!\sim\!\!\!\sim$

Loch Haven was his. Hugh stared down at the letter in his hand, his jaw clenched tight as he struggled to put a name to the emotions boiling inside him. Relief was there, aye, but so was anger, joy, stunned incredulity, and a deep, scalding bitterness that overwhelmed everything else. He felt much the same after a battle, when he found himself still alive while death and horror were piled at his feet. He felt . . . He threw down the letter and wearily rubbed his eyes. Christ, he didn't know how he felt.

Angry and impatient, he rose to his feet and stalked over to stand before the fireplace. He should be delighted at his victory, he told himself, gazing down into the flames. This was the day he'd worked toward since returning to Scotland. He should be happy, and yet that intangible emotion eluded him as ever it had done. He'd won all he'd ever wanted, and yet he felt as if he was on the brink of losing it all. It made no sense.

He was no closer to unraveling the mystery when Gregors opened the door. "Ye've a visitor," he said, his sour tone making it plain he blamed Hugh for the fact. "Do I bring him in or send him packing?"

"Who is it, Gregors?" Hugh asked, so grateful for the interruption that he didn't care if it was the king of England himself who had come calling.

"A Mr. Raghnall come from Loch Haven," Gregors informed him with an impatient scowl. "Will ye be seein' him or nae? I've no' the time to stand here blitherin' about the matter."

The mention of his old friend lightened Hugh's black mood considerably. Here was someone who would appreciate his news, he thought, a smile of welcome already forming on his lips. "Send him in," he ordered. "Oh, and Gregors," he added as the butler turned to leave, "bring in a bottle of whiskey as well. We've much to celebrate this day."

The butler gave a disapproving sniff. "The takin' o' spirits in the midst o' the day is an abomination," he said severely, then closed the door with a slam.

A few moments later there was a tap at the door, and Lucien Raghnall stepped inside.

"Lucien!" Hugh hurried forward to offer his hand. " 'Tis good to see you! What brings you to Edinburgh?"

"I've come to see you," Lucien said grimly, shaking Hugh's hand. "Rumors aplenty are flying about the village, and I thought it best to learn the truth of them from you."

The blunt words took Hugh aback. "What sort of rumors?" he asked, waving Lucien toward the pair of chairs set before the fire.

"Rumors that you've succeeded," Lucien said

without preamble. "Rumors that Loch Haven is yours, and that once more the MacColme dragon will fly above the castle keep."

An image of his family's pennant snapping in the cold breeze brought a lump to Hugh's throat. "Aye," he said softly, the joy he hadn't been able to feel before now filling his heart. "Fly again it will. Although I'd like to know how 'tis common knowledge already," he added, frowning in confusion. "I've only received final word of it this morning."

"Servants' tattle," Lucien informed him, sprawling easily in the chair. "Pickerson, the man who bought the castle from the bailiff, was ill-pleased to learn of your efforts, and was loud in his complaints to all who would listen. And a few who would not," he added with a wry smile. "He came to the inn one night to speak of it, full of bluster and moral outrage. Would you believe it? He actually expected us to take his side against yours, and seemed much surprised when we would not."

"Considering the feeling against me when I left for Bath, I would have thought there would be many who would stand with him," Hugh observed, recalling his cold reception. "My own cousin amongst them."

"Ah, but that was before you restored Loch Haven to the clan." Lucien's gray-blue eyes danced with laughter. "And as for your cousin, well, Angus MacColme was ever a bitter man. He never forgave your father for being the laird, and he'll never forgive you for the same reason. Dinna mind him."

Hugh accepted the sad truth of that with a

sigh. "What else did this Pickerson have to say?" he asked, turning his mind to other matters. "Will he make trouble, do you think?"

Lucien gave an expansive shrug. "He's threatened everything from barricading himself in the tower to burning the place down about him, but I doubt he'll do either. The bailiff made it plain that did he damage one stone, he'd be charged double the price for repairing it, and that seemed to give the limmer pause. You know how parsimonious are these sons of York," he added with a chuckle. "They put us spendthrift Scots to shame."

The arrival of the whiskey, brought by a glowering and muttering Gregors, provided a brief diversion, and Hugh waited until he had served Lucien and himself and left the room. "You said there were other rumors," he said, savoring the golden whiskey with a contented sigh. "May I ask what they are?"

"Now, that's the odd part of it," Lucien said, sipping thoughtfully. "The talk is that you've wed, and not only that, but that you've taken to wife some cold bitch of an Englishwoman with a fine title and pockets dripping with gold."

Hugh was on his feet without even being aware of having moved. "What did you say?" he demanded, a deadly fury turning his voice to ice.

Lucien blinked up at him in surprise, his glass poised halfway to his mouth. "What?"

"Repeat what you just said," Hugh ordered, fighting for control. "And remember well that you are speaking of my wife."

Lucien's jaw dropped, and he set his glass

down with a thud. "Then 'tis true?" he demanded, his eyes wide with disbelief. "You've married an Englishwoman?"

"And if I have?" Hugh growled, his hands clenching in fists.

"Then I would say you've taken leave of your senses!" Lucien shot back, rising also to his feet. "Good God, Hugh, what could you have been thinking? You must know the people would never accept a *Sasunnach* as mistress of Loch Haven!"

This was a fact Hugh had already considered, but he'd told himself that until the castle and lands were once more in his hold it didn't matter. Now they were, and the problems of Caroline and what they would next do seemed insurmountable.

"It's not a marriage that need trouble the people," he said at last, thrusting a hand through his hair and turning away from Lucien. "It's . . . temporary, I suppose you would call it."

"Temporary?" Lucien repeated in obvious confusion. "I dinna understand. How can a marriage ever be temporary?"

Hugh hesitated, wrestling with his pride and his duty. Loath as he was to discuss his marriage to Caroline and the reasons behind it, he could see no other way. Reluctantly he told Lucien how he had come to meet Caroline, and of the deal struck between the general and himself. Safety for Caroline, Loch Haven for him.

"So that is why you marred the wench," Lucien said when he was done. "It makes sense to me now. My apologies to you, MacColme, for doubting your honor. I might have known you wouldna have married one of the English without good cause."

"But you can see why I must ask that you tell no one?" Hugh cautioned, eyeing his friend warily. " 'Twould be disastrous for Caroline should the earl ever learn the truth of the matter."

"I hope I know better than to wag my tongue like a foolish woman," Lucien responded in an affronted tone. "I'll nae say a word, if that's what you wish. But dinna think I'm the only one wanting an explanation. What of your chieftains and the elders? Dinna they deserve the truth?"

Hugh busied himself pouring another glass of whiskey. "Very well," he said at last, picking up the glass and studying the amber liquor inside as if it contained the wisdom of Solomon. "You have my leave to tell them I married to secure the castle. But mind that is all you tell them," he added, fixing Lucien with a deadly look. "Do I hear but a whisper of this other business, and I'll cut the tongue from your head before I kill you."

"As you wish, laird," Lucien replied, inclining his head with grave courtesy. "I shall inform the clan of your marriage and the reasons for it. Is there anything else you wish me to tell them while I am about it?"

"Only this," Hugh said, his lips thinning in a grim line. "For all intents and purposes Caroline is my wife, the lady of the castle, and I'll have the life of any man who treats her with other than the greatest respect. Tell them that, Lucien, and make certain they understand you, for I've never meant a thing more in my life."

Lucien eyed him for several seconds before responding. "Aye," he said carefully, "I can see that you do, and I will do my best to follow your orders. But have you stopped to think what you ask may nae be possible? You've been a long time away, and you dinna know how things are. It will be difficult enough for some to accept you as laird, but if they think you have chosen an English wench above them, I—"

"*Enough!*" Hugh hurled his glass of whiskey against the fireplace. It shattered into a hundred glittering shards, and the whiskey inside stained the gray stones, darkening it as the liquid ran down the soot-stained bricks. Hugh stared at the spreading stain for several seconds, his hands clenching and unclenching as he fought to master the pain and rage inside.

"What is it you want of me?" he demanded, whirling around to confront a shocked Lucien. "What is it you all want? What else must I say, or do, or sacrifice and suffer before it will finally be enough to satisfy the lot of you?"

An uncomfortable silence followed his passionate outburst, and Lucien stared at him as if he thought him quite mad. "Hugh," he began, the awkwardness in his tone almost painful to hear. "I am sorely shamed if I have offended you. I dinna mean to insult you; I give you my word."

Hugh waved him into silence, abruptly sick and weary with it all. "No," he said, sighing as he briefly closed his eyes. " 'Tis I who must apologize to you, Lucien. I had no right to rage at you that way. I pray you will forgive me."

"I understand." Lucien's voice was soft. "And I am sorry if I pressed you too hard. It wasna my intention."

Hugh opened his eyes to meet his friend's solemn gaze. "Was it not?" he asked with a bitter laugh. "Then you are the only one with such scruples. There are times, Raghnall, when I wonder that I do not pop like a grape from the pressing."

Lucien looked much struck by the admission. "And is it your wife who presses most?" he asked. At Hugh's black glare he added hastily, "I've heard 'tis the way of wives with their husbands, which is why I have labored so hard to remain a bachelor."

Hugh knew the other man was attempting to make light conversation; still, it bothered him to speak of Caroline so disrespectfully. "No," he said, surprised to find he actually had to work to keep his tone friendly. "My wife does not press me."

Lucien poured himself more whiskey before speaking. "If you've no objections, MacColme, I am interested in knowing more of your English bride. What does she look like? Is she comely?"

An image of Caroline as he'd last seen her— her hair gloriously tousled and her face flushed from lovemaking—flashed in Hugh's mind. "Aye," he said, wishing fervently now for the whiskey he had dashed against the fireplace. "She is comely."

"And wealthy with it." Lucien gave a cynical laugh, saluting Hugh with a lift of his glass. "My congratulations, Hugh. You're a fortunate man, and clever as well, to make such good use of a temporary marriage."

Hugh felt as if he'd taken a cannonball to the gut, so great was his astonishment. For a moment he simply stared at Lucien, scarcely believing the evidence of his own ears. "And what would you mean by that?" he asked, shifting his weight on his feet in preparation to attack.

In answer Lucien indicated the rose brocade settee beneath the portrait of Aunt Egidia as a young bride. " 'Tis new, I gather, like the carpets in the hallway and the fine pianoforte I see in the corner. You've been helping yourself to her deep pockets, 'tis plain, and there's none who would think the worse of you for it. You are her husband, and 'tis your right."

Hugh warily lowered his guard, recalling Mairi's unaffected delight when Caroline had made her a gift of the expensive pianoforte. He hadn't even known his sister played, or how much she had longed for one of her own. But Caroline had known, and had presented the gift in so gracious a fashion it almost made it seem that Mairi was the one granting the boon by accepting it. He hadn't thought much of it at the time, but he did so now, and his pride gave him a belated jab at the realization of the hundreds of pounds his wife had poured into rendering his aunt's shabby residence somewhat more presentable.

"Caroline has been very kind to my aunt and sister," he muttered, wishing his friend would finish his whiskey and leave. "She is grateful for the hospitality they have shown her."

"As well she should be." Lucien gave another laugh. "Even the poorest hovel in the Auld Town would seem a castle when compared to a madhouse. Which reminds me . . ." He cast Hugh a speculative glance. "Will you be removing soon to the New Town? 'Tis all the thing for the wealthy to take up residence there."

At the end of his patience and not scrupling to show it, Hugh drew himself up with rigid pride. "Why should I do that?" he demanded, making no effort to soften his tone. "I will soon be returning to the castle, and until then I see no reason to move. Aunt Egidia's home suits me fine."

"Aye, it suits *you*." For the clever man Hugh knew him to be, Lucien seemed amazingly thick. "But what of your rich wife? She's English, is she nae, and now that they've rebuilt Edinburgh to their taste, I assumed she would wish to move there."

Hugh said nothing, despite a mounting sense of disquiet. As it happened, he and Caroline had been looking at houses, and admittedly it was the newer homes about St. Andrew Square which had most interested her. She'd never spoken of actually purchasing one, and after a while he'd shrugged aside the matter. Now he couldn't help but wonder how he would react should she insist upon buying one of the elegant homes.

"Have you any other messages you wish to convey to the clan?" Lucien had set down his glass and seemed finally ready to take his leave. "I should be happy to deliver them."

Hugh thought for a moment and then shook his head. "None," he said, feeling faintly ashamed by the sense of relief he was experiencing. Hospitality toward a guest was no small thing in Scotland, and the knowledge that he had been anything but hospitable toward a guest who had traveled so far on his behalf stung him. "Must you go?" he asked, anxious to make amends for his poor manners. "I was hoping you might stay to share supper with us."

"Thank you, no, but 'tis best I was on my way." Lucien refused the offer with a gracious smile. "The clan is anxious for word of you, and I promised to bring it quickly as I could. When will you be home, do you think?"

Home. Hugh let the beauty of the word sink inside him, stilling his rising disquiet. "Tell them I hope to be with them within a week," he said, mentally reviewing all that was left to be done. "Sooner, perhaps, if all continues to go well."

"Wednesday next, then, we shall say, just to be certain," Lucien agreed. "Pray give my regards to your family, Mairi most especially; I am sorry to have missed her. And MacColme?" He eyed Hugh solemnly. "A word of advice, if I may."

Hugh steeled himself as if for a blow. "What is it?"

"Dinna tarry long," came the soft counsel. "Come home. Loch Haven has sore need of her laird."

"Oh, Mairi, it's perfect!" Caroline stood in the center of the flagstone entryway, her eyes alight with pleasure at what she saw. "Isn't it quite the loveliest house you have ever seen?"

Mairi glanced dutifully about her. "Aye, 'tis," she agreed good-naturedly. "And considering the number of homes we've marched through these past few days, I would call that high praise indeed." She turned to give Caroline a teasing look, her green eyes merry. "Will you be having it, then?"

Caroline gave a distracted nod, her mind already whirling with tenuous plans. A long clock just there, she decided, studying the corner opposite the curving staircase, and perhaps a cherrywood side table next to the door, with a silver tray to receive the calling cards of their visitors. She gazed at the expanse of blank wall painted a soft, muted rose and lavishly trimmed with cream-colored cornices. She'd inherited several paintings upon her parents' deaths, and thought they would look quite lovely hanging there. There was nothing like a few family portraits to turn a house into a home, she mused, feeling a decided air of proprietorship.

"Caroline?" The questioning note in her sister-in-law's voice made Caroline start, and she grew red-faced in chagrin.

"Never mind," the younger girl said with a laugh before Caroline could speak. "I can see the answer plain in your face. But dinna you think you should show the place to Hugh first? He may nae like it so well as you."

The sisterly warning dimmed some of Caroline's burgeoning pleasure, and she fell into a worried silence. Hugh had accompanied her and Mairi on several of their explorations about Edinburgh, seeming to delight in showing her the fine buildings and great institutions which had earned the ancient city the sobriquet of "the Athens of the North." He'd even toured several of the houses Mairi had alluded to with them, offering witty and sometimes provocative asides that had her laughing and blushing by turns. To be sure, the subject of actually purchasing one of the houses had yet to be broached, but he had to know that was her intention.

"Do you think he will like it?" she blurted out, giving voice to the sudden uncertainties nagging her. Although the money was hers, legally it was Hugh who held the purse strings, and it would be his name upon the deed. She wondered if he would allow her to keep it once their divorce was finalized, and then winced at the sharp pain that shot through her at the thought.

"Well, he would be very hard to please did he find the slightest fault," Mairi declared stoutly, threading her arm through Caroline's. "But the devil take my troublesome brother! He will live where you tell him and like it. Now, tell me how you mean to decorate the place. I want to hear everything."

Caroline complied, eagerly describing her vision of what the house would be. She was discussing her plans for the hall when a sudden thought occurred, and she turned to Mairi.

"I am certain Hugh must have portraits he will wish to hang," she said, studying the other girl curiously. "Are there many?"

"Not so many as that," Mairi replied, looking thoughtful. "We Scots are not like the English, to be forever posing for some dolt of a painter. My father would never agree to it, and the other paintings we had were seized with everything else.

"There is my mother's miniature," she added, with a bright smile. "You might have a larger copy made to hang here. That would make a grand present for Hugh."

"Your mother's miniature?" Caroline repeated, thinking that Mairi was right, and that it would make the perfect gift.

"Aye, the one Hugh gave you after your arrival." Mairi was gazing at her with a puzzled look. "He *did* give it to you, did he not? It was meant for his wife, he always said."

A shaft of pain shot through Caroline at Mairi's artless observation. *His wife,* she thought, an uncomfortable lump forming in her throat. His real wife, he must have meant, and not the woman who would be in his life but for a year.

"Caroline?" Mairi gently touched her arm. "What is it? You've the queerest look on your face."

The rattle of the door handle announced the return of Mr. Penderson, the solicitor Caroline had engaged to help her find a house. He'd taken his leave shortly after admitting them to the vacant house, having learned Caroline preferred exploring prospective homes without him trailing after her like a puppy.

"Ah, Lady Caroline, Miss MacColme." The solicitor swept into an officious bow. "Finished already? And what did you think of the house, eh? Is it not as lovely as I promised?"

"Quite lovely," Caroline said, so grateful for his fortuitous arrival she could have wept. "In fact," she added, reaching a daring conclusion, "I believe I shall take it. Kindly have the proper papers drawn up for me to sign by tomorrow."

Greed, delight, and dismay all warred on Mr. Penderson's florid countenance before he offered her another bow. "As you wish, my lady," he said, sounding doubtful. "But will you not wish your husband to inspect the property first? He may have . . ." He fluttered his plump hands uselessly. ". . . objections."

From this Caroline concluded he meant that Hugh's permission would be needed, and she burned at the injustice of it. "I will discuss this with him tonight," she said, feigning a confidence she did not feel. "But I am certain he will be as delighted with the house as am I. Have the papers waiting."

Mr. Penderson bowed again, promising to have all in readiness by the following day. Caroline and Mairi accompanied him outside, waiting patiently as he secured the door. Caroline had hired a coach and four on her second day in Edinburgh, and it stood in readiness by the curb. The footman leaped down from his perch and was holding the door open in anticipation of their arrival, but when Mairi started forward Caroline hung back, suddenly loath to enter the well-sprung conveyance.

"Caroline?" Mairi paused and cast her a puzzled glance over her shoulder. "Are you nae coming?"

"Actually, I thought I would walk back," she said, forcing a smile to her lips. "It is such a lovely day, and I could do with a bit of fresh air. You go ahead, and I shall see you for tea."

Mairi's incredulous gaze went from Caroline to the gray and sullen skies that were heavy with the threat of a storm. "Are you daft?" she exclaimed, hurrying back to her side. "You canna walk back to Chambers Street! 'Twould be most improper!"

The idea of her fiercely independent and recalcitrant sister-in-law lecturing her on the proprieties brought forth a genuine smile to Caroline's lips. "Nonsense, dearest," she said, tugging on her gloves with brisk purpose. "In the days I have been here, I have observed many ladies of our class walking about without so much as a footman to grant them countenance, and no one seems to think a whit of it. I shall be fine, I assure you."

"Aye, but none of those ladies is a MacColme and married to my dragon of a brother," Mairi grumbled, clearly disturbed by the notion of Caroline's ambling about Edinburgh's teeming streets. "If you really wish to walk I would be happy to—"

"No," Caroline interrupted, and then softened her abruptness by laying a sisterly hand on the other woman's arm. "I am sorry, Mairi," she said, her voice gentle for all its firmness. "I have no wish to be rude, but truly I would prefer it if you returned to your aunt's home without me. I—I need to be alone."

Mairi's frown deepened. "Are you certain of this?" she asked, her green eyes frankly troubled. "I dinna mean to plague you, but Hugh willna be pleased to learn I let you do this thing. In fact, he's like to come tearing after you in a temper when he hears of it."

Knowing that was all too likely a possibility and wishing to avoid the scene that was certain to follow, Caroline thought for a moment. "You spoke earlier of needing to call upon a friend," she said, shooting Mairi a hopeful look. "Perhaps you could stop there first, instead of going directly home?"

Mairi chewed her lip bottom lip indecisively. "Caroline..."

"Please, Mairi." Caroline tightened her hold on her arm. "You must know I would never ask this of you if it wasn't important. All I am requesting is a little time alone so that I might gather my thoughts. Hugh needn't even know I am gone. Please," she repeated, guessing rightly that the other woman was weakening. "I promise to be home in time for luncheon."

Mairi regarded her for a long moment. "Is this because of what I said inside?" she asked quietly, her gaze searching Caroline's face for the truth.

"No, not at all." Caroline forced herself to meet Mairi's gaze as she uttered the lie. "I just want to walk and think; that is all."

Mairi hesitated another moment and then capitulated with a heavy sigh. "All right," she said, looking far from pleased with the situation. "I'll stop by Suzanne's on the way home to Auntie's. But I'll only be there an hour or so," she warned with a scowl. "If you're not home within half an hour after me, I'll go to Hugh and tell him everything."

Caroline did some swift calculations before nodding. Ninety minutes wasn't as long a time as she would have liked, but it was better than nothing. "By twelve-thirty, then," she said after consulting the watch pinned to her muff. "With luck, I shall even be there to greet you."

An imp of mischief danced briefly in Mairi's bright eyes. "Dinna do that," she implored with a chuckle. "For if you do, 'tis I who will find myself explaining my tardiness to Aunt Egidia, and that I would as lief not do."

Caroline could well sympathize with Mairi's plight, and renewed her promise to be home within the hour and a half's time allotted her. She waited on the sidewalk and waved good-bye until the coach disappeared around the corner, leaving her with the solitude she craved.

At first she stood there indecisively, torn between delight at her newfound freedom and a giddy sense of terror at the realization that for the first time in many weeks she was quite, quite alone. In the end her delight conquered her trepidation and she began walking, with no particular destination in mind.

As she was in the new part of the town, she explored that area first, studying with interest the many houses in varying stages of construction. Compared to the Old Town, which she found to be cramped and crowded, the New Town was quite spacious, and the elegant stone houses with their tall windows and black iron archways put her strongly in mind of Bath. She could be at home here, she mused with a sharp pang of longing. Provided, of course, she could convince Hugh to agree to her plan.

She continued wandering, pausing occasionally to peer into a shop window or gaze up at Edinburgh Castle looming high on the massive cliffs that separated the New Town from the Old. Its rugged appearance and stunning sense of isolation reminded her of Hugh, and she felt anew the sharp thrust of pain she had felt at Mairi's casual revelation about the locket. Why it mattered so much she knew not, she only knew she felt hurt and oddly betrayed by his keeping the miniature from her. If he could do that, she mused, tears stinging her eyes as she continued walking, then it must mean he did not truly view her as his wife.

Time slid away as she continued walking, brooding over the enigma that was her husband, and trying to decide what she was supposed to do about him. She soon left the New Town behind her, puffing with exertion as she climbed the steep steps leading to the area near Canongate. She wandered about aimlessly, going up and down the narrow and winding streets without thought or purpose. The skies that had been threatening rain began growing ominously dark, and at the roll of thunder overhead, she glanced up to find herself in an area of Edinburgh unfamiliar to her.

She was in one of the alleys which the Scots called closes, and although it was elegant, she felt a small frisson of unease. She gazed about her, the sudden sense of being watched making her heart race with fear. Two men dressed in the dark clothing of laborers had entered the close, and were between her and the street, their heads bent as they moved toward her. They looked harmless enough, but the sensation of danger grew increasingly strong as they neared her. She was thinking about abandoning her pride and began pounding on one of the doors opening onto the close, when one of the doors did open and a man stepped out, nearly colliding with her.

"Beg pardon, ma'am," he said, touching his finger to the broad black hat of the cleric. "Didn't see ye standing there. Might I be of assistance?"

The two men turned off into one of the narrow passageways leading to another close, and Caroline exhaled a silent breath of relief. Apparently she had let her fears get the best of her, she thought, feeling slightly foolish as she turned to give the parson a warm smile.

"I am afraid I have mistaken my way," she said. "Could you be so kind as to direct me toward Chambers Street?"

The man's bushy white eyebrows rose in astonishment. "Chambers Street?" he repeated. "Why, the Lord save ye, ma'am, ye are a good way from Chambers Street! Are ye lost, then?"

Thinking that rather self-evident, Caroline contrived to keep her smile in place. "I am afraid that I am," she said, thinking Scottish parsons were every bit as dull-witted as their English brethren. "I was attempting to find my way to my aunt's home, but I seem to have taken a wrong turn. If you could but direct me to the right way, I should be most grateful."

"Of course, madam, of course," he replied, and launched into a bewildering set of instructions that left Caroline even more confused. When he was done he gave her a polite bow and hurried away, leaving her to glare after him in helpless frustration.

Now what? she brooded, nervously chewing her lips. The one part of the minister's directions she did understand entailed walking past the passageway where the two men had disappeared, and that she would as lief not do. She hesitated a few more moments before deciding she was being unpardonably skittish. There hadn't been so much as a word of Uncle Charles in all the days they had been in Edinburgh; it was foolish of her to think she was in any danger.

With that thought firmly in mind she turned and walked back down the close, taking care to give the entrance to the passageway as wide a berth as possible. By the time she reached the street she was much more relaxed, feeling slightly shamefaced she could be so missish. She was debating whether she should attempt to find her way back to Chambers Street on her own or admit defeat and flag down a passing hack, when a closed carriage pulled to a halt directly in front of her.

Thinking someone was about to alight she stepped back, only to run into the man who had walked up in back of her. She turned to offer an apology when the man grabbed her, his hand clamping roughly down on her mouth even as he shoved her toward the waiting carriage. She struggled furiously, but she was no match for the man's bull-like strength. He lifted her off her feet, thrusting her into the carriage and then climbing in after her.

She whirled to face him, determined to do whatever was necessary to win her freedom, when she became aware of the coach's other occupant. Her uncle Charles sat across from her, a thin smile of triumph on his lips as he regarded her.

"Ah, Caroline," he murmured, inclining his head toward her mockingly. "How delightful to have you in my company once again. You might as well make yourself comfortable, my dear. I fear you are in for a bit of a ride."

Chapter 13

Hugh was looking over the day's post when there was a knock on the door. Thinking it was Caroline returned from her shopping, he set his work aside and leaned back in his chair.

"Come in," he called out, a smile of welcome on his face.

"Hugh?" Mairi opened the door and peered around the edge, her lively face set with worry. "Might I have a word with you?"

"Of course, *kempie*," he said, swallowing his disappointment. "What is it that's on your mind?"

To his surprise, she hesitated, shutting the door behind her before coming forward. "Now, before you go off in a tearing rage, I'm sure there is nothing wrong," she began cautiously. "She's lost track of time, like as not, and will be home soon. It is just she promised to be home at twelve-thirty, and it's nearer to one o'clock now. And—"

Hugh held up a hand, stopping the nervous flow of words. "Who said she would be home by noon?" he asked, a terrible suspicion dawning. "Are you talking about Caroline?"

255

Mairi gave a miserable nod. "Aye."

He leaped to his feet, his hands clenching into fists. "But I don't understand!" he said, his brows meeting in a scowl. "I thought she was with you."

"She was," Mairi admitted. "But when it was time to return home she said she was feeling restless, and wanted a breath of fresh air. She— she decided to walk back from the New Town."

"What?" Hugh roared.

Mairi drew herself up with a sniff. "You needn't take that tone with me, Hugh Mac-Colme," she informed him coolly. "I'm nae a child to be raged at and scolded."

"Are you daft? You ought to have forbade her from leaving you, instead of sending her on her way," Hugh snapped, casting a panicked glance at the clock on his desk. As Mairi had said it was nearly one of the clock, and there was no telling what terrible fate might have befallen Caroline since she and Mairi had parted company.

Mairi's green eyes grew wide with indignation. "Forbade?" she repeated incredulously. "Who am I to forbid your wife anything? And for your information, you great bully, your wife is a woman grown, and needs no one to *forbid* her to do what she would! If this is the sort of nonsense you blither at her, I dinna doubt she wanted a few minutes of peace," she continued, her manner belligerent. "I only wonder that she didna hit you over the head with a bullax instead. A Scotswoman would have split your skull for such brass!"

"Never mind that now," Hugh said, impatiently brushing his sister's scolding words aside.

"That's not important. It's probably nothing, as you say, but in light of her uncle's threats I would feel better knowing where she is."

"Her uncle!" Mairi exclaimed, shooting Hugh a horrified look. "That is another thing I wished to tell you!"

Hugh's blood turned icy with fear. "What of her uncle?" he asked slowly. "What do you know of him?"

"Only that he is here, in Edinburgh," Mairi said, looking more troubled than ever. "I was visiting Suzanne Broyleigh this morning, and while I was there Dorthea Cummings came in. She had been to call upon Iain Dunhelm's mother, and she said he had visitors, *English* visitors. An earl and a baronet, all fine airs and insolence, they were, and full of questions about Caroline. Hugh, what is going on?"

"I do not know," Hugh said, his mouth hardening as he considered what this might portend. He was fairly sure the earl was here to make mischief, and the fact that Caroline was apparently missing was troubling indeed. If something had happened to her, it was almost a certainty the earl was part of it.

Also troubling was that Westhall had aligned himself with Dunhelm. He'd not forgotten his aunt's warning about the laird of Ben Denham, nor the fact he'd tried to purchase Loch Haven after the seizure. Mayhap that was why he was helping Westhall now, he brooded. Mayhap Caroline's uncle had promised him MacColme land in exchange for whatever assistance he might render. If such was the case, the greedy laird was about to learn he had made a grievous error.

"Begin packing," he ordered. "We shall leave for Loch Haven when I return."

"Leave?" Mairi gaped at Hugh as if she feared he'd lost his wits. "Why should we do that? What matter if Caroline's uncle is here or nae? So long as you are legally wed, what harm can he do?" She broke off, gazing at him in horror. "You *are* legally wed?" she demanded, her hand going to her throat. "Caroline is your wife, and not some other man's?"

Hugh paused in his planning long enough to cast his sister an indignant scowl. "Of course she is my wife!" he said, appalled she could accuse him of such a thing. "What sort of man do you think I am? And what sort of woman do you take Caroline to be?"

"I dinna know what to think!" Mairi shot back, hands on her hips as she glared at him. "Did I smell the whiskey on you I would take Gregors's word that you are as drunk as a piper! What is going on? I insist that you tell me!"

Hugh rounded the desk, pausing long enough to deposit a kiss on his sister's cheek. "Later, *mo piuthar*," he told her, his mind on other matters. "Just do as I ask. I go to see Dunhelm. If Caroline has met with danger, then her uncle and that bastard Dunhelm are behind it. We shall leave upon my return with Caroline. Tell Aunt she is welcome to come if she wishes it. Now I must be away." With that he turned and walked from the room, ignoring his sister's frustrated cries that he return.

After pausing long enough to buckle on the sword he had Gregors fetch him from the small armory, Hugh tucked a pistol and a dirk in his

waistband and set out for Dunhelm's house near
the assembly rooms. On the brief journey there
he formulated his strategy, and by the time he
was shown into the elegant drawing room he
was ready to engage the enemy.

"MacColme! Such a surprise to see you." Dunhelm was on his feet, the false smile of welcome
pasted to his thin lips not quite disguising his
fear. "What may I do for you?"

In answer Hugh walked up to him, pulled the
sword from his scabbard, and lay the sharp blade
against the other man's throat.

Dunhelm's face went blank with shock. "What
the devil . . . ?"

"*Deasaich do chlaidheamh,*" Hugh said, calmly
issuing the ancient challenge. "Draw your
sword, laird of Ben Denham, and prepare to
die."

"What the devil are you talking about?" Dunhelm wailed, his eyes bulging in terror.

"I am challenging you to fight me," Hugh responded with the unshakable calm he knew to
be more terrifying than the loudest of shouts.
"Now you must answer, or be known the length
of the Highlands as a coward, *laird.*" He spat out
the other man's title with open contempt.

Dunhelm licked his lips, his Adam's apple
bobbing up and down as he nervously swallowed. "Why should I fight you, MacColme?" he
asked, clearly determined to brazen out the confrontation. "I don't even know you, nor have I
done aught to give offense!"

"You offer shelter to my enemies. That offends
me," Hugh continued, his voice as pleasant as if
he was but taking tea with the other man. "You

scheme to take Loch Haven from me. That offends me as well. But worst of all, most foolishly of all, you have dared to lay your hand upon my wife. For that, you will die."

"I didn't touch the wench!" Dunhelm denied, the muscles of his neck straining as he tried to move away from the razor-sharp blade without cutting himself. "I don't know what you're talking about . . . !"

Hugh ignored the sputtering protests, applying just enough pressure on the blade to have the other man paling in horror. "Do you know," he began conversationally, " 'tis possible to slit a man's throat inch by inch? It kills him, aye, but he takes a long, painful time in the dying. I've never done it myself, mind, but I've seen it done. I've seen the look in the poor sot's eyes as he feels his life and his blood draining slowly away, and I've heard the sounds he makes as he dies . . ."

"But I have nothing to do with Westhall!" Dunhelm sobbed, dropping any pretense of bravery. "Let me go, MacColme! You cannot kill an unarmed man!"

Hugh's smile was the stuff of nightmares. "Can I not?" he asked softly. "And how do you know it's Westhall I'm after? I never mentioned the *crochaire*'s name." He drew the sword gently across Dunhelm's throat, slicing the skin and bringing a welling of blood to the surface.

"No!" Tears filled the other man's eyes at the feel of his own blood dribbling down his neck. "He will kill me if I tell you!"

"And I will kill you if you do not," Hugh returned, slicing through another layer of skin for emphasis. "Tell me now, Dunhelm, or die."

"He has taken her to St. John Street! Number seventeen on the upper floor!"

St. John was less than ten minutes away; with luck he could be there in five. Hugh leaned forward until he was nose to nose with his terrified captive. "How many men has he with him?" he demanded.

Dunhelm raised a trembling hand to wipe his nose. "Just some fat fool of a doctor, and his assistant," he said. "I don't think they are armed."

But Westhall would be, Hugh was certain. He smiled, thinking of the pleasure he would get in sending the man to hell. Then he remembered what Mairi had said about a baronet.

"And what of Sir Gervase? Is he with the earl? I'm warning you, Dunhelm, if I find you've lied to me . . ."

"He is with Westhall! I—I had forgotten about him. But there is no one else, I give you my word!"

Hugh believed him; he was too intent on saving his own skin to lie. Still, he thought it advisable to take precautions.

"Very well," he drawled, "I shall accept your word. But," he added as the other man started babbling his thanks, "I'll be taking something else as well, just to be certain."

"W-what is that?" Dunhelm looked near to swooning.

"Why, you, laird." Hugh gave him another terrifying smile. "You're coming with me to rescue my wife. And if I find you've lied to me in any way, you will be the first one I kill. Now wipe your nose, you sniveling coward. We've work to do."

"Come, my dear, will you not try some of this delicious soup?" Lord Westhall queried, smirking at Caroline over the edge of his spoon. "It is really quite delicious."

Caroline remained mutinously silent, refusing to let her uncle goad her into speech. In the hours since she had been taken captive, not a word had she spoken, holding both her temper and her tongue as she struggled to remain calm. She had to be calm. It was the only way she had any chance of surviving whatever horrors lay ahead.

When her uncle had first seized her, she had done everything within her power to get out of the carriage. It was only when the doctor's grinning assistant dealt her a stinging blow across the face that she had ceased her struggles. But that didn't mean she had abandoned all attempts at escape, she promised herself silently. No matter the danger, she refused to let herself be taken to an asylum.

"Still playing the statue," her uncle said, shaking his head in disapproval. "Willful child. I see I shall have to inform Dr. Harrison to make certain he teaches you the art of obeying your elders."

Caroline's response was a cold look, her pride not allowing her terror to show. The doctor and his loutish helper were in the other room, along with Sir Gervase, who, as was his custom, was already dead to the world from drink. She breathed a silent prayer of relief for his intemperance; she shuddered to think what would happen were he awake and sober.

"You know, Caroline, this noble silence of yours is really growing quite tiresome," Uncle Charles said, frowning as he poured another glass of madeira. "In fact, if you do not answer me at once, I believe I shall call in Mr. Milkins and request that he coax you into cooperating." He smiled at her in evil anticipation. "From all reports, 'tis a skill at which he excels."

The memory of the foul-smelling man and his brutal hands was enough to loosen Caroline's tongue, and she raised her chin in an unconscious gesture of pride.

"You really cannot hope to get away with this, Uncle," she informed him, affecting a bravado she was far from feeling. "Hugh will have discovered I am missing by now, and he will start looking for me. Heaven help you when he finds me."

"Ah, yes, the noble sergeant." Uncle Charles gave a soft chuckle. "I must say I was quite vexed when you married the fellow, and poor Gervase was simply devastated. I had hoped to convince him to marry you once I succeed in having this farcical marriage of yours overturned, but now he won't hear of it." He gave her a look that made her feel in dire need of a bath. "Damaged goods, you know, and he does have the succession to consider."

Caroline fought the urge to retort that Sir Gervase's precious succession would be the least of his concerns when Hugh got his hands on him, guessing it was precisely what he expected her to say. She knew her uncle well, and knew the best way to defeat him was to keep him off-balance. He was easily distracted when angry, and if she managed to get him angry enough and distracted enough, she could make a try for freedom.

"Grandfather will disinherit you," she said, folding her arms across her chest and boldly meeting his stare. "In fact, he is already making plans to do so."

"Caroline, Caroline." He shook his head again. "Do I look that big a fool? Short of enacting a bill of Parliament, there is nothing he can do to keep the title from me, and the old fool knows it." He smirked at her. "You'll have to do better than that, my dear, if you wish to convince me to release you."

Caroline remembered the list of names her grandfather had handed Hugh on the day they had left Bath, and smiled. "That is precisely what he is doing," she said sweetly, and had the pleasure of seeing him scowl. "Grandfather has powerful friends, and they are very supportive of his cause. Your reputation precedes you, Uncle, and there are many unwilling to see you inherit Hawkeshill. Lord Gresham, for example."

The mention of the priggish duke brought a furious oath to her uncle's lips. "Gresham may rot in hell!" he snarled, but Caroline could see the unease in his eyes. "If he thinks to deprive me of what is mine, I'll soon teach him better!"

"And will you teach a similar lesson to Lord Farringdale and Sir Covington?" she pressed. "Hugh has seen them all, at Grandfather's behest, and they have sworn to lend whatever support may be necessary."

"Be silent, you little bitch!" her uncle thundered, clearly rattled. He poured out more of the wine, spilling some of it as he raised the glass to his lips. "He won't do it," he said, sounding as if it was himself he was trying to convince and not her. "Father would never risk the scandal such a thing would cause."

Caroline leaned forward. "Won't he?" she taunted, wondering how far she could push him without courting serious danger. "He has already told me that if anything happens to me, anything at all, he will see you ruined. Is my inheritance so important that you are willing to risk everything you have, or ever *will* have, just to get your hands on it?"

He glanced away from her, and she knew she had shaken him badly. "Think, Uncle Charles, think very hard. It is only worth—what? Fifty, sixty thousand pounds? Is that really worth the hundreds of thousands of pounds you will lose should Grandfather bestow his title on Cousin James?"

"Enough!" her uncle roared, glaring at her with hate-filled eyes. "I need that money, damn you! You have no right to keep it from me!"

Caroline knew she would never get a better chance than she had now. Reaching down, she grabbed the decanter of wine and leapt to her feet, bringing the bottle smashing down on her uncle's head. The heavy crystal shattered, and her uncle dropped to the floor with a low moan. She bent quickly over him, hands shaking as grabbed for the pistol she had seen tucked in his waistband. Her fingers had no sooner closed around the handle when the door to the outer room was flung open, and Dr. Harrison and Milkins stood in the doorway, gaping at her with identical expressions of astonishment.

"Stand back, I am warning you," she said, leveling the pistol at the plump doctor's belly. "I'll put a bullet in you if you take one more step!"

"Good heavens!" The doctor clapped a hand to his chest in horror. "Her uncle is right, the chit is as mad as a loon! Seize her, Milkins, before she kills us all!"

But Milkins wasn't nearly so great a fool as that, Caroline noted, seeing the wariness in the man's pig-like eyes. Evidently striking and pawing a helpless woman was a far different matter than trying to disarm one holding a loaded pistol in her hands. Taking him for the greater danger, she swung the pistol in his direction and pointed it at him.

"My grandfather is a general, and if you think I don't know how to handle a pistol, you are sadly mistaken," she said, taking a step forward and watching as they retreated. "You have to the count of three to get out of my way. One . . ." She drew back the intricately carved hammer. "Two . . ." she took better aim, bracing herself for the horror of putting a lead ball in living flesh. "Thr—"

"Here now, what's this?" Sir Gervase demanded, reeling forward and bumping into Dr. Harrison. The doctor gave a yelp of surprise and scrambled to get out of the way, and Milkins, evidently determined to take advantage of the confusion, leaped toward Caroline, his intention all too clear.

She pulled the trigger.

At the same moment, the door to the hall exploded open and two men rushed inside, one with a pistol drawn. She recognized Hugh just as he fired his pistol. Sir Gervase grabbed his arm and collapsed, blood flowing from between his fat fingers.

"Caroline!" Hugh stepped over Sir Gervase without a glance, sweeping Caroline up in his arms and crushing her to his chest. "Oh, God, my sweet, my *cridhe*, are you all right?"

"Hugh!" The tears she had been too proud to shed before now streamed down her face, and she clung to him as she at last gave in to the fear she had been holding at bay.

"I knew you would come. I knew you would come." It was all she could say, and it was the truth, she realized. It had been her absolute faith in Hugh and his abilities that had kept her sane during the nightmare of her captivity.

Hugh did not answer but only held her closer, his face buried in the tangled curls streaming down to her neck. A low groan from Sir Gervase had him raising his head, and he accepted another pistol from the man who had entered the room with him. Before she could ask him what he intended doing with it, he gently set her to one side and trained the gun on the terrified doctor.

"Take one more step, Harrison, and you're a dead man," he said.

The fat doctor froze in mid-step. Clearly thinking to brazen his way out of the situation, he turned to Hugh with a show of ruffled dignity.

"Now see here," he said, placing his hands on the lapels of his black frock coat and striking a pose. "I have no idea what this is all about, but I must insist you leave. These are private quarters, and you have not been invited."

"Cut line, Harrison." Uncle Charles spoke from the doorway, holding the back of his head and eyeing Hugh with mocking resignation. "It is obvious we have been found out."

"Found out!" The heavyset man quivered in righteous indignation. "I am sure I do not know what you mean! I am a physician here at your behest. If something is untoward, it has nothing to do with me. Call for the watch, Westhall, and throw this Scottish lout out into the street where he belongs!"

Hugh flicked the man a warning look. "Mind your tongue, you useless *mucc*, else this Scottish lout will put a ball through your throat. Provided I could find it beneath all those chins," he added with a caustic smile.

Harrison's face grew purple. "Insolence! Westhall, I insist that you do something about this . . . this ruffian!"

"Quiet, Doctor," Westhall ordered, eyes narrowing as he assessed Hugh. "For the moment it would seem the good sergeant and my redoubtable niece have us at somewhat of a disadvantage. I suppose I ought to be grateful it is Harrison you are holding at gunpoint, and not me, eh, MacColme?" And he had the temerity to smile as if much amused with the situation.

Hugh gave him a look that could have frozen fire. "Did I have you at the end of my gun, your lordship, I would blow your brains out and be done with it. And do it yet I may, if you continue provoking me as you have."

Her uncle merely raised an eyebrow, saying nothing. In the tense silence that followed, Caroline glanced nervously down at Milkins; terrified of what she would see. To her relief he was alive, although nursing a mangled wrist. Much as he might have deserved it, she knew she could not have borne it had she actually killed the man.

Sir Gervase also lived, and at Hugh's clipped orders, the doctor and the other man moved them to the far side of the room. With all four men now at his mercy, Hugh gave them a chilling look.

"We go now to Loch Haven," he said, addressing his remarks to the man he called Dunhelm, but keeping his eyes trained on her uncle. "If any man thinks to harm me or mine there, he will learn fast how hot burns the fire of the Mac-Colme dragon. And Dunhelm," he added, "mind you keep your gaze well away from the land of my clan. I don't care what this piece of dung has promised you; you'll be dead before you own so much as a stone of it."

With that he turned to Caroline, slipping an arm about her and guiding her gently to the door. They were almost there before he turned to face her uncle.

"Listen well, Westhall. The only reason I have not killed you is because my wife had already dealt with you herself. Had she not, or had she suffered the slightest harm, you would be a dead man. As it is, you are living under a sentence of death. If ever I hear of you plotting against Caroline, if ever you dare to come near her again, I will impose that sentence. Do you hear me?"

Uncle Charles dabbed at the cut on his head

with a blood-soaked handkerchief. "I hear you, Sergeant," he said, sardonic and bitter to the last. "You and my niece have caused me no end of difficulty, and I shall acquiesce to your demands. You need fear nothing further from me, I assure you."

"Did he mean it, do you think?" Hugh asked Caroline several hours later as they cuddled in the warmth of their bed.

She brushed a kiss over his chest, and curled closer. "I would like to believe so," she said, but Hugh could hear the uncertainty in her voice. "With Uncle Charles one can never tell. I know I gave him pause when I told him Grandfather would disinherit him if anything happened to me, and you most surely put the fear of the Almighty in him when you threatened him. Perhaps he will honor his pledge."

"And perhaps not." Hugh drew her closer, savoring the warmth of her safe in his arms. Did he live to be one hundred, he knew he would never forget the terror he had felt when he had burst through that door. He'd wanted to kill every man there, shrieking as his ancestors shrieked when they descended like the Furies on their enemies. Indeed, leaving her uncle alive had been the hardest thing he'd ever done, but in the end he'd been unable to cold-bloodedly kill a man who posed no immediate physical threat to either Caroline or himself. It would have been too much like murder, and he refused to sully his honor with so foul a crime as that. A foolish distinction, he knew, considering the number of men he had killed in battle. But that was war, and honor was often made up of such foolish distinctions.

"Did you mean it when you said we are leaving for Loch Haven?" Caroline asked, yawning delicately. She was finally beginning to wind down from the events of the day, and Hugh prayed she would soon fall asleep.

"Aye," he said, stroking her hair with gentle fingers. "I had meant to leave tonight, but it will be better, I think, to leave tomorrow morning when you've rested."

"Mmm." She gave another yawn, and he felt a contented sigh ease out of her. "Tell me about Loch Haven. What is it like?"

He took a few seconds to pull his lascivious thoughts away from the clamoring demands of his body, conjuring up an image of Loch Haven to describe to her.

"It's the most beautiful place you'll ever see," he said, his voice soft with love and memory. "In the winter, it's so gray and desolate it looks like the ends of the earth. But there's a beauty to it, and a majesty that will take your breath away. And in the spring, the Highlands are alive with thousands of flowers, the smell of them sweet on air ringing with birdsong. And in the summer . . ." His voice trailed off when his wife gave a soft snore, and he realized she had drifted off to sleep.

Thank God for that, he thought gratefully. He'd been terrified she would be too frightened to sleep, but she'd adamantly refused the laudanum Aunt Egidia had attempted to force on her. The memory of the way she'd stood up to his fearsome relation, going nose to nose with the old tartar, was an image he would long hold close to his heart.

"Ah, Caroline MacColme," he murmured, pressing a kiss to the top of her head, "we'll make a Highland lass of you yet."

Chapter 14

‿‿◯◯‿‿

The first weeks at Loch Haven passed slowly for Caroline. The castle itself was like something out of a dream, its huge stone walls and massive rooms as intimidating as they were uncomfortable—something she would sooner die than admit. Not only did she have no desire to insult her husband's ancestral home, but she could only imagine how such a comment would be received by the castle's sullen staff. They were efficient enough, she supposed, but she was always aware of their disapproval; a disapproval she noted they were careful to hide whenever Hugh was about.

The villagers seemed to share the staff's animosity. At first she put down their behavior to shyness, or a villager's natural wariness with outsiders. But after a fortnight passed with no warming on their part, she came to realize they truly disliked her, and she could find only one explanation for such dislike. She was English, and in the Highlands the English were not wanted.

Such prejudice was becoming more blatantly obvious, and Caroline was finding it harder to hold her tongue. And there were times, such as now, when it proved an almost impossible task.

"Are you quite certain you are out of rum balls?" she asked, struggling to keep her tone pleasant as she confronted the recalcitrant shopkeeper. "Mairi said it was your specialty."

"Aye, and so 'tis," the older man returned, wiping down the gleaming counter with suspicious industry. "Which is why we no' have it on the shelves. You're welcome to send to London for some, if you've a mind. I'm sure they will be more to your liking." And he shot her a pointed smile.

"The balls are not for me," she said, making one final try at reasoning with the stubborn Scot. "They are for Mrs. Sinclair. When she learned I was coming to the village, she asked that I bring her some. She speaks most highly of them."

The shopkeeper stopped in his polishing. "For Mrs. Sinclair, are they?" he said, reaching up to scratch his beard. "Well now, I suppose I might send a box of them up to the castle for her when they are made. She's a fine lady, is Egidia Sinclair."

Caroline accepted the insult and defeat with determined calm. "Yes, she is," she said, a tight feeling of pain in her chest. "Also, when you have made the rum balls, will you kindly send a box of them to Mrs. MacDouhal? She has been ill, and I hear she has a fondness for sweets."

The shopkeeper seemed taken aback by her request. "That she does," he said, regarding her curiously. "But I did not know the poor woman to be ill. How did you hear of it?"

Caroline allowed herself a tiny smile. "The

lady is one of my husband's oldest tenants," she told him coolly. "And as lady of the castle, it is my responsibility to see to her welfare. Good day to you, Mr. Addams." She turned and left, her pride refusing to let him see the tears stinging her eyes.

After leaving the sweetshop she went next to the grocer's, hoping to purchase some fruit for the table. She found several apples and baskets of sweet strawberries, but the pursed-lipped woman behind the counter was forever in writing up her order. The same thing happened when she stopped at the church to speak with the vicar, and by the time she climbed into her carriage for the ride back to the castle, she was shaking with fury and hurt.

Her feelings of ill-use increased when she arrived home and was met by the surly butler who refused her request to serve tea on the rear terrace with a cool "Mistress Mairi and Mrs. Sinclair wouldna like it."

That's it, she decided furiously. Temporary mistress of Loch Haven though she might be, this was still her home. And although it was a home where it was rapidly becoming obvious she was not welcome, it was time she made a stand. She'd resisted telling Hugh of her difficulties, not wishing to upset him, but now she didn't feel she had a choice. Ignoring the butler's sharp admonishment that "the laird wasna to be bothered." She brushed past him, storming into the study with her jaw set.

"Hugh, I must speak with you," she began, breaking off at the sight of a dark-haired man in the gray and heather plaid of the MacColme standing beside Hugh.

"I beg your pardon, Mr. Raghnall," she said, belatedly recognizing one of Hugh's chieftains. "I didn't know you were here. I will come back later." She made as if to withdraw.

" 'Tis all right, Lady Caroline," he assured her with a low bow. "I've finished my meeting with the laird, and was about to take my leave." He turned to Hugh and rattled something off in the language she now recognized as Gaelic. Hugh answered in the same tongue, although his gaze remained fixed on Caroline.

She waited patiently until the door had closed behind the man before turning to Hugh. "One of these days, sir, I shall have mastered Gaelic, and then you won't be able to speak in front of me without my understanding every word you say."

He shot her a piratical grin, his green eyes dancing with amusement. "The day a *Sasunnach* understands the ancient tongue, *leannan*, 'twill be a day when pigs fly."

She raised her chin. "Indeed?" she said coolly. "Well, as it happens, I speak it well enough to recognize that word."

He walked over to where she was standing and gathered her in his arms. "*Leannan?*" he said, bending to brush a teasing kiss across her mouth. "And so I think you would, my sweet, for I say it often enough when we are in bed. It means *lover*."

"I know that." She looped her arms about his neck and pressed closer. "I meant the other word."

He paused in the act of brushing more kisses

down her neck. "*Sasunnach?*" he repeated, raising his head. "Where would you have heard that?"

"Here and there," she said, her curiosity piqued by his reaction. "What does it mean?"

A look of hard anger settled on his face. "An Englishman or in your case, an Englishwoman, and 'tis nae a compliment," he said, his mouth hardening in a thin line. "Has someone called you that, Caroline? If so, you must tell me their names. I willna have my wife insulted."

Now that the moment was here, Caroline was suddenly loath to continue. Hugh had looked so happy, so relaxed, she couldn't bring herself to place him in a situation where he might be forced to chose between his people and her.

"Caroline?" He scowled down at her. "Answer me. Who called you a *sasunnach?* I would know so I can have words wi' him."

She gave herself a mental shake, and pinned a teasing smile to her lips. "Then you had best be prepared to talk to everyone in the glen," she said, trying to inject a rueful note in her voice, "for I hear it nearly everywhere I go. It's to be expected, I suppose. I *am* English, after all."

His arms remained closed about her waist. "Aye," he muttered, looking far from pleased. "But you are my wife as well, and I cannot stand by and do nothing when you are offered such blatant insult. How long has this been going on?" He added, fixing her with a stern gaze, "And why did you not tell me until this minute?"

"Almost since the moment of our arrival," she admitted, deciding to tell him the entire truth of the matter. "And I didn't tell you because I didn't want to upset you. I know you are working hard to regain your people's trust, and I didn't want to add to your burdens."

He gazed down at her a long moment, and then gave a weary sigh. "They're good people, Caroline," he said, pressing her head against his shoulder. "Good people with long memories and a bitter hatred of the English. So much was taken from them after Culloden and even long before, that I suppose I ought to have guessed how it would be. Lucien tried to warn me, but I would not listen. I am sorry, love, if your feelings have been hurt."

Hearing his words, and knowing he truly regretted what had happened helped ease the hurt in Caroline's heart. It also relieved her of one of her most secret worries—that perhaps Hugh was beginning to share his people's dislike of her. She sent a silent prayer of thanks winging heavenward that it was not so.

"I'll speak with the chieftains tomorrow," he told her, cuddling her close. "I'll remind them yet again that *sasunnach* or nae, you are still the laird's woman, and no disrespect of you will be tolerated."

His protective words warmed her, and she raised her head to send him a provocative grin. "The laird's woman, am I?" she drawled, thrilling at the feel of his rising male flesh beneath the soft wool of his kilt. He'd worn the garment from their first day in the castle, and the sight of him in it always made her senses swim with the most wanton delight.

He pressed closer to her, making her even

more aware of his arousal. "Aye," he said, his voice a husky purr. "Have you a problem with that, my lady?"

"And if I do?" She rose on tiptoe and nipped his chin.

His lips curved in a smile that fired her blood. "Then I think, *mo cridhe*, 'tis time I was taking you for a picnic."

For a woman expecting to be swept off her feet and carried away for a passionate bout of love-making, this was hardly a welcome suggestion. "A picnic?" she repeated, her mouth forming a sulky pout. "Now?"

He gave a lusty laugh, sweeping her into his arms and swirling her around in a circle before depositing her once more on her feet. "Aye, now," he said, dropping a smacking kiss on her lips. "And dinna look so put out, sweeting. 'Tis a Highland picnic I mean to take you on."

Deciding that sounded as if it might have definite possibilities, she pretended to pout a little longer. "And what, sir, might a Highland picnic be?"

His grin grew wider. "Go fetch your shawl, lassie, and I will show you."

"Oh, Hugh, how beautiful!" Caroline stood beside Hugh, her arm draped companionably about his waist as they stood on a rock cropping high above the valley. "I've never seen anything half so lovely!"

"Do you truly like it?" Hugh asked, gazing slowly about him with a heart overflowing with joy. As a lad this had been his favorite place in all the world, and sharing it with Caroline made

him happier than he had been in years. Up here
with only the wildflowers and the larks for company and Loch Haven spread out below their
feet, he felt both the laird and the lover, and he
burned with the desire to make love to his wife
with only openness between them.

"How could I not love it?" she asked, brushing
a windblown curl from her cheek as she turned
to give him a smile. At his request she'd left her
long blonde hair down, and the soft breeze, ripe
with the smell of heather, blew it playfully about
her face. "I do not think even Shakespeare himself could do justice to so lovely a sight."

"Of course he couldna do so," he teased, deciding they'd wasted enough time admiring the
view. "He's an Englishman, and what would
they know of the beauty of the Highlands?" He
took her hand and led her back to where he had
spread out a blanket.

"Some wine for you, *annsachd*?" he asked,
pouring out some of the golden wine and handing it to her. " 'Tis almost as sweet as your
mouth, and it heats my blood near as hot as your
kisses."

She accepted the silver goblet silently, her eyebrows arching at his provocative praise. "There
is another word I am beginning to recognize,"
she said, after sampling the potent wine. "It
means *dearest*, does it not?"

"Or *darling*." He bent his head and lightly
kissed her neck. "Or *beloved*. *Is tu mo annsachd*:
thou art my best beloved."

"Mmm." She tilted her head back and
threaded her fingers though the hair he had also
left down. "Gaelic would seem to have as many

pretty phrases in it as French. And you speak it most eloquently."

His hands went to the back of her gown to begin untying her laces. "I've many words I'll gladly teach you, my love. Just mind you pay close attention, for I believe in teaching a most thorough lesson."

He pressed her back down against the blanket, covering her mouth with ardent kisses. *"Bheóil,"* he whispered teasingly. *"Mouth.* Yours is as sweet as a summer berry, my darling, and nearly as tempting."

He deepened the kiss, his tongue engaging hers in a passionate duel until she was moaning with delight. *"Teanga, tongue.* And how cleverly you make use of yours. You make me mad from wanting you."

"Hugh." She arched beneath him, clearly delighting in his ardent instruction. "Oh, Hugh, you make me burn!"

He slid his mouth down her neck to the gentle slope of her shoulders. *"Gualainn,"* he told her, slipping the loosened gown from her shoulders. *"Shoulders,* and how smooth and creamy yours are, *annsachd,* like the richest of desserts."

He removed her gown and undergarments with more teasing words and gentle caresses until she lay naked beneath him. He stopped to pull his shirt over his head, unwrapping his kilt and using it as a pillow for her head. His body was screaming for release, but he was not yet ready to abandon his play. He returned to her, his hands gently cupping her full breasts.

"Broilleach," he said, using his fingers and tongue to tease her nipples to hardness. "And

these lovely things are called *ceann na ciche*. I love kissing them, touching them. Do you like it as well, Caroline?"

He took her breathless moan for assent, and pressed a wet kiss to her quivering stomach. "*Stammac*," he said, chuckling as he teased her navel with the tip of his tongue. "An easy word to guess, I'm thinking. And this . . ." He slipped his fingers into her wet, feminine folds in an audacious caress. ". . . is called—"

"I don't care what it is called," she interrupted, twining her fingers through his hair and lifting her hips in a demanding plea. "Stop talking, you wretched man, and make love to me!"

Her imperious demand delighted him, and he pressed another kiss on her stomach. "As you wish, my lady," he said with a low chuckle, and then lowered his mouth to kiss her sweet femininity with a daring that soon sent her soaring over the peak.

He had never wanted her more in his life, and he drove himself and Caroline to madness as he dined on the sweetness of her. Finally he knew he couldn't wait any longer, and moved over her to claim her at last.

"Caroline, *mo cridhe*," he groaned, slipping eagerly into the liquid warmth of her. "*Annsachd*, tell me you want me. Tell me you adore me."

"I want you, Hugh," she moaned, her face flushed and her eyes squeezed closed in ecstasy. "I adore you more than I can say."

He thrust deeper, burying himself in the heart of her. "Tell me in Gaelic," he demanded, bending his head to lightly bite her soft shoulder. "Let me hear you say it in my tongue."

She moved her head restlessly, her breath coming in fast pants as she neared yet another peak. *"Annsachd,"* she repeated, her slender legs wrapping around his surging hips. *"Leannan.* Oh! I cannot think of the words! Now, Hugh, now!"

Her gasped words delighted him, thrilling him in a way he could never have anticipated. He slipped his hands beneath her, his palms cupping her as he thrust deeper and harder. Emotions he couldn't give name to exploded inside of him and he groaned out her name, shuddering with release as he swept them both to glorious ecstasy.

The following afternoon, he was in his study with his accounts spread out before him, but his mind on the windswept meadow where he and Caroline had made such passionate love. He remembered her shyness afterward, and the way she'd laughed later that night as she plucked out the wildflowers tangled in his hair. How was he supposed to honor their agreement? he wondered bitterly, closing his books and rising to his feet to prowl about the room. How was he to stand back and let her walk away when every instinct he possessed screamed at him to hold her close for all time?

It was like being trapped in the deadly marshes of the Carolinas. Marshes that looked sound and safe until a man had blundered into them too deep to retreat, and then the treacherous sands sucked him down into death. Struggling only hastened the inevitable, for the harder one struggled, the deeper and faster one sank.

There was no going forward, no going back. Like now.

"Devil take it!" he muttered, impatient with his morose thoughts. A breath of fresh air was what he needed, and on impulse he decided to ride into the village. It had been several days since he'd last been there, and there was much he needed to see to.

Bypassing the main keep where the women were hard at work, he slipped out the back and down to the stables. One of the first purchases he'd made upon reclaiming the castle was a fierce black stallion, the first mount he'd owned in more years than he could count. He'd named him *Nathrach*, Dragon; the name well suited the great beast whose fiery temper and strong will nearly matched his own.

The promise of summer was soft in the air as Hugh rode down from the castle and into the slumbering village. Several people called out to him and a few came up to speak with him, offering compliment or complaint as was their nature.

After promising an elderly crofter he would see to the repair of the man's pig shed, he was about to ride away when the man said, "And a blessing as well on she who is your wife. A fine lassie she is, and nae the icy bitch as some would name her."

Hugh pulled up sharp on Nathrach's rein, making him dance with impatience. "Who called my wife an icy bitch?" he demanded, his voice low and dangerous with fury.

The elderly man shrugged his skeletal shoulders. "Everyone, laird. They see her in her fine clothes, in her fine carriage, and curse as she drives by. But that is because they dinna see her sweet smile, as I do," he added, offering Hugh his own broken-toothed smile. "She does Loch Haven and its laird proud."

By the time Hugh burst into the smoky taproom of the inn, he was spoiling for a brawl. The first person he saw was Lucien, and he stormed over to confront him.

"You've done a poor job of explaining things, Raghnall," he said coldly. "And I'm fair displeased with you. When I give an order, I expect it to be carried out."

"What order?" Lucien asked, setting down his tankard with an astonished expression on his face. "What have I nae explained? Truly, Hugh, I dinna know what you are talking about."

Hugh laid his hand on the bar and leaned down until he was eye to eye with the other man. "I made it plain to you that I would brook no insult to Caroline," he ground out, his voice low and tight with fury. "I told you I would have the life of any man who hurt her. Did you nae believe me, Raghnall? Or did you nae think I could enforce the bond of my word? Either way, laddie, you've made a grievous error."

Lucien swallowed uncomfortably, his eyes showing both alarm and indignation. "I did as you asked, laird," he said with quiet dignity. "I spoke with the chieftains and their men. I warned those in the village that the lady of Loch Haven was to be accorded every degree of honor, but it did no good. It is as I tried to tell you, Hugh. Your wife is English, and the people are of no mind to accept her."

Hugh thought of his wife's sweet nature, and the open way she showed affection for his sister and even his impossible aunt. She was one of the kindest people he had ever met, and the notion of her warm generosity being spurned because of her nationality filled him with murderous rage. Caroline might only be his wife for a brief period of time, but so long as she bore his name, he would do what he must to protect her.

"Then mind you tell the people this," he said, fixing Lucien with a hard stare. "Tell them the goodwill of the laird is dependent upon the welcome accorded his wife. If they continue offering her insult, I withdraw my aid. 'Tis that simple."

Lucien gaped at him in horror. "You canna do that!" he gasped. "You canna choose one of the English above your own people! 'Tis treason!"

"I do nae choose!" Hugh fired back, slamming his fist onto the bar. "Or if I choose, 'tis because they have forced me to do so! Caroline is my *wife*, and protect her I will!"

"Your temporary wife," Lucien corrected, although he was careful to keep his voice pitched low. "Think, man; think of all you have sacrificed and sweated for. You have it now, here in your hand; why should you risk it all for her? Why should her feelings matter to you, when in a year's time she will be gone and back in London where she belongs?

"Hugh." Lucien leaned forward and grasped Hugh's arm, his expression earnest as their gazes met. "Listen to me. Let me tell the others the truth of your marriage. Let me tell them your wife will soon be away, and they need nae worry about her again. If they know that, 'twill make it easier for them to swallow their hatred of her.

"I understand you feel you must protect the wench," he continued when Hugh remained silent, "and I admire you the more for it. But dinna put your sense of duty to her above the duty you owe to your people. She will soon be gone, but they will still be here, and if you choose her above them, it is something they will remember always. Think of that, Hugh. That is all I ask of you."

"Ouch!" Mairi cried out angrily, dropping the shirt she was hemming and sticking her wounded finger in her mouth. "That is the third time this morning I have stuck myself! The plague take this insufferable sewing! Why must we do it?"

"Because the sewing of clothes for the poor is the duty of the ladies of the castle, you ill-mannered *kempie*," Aunt Egidia informed her sourly, peering at her over the edge of her spectacles. "You dinna hear Caroline complain, do you? And she's sewn double the amount of clothes as you! Hush now with your wheeking, and get on with it. We've a dozen more shirts to hem before nuncheon."

"And I shall be as full of holes as a crofter's shift," Mairi grumbled under her breath, directing a scowl at Caroline. "And you," she said crossly, "the least you might do is not sit there smiling like a saint. Are you nae as sick of this as me?"

Caroline's smile deepened at what she knew to be no more than good-natured teasing. "I've always enjoyed sewing," she replied, passing her needle in and out of the sturdy fabric. "It's quite soothing, really, once one gets the hang of it."

"Soothing?" Mairi gave a disgusted snort, even as she resumed her hemming. "Boring, 'tis more the like of it. Well, if we must pass the time in such a ladylike manner, then we might as well do what all fine ladies do, and gossip about our neighbors. Have you heard about Flora Mac-Gregor?"

"Who?" Caroline asked, not really interested, but always willing to indulge Mairi.

"The daughter of the village miller," Aunt Egidia provided, her lips thinning in obvious disapproval. "And aye, I've heard the tale, though I dinna think 'tis a proper topic for unwed maidens to be discussing." A hard stare was directed at Mairi, who merely laughed.

"Now come, Auntie, and how are we poor unwed maidens to learn of the dangers that lurk from dallying with men, if we canna discuss the results?" She turned to Caroline, her green eyes bright with mischief. "Flora dallied with a man from the glen near the loch, and now she's three months gone with child. Her father's for shooting the fellow, once he's wed Flora, of course, but 'tis said he's already taken himself off to Aberdeen. Poor Flora. It doesna look so sunny for her."

"The hizzie ought to have known better than to be lifting her skirts without taking the proper care," Aunt Egidia opined with another sniff. "What Highland lassie doesna know the good of a visit to a wisewoman? She was after getting herself with child, if you want my thought on it, so that she could force the man into marrying her."

"What is a wisewoman?" Caroline asked, all this talk of children making her nervous. "Do you mean a witch?"

Aunt Egidia glared at her. "An English word, is *witch*," she said with a frown. "Here in the Highlands where we dinna have fine doctors waiting to attend our every hurt, 'tis the wise-women and the healers who see to people's needs. A wisewoman knows many things, including what herb a lass might eat to make certain a man's seed doesna find a home in her belly. If Flora MacGregor had kept her wits about her, she'd have gone to the wisewoman near the cairns and seen to the matter. But as she didna . . ." She lifted her shoulders in an indifferent shrug.

"I heard Annie talking, and she says Flora never even guessed she was breeding," Mairi continued with a shake of her head. "It was only when she began losing her breakfast each morning that the truth of the matter dawned on her."

Caroline winced as she jabbed the needle in her hand. For the past several mornings, the smell of food had been enough to set her stomach churning. And this morning she'd had a brief dizzy spell when coming down the front steps. If she hadn't grabbed the banister, she was certain she would have fallen. What if . . .

"Aye, the girl was ever as thick as a plank of oak," Aunt Egidia agreed. "The stopping of her monthly flow ought to have told her something, but expecting wit from a MacGregor is like expecting eggs from a cow. 'Twillna happen."

Caroline did some quick calculations. She and Hugh had been man and wife for over three months, and in all that time she'd had but one flow. Dear God! She dropped the shirt she was hemming, her eyes going wide with shock. Was it possible she was breeding? The idea brought a dreamy smile to her lips.

"Well, I'm glad you can find humor in the poor girl's ruin." Aunt Egidia had noted the smile and was frowning at Caroline reproachfully. "For as the lady of the castle, 'twill fall to you to find a position for her and the bairn if her father canna force the man to do what is right."

"Mayhap Hugh might find a husband for her," Mairi suggested. "Douglass Badenoch lost his wife last fall, and he's three small ones in need of a mother. 'Tis something you might want to mention to him, Caroline. Caroline?"

"What?" Caroline looked at her, then blinked as she realized some reply was expected. "Oh. Oh, yes, Mairi, thank you; I shall be certain do to that."

The topic turned to other matters: who was flirting with whose wife, and what handsome young man had more than his fill at the taproom and got miserably sick during services the following morning, but Caroline listened with only half an ear. *A baby*, she thought, laying a gentle hand on her stomach. A son, perhaps, with Hugh's hair and eyes, and his fiery sense of honor. Or a little girl, mayhap, with red curls and a shy, sweet smile. Mairi was lovely as a picture, and she was certain her daughter would surely favor her aunt.

In the next moment her eyes were burning

with unshed tears. The arrangement she and Hugh had entered into had made no mention of children. What would happen if she was breeding? And what if the babe was a boy, an heir to the MacColme name and lands? She knew Hugh too well to think he would allow her to take his son with her when she left. Would she be forced to leave her child behind, as well as the man she was coming to care for more and more with each passing day? Tears began flowing down her cheeks at the thought.

"Caroline!" Mairi gave a horrified cry, tossing her mending down and hurrying to Caroline's side. "Dearest, what is wrong?"

"Nothing," Caroline denied, laughing unevenly and dabbing at her eyes. "It is only the mending that is making my eyes burn. The light in here is very poor."

"I'll fetch another brace of candles for you," Mairi promised, rising to her feet. "In the meanwhile, mind you rest your poor eyes. Auntie, keep watch on Caroline while I am gone, will you? Dinna let her work anymore." And with that she turned and hurried from the room.

"Aye," Egidia said softly, her gaze sharp with speculation as she studied Caroline. "I'll keep an eye on her, all right."

Chapter 15

The letter from Edinburgh was waiting for Caroline when she came down to breakfast the following morning. The return address was that of the solicitor she'd engaged to help her find a house, and she quickly opened it, curious as to why he should write her after all these weeks. Curiosity turned to delight when she read that the house she and Mairi had toured that momentous day was still available. The developers were most anxious to sell, Mr. Penderson assured her, and she would need to give them her answer as quickly as possible. He then went on to quote a price that had her smiling, it was so low. She was still smiling when she walked into the morning room and found Mairi and Aunt Egidia already tucking into their food.

"Good morning!" she said, giving both ladies an affectionate kiss before taking her seat. "How are you this fine morning?"

Mairi's gaze went to the window, where storm clouds were dulling the weak sunshine. "A fine morning, is it?" she said, her green eyes bright with laughter. "When we'll have a Highland storm before lunch is served? It's an odd sense of *fine* you must have, to be saying such things."

"Quit your blitherin', you ill-mannered child, and let the poor girl have her porridge in peace!" Aunt Egidia snapped, bending a fierce scowl on Mairi. "How many times must I be telling you to mind that tongue of yours?"

Mairi sent Caroline a saucy wink. "Times out of telling, Auntie," she said serenely. "And you can see yourself the edifying effect it has had upon me."

Even Aunt Egidia had to laugh at that, giving the younger woman's hand a teasing slap. "It's a spinster you're fated to be, Mairi MacColme, with that will of yours," she said, shaking her head in resignation. "I can think of no man with either the patience or the courage to tame you."

"Then I am better off a spinster, aren't I?" Mairi asked with an indifferent shrug. "And for your information, Auntie, I'd rather spend all my days alone than handfasted to some great bore of man who thinks to tame me to his hand." She gave Caroline a conspiratorial grin.

"I want a marriage like Caroline's and Hugh's. It's openness and trust they have between them, and respect as well. I want that, and if I canna have it, I'll have nothing at all."

Caroline's smile faded, and she applied herself to her bowl of porridge with an enthusiasm she seldom showed for the thick, heavy cereal Aunt Egidia insisted be served each morning. *Openness and respect*, she thought unhappily. Was that really how Mairi saw her and Hugh's marriage? If only it were so.

"I have a letter from Mr. Penderson," she said, hiding her troubling thoughts behind bright chatter. "Do you remember the house we looked at in Edinburgh, Mairi? The one on St. Andrew Square?"

"Only the rich and the foreigners live on St. Andrew Square," Aunt Egidia observed sourly, dipping her toast into her egg.

"Aye, I remember it," Mairi said, replying as if Aunt Egidia hadn't spoken. "It was a grand place, with a large entryway and the prettiest rooms. You wanted to buy it, didn't you?"

"Very much so," Caroline assured her, remembering her delight in the stunning house. "I even asked Mr. Penderson to have papers drawn up, but then—" She broke off, paling at the memory of all that had followed.

"Is the house still available?" Mairi reached out to give Caroline's hand a reassuring squeeze. "Is that why Mr. Penderson has written you?"

In answer Caroline handed Mairi the letter. She read it quickly, her eyebrows climbing in surprise.

"Four thousand pounds!" she exclaimed. "For a single house? That's rather dear, isn't it?"

"I thought the price more than reasonable," Caroline replied, surprised by her reaction. "In London, homes of this sort go for two and sometimes even three times that amount."

"That's because in London there are fools willing to pay," Aunt Egidia retorted, snatching the letter from Mairi and reading it as well. "Hmph! Presumptuous fellow, isn't he? Offering to come to the castle to have the papers signed. It's English he must be, to be so bold."

Although Caroline knew the old woman meant no ill, her words still stung. Was that how

Hugh felt? she brooded. The Scots bore the English such enmity, and the more he was with his people, the more Scots Hugh became. Would he soon come to share their feelings? To regard her as no more than an interloper, an enemy who was never to be welcomed amongst them?

"Caroline?" Mairi was studying her curiously. "Is everything all right? Did you not hear Auntie?"

Caroline shook off her dark musings, and pinned a smile to her lips. "Yes, I heard her," she said, pushing her bowl away from her, her appetite gone. "I was only thinking I would tell Mr. Penderson to bring the papers. I've decided to buy the house."

Mairi gave her her enthusiastic congratulations, offering several suggestions for colors and fabrics for the drapes and carpets Caroline would need. Aunt Egidia remained oddly silent, holding her tongue until after Mairi had dashed off in search of a cabinetmaker's book she had in her room. An uneasy silence fell between the two ladies, and in her blunt way, Aunt Egidia was the first to break it.

"I hope you took no offense by what I said, child," she said, her faded eyes direct as she met Caroline's gaze. "I meant no harm; upon that I give you my word."

Caroline believed her at once. "I know you didn't, Aunt," she said gently. "And I'm not hurt—"

"Yes, you are," Aunt Egidia interrupted, scowling. "And for that I am most heartily sorry. Hating the English is as natural to a Scot as drawing breath, and there are times I forget you are nae of the clans. Am I forgiven?''

"Of course you are."

"Good." Aunt Egidia gave a decisive nod. "Then you won't mind my telling you you're doing a foolish thing by buying this house without first consulting Hugh. He has his pride, you know, and it will chafe sorely at your making such a purchase without so much as a by-your-leave."

Caroline conceded the truth of that, but she was nonetheless adamant. She was fairly certain she was with child, and if so, she knew she could not return to England as she had originally planned. Even if she and Hugh divorced as intended, she couldn't leave Scotland. She had grown to love it too much.

"I will think about it," she temporized, knowing Aunt Egidia would argue her into the ground if she refused outright. "Much as I want the house, I wouldn't wish to upset Hugh."

Aunt Egidia gave her a suspicious scowl. "Then you mean to discuss this with him?" she asked.

"Certainly," Caroline assured her. "Why should I not?"

"Mayhap because of the way you keep other matters from him," Aunt Egidia said, eyeing Caroline knowingly. " 'Tis none of my business, I am sure, but there are some secrets, lassie, that cannot be kept forever. Some cannot be kept beyond a few months."

The older woman's remarks weighed heavily on Caroline's mind as she strolled about the gardens later that morning. Hugh had left strict orders she was always to be accompanied when she left the house, but since she didn't intend to leave the grounds, she saw no reason why she should wait until one of the men Hugh deemed a suitable escort could be found. And, she admitted with a flash of honesty, she was in no mood to obey her masterful husband.

At first she kept to the well-tended gardens, pausing occasionally to sniff a rose or listen to the sweet sound of a lark's song. But as she worked through the puzzle of her marriage to Hugh, and what would happen when she told him of her suspicions, she forgot her innocent intentions. Instead of turning back when she reached the outer walls, she wandered through the gates and off into the Highlands, in search of answers to questions she yet possessed the courage to ask.

By the time she realized her mistake she was a good mile from the castle, and it took her almost forty minutes to find her way back. She walked around to the back of the house, hoping to slip in unnoticed and thus escape a scolding should Aunt Egidia catch her. She had just reached the door leading into the library when it was suddenly flung open. Hugh stood there, his arms folded across his chest and a look of black fury glittering in his eyes.

"You little minx!" he exclaimed, glowering down at her. "And just where the devil have you been?"

Hugh glared down into Caroline's face, torn between the desire to shake her and the equally strong desire to toss her over his shoulder and carry her up to their room and make love to her until they were both too spent to move. He'd lived a lifetime in the hour since Mairi had come to tell him that his gently reared wife was out traipsing across the Highlands without so much as a scullery maid to protect her, rather than being tucked safely in her room as he'd thought.

He'd been about to set off after her when he'd glanced out the library window to see her scurrying up the walk. The sight, welcome as it was, had been all it had taken to set light to his temper, and now he was ready to do battle. If it was the last thing he accomplished, he vowed she would pay for the hell she had put him through this day.

"Well?" he prodded, his impatience mounting as she maintained her mutinous silence. "I am waiting."

One of her blonde eyebrows arched in icy inquiry, and her blue eyes were glacial as she returned his angry stare. "Indeed, Mr. Mac-Colme?" she said, using his family name in a way she hadn't done since their first introduction. "And might one ask what it is you are waiting for?"

Those prim words, spoken in that precise, condescending tone, made his mouth tighten, and he made a Herculean effort to rein in his mounting ire. "Don't press me, wife," he warned, his accent thickening with his emotions. " 'Tis sore mad I am with you, and 'twill take little to make me truly furious. I ask you again, where were you?"

Her chin tilted up, and he was beginning to think he would have to do something truly drastic to prove his point when she capitulated with an impatient sigh.

"I was out walking," she said, her defiant manner daring him to object. "I went a little further than I meant to, and so was late in getting back. That is all."

Her audacity rendered him speechless, but only temporarily. "All?" he repeated, feeling the pulse pounding in his temples. "You can say 'all' to me when I've spent the past hour terrified your bastard of an uncle may have broken his word to us, and was even now carrying you back to Oxford? When I have been pacing the floor and thinking of you lying dead and brutalized in some filthy hole? *All?*" He shook his head in patent disbelief. "My God, woman, are you insane?"

"No, I am not," she retorted, not seeming in the slightest bit intimidated by his black fury. "Nor am I some weak-spirited miss to be scolded and shouted at as if I were no more than a disobedient child. I once told you I would not tolerate such high-handed behavior, and I meant it."

"And I told you I wasna the man for soft words and gentle ways," he shot back, curling his hands into fists to keep them from grabbing her by the shoulders. "Don't do this to me again, Caroline," he warned, making one last, desperate effort at control, "or by heaven, I will give you cause to regret it."

There was another silence, and then she bowed her head with mocking deference. "Very well, laird," she said, her voice cool as she met his gaze. "Now if you are done ringing a peal over my head, there is a matter I would like to discuss with you."

"What matter?" he asked warily, not caring for her reference to his title. It was the first time she had done so, and given the circumstances, he was fairly certain she didn't do it out of any new-found sense of respect for him.

"Mairi and I looked at a house the day I was kidnapped, and I should like to purchase it."

The forthright words made him scowl. "A house?" he asked, remembering his conversation with Lucien about Caroline's money.

"Near St. Andrew Square," she said, the ice in her countenance melting as her enthusiasm grew more obvious. "It has only just been completed, and it is really quite lovely. There are several bedrooms, and I thought perhaps Mairi might stay—"

"No."

His blunt interruption made her pause. "I beg your pardon?" she asked, her eyes narrowing as she studied him.

He didn't pretend to be deceived by her brittle civility. In the weeks since their wedding he had come to know Caroline well, and 'twas plain to him his usually good-natured bride was spoiling for a brawl. Unfortunately for them both, he was just of a mind to oblige her. He squared his shoulders, crossing his arms in a deliberately antagonistic stance as he met her gaze.

"I said no."

Her chin tilted up another notch. "No, you do not wish Mairi to stay with us, or no, you do not wish to purchase a home?"

"No, I do not wish to purchase a home," he

returned, making no effort to soften his tone. "We shall stay with Aunt Egidia when we are not at Loch Haven, and a new house would be a foolish waste of money. I will not allow it."

Caroline's head jerked back as if he'd struck her. A raw hurt showed in her eyes, and then she was drawing herself upright again. "I see," she said, her voice taking on a note he'd never heard. "And if I decide the money is mine to waste, what then?"

Hugh hesitated, not certain how to proceed. He and Caroline seldom quarreled, and when they did it had always been like a summer storm—loud and violent while it lasted, but soon over, and with no harm done to anyone. But this was like a blizzard in the Highlands, all the more deadly for the cold and the ice of it. Suddenly he no longer wished to continue but he knew he could not withdraw. The battle was joined, and now there was only victory or defeat.

"Then the answer remains the same," he said, unconsciously softening both his stance and his voice. "I have duties which hold me here, and I will not let you go alone to Edinburgh. Your uncle is still too great a danger to my way of thinking, and I've no wish to let you out of my sight. You are my wife, Caroline; you must allow me to do what I see as right."

Tears glittered in her eyes, but she did not allow them to fall. "And if I disagree?"

"Then you will still do as I say," he said, the feeling he was fighting an enemy he couldn't see growing stronger. "Your grandfather charged me with your care, and I've no intention of failing him. I owe him too much to go back on my end of the bargain. I am a man of my word."

The glitter in her eyes grew more pronounced as she gave a bitter laugh. "Ah, yes, your bargain with Grandfather—how could I have forgotten? You must be very grateful for his help in regaining your castle and lands."

"Aye, that I am. He was of immeasurable help," Hugh agreed, his frown deepening. His pride would have preferred she not know he'd come to her all but a pauper, but in the end he didn't see that it mattered. Surely she must have known he had some reason for marrying her other than the money she had once offered. He studied her too-calm expression with mounting worry.

"Caroline," he began, reaching tentatively for her. "What ails you? Why are you behaving like this? We have always had the truth between us; you knew I never married you for love. You didn't marry me for it, either, if it comes to that. Why should it matter so much to you now?"

She stepped away from him, her spine so straight he wondered it didn't snap. "You mistake me, sir," she informed him coldly. "It matters not at all. If we are quite finished, I should like to retire to my room. With your permission, of course," she added, her lips twisting in a parody of her usual warm smile.

Hugh could think of nothing to say, too heartsore to argue any longer. He merely nodded, his eyes brooding as he watched her walk out of the room. Even after she was gone he remained where he was, his heart and mind conducting a war that threatened to tear him apart. He'd just decided to go up to their room and demand an explanation for her odd behavior when there was a rap on the door.

"Come in," he called out, hoping whoever it was would not keep him overly long. If not, he had no compunction about hurrying them on their way.

Mairi stormed in, her eyes narrowed with fury as she advanced on him with a purposeful stride.

"To the devil with you, Hugh MacColme!" she said, shaking her finger at him in a fair imitation of Aunt Egidia at her worst. "You have been quarreling with Caroline, haven't you?"

Hugh thought of the bitter words that had passed between him and Caroline, and gave a harsh laugh. "Aye," he said, walking back to stand before the fireplace. "We quarreled."

"And you scolded and shouted at her like Father used to rage at you," Mairi said with a sister's unerring perception. "No wonder she stalked out of here with tears in her eyes! Shame on you, you beast, to be so cruel to your wife!"

"Me?" Hugh's masculine outrage rose at the unfairness of the accusation. "What of her? She did her own raging and scolding, I can tell you!" Then he frowned. "Caroline was crying?"

Mairi sighed, raising her eyes heavenward in a plea for guidance. "On the inside," she told him gruffly. "Where the tears are the deepest. What did you argue over? The house?"

Hugh studied her through narrowed eyes. He supposed he could refuse to answer, or he could order Mairi from the room, but he did neither. Oddly, he found he wanted to talk, and who better to listen to him than his own belligerent sister?

"Aye, about the house," he admitted, thrusting a weary hand through his hair. "And for leaving the house without escort. After what happened in Edinburgh, you cannot fault me for my concern when I learned she was gone."

"For your concern, no, but for your shouting at her for wanting to buy a house, aye, I can fault you plenty." Mairi shook her head at him. "What were you thinking, Hugh? No woman, not even an Englishwoman, could stomach such tyranny."

His sister's words called to mind the bargain binding Caroline to him—a bargain he had deliberately put from his mind. "But Caroline *is* English," he said, as much for his benefit as for Mairi's. "And that is something we had best both remember. It will make her leaving the easier to bear."

Mairi's face went blank. "Leaving? What do you mean, leaving?"

Hugh instantly wished his words unsaid. "Mairi—"

"No," she said, shaking her head angrily. "I would know what you mean. Where would she go? And more to the point, why should she wish to go there?"

Hugh opened his lips to answer, then abruptly closed them, unable to find the words to explain either himself or the bargains he had struck with Caroline's grandfather. "Leave it, Mairi," he ordered his sister, his tone harsher than he intended. "It is none of your concern; this is between Caroline and myself. Stay out of it."

"But—"

He whirled around to face her, his eyes full of bitterness. "I said stay out of it!" he roared, and before Mairi could utter another word, he turned and stalked from the room, slamming the door hard enough to shake the house.

Caroline sat before her dressing table, repairing the ravages to her complexion and doing her best to control the pain that was shredding her heart. *You knew I never married you for love.* Hugh's words echoed in her mind, magnifying the folly of her own errant emotions. She loved him, she realized, staring at her reflection with wide eyes. She loved him, and he still regarded their marriage as little more than the simple business transaction they had made all those weeks ago.

When had it happened? Had it begun the first night he had made such sweet, gentle love to her? Or had it been afterwards in those early days and nights when they had slowly opened themselves up to one another, coming to know the person behind the stranger?

Perhaps it had been there from the moment she first saw him, she mused, turning fanciful. Upset and determined to win her grandfather's aid though she'd been, he was still the first thing she'd noticed after barging into the parlor. He'd been dressed in black, and although he looked every inch the gentleman, there had been something wild and dangerous about him that had caught and held her interest.

And, her heart whispered treacherously, was her awareness of him not the reason she'd acquiesced to her grandfather's scheme with scarcely a whimper? Granted she'd had precious few choices in the matter, but had she not felt such an intense reaction to Hugh, would she have been so willing to marry a man she didn't know? She was no closer to discovering the answers to these puzzling questions when Mairi came rushing into the room.

"Caroline!" Mairi took one look at her face and flew to her side. "You've been crying!" she exclaimed, dropping to her knees in a flurry of petticoats and satin. "That black-hearted devil of a brother of mine! Just wait until I get my hands on him!"

Touched and more than a little amused at the younger woman's passionate defense, Caroline gave her an impulsive hug. "I'm not crying, dearest," she said, drawing back with a smile. "Although I will own to being quite hipped with your brother. He is an autocratic, impossible despot who still thinks himself to be in command of a squadron of regulars."

"Aye, he told me you'd quarreled about the house and your going about on your own," Mairi said, settling her skirts more comfortably about her and leaning against Caroline's knee. "It's a wonder he didn't scold *me* for 'allowing' you to do it, as he did last time, the overweening sot. I told him then he ought to be grateful you didna hit him over the head with a bullax."

Not knowing what a bullax might be, Caroline merely smiled. "It's a tempting thought, but in Hugh's defense, I must say that on that previous occasion he did have cause for concern. Although I am certain I am perfectly safe here in Loch Haven."

"Aye," Mairi agreed, although her green eyes were troubled. She paused, chewing her lip and eyeing Caroline with open curiosity.

"Caroline," she began tentatively, "you dinna have to answer if you've no wish to, but Hugh said something else. He said you would be leaving. What did he mean? You're nae returning to England . . . are you?"

Oh, God, how to answer that? Caroline thought, briefly closing her eyes. She thought about lying or putting the other girl off with some excuse, but the effort seemed too much. Perhaps the time for the truth had finally come. And perhaps in telling Mairi, she would remind herself of the truth as well.

"Not for several months," she said, opening her eyes to meet Mairi's concerned gaze. "But England is my home, and that is where I will go when Hugh and I have our marriage overturned."

"Overturned?" Mairi gasped, clearly shocked. "You canna mean so! 'Twould be a dreadful scandal!"

"Perhaps." Caroline gave a delicate shrug. "But not so great a scandal as it would have been in my country. Scottish law is far more lenient than English law, and here a divorce is more easily obtained. It was Grandfather's idea, actually. A temporary marriage to Hugh to protect me from my uncle, and in exchange he helped Hugh regain title to the castle. Really, it's quite practical when you think of it."

Mairi was staring at her with horror. "It doesna sound practical to me!" she exclaimed, her hands on her hips as she glared at Caroline. "It sounds cold-blooded as hell!"

"Of course it is cold-blooded," Caroline said, and was proud at how cool she sounded. "But what else did you expect? I am English, you know."

Mairi bit her lip and looked near to crying. "Caroline . . ."

"If you will excuse me, Mairi, I have a bit of a headache," Caroline said, picking up her brush and drawing it through her hair. "If you don't mind, I should like to be alone."

Mairi rose to her feet, dignity and fury obvious in her rigid posture. "Och! To the devil with you and that stiff-necked brother of mine!" she cried. "You're exactly the same, the pair of you! So cold and proud, you'd sooner cut off your nose than see what's under it! I wish you joy in each other!" And with that she stalked out of the room, her red hair flying like a banner behind her.

Chapter 16

❦

S ummer burst upon Loch Haven in a brilliant explosion of color. Hugh spent nearly every day out of doors, riding from croft to croft and reacquainting himself with the land and the people. The work was backbreaking at times, but he reveled in the effort, finding solace in the grueling labor as he finally made peace with himself and with his clan. Peace between him and Caroline, however, was proving a more difficult matter.

Following their bitter argument, she had retreated behind a wall of coolness he could not penetrate however hard he tried. And he had tried, he told himself bitterly. He'd tied his tongue into knots apologizing to her—groveling, in his eyes, to get her to forgive him. He'd even reversed his opinion on the house she seemed to want so desperately, but no matter what he did, he couldn't breach the fortress she had erected about her.

Despite the distance between them Caroline continued working with him, seeing to the needs of his people with gentle kindness. The grumblings against her lessened, but he still kept a watchful eye upon her when they were out together. When he couldn't be with her, he continued making certain either Lucien or another trusted man rode with her. He didn't think any of his clan would attack her, but he preferred not to take any chances. There was also her uncle to consider. Caroline's safety was too important to him to believe blindly in the earl's vow to leave them in peace.

Remembering Lucien's remarks about the resentment caused by Caroline's carriage, he had purchased a mount for her, requesting that weather permitting, she ride when carrying out her duties as the lady of the castle. He was certain that once the people came to know her as he did, they would see what a fine and noble lady she was. It seemed to be working, and he watched hopefully as she blossomed under her newfound acceptance.

One day nearly a week after the confrontation in the library, he and a group of men were on the far side of the valley repairing a crofter's roof. It was a rare hot day, and in the heat of the day he'd taken off his shirt, baring his back to the sun. He felt the curious glances of his men when they saw the scars on his back, but to his relief they kept their own counsel.

It was approaching noon when he saw two figures approaching on horseback. He recognized Caroline first, and then William King, as they rode toward them. He started reaching for his shirt to cover himself, but abruptly changed his mind. To the devil with propriety, he decided, setting his jaw. 'Twas not as if Caroline hadn't seen his naked back. She was his wife, and mayhap seeing him like this would remind her of that fact. He leaned against his rake, watching with narrow-eyed patience as she rode up to the cottage.

"Good morning to you, Mr. MacColme," she called out, shielding her eyes with her gloved hands as she smiled up at him. "I've brought you and these other gentlemen a bit of lunch."

Her consideration stunned him as much as it delighted his men. By the time he'd climbed down from the roof she was surrounded by hungry laborers, their dirt-stained hands reaching eagerly for the large hamper of food she'd brought them. There was cold chicken and ham, along with a selection of cheeses and crusty chunks of freshly baked bread. After leading Caroline to the shade of a tree well away from the others, Hugh dug into the food with the same enthusiasm as his men, his appetite sharper than it had been in days.

"I also brought some cool cider," Caroline told him, hands folded primly on her lap as she watched him eat. "I thought perhaps you and your tenants would want something other than Highland water to refresh yourselves."

Hugh glanced over to where his men were passing about a ceramic jug of whiskey. "Aye," he said, smiling as he took another bite of the delicious chicken. "I'm sure the cider won't go amiss, *leannan*. Thatching works up a powerful thirst in a man, especially on a day so hot as this."

He felt the touch of her gaze upon his chest, and resisted the urge not to preen. Instead he leaned back on his elbow, his legs crossed beneath his kilt as he lounged on the sweet grass, as smug as a pasha in a harem. He spoke casually of the work he was doing, drawing her into the conversation as he inquired after the tenants she had seen that morning.

"Mrs. Muir is feeling more the thing," she told him, brushing at a fly buzzing about her face. "The beef tea I brought her seems to be helping."

"That is good," he approved, his body stirring with desire as he studied her. He was certain she thought the straw bonnet and serviceable riding habit she wore were all that was modest, and wondered what she'd say if he told her they were having an opposite effect upon him. It had been over a week since they had lain together, and the sight of her made him ache with longing.

"Your aunt is to thank for suggesting the treatment," Caroline continued. "When I mentioned Mrs. Muir's symptoms to her, she said it sounded like a complaint of the liver, and told me to bring the tea and wine." She cast him a curious look. "You never told me your aunt was a wisewoman."

"The only thing my aunt is, is a royal pain in the arse," he grumbled, wondering what his chances were of talking her into riding off with him for another romp in the wildflowers. There was a meadow not far from where they were, and it was secluded enough to guarantee privacy while he made love to her.

Following lunch he dismissed his men for the day, declaring it too hot for work. He also dismissed William King, and as he and Caroline rode back toward the castle, he decided to have it out with her. Their foolish separation had gone on long enough, and it was time to put an end to it.

He turned to her, but before he could open his mouth she said, "What is that?"

Something in the question had him bringing Nathrach to a plunging halt. "What is what?" he demanded, his hand going to the sword he wore at his side and his eyes scanning the horizon for any sign of danger. He thought he detected movement just below the ridge on their right, but he couldn't be certain.

"There." She pointed a slender finger in the direction he'd already noted. "I thought I saw a flash of some—"

"Get behind me! Now!" Hugh shouted, kicking his mount in the ribs and trying desperately to interpose himself between her and the ridge. As if in a dream he saw Caroline turn, saw the questioning expression on her face as the crack of a musket shot split the air. He saw Caroline jerk, saw the reins falling from her hands as blood blossomed on her shoulder.

"Caroline! No!" The words were torn from his throat, and he urged his horse forward, his arms reaching out to catch her as she tumbled from her saddle.

"Oh, love, love, no, no, no," he said, unaware he was even speaking. More than anything he wanted to tenderly lay her on the ground and examine her wound, but they were still in the open and vulnerable to the unseen enemy who had fired upon them. Catching her against his chest, he wheeled Nathrach around and charged for the stand of pines, doing what he could to shelter Caroline with his own body.

The moment they reached the safety of the trees he half-leaped, half-fell out of the saddle, gently easing Caroline to the ground. The prim habit he so admired was already stained with her blood, and the pretty little hat was crushed and broken. He untied the ribbons with hands that were unsteady, his gaze never leaving the slow rise and fall of her chest as he laid the hat to one side.

"Hugh?" Caroline's eyes fluttered open, and she gazed up at him in dazed confusion. "Did I fall?"

"Yes, *annsachd*," he said, fearing that learning she'd been shot might prove too much for her. He tore a wide piece of cloth from the hem of her riding skirt and hastily fashioned a pad which he pressed to her shoulder. "Lie still now, my love, while I tend to your arm. I fear it may be sprained."

She winced slightly, but didn't cry out. "All right," she said, her bloodless lips lifting in a tired smile. "I've never fallen before. It hurts quite dreadfully. Hugh?"

The bleeding seemed to have stopped, and he tore another strip of cloth and used it as a bandage to help secure the pad. "Yes, my love, what is it?" he asked, his trained gaze scurrying over her as he searched for any other sign of injury.

"Don't frown," she said, raising her good hand to lightly touch his cheek. "You look so fierce when you frown." Then her hand dropped to the ground, and she fell into unconsciousness.

The ride home was a blur in Hugh's mind. He drove Nathrach brutally, his only thought to reach the safety of the castle as quickly as he could. Caroline's wound reopened during the rough journey, but she thankfully remained insensate, her head lolling against his shoulder. He rode the sweating horse into the great courtyard, shouting for help as he leaped down from the saddle. Servants came running from inside the house, Mairi hot on their heels. She skidded to a halt at the sight of Caroline clasped in his arms.

"Mother of God! What has happened?" she cried, stumbling back as Hugh brushed past her.

"Send for the doctor," he called out over his shoulder, taking the steps two at a time. "And then order every man in the glen armed and ready to ride within the hour. Send Lucien to the north meadow with a party of men, and order it secured until I arrive."

"But what happened?" Mairi picked up her skirts and dashed after him. "What is going on?"

He kicked open the door to their rooms, striding forward to carefully lay his wife on the soft bed. "Caroline was shot," he said, his voice raw with torment as he let himself touch her pale cheek. "Some black-hearted whoreson shot her, and when I lay hands upon him, he is a dead man."

"Oh, Hugh, no!" Mairi gasped, her hands fluttering to cover her mouth. "Who would do so vile a thing?"

"I don't know," he replied, stripping off his wife's riding gloves and tossing them onto the floor. He examined the nails on her injured arm, breathing a silent prayer of relief when he saw their pinkish color. Had they been blue, or worse still, white, it would not have boded well for her.

Aunt Egidia arrived, summoned by the shouts

of the servants. She took one look at Caroline and ruthlessly elbowed Hugh to one side. "We will take charge of your wife, Hugh MacColme," she said, sparing him a burning glare. "You rally the clan and find the *diahbol* who did this."

Reluctant as he was to leave Caroline, Hugh accepted the wisdom of his aunt's commands. He was a master at hunting down and destroying the enemy, and he could better serve his wife doing just that, instead of hovering like an old maid about her sickbed. He laid his hand on Aunt Egidia's arm, staying her.

"Send word," he ordered, holding her gaze. "If there's the smallest change send word, and I will ride directly home."

Egidia nodded. She seemed to know Hugh meant to notify him only if the change was for the worse. "I will send word." Then she astonished him by leaning forward to kiss his cheeks. "Go now," she told him gruffly, "and avenge your wife."

The men were mounted and waiting when he ran back downstairs. A new horse was saddled and waiting for him, and he led them away without saying a word. They reached the place where the ambush had occurred in a little under twenty minutes, but even after an extensive search, there was no sign of the intruder to be found.

"Whose land lies to the east?" Hugh asked, doing his best to tamp down his white-hot rage. He had to keep iron control on himself, else he feared he would descend into howling madness like a rabid dog. If he let himself think, he remembered watching Caroline get shot, so he kept his mind tightly focused on what was next to be done.

"That would be Ben Denham land now," a grizzled Highlander offered, scratching his badly scarred cheek. "The *meirleach* bought it last year when it came to auction."

Hugh swallowed the fury that threatened to choke him. He turned to three of his most trusted men. "Ride there," he ordered in a clipped voice. "Search hard, and if you find a man riding who has a musket, I want him brought here. Even if it's the laird himself," he stressed, meeting each man's gaze in turn, "I want him brought here."

After they rode off he divided the rest of the men into search parties, ordering them to fan out in ever-widening circles before doubling back. If the attacker had been a stranger and was still on MacColme land, they would have him within the hour. That done, he rode up to the site where he gauged the shot had come from, and dismounted to begin examining the ground with senses trained through almost fifteen years of combat.

"One rider," he determined, studying a set of hoofprints. "And he wasna riding a Highland pony. The hooves were shod."

Lucien followed him. "How can you tell that?" he asked, leaning forward to peer at the tracks. "I canna see a thing."

Hugh continued walking, his gaze never leaving the ground. "That is because you were never trained by an Indian guide, as was I," he said, noting that the tracks turned to the east.

"The man who shot my wife waited by that small tree for us to ride past. He dismounted to shoot; you can see his boot print there." He indicated a mark on the ground. "And after shooting Caroline he remounted and rode east . . . to Ben Denham land." He spoke the name with a savage ferocity that had Lucien studying him with marked concern.

"Hugh," he began cautiously, "I understand your anger, but I urge you to practice every restraint. A feud between the clans just now would play into the hands of the English, and that would do none of us any good."

Hugh turned his head to sear him with a glare. "Dunhelm shot my wife," he ground out, his hands clenching into fists. "What do you expect me to do? Kiss him for it?"

"Wait until you have proof," Lucien urged, his gloved hand closing over Hugh's wrist. "With that you can see him hang, but if you act without it, you'll only cause bad blood between our clans. Besides," he added with a frown, "what makes you so certain it was Dunhelm as did this?"

Hugh rubbed his hand across his eyes, trying to force himself to think with his mind instead of his heart. "We had words," he said, and told Lucien the details of Caroline's kidnapping. "That bastard Westhall was there," he concluded, his jaw tight as he remembered the earl's parting words. "He promised to stay well away from us, but that doesn't mean he didn't convince Dunhelm to do his foul work for him. Doubtlessly he got Dunhelm to do away with Caroline as a means of avenging himself."

"You sound convinced of that," Lucien said, watching him.

"I am," Hugh said grimly. "And when I get my hands on Dunhelm, I will convince him to admit as much." He gave the other man a smile that made him blanch. "Tracking the enemy isn't the only thing I learned from Sesquadech, Raghnall. Dunhelm is as soft as a girl, and I doubt he'll last long once I start on him."

"You'd *torture* him?" Lucien's eyes threatened to pop from his head.

"With the greatest of pleasure."

Lucien shuddered, then drew a deep breath before speaking. "Dinna you think you had best consider every other alternative first?" he asked carefully. "Dunhelm is too much a feardie to shoot at anyone. And try as I might, I canna see him having the wit and the patience to sit and wait for you and your wife to come wandering by. And what is his reason? What is his prize? He may well be kittled with you, but do you really think he would shoot an innocent woman to salvage his pride?"

Hugh's head was beginning to ache. He wished Lucien would cease his prattling; he was making him think, and he didn't want to think. He wanted to stain his hands with the blood of those who had dared harm his Caroline. He wanted them dead and burning in hell for hurting her so grievously, but how could he do any of these things if he couldn't find those who were to blame?

"It has to be Dunhelm, or that pig of an uncle of hers," he said wearily. "Who else had cause to harm her?"

Lucien's protracted silence drew Hugh's notice, and he raised his head to give the other man a wary glare. "Raghnall? Is there something you're nae telling me?"

Lucien fidgeted uncomfortably for several seconds before answering. "I've tried telling you the feeling ran hard against your English bride, but you wouldna hear of it," he said with visible reluctance. "I know you thought to bend the others to your will, but you of all people should know how strongly a Highlander would resent being led where he wouldna go."

For a moment Hugh feared he would be ill. He could feel the puke rising in his throat, and the sickly sweat dappling his forehead. "Are you saying one of my men, a man of my own clan, shot Caroline?" he asked, horrified to realize that Lucien's words made a dreadful sort of sense.

"I'm saying that before you lash Dunhelm to a burning stake you at least consider the possibility," Lucien replied with a surprising note of gentleness in his voice. "I know it must pain you to think so, Hugh, but I fear it is something you had best consider. I am sorry."

Hugh didn't answer, speech beyond his capabilities. Not even his father's denouncement had hurt him like this. This was a betrayal so vile, so stunning, he couldn't seem to find his way past it. A MacColme or one under their charge had lain in wait for them. He had raised his rifle, trained it on Caroline, and he had pulled the trigger. That he'd meant to kill her was obvious, for had she not turned just then, the bullet would have struck her full in the chest.

"Why?" He wasn't aware he had spoken until he heard the word leave his lips. He turned to Lucien, shaking so hard he feared he might fall. "In the name of God, Lucien, why?"

Lucien laid a comforting hand on Hugh's

shoulder. "As to that, I canna say. Perhaps he felt justified in what he did, or perhaps he was too filled with hate to care, but either way I dinna see that it matters. You must surely see that you no longer have the choice of letting your wife remain at Loch Haven. When she is recovered, you must send her away."

"Send her away?" Hugh echoed, gazing at Lucien in shock. "Why the devil should I do that?"

"Because if we are right, and 'tis a MacColme who is responsible for this, what is to keep him from trying again?" Lucien pointed out with deadly logic. "And next time, what is to keep him from succeeding? You must send her away, laird. It is the only way you can guarantee she will be truly safe."

She hurt. Caroline lay on her bed, her brow puckering as she moved her head restlessly on the pillow. She was also roasting, and she wondered why the maid had piled so many blankets on top of her. She tried to push them off, but the small movement sent agony shooting through her and she cried out in pain.

"Hush now, love," came Hugh's voice, and she felt the gentleness of his touch as a cool cloth was laid upon her forehead. "It's all right. You'll soon be fine, I give you my word on it. Shh."

The words were meant to reassure, she was certain, but they vexed her instead. She opened her eyes with a surprising amount of difficulty, and scowled up at him. "What rot," she said, her voice sounding as if she had a cold. "How can all be fine when I am near to burning from all these blankets? Get them off of me."

A slow smile lit his eyes. "So 'tis up to giving orders you are," he murmured, reaching out to touch her face. "I might have known 'twould take more than a musket ball to take the thorns from my English rose."

Caroline glared up at him, wondering if he'd been at the whiskey while she was resting. He certainly looked as if he'd been imbibing, she brooded, staring into his face and seeing the shadows beneath his light grey-green eyes, and the tired lines bracketing his full mouth. His jaw was heavily shadowed by stubble, and his hair hung in lank strands about cheeks that looked decidedly leaner than she remembered them being.

"What has happened to you, Hugh?" she asked, holding her hand out to him. "Have you been ill? Tell me truly, now."

To her horror a silver tear escaped his eyes to trickle down his face. "No, *mo cridhe*," he said in a voice that shook with emotion, " 'tis not me who has been ill, but you."

"Me?" she exclaimed, and then in a rush a confusing tangle of images unraveled in her mind. She could see herself riding back toward the castle with Hugh, and then she could see him shouting at her, warning her to get behind him. She could remember turning, and then she remembered the white-hot pain that tore through her, sending her into a black pool of darkness.

"Musket ball," she whispered, and then another image of an older man's face dripping with sweat filled her mind. She remembered the smell of blood, and the stomach-churning pain as he poked and prodded at her arm. *"Got it!"* she remembered him saying, a look of triumph on his face as he held up an ugly black piece of metal. *"Got the bastard!"*

"I was shot?" Her voice shook as she put the images together and reached the horrifying conclusion.

Hugh's face grew ashen. "Yesterday afternoon," he said, kneeling down to gently kiss her cheek. "We were riding back from the Browns' cottage, and were ambushed. I am sorry, love."

"S-sorry?" Caroline repeated, her eyes filling with tears. *The babe!* she thought, her heart rending in two. Oh, God in heaven, had she lost the babe?

"I should have had a better care of you," Hugh said, his voice filled with remorse. "I've been a soldier nearly half my life, and I led you straight into that ambush like a lamb to the slaughter. 'Tis my fault, and I am sorry, so sorry, dearest." His voice broke on the last word, and he buried his face against her neck, his grip desperate as he held her.

Caroline was unsure what to think. If she had lost the baby he would surely have said something, wouldn't he? She reached up to stroke his hair. That he had not filled her with cautious hope, but she wouldn't let herself rest until she knew for certain. She glanced up and saw Aunt Egidia hovering by the foot of the bed, and scraped up a weak smile.

"Is the doctor here?" she asked, wondering how she'd manage to have a private word with him.

"At this time of night? I should say not!" Aunt Egidia snapped, her lined face set with grim annoyance. "Besides, once the bullet was out we had nae use of him. I can tend a sickling better than some black-coated *sgoitiche* from Edinburgh."

"Dr. Stephenson is nae a quack, Aunt." Hugh raised his head to send his aunt a reproving frown. "He did as fine a job as I have seen getting the ball out." He glanced down at Caroline, and offered her a poor attempt at a smile. "You'll have a scar now, *leannan*, like mine. Do you mind?"

"No," she whispered, thinking that if a scar was the worst she got from this, she would thank God every day of her life.

"Wheest! Do the pair of you mean to go on blithering half the night?" Aunt Egidia grumbled, rudely elbowing Hugh to one side. "'Tis past midnight, and I would be seeing my bed before the cock's crow! Here, drink this now," she ordered, thrusting a glass strong with the smell of wine beneath Caroline's nose. "Hugh, lift the child's head for her. Do you expect me to do all?"

Hugh's hands were gentle as he carefully lifted her up, supporting her so she could accept the glass.

"What is in it?" she asked, sniffing the contents warily.

"Sweet red wine heated wi' spices and an egg whipped in it," Aunt Egidia snapped. "And 'twill do you no good to turn your nose up at it either, for drink it you will, if I must pour it down your throat. Now, stop this fussing and get on wi' it. I've no time to waste pampering you."

The grumbling complaint made Caroline

smile. "Yes, Aunt Egidia," she murmured, and dutifully did as she was bid. To her surprise the drink was quite delicious, and she needed no urging to finish the glass. When she was done Hugh lowered her back down on the pillow. She glanced slowly about her, taking in more of her surroundings as her senses returned.

"Where is Mairi?" she asked, noting the other girl's absence with some surprise. She would have thought nothing could have kept her sister-in-law from her side if she was truly ill.

"Asleep," Aunt Egidia said. "The poor lass was near to collapsing before I insisted she lay down. I tried sending this great lout off as well, but he is as stubborn as ever he was." She glared at Hugh with marked annoyance.

"I'll nae leave my wife," Hugh said simply, wrapping his fingers around her good hand. "You go to bed, Aunt, I'll sit with Caroline until she sleeps."

Aunt Egidia's great beak of a nose twitched with obvious displeasure that Hugh would defy her. "Well, if you're going to be a fool, Hugh MacColme, dinna be a bigger fool than you can help," she said tartly. "Climb into bed wi' the lassie; that way at least you might get a few hours' rest. But no loving, mind," she added with a shake of her gnarled finger. "You're nae the one of you in the shape for it."

After she'd gone there was an awkward silence, then Hugh gave a reluctant chuckle. "The army is mad for not admitting females to the ranks," he said, humor melting some of the bleakness from his eyes. "Can you imagine the general that one would have made?"

"She would have made Grandfather pale in comparison," Caroline agreed, her smile fading as she saw the fatigue that was stamped in Hugh's face. "But she does have the right of it, you know," she added, giving him a wifely frown. "You look exhausted. Come to bed, Hugh, before you collapse."

He studied her for a long moment. "Are you certain, my love? I fear I may do you some injury if I move wrong in the night."

"You won't hurt me if you lie on my good side," she said, patting the mattress beside her. When he still hesitated, she smiled sweetly. "I will sleep better if you are with me."

His lips twitched with reluctant humor. "You have been too long about Aunt Egidia, *annsachd*," he murmured. "You'll soon be as clever a conniver as she is."

"A truly terrifying thought," she said, smiling. Her eyes were beginning to grow heavy, and she strongly suspected the drink Aunt Egidia had pressed on her had been laced with something other than a whipped egg. Fighting the drug's effects, she lay quietly on the pillows, watching her husband disrobe with loving eyes.

To her surprise he donned a nightshirt before climbing into the bed, and when he settled carefully against her side she said, "This is the first time since our wedding night you've worn anything to bed. It seems rather strange."

He pressed a gentle kiss to her tousled curls. "Don't get used to it, sweeting. I'm only wearing it in case you take a turn in the night, and I need to fetch someone in a hurry. I would swoon from embarrassment did Aunt Egidia see me with naught a stitch to cover me."

The image brought a sleepy grin to her lips. "I daresay that would prove somewhat disaccomodating," she murmured, unable to keep her eyes open another moment. Hugh was stroking her hair, and the comforting warmth of his body next to hers acted as a soporific, lulling her into a gentle sleep.

When she awakened several hours later Hugh was still beside her, his face buried against her neck and his arm wrapped loosely about her waist. Her arm was beginning to throb most painfully, and she decided that must have been what awakened her. She wondered if she should rouse Hugh and ask him to fetch her some laudanum, but one glance at his face dissuaded her. *Poor darling*, she thought, her heart aching with love. She would wait a little bit longer, and if the arm continued paining her she would wake him then.

While Hugh slept on Caroline lay quietly beside him, trying to remember more details of what had happened. She had brief flashes of Mairi, tears in her beautiful green eyes, bending over her, and talking to someone she couldn't see. Other images, these of Hugh, his face hard as he spoke in low, furious tones about revenge, came next, and she wondered who he had been speaking to. Had they found the man who shot her? she wondered, and shivered at the thought. Her movement, small as it was, brought Hugh jerking up, and she saw the panic flare in his eyes as he came more fully awake.

"Caroline?" he said, his arm tightening about her waist. "What is it? Are you in pain?"

"No, I am fine, *leannan*," she lied, not wishing to alarm him. "My arm is a trifle sore, but it is not more than I can bear."

He levered himself up on one powerful arm and stared down into her face. "Are you certain?" he asked, his eyes filled with shadows as he studied her. "The doctor left some powders we were to give you when you awakened. Shall I fetch them?"

Caroline started to say yes, but then her stomach gave a sickening roll and she changed her mind. "No, that is all right," she said quickly. "If I am careful and do not move suddenly, it should soon settle down."

He studied her for several more seconds, his face working as if he was fighting back tears. She was about to ask him what was wrong when he reached out a shaking finger to lightly stroke her bandaged arm.

"I can't bear the thought of you in pain," he said, his voice raw with agony. "I would do anything, give anything, to take the hurt from you. I would die gladly, if it meant I could take the bullet instead of you."

"Hugh!" She gazed at him in horror. "You can't mean that!"

He gave her a tired smile. "Can I not?" he asked, then shook his head. "I was in the army near to fifteen years, and in that time I have seen a hundred men fall, a thousand. I thought witnessing such carnage had prepared me for any horrors I might see. But when I saw you jerk, when I saw the blood on you and realized you'd been shot, I knew I was prepared for nothing."

"But it wasn't your fault!" she said, tears in her own eyes as she realized how fully Hugh blamed himself for what happened. "How could you know someone would—would—" She could not continue.

"Would shoot you? Would cold-bloodedly try to kill you?" he finished for her, his lips twisting in a bitter sneer. "Aye, perhaps there is no way I could have *known* it, but I should have been expecting it, waiting for it, planning for it. I should have known better than to think your uncle would simply shrug his shoulders and walk away. I should have known that, but I didna. And because of that, you near died."

Although she also suspected her uncle's involvement in the attack, hearing it was a painful blow. "My uncle?" she asked, her voice quavering despite her best efforts to steady it. "He—he is the one who shot me?"

"We've no proof of that yet," he said cautiously, as if regretting his impetuous words. "But I suspect as much, or that he ordered it done, which is more likely. We traced the man who did the shooting as far as the old ruins on Ben Denham, and that could implicate Dunhelm. If he is involved, that implicates the earl as well."

Shock rendered Caroline speechless. She'd always known her uncle to be a cold, greedy monster capable of any number of vices—but murder? Could he truly order her death when it would avail him of nothing? If she died, Hugh would inherit her vast fortune, and it was certain to risk a scandal that could cost her uncle everything, his life included. Would he really have done such a thing? Then she thought of the odd way Hugh had phrased his reply, and cast him a confused look.

"You said *if*," she said slowly, trying to force her frozen brain to think. "Does this mean there is some doubt in your mind that Uncle Charles could be involved?"

He paused, then gave her an admiring look. "You are too sharp by half, dearest. Yes, there is a doubt, a small one, mind, but a doubt nonetheless. Still, I have written your grandfather to inform him of what happened and asking for his advice. When his answer arrives, I'll know better what is to be done."

She decided she didn't like either his words or the ominous tone in which they were spoken. "And what do you mean by that?" she asked, frowning at him in disapproval.

He reached out to twine one of her curls about his finger. He turned it to the light, studying the play of color in the soft sunlight streaming through the partially opened shutters. "He tried to kill you, *mo cridhe*," he said quietly, his eyes filled with cold rage as he met her gaze. "Do you truly think that knowing that, I will let him live?"

She considered that and realized she expected nothing less from a man as hard and single-minded as Hugh. "And if it was not my uncle, who is to blame?" she asked, curiosity spurring her on.

"Whoever did it is dead," came the calm reply. "I am MacColme of Loch Haven; no man attacks me or mine with impunity. Whoever did this, I will find him. If it takes one day or a thousand years, I will find him. And when I find him, I will kill him. I pledge this to you, my wife."

Chapter 17

❦❧

"Will you nae have some tea, Caroline?"
"Finish your sops and broth, and mind you eat every bite."

"*Annsachd*, are you cold? Do you need a shawl?"

To Caroline it seemed as if the entire world had entered into a conspiracy to coddle her into an early grave, and after a sennight of such unceasing devotion she decided she'd had enough. Her arm was a long way to being better, but if the fussing didn't stop, she feared she would go mad.

"Enough!" she exclaimed, glowering up at the three people hovering over her chaise. "Will you please stop fretting over me, and go away? I am fine, I tell you!"

Hugh, Mairi, and Aunt Egidia all drew back in stunned silence, the amazement on their faces such that Caroline was hard-pressed not to laugh. Indeed, she would have laughed, had she not feared they would take it for a sign of hysteria and send at once for the doctor. She'd escaped being bled so far, but it had been a very near thing.

"Leannan." Hugh was the first to recover, his expression tender as he bent over her. "Is your arm paining you? Shall I carry you back to our room so that you can rest?"

Her arm was still too sore for her to fold it across her chest, and so Caroline had to make do with her most intimidating stare. "I am not tired," she said, her voice crisp with annoyance. "And if I did need to go upstairs, I am more than capable of getting there under my own power, I assure you."

"Then what is it you want?" Mairi was next to venture closer, her face set with worry. "Tell us what it is, and we shall do it."

Caroline gave a heavy sigh, defeated as she often was by the burden of their obvious concern. It was hard to rage at people who wanted only to help one. She sighed again, searching for the proper words to send them on their way without giving offense. She was no closer to finding them when Aunt Egidia spoke.

"Ah, I ken, the lassie wants to be left alone," she said, nodding her head briskly. "Why dinna you say so sooner? There was nae a need to peck off our noses, you know."

As usual, the older woman's acerbic manner made Caroline smile. "I hadn't meant to peck them off," she replied wryly. "But only to nip hard enough to send you scurrying on your way."

"English humor," Aunt Egidia grumbled, albeit hiding a smile. "Well, come along, Mairi." She prodded the younger girl with her bony elbow. " 'Tis plain we are not welcome here. But dinna think this will get you out of your afternoon's rest," she added, casting a final glare at Caroline. "You'll lay down for two hours, or I'll know the reason why!"

"Yes, Aunt Egidia." Caroline was generous enough in victory to appear cowed. "I promise."

"Hmph!" Aunt Egidia gave an inelegant snort, and, still muttering, led a protesting Mairi away.

Hugh watched them go, a half-smile touching his mouth. Staring at it, Caroline realized she hadn't truly seen him smile since the day of the shooting, and she wondered if she would ever again see that sly grin of his that always set her blood aflame.

"So, *mo cridhe*, you've given us our marching orders, have you?" he said, reaching out to tenderly tuck a wayward strand of hair back beneath her cap.

"Aye, and so I have," she replied, imitating the husky brogue that was becoming more pronounced with each passing day. It seemed the longer they were in Scotland the more Scots he became, and she fell deeper in love with him because of it. Here was a man, she thought with wifely pride, smiling up at the deeply tanned face, surrounded by the soft waves of russet-colored hair. She had long since recovered from the scalding hurt she had felt at their foolish quarrel, and was anxious to spend what time she had with him loving him.

"Lass, if it's on my way you mean to send me, don't smile at me like that," he warned, his hand stealing down to give her waist a gentle squeeze.

She thrilled to his touch, for it was the first time he'd touched her in any way approaching an intimate manner since that dreadful day. She might not yet be ready for the pleasures of the marriage bed, but she ached for him to touch her as a man touches a woman.

"And what is wrong with my smile, sir?" she asked, leaning closer until the tips of her breasts were brushing against the front of his cambric shirt. His arm tightened and his eyes darkened with passion, but just as she was certain he would kiss her, he gently pushed her aside and rose to his feet.

"I must be away," he said, his voice suddenly as cool and brisk as the wind off the loch. "MacDouglass has come from Ardrossan to discuss clan matters with me, and I've kept him waiting longer than I should." He thrust a hand through his hair and cast her a brooding look. "Do you truly wish to be alone, Caroline?" he asked worriedly. "I cannot like the thought."

Caroline smarted from his rebuff, and it was several seconds before she could answer civilly. "I do wish a few minutes to myself, yes," she said, so frustrated and angry she felt like shrieking like a virago. She knew he was still upset by what had happened, and was understandably wary of making love with her, but she didn't see that meant he should treat her as if she had suddenly become a leper.

"What will you do?" he asked, still taking care to keep his distance from her.

"I don't know," Caroline replied petulantly. "Read, perhaps. Or go out into the gardens for some air. I haven't—"

"No!" he interrupted, his eyes glittering savagely. "You're nae to step a foot outside the great hall unless I or one of my chosen men is with you! Your word, Caroline, give it to me!"

Caroline raised her gaze to heaven in a mute plea for patience. His overprotective manner would be the death of her yet. "Very well," she grumbled, knowing she was behaving like a spoiled child, but not particularly caring. "I promise not to leave the hall without you or your men."

"See that you do," he said, and turned and stalked toward the door. When he reached it he paused, his fingers gripping the handle as he turned to send her an anguished look. "I came so close to losing you once because of my carelessness," he said, the familiar note of guilt darkening his voice, "I'll nae risk you again." And he opened the door and closed it quietly behind him.

After he'd gone Caroline lay back down on her chaise longue to brood over his odd behavior. Her temper cooled, and the more she considered it, the less sense it made. Why should he be so set against her going outside for a breath of air? She tucked her hand under her cheek and stared at the flames dancing in the hearth. And why should he be so adamant she have one of his hulking men-at-arms about at all times? Surely he couldn't suspect Uncle Charles would still be hanging about the area? She'd overheard two of the maids whispering, and knew Hugh and his men had conducted a thorough house-to-house search of the entire valley, but no sign of her uncle had been found.

Or perhaps it wasn't her uncle he feared, she thought, recalling their cryptic conversation on the day after she'd been wounded. She'd tried reopening the matter several times since then, but he either abruptly changed the subject or ignored her. She found such secretiveness decidedly vexing, but in the end she could not hold it against him. He was not the only one to keep secrets, she thought, laying her injured hand upon her stomach.

She was now certain she was indeed with child. The sickness that had plagued her before the shooting was back, and she found she wanted only to sleep. Thankfully these symptoms were accepted by Mairi and the attentive maids as being caused by her injuries, and no one seemed to think more of it. There were times when she'd catch Aunt Egidia watching her with a speculative gleam in her eyes, but as she didn't demand answers, Caroline didn't feel obliged to offer them.

Thinking of the babe made her think of the father, and she wondered yet again when and how she was to tell Hugh. She loved him quite desperately, but feared confessing the truth to him. She knew he had feelings for her, and before their argument she was even beginning to cautiously hope he might return her love, but now she didn't know. He blamed himself so completely for what happened, she knew he would do or say whatever it took to make amends. If he learned she was with child, she knew he would at once confess undying love if that was what it took to keep her at his side.

But she didn't want empty words inspired by duty and remorse, she realized bleakly. She wanted Hugh as deeply and passionately in love with her as she was with him, and that, she feared, was impossible. Hugh had entered into their marriage with the understanding it would be over in a year's time, and in all their weeks together he'd given no indication he wanted it any other way. He cared for her, desired her, but that was all. And when the time came when she could no longer hide her condition from him, she wondered if that would be enough to make her stay.

"Wheest, lad! Are ye gone deef as well as daft?" Padruig MacDouglass growled, his jet-black eyes glittering with outrage beneath his bushy red eyebrows. "I said I'll nae take the Dunhelm's side agin ye in this feud, and I mean it! If my oath 'tis nae enough for ye, then to the devil with ye!"

"And I tell you, MacDouglass, there is no feud. Not against Iain Dunhelm nor any man of Ben Denham," Hugh responded, doing his best to keep his temper in the face of rising frustration. He'd come into the keep to find MacDouglass and twenty of his men fairly bristling with weapons and the need to make use of them. News of the attack against Caroline had circulated amongst the clans, and now many were choosing sides and lining up for a war Hugh was frantically trying to avoid. Whatever his feelings about Dunhelm's involvement, he considered the matter a personal one, and was determined to avoid clan warfare at all cost. As Lucien had said, it would take but the hint of such a thing to bring the British army marching back into the Highlands.

"No feud, when the black-hearted bastard

shoots yer wee wife from ambush like the *clad-haire* that he is?" MacDouglass lumbered to his feet, his huge size dwarfing even Hugh. "Christ, man, where are yer balls? Have yer years wi' the English left ye nae more than a poor *segg*, with nothing a'tween yer legs?"

Hugh flushed a deep red, MacDouglass's crude barb striking perilously close to home. "If I believed without a doubt that Dunhelm had aught to do this, I would cut his head off and display it to all," he said, infusing the cold fury he felt into each word. "But I *do* have doubts, and that is why there will be no feud. You honor me with your loyalty, MacDouglass, and I thank you truly for it, but I will not be the one to break the peace between the clans. I'll not bring war to Loch Haven."

At first he thought his words in vain, but slowly the fire died in the huge Scot's eyes, and he lowered himself back onto his chair. "Ye're a different man from yer father," he said after a moment, folding his arms across his massive chest and eyeing Hugh with open speculation. "Douglas MacColme would bluster and rage, like me, and go off like a half-grown laddie with nae a thought to the consequences. But ye, ye're colder, I ken; more watchful-like, and sharp as the blade of a claymore." A wide grin split his bearded face. "I dinna think I would choose to ride against ye, laird. Ye would make a fearsome enemy."

"And I would hope, a better friend." Hugh rose to his feet to offer the other man his hand. "Thank you again, Padruig. It means much to me to know I have your support."

The laird of the MacDouglasses stood to his full height, his ham-sized fist giving Hugh a thump to the back that all but sent him sprawling. "Aye, that you have, MacColme," he roared. "Even though ye'll nae let me and my chieftains have our bit of fun and slay a few of those useless sots. They're Dunhelms, lad. 'Tis nae as if they'd be missed!"

When Hugh had recovered from the friendly blow he offered MacDouglass and his men some whiskey to ease their parched throats, an offer they welcomed with the same enthusiasm as they would have welcomed a war. Hugh escorted his guests to the great hall, making certain they had all that they required before excusing himself. Clan custom required he stay to drink with his guests, but he disliked the idea of leaving Caroline alone for very long. And, he admitted with a self-deprecating grin, because he much doubted he could keep pace with the amazing quantities of whiskey being drunk. He hadn't the head or the stomach for such excesses.

He checked to make certain there would be beds for all who drank themselves into stupors, and then quietly slipped away. He was walking up the stairs to return to his room when he heard his name called, and turned to see Lucien Raghnall standing there.

"A moment of your time, MacColme, if I may," he said, his expression somber. "I have news for you."

Hugh tensed, a cold feeling of dread settling into the pit of his stomach. He'd assigned Lucien the sensitive task of finding proof if a member of his own clan had shot Caroline, and from the looks of him, 'twould seem he had found it.

"In my study," he said, his blood turning to ice as he silently led the way into the back part of the castle. *Don't let it be true*, he thought, schooling his own face to show nothing of his raw emotions. *Dear God, don't let it be true.*

Once they were inside the study, Hugh did a quick search of the small anteroom adjacent to the study to make sure they were truly alone, and only when he was certain did he turn back to Lucien. "Tell me what you have found," he said, steeling himself.

But instead of answering, Lucien leaned back in his chair. "I see you've convinced Mac-Douglass there's nae a fight to be had, and still he's happy," he said, his eyes looking anywhere but at Hugh. "You're to be congratulated, laird. I dinna think it possible to placate that great bear once he'd caught a whiff of blood."

But Hugh would not be diverted. He sensed the other man was stalling, and it only added to the pain he was feeling. "Lucien," he ground out between clenched teeth, "tell me."

Lucien looked at him then, and the pity that he saw there gave Hugh the answer he had been fearing . . . and expecting.

"There's a young crofter, name of Labhruinn," he began carefully. "He's nae a MacColme, although his mother has claims upon the clan. He came to Loch Haven about two years ago, and a surly, disagreeable sort he has been from the first. He hates the English most especially, and I have myself heard him saying some unflattering things about your wife."

Hugh's hands clenched into fists. "And you

didna think to tell me of this?" he demanded furiously. "Even when I most specifically charged you to do so?"

"Hugh, you must believe me—had I thought for even one moment that he posed a true danger to you or your wife, I would ha' told you at once! But I took him for naught but a drunkard and a fool, a *bragoil* who too well liked the sound of his own mewling. I never paid the slightest mind to his threats and his mutterings, but now I wish I had."

Now that he had a name to go with the hate building inside him, Hugh could let himself relax. "Where is Labhruinn now?" he asked, his voice utterly calm, utterly devoid of the smallest inflection of humanity. In his mind's eye he was already at the crofter's rough hut; already killing him.

"That is what convinced me of his guilt," Lucien said with visible regret. "The lad's gone."

"Gone?" Hugh scarcely recognized the sound of his own voice.

"Him and his musket, both gone, and none have seen him in near to a fortnight," Lucien admitted, eyeing Hugh nervously. "I dinna remark on it at first because the lad's taken himself off half a dozen times before, and always he has returned. But this time it is different, for 'tis not just his musket he took, but all his clothes and every scrap of money his poor mother had as well. She said he spoke of going to Glasgow, but who can tell?"

Hugh couldn't believe it at first. The vengeance he had hungered for, lived for all these endless days, was for naught. If Labhruinn had indeed taken himself to Glasgow all those days ago, then the chances of his still being there were all but nonexistent. Glasgow welcomed ships from every corner of the globe, and he could be anywhere, anywhere in the world, safely away from Loch Haven and his reach.

"God damn you for a useless fool!" he roared, shaking with the strength of his fury. "Why did you nae tell me of him sooner? You let him get away! The stinking bastard shoots my wife, and you let him get away! You cursed whoreson! I could kill you for this!"

Lucien rose at Hugh's words. "Then kill me, laird, if 'twill make you feel better," he said quietly, meeting Hugh's molten glare with cool equanimity. "Curse me, strike me, if that is your pleasure. For whatever you do to me, 'tis no less than I would do to myself for failing you. I am most heartily sorry."

His soft words defeated Hugh, leaving him even more at a loss. He whirled away, turning to stalk the narrow confines of the room. So many emotions rioted inside of him, he thought he would surely go mad from the cacophony. The only thought to emerge clearly from the chaos was that he had failed Caroline. He had failed to protect her, and now he had failed to find the man who had wounded her so grievously. The bitterness of that knowledge all but broke his pride, and his heart.

He loved her, he thought, amazed he hadn't realized the truth of that until just this very minute. He loved her, and he had failed her.

"No, Lucien," he said heavily, turning to face the other man with as much dignity as he could muster. "Once more, 'tis I who must apologize to you. I am bitter disappointed I couldna avenge myself on Labhruinn, but the fault is more mine than 'tis yours. Will you forgive me for my temper and my words?"

Lucien gaped at him before replying. "Aye, Hugh, of course!" he said, his cheeks growing as pink as a schoolboy's. "But as I said, I blame myself for nae telling you sooner of my suspicions. If I had, mayhap we would have caught the *bleek*."

"And mayhap we would have not," said Hugh, painfully accepting the truth of the matter. "Do something for me, Raghnall, if you would."

"Anything, laird."

"Send a man . . . no, two men to Glasgow, and have them make inquires to see if any trace of Labhruinn is to be found. Have them check all ships that have set sail in the past two weeks, and order them to report back to me the smallest scrap of information they find."

"Aye." Lucien nodded eagerly. "Will there be anything else?"

Hugh thought a long moment. "You said he took all his mother's money when he left," he said in a heavy voice. "Have my steward check on her. Be certain she doesna lack for anything. I willna have her suffer for the sins of her son."

Lucien looked much-struck by his generosity. "I will see to it at once," he vowed. "And if you dinna mind my saying it, 'tis a rare kindness you are showing. You are a good laird, Hugh."

"Am I?" Hugh asked, his shame all but choking him. "I am glad you think so, Raghnall, for God knows, I do not."

By late the next evening, Caroline felt well enough to insist she be allowed to take her dinner in the dining hall with the rest of the family. Hugh protested at first, citing her poor health and delicate constitution, but when she persisted he finally acquiesced. With provisos, of course.

"Really, Hugh, you need not carry me down the stairs, you know," she scolded, wrapping her arms about his neck. "It was my arm that was injured, not my leg."

"Hush, wife, and mind your wicked tongue," he ordered, his stern tone belied by the twinkle in his eyes. "I am your husband, and 'tis my right to carry you when and where I will."

Caroline pretended to pout, even as she secretly thrilled to the commanding words. For reasons she couldn't fathom, her hunger for her husband was reaching decidedly unladylike proportions, and she feared that did he not make love to her soon, she would attack him in his sleep. In fact, she mused, her lips curving thoughtfully, that sounded like a most interesting idea. Hugh gave a sudden groan, and her lascivious thoughts were instantly forgotten.

"What is it?" she demanded, horrified to see he had clenched his jaw, and that sweat was beading his brow. "I'm too heavy, aren't I?" she cried, aware of the weight she had gained, despite her injury. "Put me down, Hugh, before you harm yourself!"

Instead of being touched by her solicitousness,

he seemed to take it greatly amiss. "Will you stop wiggling, blast it!" he roared at her, his grip tightening about her. "You'll overset me, and then we'll both end up on our arses!"

Mindful of anything that might bring harm to the babe, Caroline stilled at once, although it was hard. *Impossible brute*, she thought, the pout on her lips now genuine. He was becoming entirely too masterful for her liking.

She was pleased and more than a little relieved to find they would be dining *en famille* tonight. Although she had kept to her rooms last night as befit an invalid, she was well aware of the company they had. Indeed, she would have to have been deaf to have missed the wail of the pipes and the general sounds of merriment coming from the great hall. 'Twas the Mac-Douglasses, a giggling maid had informed her proudly. And there was nothing a MacDouglass liked better than to make merry and make music. She'd met the laird of the MacDouglass this morning when, at his insistence, Hugh presented the behemoth to her. She'd been torn between astonishment and laughter when the huge gentleman, with his great mane and beard of flaming red hair, had bowed over her hand with all the grace of a courtier, pronouncing himself her most ardent protector. He was charming indeed, and she was heartily grateful to be shed of him.

Dinner was pleasant, and if Mairi and Aunt Egidia did tend to watch her like two broody hens fighting over a lone chick, at least they did not nag her to death. Hugh alternated between attentive care and blank disinterest, spending much of the evening scowling off into space. At the end of the meal they retired to the music room, where Mairi played the pianoforte Hugh had had shipped from Edinburgh as a surprise for his sister. The music was lovely and soothing, and to Caroline's everlasting embarrassment, it soon had her nodding over her sherry.

"Hugh, you thoughtless brute!" Aunt Egidia was quick to notice her sleepiness, and quicker still to blame Hugh for it. "What can you be thinking to keep the poor lassie up all hours, when she is fresh from the sickbed? Take her up at once before she falls asleep where she sits!"

"I'm all right, Aunt Egidia," Caroline protested, then spoiled the words by giving a huge yawn. The older woman turned upon her with a fiery scowl.

"And there will be no more impertinence from you this night, young lady," she said, shaking an admonishing finger at Caroline. "If I say you're tired, than tired you are, and I'll nae hear another word about it! Off with you now!"

Bowing to the voice of authority, Caroline allowed Hugh to escort her from the room, and once more he swept her into his arms and began carrying her up the stairs.

"I really wish you would not do this, Hugh," she reproved, although she was careful to remain perfectly still. "I have eaten so much these past several days that I feel quite the pig. I am afraid I am too heavy for you."

"Nonsense, *annsachd*," he assured her, pressing a tender kiss to her forehead. "You scarce weigh more than a puff of air. 'Tis no strain to carry you, I promise you."

She let herself be mollified, for truth to tell, she

rather enjoyed being carried so in her husband's arms. A scheme had come to her over dinner, and she was most anxious for them to reach the bedroom so that she could set it into action. It had been too long since she'd known the shattering ecstasy of Hugh's lovemaking, and she was ready to put an end to the drought. All she needed was to wait for the right moment.

The embers in the fireplace cast a reddish-gold glow, providing more than enough light as Hugh elbowed opened the door and carried her inside. The bed could be clearly seen, the bedclothes already turned down and waiting for them. She waited, biding her time until Hugh leaned forward to set her down, and then she gave a hard tug.

"What the—!" she heard him exclaim, and then he tumbled down on the bed beside her.

"Caroline!" he scolded, glaring down at her with a mixture of irritation and concern. "Mind what you're doing! I might have landed on you and hurt your poor arm!"

"My poor arm is fine, you thickheaded oaf!" she told him, and to prove her point she gave another tug, this time bringing his mouth down to hers. She kissed him with all the love she took such pains to hide, and with the blazing passion that threatened to consume her alive. She loved Hugh, she desired him, and if it was the last thing she did this night, she was determined to have him. She opened her lips, teasing his tongue with hers in a way which never failed to drive him wild.

"Caroline, *annsachd*," he groaned, his body

hardening with desire. "Dearest, we cannot. You are yet hurting . . ."

"Yes," she said, fear she would fail driving her to greater acts of boldness. "I hurt. I hurt here . . ." She took his hand and placed it upon her aching breast. "And here . . ." She lifted her hips until her femininity was cradling his hard male flesh. "Make the ache stop, *leannan*, else I fear I shall die from the pain!"

Whether it was the sound of his language on her tongue or the insistence of her caresses, Hugh ceased his protestations. He leaped from the bed and began tearing off his clothes, with little care for their cost or condition. When he was splendidly nude he returned to the bed, and Caroline trembled with excitement at what she knew would come next. But instead of falling on her and loving her with the ferocity she was expecting, he turned as coy as a young lad faced with his first maiden, taking his own time as he removed each item of her clothing piece by piece.

"A silly piece of frippery," he announced, tossing her corset onto the floor. "An Englishman must have designed this," he declared of her stiffened petticoats, before removing them one by one. Finally, when she was as naked as he, he leaned back to enjoy the fruits of his handiwork.

"Mayhap you *are* gaining the smallest bit of weight," he decided, reaching out to stroke her breasts, noticeably fuller now than they had been even weeks before.

"Beast!" She slapped his hands, feigning indignation lest he guess the truth. "That was most ungentlemanly!"

He raised an eyebrow in mock reproof. "Did I

say I was complaining?" he asked, his fingers teasing the pouting nipples to hard points. "You're very beautiful, love. And these are like ripe strawberries, begging to be plucked." He gave them a gentle pinch that had her biting back a moan of pleasure. "I've always had a weakness for the fruit," he said, and dipped his head to gently tug one of the nipples into his mouth. The hot suction of his mouth was all it took to drive Caroline over the edge. She clung to him, sobbing her joy and arching against him with helpless abandon. When he entered her she peaked a second time, calling out his name as he made love to her with a fierce passion that more than equaled her own. The third climax was beckoning when he began thrusting harder and deeper, joining her in shimmering wonder as release shuddered through both of them.

It was the rattle of dishes and the loud whispering of the maids that awoke Caroline late the next morning. She opened her eyes to see one of the maids holding up one of her discarded stockings and giggling. She gave judicious thought to closing her eyes and feigning sleep until the servants left, when she suddenly became aware she was alone in the bed.

"Hugh?" His name left her lips without her being aware of it, and she raised her head to glance around the room.

"Oh, he's been up and gone for hours, my lady," the bolder of the two maids offered, bustling forward to smile at Caroline. "An English nobleman, a duke, has arrived all the way from

Bath, and the laird did go down to bid him welcome."

The news brought Caroline bolting upright in bed, the bedclothes clutched protectively in front of her. "Grandfather is here?" she exclaimed, delighted at the prospect of seeing him after all these weeks. "Why was I not told?"

"The laird said you were nae to be disturbed," the second maid said, clearly not willing to be left out of the conversation. "But he did leave word to join him and the duke in his study once you had awakened and had breakfast."

The mention of breakfast made her always-uncertain stomach twist, and Caroline decided to forgo her morning meal until later. Besides, she didn't want to wait another moment to go and greet her dearest grandfather.

She rushed her maid through her morning ablutions, fidgeting with mounting impatience. A small skirmish ensued when she refused to let her stays be completely laced, but she was able to overcome the maid's fashionable sensibilities by explaining she was still hurting from the wound. She knew that the truth would be obvious in a few weeks, but until then she was determined to keep the matter secret. The moment the maid pronounced herself satisfied, Caroline bolted from the room and ran down the steps to find Hugh.

She was about to start down the long corridor leading to the study when she remembered the shortcut Hugh had shown her their first few days in the castle. It led through a confusing array of rooms and ended in a small anteroom on the other side of his study, and on impulse she decided to take that route. Not only would it save considerable time, but it would allow her to pop in on her grandfather and Hugh by surprise, an idea she found childishly pleasing.

The rumble of male voices greeted her when she walked into the anteroom, and she was about to open the door when she heard her grandfather say, "Charles has ever been a liar and a coward, but he's not foolish enough to lie to me when I am threatening to disinherit him. He swears by all that is holy he had naught to do with the attack on Caroline, and damned if I don't believe him. Besides, he was in London when it happened."

"Men like your son, General, dinna sully their hands directly with something so base as murder," Hugh's voice was filled with icy disgust. "But as it happens, I have cause to believe in his innocence. For the moment . . . at least."

Caroline hesitated. Loath as she was to eavesdrop, this was her first chance to learn the full truth of what had happened on the day she was shot. Hugh refused to even mention the matter to her, and she strongly suspected he had instructed everyone else in the household to be equally as tight-lipped. This might be the only opportunity she would have to learn something of import. Her curiosity battled her conscience, and her conscience promptly lost. She leaned closer to better hear what was being said.

"It sounds interesting, Sergeant Major, and I shall certainly expect a full report before Captain Dupres joins us. But in the meanwhile, tell me how our other little mission is coming along. Is everything proceeding accordingly?"

Chapter 18

"**S**ergeant?" General Burroughs was scowling at Hugh with marked impatience. "Did you not hear what I asked? I asked—"

"I heard you, General," Hugh replied, the familiar taste of betrayal and dishonesty foul in his mouth. Since the first time he'd made love with Caroline, not a day went by but he didn't bitterly regret the offer the general had made at the Gilmore's ball. Telling himself he'd had no other recourse did little to remove the taste, nor did the knowledge that when he made love to Caroline, his agreement with her grandfather was the farthest thing from his mind. He loved Caroline passionately, endlessly, in ways that had nothing to do with bargains or agreements, and he felt as if he had betrayed her in the cruelest way there was.

"Well?" The general was all but hopping up and down on his chair like a lad waiting for school to be out. "Tell me! Is my granddaughter breeding, or is she not? It's one or the other."

"I don't know," Hugh blurted out, deciding that was close enough to the truth to suffice. "After the doctor had removed the bullet I asked him about the possibility of a babe, but he said he couldn't be certain. I know I was hoping she was not," he added, remembering how pale and still she'd been on the long ride back to the castle. "I feared a babe would be too much for her after . . . after what had happened."

The general frowned, his blue eyes growing grim. "Aye, there is that," he muttered, looking troubled. "And I know you to be too much a gentleman to importune her while she is recovering. Ah, well, mayhap in a month or two. Only mind you do not dally overly long," he warned with a waggling finger. "I've not a great deal of time left, you know."

Another person he had failed, Hugh thought bleakly. It would seem he had made a sad job of things since returning to Scotland. He was also glad the general could not read minds, else he would know that he'd done a great deal more than importune Caroline last night. She might have initiated their lovemaking—a boldness which, if he thought about it, would have him grinning like a moonling—but he had been the one who'd been without a shred of control. Even when she'd lain weak and exhausted in his arms, he kept touching her and kissing her, offering his love to her in the only way he dared.

". . . would be the sensible thing to do, eh, MacColme?" the general concluded, gazing at Hugh impatiently.

Hugh flushed slightly, embarrassed at having been caught paying such poor attention. "My apologies to you, General," he said, shifting uncomfortably on his chair. "I fear I was not attending. What did you say?"

The general peered at him reprovingly. "Civilian life has made you weak, Sergeant," he reproved. "You used to pay far better notice at our briefings."

Hugh's flush deepened. "I am sorry, sir."

"Never mind, lad, I shall overlook it this time. What I said was that what was needed here was a board of inquiry, such as we hold in the army. No better way to learn the truth of what occurred, and ferret out the guilty party. I will help you."

"That is all right, General Burroughs," Hugh said, although he thought the suggestion a good one. "As it happens, I already have a good idea as to the guilty party's identity. Unfortunately I fear he has already left the country."

"The devil you say!" the general exclaimed, incensed. "And who let him get away, I should like to know? I cannot imagine you being so derelict in your duty as that."

Hugh didn't know how to answer that, for he greatly feared he *was* to blame. Had he paid more mind . . . His head snapped up as he caught the sound of the door to the anteroom being closed. He shot out from around his desk, his dirk in his hand as he rushed toward the door. The general also leaped to his feet with surprising nimbleness, considering his advanced age and poor health. A deadly-looking pistol was in his hand, making it plain the older man was still every inch the seasoned campaigner.

Hugh motioned him to one side, carefully wrapping his fingers around the door's handle and gently easing it open. His field of vision encompassed most of the small room, and when he saw it was empty he eased further into the room, his eyes scanning for any sign of an intruder. There was nothing.

"What is it?" General Burroughs asked, peering around as well. "Enemy spies, do you think?"

"Perhaps." Hugh kept his dirk at the ready as he moved on to explore the withdrawing chamber next to the anteroom, only to find it empty as well. "And perhaps I was only imagining things."

The general gave a loud sniff and pocketed his pistol. "Never known you to be the imaginative sort," he said, his expression glum. "Always did have ears as sharp as a hound. Well, what's next? You'll be posting sentries, I'll warrant?"

Hugh nodded, thinking it a wise precaution, and one he obviously should have employed before now. He tried to think if either the general or himself had said anything of a sensitive nature regarding the attack, and breathed a sigh of relief when he realized they had not. He was about to suggest they return to the study when he suddenly froze in horror.

What if whoever had been lurking in the anteroom had heard the general's remarks about Caroline? he thought, an icy feeling of sickness settling in his stomach. On the surface it didn't seem so incriminating, but dear God! The damage it could do should Caroline ever hear of it!

"MacColme?" The older man was regarding him with anxiety. "I say, lad, are you all right? You look dashed queer, if you don't mind my saying so. Is there something you're not telling me?" he added with a suspicious scowl.

"What?" Hugh stared at him blankly for a brief moment, and then gave himself a mental shake. "No, sir," he said, taking a firm control of his wild emotions. "I was but wondering if Caroline was awake. I know she will be delighted to see you."

"As I will be happy to see her," General Burroughs said, a fond smile softening his features. "But it's doubtless best to let her rest. Gunshots can be the very devil to recover from, you know. I recall back in sixty-three when I was fighting my way out of an Iroquois ambush . . ." And he went on reminiscing about one of the bloodier battles of his illustrious career.

I am inquiring if you have kept your end of our bargain. Is Caroline with child as yet?

Her grandfather's words echoed in Caroline's mind with the cruelness of a lash. For as long as she lived, she knew she would never forget the horror of hearing the casual words that had shattered her world beyond any hope of repair. How she got out of the anteroom without being violently ill, she knew not. As it was, she barely reached the safety of her own room before grabbing the slop jar and disgracing herself thoroughly.

The maids rushed to her side at once, hurrying her back into the bed they had just made. While one helped her out of her clothing, the other offered to send for her husband, but she refused so vociferously they quickly withdrew, leaving her in blessed peace. The moment she knew herself to be alone she gave in to tears, weeping so hard she was sick a second time. When it was over, she collapsed against her pillows, too weary to think.

Under such circumstances she would have thought sleep to be an impossibility, but she hadn't reckoned with the demands of her ripening body. When she next awoke, her first thought was that it had all been a dream—a hope that quickly died when she opened her eyes to find her grandfather sitting beside her bed.

"Well, good afternoon, poppet," he greeted her with an indulgent smile. " 'Tis about time you have decided to honor us with your presence. It's gone past noon, you know."

"Grandfather?" Surprise seemed the safest emotion to feign, and so she allowed herself to act startled to see him. "What are you doing here?"

"And where else would I be, after MacColme informed me of what happened?" he chided, a puzzled look stealing into his eyes. "What is it, child? Aren't you pleased to see your grandpapa?"

She managed an edgy smile. "Of course I am," she lied, and knowing there was no hope for it, sat up and gave him a hasty embrace. "I'm sorry," she said, withdrawing as quickly as she could. "I fear I overdid things yesterday, and am paying the price for it today. I only ask that you not confess as much to my husband," she added with a credible chuckle. "He will only lord it over me for having been proved right."

"Ah, like that, is it?" he replied, giving her

hand a paternal pat. "Never fear, dearest. I am an old hand at keeping mum. Your secret is safe with me, I promise you."

Caroline listened in silence to her grandfather's chattering, resentment and fury rising like bile in her. She want to scream and rage, to lash out at Hugh and her grandfather and make them hurt as much as they had hurt her. Instead she merely smiled and nodded, her expression growing warmer even as her heart iced over with bitterness.

"But listen to me rattling on when you are looking so pale and tired," her grandfather concluded, rising to his feet. "You ought to have sent me packing, my dear, with a boot to my rear."

"Oh, no, Grandfather," she said, grimly pleased with her newfound ability to smile and lie at the same time. "I was enjoying listening to you talk. I have missed you."

"And I you, little one." He bent to deposit a quick kiss on her cheek. "But I am still making myself scarce before that fierce Scot you married comes in here and whacks off my head for keeping you from your rest. He is very worried about you, you know," he added. "When he heard you had taken to your bed he was all for sending for the physician at once, but that sour-faced aunt of his said there was naught wrong with you sleep couldna cure." His credible imitation of Aunt Egidia won a genuine chuckle from her.

"Where is Hugh now?" she asked, praying she wouldn't have to face him just yet. She needed time to harden her heart against him, and feared she might burst into tears at the sight of him.

"Riding off to visit one of his tenants, I believe he said. A friend of his father who has only just returned from the north. He offered to let me accompany him, but truth to tell, I am feeling the smallest bit fagged myself, and believe I shall have a bit of a lie-down. My heart is not what it used to be, I fear," he admitted, sighing as he patted his chest.

Caroline felt a sharp stab of concern, but she ruthlessly cut off the errant emotion. "Perhaps that might be wisest, sir," she said, contriving to look worried. "I wouldn't wish you to become overly tired."

"I am sure I shall be fine after a few hours' rest," he assured her. "Which reminds me, shall we be seeing you for dinner?"

The thought of eating food with the two men who had so viciously betrayed her made Caroline fear she would disgrace herself yet again, but she choked it down. "We shall see," she prevaricated, a daring plan beginning to form in her mind. "I believe I shall rest just a little bit longer. That way perhaps I shall feel more up to joining in the festivities."

"A wise plan," he approved with a nod. "Shall I leave word you are not to be disturbed? That way you can sleep secure in the knowledge no one else will wander in to chatter at you."

"What an excellent notion, Grandfather!" she said, beaming at him in unaffected delight. "I would appreciate that very much."

"Consider it done," he said, patting her hand one final time before taking his leave, closing the door firmly behind him.

The moment she was certain she was alone

Caroline rose and cautiously made her way to the washstand to wash her face and hands. She needed to think, and she would do a better job of it when she was feeling fully alert. After she had restored her appearance to some semblance of order she began pacing, seeking refuge from her pain in plotting how best to get away from the castle without being discovered.

The plan had actually come to her while she was standing in the anteroom, listening to the destruction of the fragile world she had built for herself. Running away was a solution that was vastly appealing, but because of the shooting, it was a solution she rejected out of hand. Had it just been herself she might have been willing to take the risk, but she had another life depending on her now, and there was no way she would risk her babe to an assassin's bullet.

But there was no assassin now, she thought, remembering Hugh's words. The man he believed responsible wasn't even in Scotland any longer, and if her uncle was innocent of attempting to hurt her as her grandfather insisted, then it meant the danger to her had passed. She was free to leave without fear of another ambush, and after a moment's hesitation that was precisely what she decided she would do.

Fleeing from her uncle's had given her experience in how such things were done, and she began packing with ruthless efficiency. Using the cloth valise she'd seen on top of the wardrobe, she packed only one change of clothing, deciding she could purchase whatever she needed once she reached Edinburgh. With that thought in mind she hurried over to the safe

Hugh had shown her hidden in the wall, and removed large piles of banknotes and several pieces of jewelry. She had no idea how long it might be necessary for her to hide, and she wanted to make certain neither she nor the baby would lack for anything.

Once that was done she dressed quickly, donning one of her oldest and plainest gowns, and covering all with the plaid wool cloak Mairi had woven for her. The MacColme plaid, she thought, treacherous tears burning her eyes at the sight of the gray and lavender stripes. She blinked them back, and tightened the cloak about her. She would buy another when she reached Edinburgh.

Finding a way to sneak from the house proved more daunting than she feared, for there seemed to be men everywhere. She was chewing her lip and weighing her options when she heard the sound of a footstep behind her. She whirled around and found herself facing Lucien Raghnall.

"Good day to you, Lady Caroline," he said, his gaze going to the valise in her hands. "Are you going on a journey?"

Caroline shifted her valise from one hand to another, trying to think of some plausible tale to spin, but her imaginative powers seemed to have deserted her. She was no closer to finding an answer when he asked, "Do you need a ride into the village, perhaps? If so, I should be happy to offer you one."

"Yes! The very thing!" she cried, scarcely able to believe her luck. "Something has arisen which requires my immediate return to Edinburgh. I should be most grateful for your help," she added, lowering herself to flutter her lashes at him like a coquette.

He stared at her for several seconds before responding. "Aye," he said at last, an odd look on his face. "I suppose as a loyal friend to your husband, the least I might do is see his wife safely from Loch Haven. Aye," he said again, and gave her a dazzling smile. "Very well, my lady, if that is your wish. 'Twill be my pleasure to be your escort. Shall we go?"

"Keir Labhruinn shot yer wife?" James Callamby spat out the sip of ale he had just taken, his blue eyes wide with shock. "Christ, man, is it sheep *cacc* ye have for brains? However can ye believe such nonsense?"

Hugh frowned at his father's old adviser's reaction. He'd expected shock, aye, but shock over the deed, not over the perpetrator's identity. And Callamby wasn't shocked, he realized in mounting confusion; he looked as if he considered it a rare joke. "I have it on good authority he was heard speaking ill of my wife," he said, wondering what the devil was going on. "He disappeared a day or two before Caroline was shot, and his musket went missing with him as well," he added grimly, lest James fail to take in the significance of his words.

"Aye, in times like this who doesna travel wi'out a flintlock at his side?" Callamby said, and then shook his head. "For all the good it would do Labhruinn. The lad is accounted the worst shot in the whole of the glen. He couldna hit the walls of the castle was he standing four feet from them. And as to his going missing, so he did, wi' Flora MacGregor's father hot on his heels. It seems the father to her bairn was a good sight closer than the loch," he added with a knowing wink.

Hugh raised a shaking hand to his head, trying to make sense of the thoughts rioting in his heads. "But Lucien told me it was Labhruinn," he said, a terrifying suspicion making him sweat. "He told me the lad hated my wife . . ."

"Raghnall." Callamby gave a contemptuous snort. "He's the one to harden the people's hearts agin yer wife. I warned him more than once to mind his viper's tongue. I remarked it odd, I remember, for he seemed to think so well of you. And your wife is so sweet and lovely, who couldna love her, even if she is English," he added with an apologetic shrug.

Hugh sat in silence, so many things he had seen but not understood now becoming appallingly clear. When Lucien had joined the search on the day of the shooting, the alarm had scarcely been sounded, but he was already armed, a musket cradled in his arms, Hugh remembered, swallowing a ball of nausea.

"That son of a bitch!" He shot to his feet, his face set with rage. "It was him! It was him all along!"

"Raghnall?" James echoed, and then a resigned expression settled on his face. "Aye," he said, sounding every one of his sixty-plus years. "Aye, it makes sense. It makes a terrible sense." He studied Hugh grimly. "I'll ride wi' ye," he said, pushing to his feet to stand beside him. "Ye'll need a witness to the duel to swear ye dinna kill him in cold blood."

They started toward the front door of Callamby's modest home when it flew open and Mairi dashed in, her hair in wild disorder about her face. "Hugh, Caroline is gone!"

The room dipped and swayed so alarmingly, Hugh feared he would swoon. He grabbed Mairi's arm, holding tightly and blinking his eyes until his graying vision cleared. "What do you mean, gone?" he asked, clinging to what remained of his control with an uncertain grip. "She is missing, do you mean?"

In answer Mairi nodded her head, her eyes brimming with tears. "I would never have believed it had I not seen it with my own eyes," she said, swiping at her cheeks with unsteady hands. " 'Tis Lucien, Hugh," she whispered brokenly. "Oh, I am so sorry to hurt you like this! I know he is your dear friend, but I saw them myself. She had a valise with her, and he helped her on his horse and they rode off together!"

"Where?" He shook her, panic clawing at him and making him wild. "Which way did they ride?"

"To the west, toward the cairns," Mairi replied, managing to sneak in quick hug. "Does this means you will ride after them?"

"Aye." He turned to Callamby who was already conferring with three of his strapping, grown sons. "James, notify the men, and begin the search. He is to be located, but nae killed. No one kills him but me. Is that plain?"

"Aye, laird." Callamby nodded solemnly. "My oath to you, my life for yours; I swear this."

Hugh accepted the ancient vow of allegiance, then turned back to his sister who was starting to look more than a little confused. "At the castle, who knows of this?" he demanded.

Mairi's frown deepened. "Aunt Egidia," she said. "And Caroline's grandfather. He was readying himself to ride when I came in search of you."

"Ride back and tell them I want the men assembled," he said decisively. "Have them divided into parties to begin the search."

"Aye," Mairi promised, and turned to go.

Hugh grabbed her arm and swung her back to face him. "Tell them this as well," he added, his voice as cold as his soul. "If they find them, they are not to hurt Raghnall. Make certain they understand that. Raghnall is mine, and I shall be the one to kill him."

They hadn't been riding for more than half an hour when Caroline began to suspect something was amiss. Granted her sense of direction wasn't well-developed, but she specifically remembered that one rode down the mountain to reach the village, and for the past fifteen minutes Mr. Raghnall had been riding up, further into the sharp crags of gray rocks jutting into the sky. Perhaps he knew a shortcut, she told herself. But when they left the rough road and began riding in open country, she decided it might be prudent to say something.

"Mr. Raghnall," she began cautiously, knowing how tender was men's pride on such matters, "I do not wish to appear critical, but are you quite certain you have not mistaken the way? I believe the village to lie down there." She gestured in the direction from which they had just come.

In answer he tightened his grip about her waist. "I am not mistaken, my lady," he said, something in his voice making her frown. "I know precisely what I am doing."

They rode in silence for several more minutes, her sense of unease growing ever stronger. Evidently she had misjudged Mr. Raghnall's credulity, she mused. He had evidently tumbled to her scheme, and was returning her to Hugh instead of aiding her in her escape. But if that was so, wouldn't he have turned around by now? They were a good three miles from the castle, she judged, going higher into the mountains where the shooting had occurred. The realization sent a frisson of fear through her, and she had an abrupt change of heart.

"Sir, I believe it is too late in the day for me to start for Edinburgh," she said, doing her best to remain calm despite the way her instincts were clamoring at her to get as far from him as was possible. "Please turn around and return me to the castle. I wish to go home."

The arm about her waist tightened so painfully as to make her cry out. "I am afraid I canna do that, *Sasunnach*," he said, his voice dripping with cold menace. "I have plans for ye." As if to drive home his point he pulled a dagger from his waistband and laid it against her throat. "English bitch," he said, pressing the blade cruelly against her flesh. "This time I'll make certain I dinna miss."

Understanding dawned in a wave of nauseating terror. He was the one who had shot her! she realized, the blood draining from her face. He was her deadliest enemy, and she had put herself and her unborn babe at his mercy. A tremor she couldn't suppress rolled through her at the thought. Her babe! Tears filled her eyes. He was going to kill her babe!

Even as she was absorbing the horror of this, a band of horsemen came thundering from above them, and as Raghnall wheeled around to face them, Caroline saw Hugh at the head of the men, his sword held high in his hand.

"Let her go, *fear-brathaidh*," he ordered, his hair and plaid cape whipping wildly about him. "Let her go and fight me like a man! I challenge you to the death!"

Lucien's arms tightened, and he dropped his reins to wrap his hand more firmly about Caroline's waist. "Traitor?" he roared, his face twisting with hatred. "You have the gall to call me a traitor when you have betrayed all you once swore to protect? When you've made a mockery of the clan whose name you bear? You're the traitor, and a fool if you canna see it!"

Hugh's deadly anger was replaced by momentary confusion. "What have I betrayed?" he asked, clearly puzzled. "What have I done to make you hate me so?"

"You *love* her!" Lucien roared, and Caroline was grateful for the brutality of his hold, for without it she would most surely have tumbled from the saddle. "That is your betrayal! You may have married her for Loch Haven as you claim, but you love the bitch now! You chose her against your own people, and that was when I knew she had to die. It is the only way to restore the honor you have sullied with your foul love."

Hugh loved her. Caroline shook as the shock of the realization hit her. He loved her! She could see it in the anguish in his eyes, in the way his face contorted with hatred and fear.

"Then kill me," he said, his voice raw with emotion. "If the sin is mine, then so let the punishment be. Kill me, Raghnall, and let my wife live."

The other men cried out, and behind her she could hear the thunder of more approaching horses. She felt Raghnall tense, and he began to turn to face this new danger. Knowing she might have no other chance, and praying she would survive without getting her throat slit or losing the babe in the fall, she sent Hugh a final, desperate glance.

Her fingers tightened on the handles of her valise as she shifted away from her captor. He leaned forward, just as she expected, and she slammed the valise down as hard as she could against his groin. He gave a strangled cry, and the moment she felt his grip loosen, she used her arm to knock away the knife and threw herself to the ground, doing what she could to protect her stomach.

Above her she could hear the sounds of men shouting and fighting, and the sound of flesh striking flesh. A pair of strong arms reached out and snatched her up, carrying her away from where the battle raged. She sat up, watching in horror as Hugh lifted his sword a final time, and plunged it into Raghnall's belly. The man gave a keening cry, and then grew still, his body twitching once as death claimed him.

Hugh stood over him, his cheeks streaked with blood and sweat, a look of terrible desolation on his face. It was that look that had her on her feet, her pride and her pain forgotten as she ran to him. "Hugh!" she cried, throwing herself into his arms. "Oh, Hugh, thank God you have not been hurt!"

He dropped the bloodstained sword, his muscular arms shaking as he gathered her against him. "Caroline," he groaned, and she could feel the wetness of his tears against her neck. "Love, love, never leave me! I dinna want to live without you!"

"Hugh..." she drew back, her own eyes streaming with tears as she gazed lovingly up at him. "I—"

"Quick! Quick! Come quick!" an agitated voice cried out. " 'Tis the old general!"

Hugh and Caroline turned as one to see that the second group of riders had dismounted, and were clustered around a figure lying in the dust. Raghnall was forgotten as everyone rushed over to cluster around the fallen figure of the old man, who looked like a broken toy a careless child had tossed aside.

"Grandfather!" Caroline fell on her knees beside him. gently laying a hand on his grayish cheek. "Oh, please, do not die! I cannot bear to lose you now!"

"I told the old gentleman the ride would be a hard one, but he wouldna listen," a bearded man apologized earnestly. "Indeed, he led the way for near half the ride, but when he heard Raghnall's evil shouting it seemed more than he could take.

He clutched at his chest, and tumbled from his mount. 'Tis his heart, I fear."

"Caroline?" Her grandfather's eyes fluttered open, and he gazed up at her as if through a fog. "Is that you, child?"

"Yes, Grandfather, yes." Caroline clung to a hand that seemed surprisingly warm. "Hugh saved me, Grandfather. He saved me! Everything will be all right now. But you must be all right too, else how shall I ever be happy?"

Her grandfather gave a sigh that was little more than a puff of air. "Knew he would be the man for you," he said. "I took one look at the two of you together and I knew. You heard us, Caroline, didn't you? You heard us talking this morning."

She felt Hugh jerk and sensed his horrified gaze upon her. "Yes, Grandfather, I heard you," she said, cradling his head in her lap. "But I forgive you. I know you and Hugh were only doing what you thought right. Please don't worry."

"I could tell the lad loved you the moment I saw him in London." The general continued as if she hadn't spoken. "Saw his face and I knew. Now if I knew you loved him as well, I would know I had not failed you. I haven't failed you, have I, popppet?"

"Oh, no, Grandfather, no!" Caroline was shaking with grief. "You haven't failed me at all!"

"Do you love him, Caroline?" His fingers tightened weakly about hers. "Do you love the man your grandfather picked for you? Tell me the truth, dearest, that I might die in peace."

Caroline didn't hesitate, but reached out to grab Hugh's hand, laying it on her belly and covering it with her own. "Yes, Grandfather," she vowed, her voice shaking with intensity. "I love him with all my heart. And I am with child, do you hear me? I am with child. You will have the great-grandchild you want."

"What?" The general's eyes flew open, and he popped straight up, his eyes bright with pleasure. "That's marvelous!"

Caroline stared at him in disbelief. "You wretch!" she cried, torn between shaking him and kissing his lined cheeks. "You were faking!"

The general drew himself up haughtily. "What nonsense," he said, his voice cool with pride. "I was acting, and very credibly too, if I do say so myself. Do you know," he added, tipping his head to one side as if considering the matter for the first time, "I've always thought it rather a shame that those of our class do not tread the boards. I'd have done rather well, I think."

Caroline and Hugh looked at each other, at the general, at each other again, and then they were laughing. Hugh caught her in a passionate embrace, crushing her to his heart and kissing her as if he would never get enough of her.

"Well, *leannan*," he said, drawing back to gaze down at her with green eyes shining with love, "is it true, then? Do you really love me?"

"Aye," she answered in kind, pressing a kiss to his smiling lips. "I love you, *annsachd*, more than words can say."

His hand caressed her belly, his fingers cupping her protectively. "And you carry my son inside you?"

"Or your daughter," she reminded him softly, her heart so filled with joy she felt like she could float away. "What say you to that, laird of Loch Haven?"

"I say welcome home, lady of Loch Haven," he murmured, pulling her close for another kiss. "Welcome home—and this time, mind that you stay there."

Dear Reader,

If you loved the Avon book you've just finished, then you should know that Avon's commitment to publishing the very best in romantic fiction is ongoing. Each and every month brand-new Avon romance novels become available at your local bookstore.

Sensuous, powerful, and packed with emotional intensity, Karen Ranney's love stories are a must-read for lovers of historical romance. MY WICKED FANTASY, her latest, has a rakish hero, a strong-minded heroine and not-to-be missed love scenes. Don't miss this compelling romance and discover for yourself why *Affaire de Coeur* has called Karen an "uncommon talent."

Westerns are always a favorite setting, and Nicole Jordan's latest THE HEART BREAKER comes complete with a rugged cattle baron who needs a wife and mother to keep the ranch in order. But when he enters into what he thinks is "just" a marriage of convenience he soon discovers he's gotten more than he'd bargained for.

Rosalyn West's new miniseries THE MEN OF PRIDE COUNTY is sure to captivate readers who like strong heroes who find redemption through love. A bitter Civil War veteran returns home to Pride County to find that the woman who owns his heart, and the entire town, have branded him a traitor. He must regain his honor—and her love—in this unforgettable love story.

And for lovers of *contemporary* romance . . .

Award-winning author Sue Civil-Brown, who you might also recognize as Rachel Lee, has written a sexy, light-hearted romance, LETTING LOOSE, filled with rollicking good fun. Jillie MacAllister has a new life, a new job . . . and is newly single after dumping her philandering, no-good ex-husband. But when a matchmaking maven decides to fix Jillie up with the sexy Chief of Police Blaise Corrigan, her life gets even more confusing . . . but in some very wonderful ways.

Happy reading!
Lucia Macro
Avon Books

AEL 0198

Avon Romances—
the best in exceptional authors
and unforgettable novels!

SCARLET LADY	**by Marlene Suson** 78912-4/ $5.99 US/ $7.99 Can
TOUGH TALK AND TENDER KISSES	**by Deborah Camp** 78250-2/ $5.99 US/ $7.99 Can
WILD IRISH SKIES	**by Nancy Richards-Akers** 78948-5/ $5.99 US/ $7.99 Can
THE MACKENZIES: CLEVE	**by Ana Leigh** 78099-2/ $5.99 US/ $7.99 Can
EVER HIS BRIDE	**by Linda Needham** 78756-0/ $5.99 US/ $7.99 Can
DESTINY'S WARRIOR	**by Kit Dee** 79205-2/ $5.99 US/ $7.99 Can
GRAY HAWK'S LADY	**by Karen Kay** 78997-3/ $5.99 US/ $7.99 Can
DECEIVE ME NOT	**by Eve Byron** 79310-5/ $5.99 US/ $7.99 Can
TOPAZ	**by Beverly Jenkins** 78660-5/ $5.99 US/ $7.99 Can
STOLEN KISSES	**by Suzanne Enoch** 78813-6/ $5.99 US/ $7.99 Can

Avon Romantic Treasures

*Unforgettable, enthralling love stories,
sparkling with passion and adventure
from Romance's bestselling authors*

EVERYTHING AND THE MOON *by Julia Quinn*
78933-7/$5.99 US/$7.99 Can

BEAST *by Judith Ivory*
78644-3/$5.99 US/$7.99 Can

HIS FORBIDDEN TOUCH *by Shelley Thacker*
78120-4/$5.99 US/$7.99 Can

LYON'S GIFT *by Tanya Anne Crosby*
78571-4/$5.99 US/$7.99 Can

FLY WITH THE EAGLE *by Kathleen Harrington*
77836-X/$5.99 US/$7.99 Can

FALLING IN LOVE AGAIN *by Cathy Maxwell*
78718-0/$5.99 US/$7.99 Can

**THE COURTSHIP OF
CADE KOLBY** *by Lori Copeland*
79156-0/$5.99 US/$7.99 Can

TO LOVE A STRANGER *by Connie Mason*
79340-7/$5.99 US/$7.99 Can